The ICARUS JUMP

by John Yearwood

Printed by CreateSpace, An Amazon.com Company
Available from Amazon.com and other online stores.
Available on Kindle and other devices

Library of Congress Control Number: 2016902383
CreateSpace Independent Publishing Platform, North Charleston, SC
John Yearwood   Copyright 2016

ACKNOWLEDGMENTS

Every author needs help, and me most of all. I want to say thank you to all the many people who have helped along the way, bailing out my little one-oared boat and pulling me from dangerous shoals. Among these generous people and institutions, some stand out at the end of this four year writing project: the Black Lab Pub in Houston for unlimited wifi and patience, Cory Elliott for help with Greek, Adam Brochtrup for helping me to understand a Ranger's training, Alice B. Acheson and Marcy Posner for invaluable professional advice early on, and Sarah Kate Hackley for her editorial assistance. My writer's dream team of beta readers included Marta and Gary Gattis, Natasha Williams, Megan Biesele, Mike Geehan, Carissa Filip, Donna Birdwell, and John Montalbano, and for their many suggestions I am most thankful. Most of all I owe everything to my brilliant and loyal spouse Steffi for her endurance, multiple rough draft editing, her patience, and her loving help.

ONE

A t 21,000 feet three hours east of Germany's Ramstein Air Base, bitterly cold night wind roared past the lowered cargo ramp of the C-130, unseen, tornadic, solid, torn into invisible vortices by the plane's 330-knot speed and the noise of its four turboprops. A red jump light glowed next to the ramp, faintly illuminating Charles Shelby, former US Army Ranger, who gazed through the opened hatch at the maw of black night and the divine solitude of high altitude. It was like standing on the edge of civilization. Or the edge of time. God-like. Outside, a slim moon silvered the tops of distant clouds. Far away and down, tiny farm lights, perhaps an occasional vehicle, glittered on the dark globe.

At thirty minutes to launch, the German jumpmaster signaled "Make Ready."

Shelby moved to the carbon fiber winged capsule. He had already checked all his equipment, using his little LED flashlight to peer into crevices of the stubby-winged glider hidden in the dim light of the C-130's belly. Being a civilian consultant with NATO meant he didn't need much for this jump. No rifle, no explosives, no Kevlar-lined Rhodesian vest, no complicated gear, no 100-pound combat pack. No dropping into active war zones, as he had done several times a year for the last twelve years. Tonight, he expected to land in the dark and for his radio locator beacon to activate automatically. He might put up a tent, might sleep, but at first light the recovery helicopter would appear. That was the plan.

Back at Ramstein, he made up his small grab bag for tonight's jump in about fifteen minutes. He kept his quarters neat, everything in its place. All he needed to do after preparing the pack was to re-shelve his books on Mediterranean history and dictionaries of classical Latin and Greek. Other guys went drinking or chased women or worked on cars. Shelby had always been fascinated by the history of the Mediterranean. History and classical languages were his hobby. He loved decoding them, fitting together the shards and remnants of long-dead civilizations, and he was good at it. For the jump he had briefly considered packing his copy of Herodotus, but decided against it. Despite all the hours of waiting involved in this test jump, he didn't want the extra weight of the ancient Greek storyteller, the "father" of history. Instead, he opted for three days of MREs, some fundamentals, and, yes, a flask of whisky. Not regulation, he knew, but the Germans didn't care. These personal conveniences were in case his retrieval were delayed for some reason, which happened fairly often. Still, it was just the last test jump before this glider the Germans named "Gryphon" went into its next phase of development.

The dark sky beckoned, and he was ready. He switched on the heads-up display of his flight helmet, satisfied to see the green glow displaying GPS, winds aloft, and altimeter readings. With the ramp down and everyone on oxygen, only his headphones connected him to the rest of the flight crew, crackling with NATO radio traffic and airplane intercom. Nevertheless, he double-checked his oxygen bottle and the critical quick release trigger to pop the glider open. When he pulled that trigger at about a thousand feet, his chute would deploy. The glider would pop its own chute as it detached. Over the past months German engineers worked the kinks out of this apparatus, and now, one last nighttime test near the Ukraine border, just to see if the Russian air defenses alerted to his presence.

"They won't," he thought. "I'm too small, and after the hydrogen peroxide rocket pack fires, I will move too fast and have a heat signature cooling off so quickly they won't be able to see it. The rocket will leave a contrail of water vapor and oxygen like a long hooked claw, but the slender contrail won't be visible near a landing zone. This rig is perfect for clandestine operations, capable of propelling black ops parachutists up to 600 miles from the aircraft that drops them."

He lay prone on a wheeled dolly, his feet toward the rear of the plane and twenty degrees above his head so the nose of the glider entered the slipstream first, his mind rehearsing the advantages and faults of the device.

"The Germans may call it the 'Gryphon,'" he thought. "That's a monster with the head and wings of an eagle and the body of a lion, and about as clumsy. It's hard to get into the air, but it's fun when it does. Falling out of a plane into a slipstream with a rigid wing attached to your back tosses you around like a playing card," he thought. "You can go into a tail spin and never recover."

This was why Shelby called it "The Bitch." Even with modifications to the launch system, it was always a violent launch, his helmeted head banging side to side inside the plexiglass canopy of the capsule.

He lay in the Gryphon suspended on a gurney that dangled from a system of girders projecting beyond the airplane's loading ramp. With the plane's motion, the Gryphon swayed and vibrated gently, like a lion shifting his haunches just before an attack. Shelby was silent, intent, preparing himself, feeling the almost thousand pounds of propellant, electronics, and other gear that made up the Gryphon. "Once you're in it," he thought, "you're at its mercy, spread-eagled, arms trapped in the wings and fingers on the ailerons. No sense of freedom in free fall, which is what I really loved about jumping out of planes. But then, it soars. It's fun to soar."

In the dim cabin sixty feet feet ahead, the pilot eased the nose of the plane up, changing the aircraft's angle of attack to give an additional gravity boost to his launch. The other cargo creaked against its lashings — a Humvee outfitted as an ambulance, boxes of medical supplies headed to Turkey, other things. One of the design features of the Gryphon was deployment at cruising speed instead of slowing to the 125 mph of standard parachute jumps. "More wind on the wings, more things to go wrong," thought Shelby, "more equipment, more problems. Shit. Sua sponte, I guess. Again." He clenched his teeth anticipating the hazard.

"It's funny how your mind jumps around when you're waiting," he thought. He had jumped from images of his room in Ramstein with its green covered Loeb Classics, to the German love of mythological monsters, and now to "sua sponte," the Ranger motto in Latin that means "to do his will." In other words, to volunteer for the mission, no matter what it is, to execute the orders as given. "Always it goes back to those old classics," he thought.

Waiting for the red light to go green, his mind jumped involuntarily to his last tour in Afghanistan, images of explosions, gunfire, a bullet into his shoulder. He jerked himself back, willing himself from the memory.

"I won't go there," he thought to himself, turning his mind from the massacre. His wound. His rage.

"Ein minute," the jumpmaster finally said over the helmet radio.

"One minute to go," he thought. "This is when time stands still. Every second is an age." He felt his pulse quickening. No matter how many times he did this, it was exhilarating. "Sua sponte." He flexed his fingers, felt the ailerons move, and pressed his leg against the side of the capsule to remind himself of the SOG knife attached to his calf. He ran over a mental checklist, ending with the hope that he would not get banged around too much on launch. But this final minute: this terror, this joy, wrapped into a single vortex of time. It was the longest minute, always the longest minute.

"Dreissig secunden," the sausage-nosed German jumpmaster sneered into the intercom.

"Thirty seconds to go," he thought, inhaling deeply and slowly, slowing his racing pulse but not his racing mind.

Later, when he tried to remember the launch, to figure out what went wrong, he was sure he saw the light turn green. After that, nothing.

TWO

His abdominals shuddered, cramped, as he came to. He shook his head and slowly his vision returned, expanding out of blackness. He was gliding through the night. Below him, he saw the peaks of mountains illuminated by a slim crescent moon, a dark horizon stretched before him, and no traffic on highways below. No farm lights. The world was dark.

Surrounded by puffy cumuli, cotton-ball clouds loomed everywhere, glowing faintly in the moonlight. He glided silently into one and was lost in a gray fog, little streamers of water forming on the windshield of the capsule. Then, he was out in open air again. He tested the ailerons and banked left, then right, satisfied that he still had some control.

He must have blacked out on launch. But, for how long? His helmet was quiet. No heads-up display. His arms secured in the Gryphon meant he could not check the batteries, the on-switch.

"Maybe it got knocked off," he reasoned. "Must have been a violent launch."

The radio was off, too.

From the dim appearance of the ground in the tricky moon-light, he thought he was about 5,000 feet above the mountains. But what mountains? No mountains were in the landing zone, and coming down in the mountains anywhere was always a bad idea.

He pulled the rocket trigger to gain altitude and distance, but nothing happened. No rocket.

"Shit," he thought, "did I fire it while I was unconscious? Is it a malfunction? What happened?"

The glider descended another thousand or so feet and he

saw nothing but broken mountainsides, steep gullies, and dense forests. The world looked primeval, with not a shred of human habitation anywhere. No lights, no roads, no dams, no fields lying bare in the moonlight. Nothing but vertical walls of stone, piles of boulders, and huge trees.

"I'm going to come down," he finally said to himself out loud. "And it's going to be a damned rough landing."

With the restricted motion of his helmet inside the glider, he saw that he was already sailing below some of the taller peaks.

"What mountains are these?" he asked himself. "Alps? Caucasus? Am I in Montenegro?" He was supposed to be landing in the broad plains of Romania, not in mountains.

In the distance, he saw a football field-sized pond in a level shelf midway down a cliff, glinting in the moonlight, its surface gently rippled. Tall trees, tumbled terrain were everywhere else.

"The only clear spot," he thought.

He made for the pond, raising the nose of the glider to slow to stall speed. When he pulled the trigger, the clamshell of the Gryphon broke apart flawlessly, just like it was supposed to. For an instant, he was motionless and free in the night air, then gravity tugged at him and his chute deployed above his head.

Looking behind, he saw the Gryphon floating away on its own small chute. It was headed for treetops on the steep slope, but a helicopter team could retrieve it.

His hands freed at last, he felt for his helmet and located the switch to turn on the avionics. Nothing happened.

"No problem," he thought. "I've landed without instruments many times."

Boots down, he drifted in circles toward the pool.

"It's not too big, but it'll do," he thought. "It's open enough for a clean splashdown, maybe 100 feet wide. I can do this. I've landed in water plenty of times, and in tighter spots, under fire. This is the easy part."

Big breath.

Splashdown.

The water was deep, maybe 30 feet. He released his floating chute while still submerged and swam toward shore, his boots crunching on pebbly bottom when he neared the water's edge, making an easy walk out to the grassy verge among tumbled rocks. The pond was bordered on three sides by steep bluffs of rock. The uphill bluff was a high cliff, rising into dark shadows out of sight. The downhill bluff was much lower, with a small channel where the water from the pond flowed out. On the other two sides were six to ten foot high rock faces, mostly perpendicular but also slightly concave in places where ancient water flow had undercut the rock. Trees grew densely beyond the rock rim and loomed over the pool, casting darker shadows against a starlit grassy verge with clumps of bushes and boulders. To his right against the uphill cliff, a rock cleft nearly level with the pool disappeared into what looked like a small cave. From the cleft a shallow foot-wide stream trickled, dancing in the moonlight into the pool itself and rippling through the little channel downhill to his left with pleasant sounds of gentle cascade as it sought the sea.

Dripping in the warm night, he assessed his situation.

"With no radio," he thought, "I'll probably be stuck here for a day or two until the recovery teams find me. I have my knife. The water looks clean in this light. I have water purification tablets anyway, and might be able to fish the chute out if I need to. Thank God, I stuck that flask of blue corn whiskey in my pack. A little shot of that will perk me up during the wait. But first, gotta get off these wet clothes."

Later, a kind of camp set up, Shelby hid his pack and helmet by force of habit. Then he walked the perimeter of the pool, stopping finally at the cleft where he found the entrance to a cave. Stooping his 6'2" frame to enter, he shone his flashlight around.

At first, the flashlight beam was lost against the darkness, then shapes emerged on the stone walls receding into the distance as the cave widened out.

He stared, awe-struck.

Primitive paintings glowed on every surface. Shapes outlined in red and yellow showed women in all manners and states: pregnant, nursing, stooping to gather, fixing each other's hair, some naked, some clothed, some wearing short skirts apparently made of strings. One elegant female with a curved back held a string of fish, a ribbon of some kind tied in her hair, her breasts curved upward. Her eyes, white with dark irises, stared directly at him like a dare.

"Ancient," he thought, whistling at the sight, but some looked much older than others as though created by different generations. At the center of the left hand wall, a large seated woman dominated the cave, hands on knees, her wide eyes glittering like diamonds.

On the floor near the walls, the flashlight beam highlighted the imprints of naked feet in the dust, feet much smaller than his own. Hundreds of footprints, thousands, not much larger than children. A trail led toward the back of the cave, perhaps 100 yards — too far for his flashlight.

"Am I the first person in thousands of years to walk here?" he wondered. "Certainly I am the only one to walk in shoes."

He followed the rippling water further into the cave, making sure to step only on bare rock or in the little stream bed, careful not to disturb anything for the archaeologists who must surely come.

As he peered into the darkness, he thought the images on the uneven surface of the cave moved as his light moved. The ancient women, with their shining white eyes and dark irises, seemed to follow him, murmuring to themselves inaudibly below the rippling water. It was spooky and he shuddered involuntarily.

At the back of the cave, the stream quietly gurgled from under a large, red boulder. Above near the roof of the cave, he saw the sheared rock from which the boulder fell and an opening at the top of the boulder suggested space beyond it, but it was too high up and too sheer a climb to investigate. If the cave extended beyond this boulder, he would explore it when he came back.

"Later, I'll do that later, and maybe I will find treasure beyond that boulder," he smiled grimly to himself.

Retracing his steps, he shone his flashlight higher and higher on the walls. Everywhere women engaged in domestic chores, weaving, tending animals and children. Near the entrance, he found a scene of mourning: grief-stricken, wailing women tending the punctured body of a dead male warrior, the only painted man in the cave.

THREE

He knew the cave would be important to archaeology. He imagined the reactions of some professors he studied with and his aunt in New York was friends with some archaeology profs at Columbia. He made a note to call her when he got back to Ramstein. Well, to call her after he came back and climbed that boulder. If the deeper cave contained treasure, he wanted to see it first. "Let's keep things in perspective," he reminded himself.

A biting slug of whiskey from the flask finished off a tasteless MRE and spread tentacles of warmth across the pit of his stomach, relaxing him. He took one more pull on the flask, and lay back on his ground cloth, naked to the night sky, his clothes and boots spread out to dry. The low humidity in these mountains would dry his clothes quickly, he thought, and meanwhile the night air was gentle, caressing. It was a perfect night to lie out in the nude.

On his back, he stared up at the brilliant stars, contemplating this discovery. He'd found the cave, and he would come back with the proper gear and lights. He had nothing more to do tonight but wait to be rescued, and to dream. He thought briefly about the parachute in the water wondering if its transponder turned on. They nearly always did, though. When he had more light in the morning, he'd fish it out and check. Meanwhile, all he had to do was wait, and maybe sleep.

As a wisp of breeze off the pool stirred his pubic hair, his mind drifted to the possibility of treasure in the hidden parts of the cave. But the paintings alone were remarkable treasure. And how old, he wondered. Ten thousand years? Twenty thousand? They might reach back to the dawn of civilization. And staring at the great wheel of the sky, his arms behind his head, Shelby dozed.

Sometime later, he woke with a start to a canine wail like a coyote shrilling over the night air, its haunting seven-note call pouring into his sleeping brain like ice water. In the American west he had heard coyotes at night, and once or twice a pack of wolves, but never anything as melodious and eerie as this.

"Where the hell am I?" he wondered. "It would be nice to know what creatures I need to guard against."

Answering calls — jackal? — from distant hills and valleys echoed like arias in some senseless midnight opera, dying away into the dark night.

The whiskey and the adrenaline worn off, he began to feel chill in the cooling mountain air. Before he could reach for his clothes, however, something heavy moved in the dark woods and underbrush on the far side of the pool. He heard it distinctly and thought he saw a dark shape on the top of the stone bluff that surrounded the pool. He froze, motionless.

One foot tread. Another. A shuffle. Then stillness. Another foot tread. The shape moved, black against shadow, hunched and large.

Shelby eased himself backward toward a slight concavity in the rock face, very slowly and gently tugging his gray ground cloth. He hoped to hide in a shadow, making as little noise as possible until he knew what was moving. He was too far from the cave to seek shelter there.

He regretted his decision to sleep naked, and pulled the ground cloth closer, worrying that his jumpsuit could be seen on the rocks where he spread it to dry. Rocks and brush obscured his pack with his knife, but it was out of reach. "Why tonight, of all nights, did I not keep my SOG knife with me?" he wondered.

Another sound, then the dark shape descended slightly, and a branch quivered. A single leaf drifted onto the grass verge of the pool, lazily slipping through the air in its careless spiral, lit by what was left of the slim moon. Above and behind him, he heard a different grunt and knew there were two somethings. Two humans, two bears, two lions. Two somethings. One was overhead on the rocks above him, the other across the pond.

"Fucking bear?" he thought. "I'm being hunted by bears? Lions?"

The lonely song of the jackal sounded again, farther away.

Shelby stared at the dark shape across the pond, but it had gone still.

His only weapons would have to be rocks, which were plentiful. Feeling around with his hand under the cloth, he discovered a piece of heavy wood, possibly olive wood, he could use as a club. And then his hand brushed the parachute cord tied to a grommet in the ground cloth and he brightened. With the cord, he'd have a variety of weapons he could improvise. Garrote. Sling. If he were cautious and moved slowly, he could detach at least four and maybe six pieces of three-foot parachute cord without alerting those dark presences, whatever they were. Parachute cord was not a Kimber .45 caliber pistol, but it was better than nothing.

For a brief moment he allowed himself to regret not having his boots on. Clothing was neither here nor there, but boots were different.

He stayed silent, watching, sitting in the shadow of the rock for the rest of the night. After his years in the Rangers, he knew about surveillance and hunting. From time to time, though, while his physical senses remained vigilant, his mind drifted.

He was hiding behind rocks at an ambush in the Hindu Kush. Overhead, insurgents milled around, calling out in hoarse whispers as they positioned mortars to attack the Army column approaching below. He dreamt he could see every unbathed murderer through the rocks. He would get them in a moment, with stun grenades, frags, automatic fire. Everything was ready, but, for now, just steady, silent breathing.

He roused, then drifted again: and he was lying on his belly, a sniper rifle focused on a distant Somali camp, watching as a huge man with a machete brutally maimed little children. He couldn't fire at the man: it would give away his position. Air support did not come, did not come, did not come. If the warlord showed, Shelby had permission to take him out. Otherwise, he must sit there, sick to his stomach, waiting for the Air Force. The man fondled the children, rubbed their heads, made them look up at him with terror in their eyes, then whisked off each child's right arm below the elbow, and laughed. Shelby could not fire, and anger seared him like a brand. A pile of small limbs bled into the dirt.

Each vision forced him to suppress it, to shove it back down, safely out of sight, into his subconscious. So many wartime visions scrabbled around in that box, angrily rattling around, wanting to get out. He felt himself tensing, his heart racing at the memories, a growing sense of revulsion.

"Somalia just happened, that's all," he told himself. "It was bad, worse than bad, but I don't have to think about it. Focus on the present. Maybe that guy up the rock there is just hunting for food."

The sky finally began to lighten. Once or twice he heard movement overhead, and then further down the bluff. To his right, the grassy verge below the rim of the bluff was quiet.

Sitting absolutely still under his ground cover, just peering over its edge, he watched sunshine creeping onto the surrounding high peaks. The dark shape across the pool was still motionless, but still there, lying lengthwise maybe five or six feet above the verge, mostly out of sight. As the sunlight shifted over the area, it caught something metallic next to the shape, something that glinted briefly.

He'd heard nothing from overhead for some time, but then, suddenly, he heard female voices.

At first he thought their voices came from the cave, but that didn't make sense. He glanced away from the shadow on the far wall and saw a flash of movement at the top of the precipice to the right of the cave. When he looked back at the shadowy shape, he saw a darkly dressed man slowly rising in the shadows. Although he was only 100 feet or so away, the covering branches kept Shelby from seeing him clearly. Still, it looked like he carried a spear and had a sword belted to his side. "Not a bear," he thought.

Overhead, he heard a grunt and the shifting of another large body.

FOUR

C raning his neck to the right, Shelby saw bare legs coming down through the brush on a path that would end at the pool. The females were chattering and giggling in a language that sounded something like his aunt's Greek, but he could not quite understand it. Was it a Balkan dialect? More like Homeric Greek? He was certain it was some form of Greek. They were sharing confidences, something about a father, their melodious voices echoing over the still surface of the pool.

"They are walking into a trap," he thought. "Are these guys hiding up there just to watch the girls?"

"No," he concluded, "too much weaponry. This is a rape or kidnapping or both. But not in front of me, it's not. I have had it. I'm not standing by and watching defenseless people get maimed or murdered any more. Fuck the Air Force, fuck the Army, fuck orders. This is me, and I'm stopping this!"

The women were much closer, now, three of them. A girl, a young woman, and an older woman. He could see them clearly. Their muscular limbs glowed in the early sunlight, with dark hair and pale blue old-fashioned drapery. They were happy, laughing to one another, but so short. Barely five feet tall, maybe shorter. A wry comment sent them into gales of laughter and their footsteps scattered rocks down the path. The young woman and girl carried baskets, balancing them on their heads as the older woman picked her way gingerly in their wake.

At the water's edge, they put down their baskets, still giggling. Then all three turned from the pond and disappeared into the cave where echoes magnified the rise and fall of their melodious voices.

At their entry into the cave, the man across the pool dropped quietly down onto the grassy verge and began creeping along the face of the bluff, obscured by bushes and rock, toward the cave entrance. The overhead man almost simultaneously eased himself down the rock only six feet away, but his back was turned and he did not see Shelby. Instead, he too moved intently toward the cave, loosening his sword from his belt and hefting his spear, crouching, all his attention focused ahead. He was so close that Shelby smelled him. This man, too, was short, barely five feet, if that.

On the other side of the pool, the intruder passed out of sight behind a clump of low bushes at the base of the rock face.

"Now or never," Shelby thought, and silently sprang up. Three steps sideways in the silent lope they teach in combat school, and he took the short man from behind in a sleeper hold, putting him out in seconds. He moved the unconscious man behind a small pile of brush-covered rocks next to the rock face, out of sight of the other man, the slight rustle of the movement covered by the echoing chants from the cave. Using parachute cord, Shelby secured the man's hands and feet.

He hefted the man's seven-foot spear in one hand and the sword in the other, noticing only that the spear's tip was a deadly looking sliver of flint. The sword was bronze.

"Bronze?" he thought to himself. "Who the hell carries a bronze sword?"

Peering through the screen of brush, Shelby saw the dark man across the pool still moving stealthily toward the cave mouth, attention riveted to the cave mouth, his gaze fixed. The melodious voices stopped, and the females emerged from the cave entrance onto the level pebbly ground at the head of the pool, loosening their clothes as they approached the water.

Crouching, Shelby crept toward the unsuspecting women, trying to remain unseen, timing his approach to match the dark man's so they would arrive at the women at the same time.

Suddenly, the tenor of the women's voices changed: they saw the intruder only twenty or thirty feet away and cried out in alarm. The older woman clutched her loosened clothes in front of her. The youngest one, the girl, already nude, picked up rocks from the edge of the pool and threw them clumsily. The young woman, maybe 20 and still dressed, also began throwing rocks. Her aim was good and her baseball-sized stones enraged the man. At the second blow to his forehead, he charged head down, eyes glaring under his lowered brows and leading with his spear. The females screamed with fear and anger.

At the same moment, Shelby charged too, from behind the women. The intruder ignored Shelby for a moment, focusing on his prey, while the females pelted him with rocks. Then he realized that Shelby was not his partner and plunged by them, lashing his spear at the girl in passing, ripping her side. She went down into the water howling with pain to the shriek of the other two women. A split second later, the intruder thrust his spear at Shelby.

Shelby leapt aside and hit the ground, rolling. The other's spear struck again, deeply into the dirt just beside his head, but Shelby was out of the way. Coming up, he thrust his own spear, catching the man in the inner thigh and drawing blood. He thrust again, but now the man's spear was up again and he charged, his face bleeding, bloody mist spewing from his beard. Shelby parried the thrust to his right with his own spear held in one hand and then uppercut the man's right arm with the sword in his other hand. The sword caught him under the armpit and the spear dropped, blood spouting from the artery, the arm limp. The man danced sideways, grabbing at his own sword with his left hand and raising it to charge again. Then, he checked in mid movement, a stunned look on his face. His eyes went blank. He fell slowly to his knees, and then face forward into the dirt.

The young woman had struck him solidly with a rock in the back of the head.

Now she and the older woman rushed up, the woman shouting orders, their clothing flapping. The young woman grabbed the man's sword with both hands and plunged it into his back, aiming for the kidney, then several times into his ribs. Her draperies flapped loosely as she swung, showing her young breasts swinging with each thrust. Holding one of her hair braids in her mouth to keep it out of the way, she hacked away at the back of his neck. She would have continued until the head came away from the corpse, but Shelby touched her bare shoulder and said softly, catching his breath, "Stop now."

FIVE

For the rest of his life, Shelby remembered the shock of touching her bare shoulder; her skin, flushed with fury, glistening in the morning sun; her breasts swinging free of the loose clothing.

The young woman stopped, but reluctantly. He felt her exerting control, trembling, then she looked at him defiantly for an instant before dropping her eyes. The sword lowered as she exhaled.

From the water's edge the girl's sobbing caused him to break the contact. She was kneeling in the water, holding her stomach, naked, blood streaming through her fingers. He rushed over and lifted her out, the older woman following behind, and carried her up to a flat rock where she could stretch out. Her little acorn breasts heaved with terror and pain. She was maybe 10 or 11 years old, he thought. Only the faintest down of pubic hair.

Her wound wasn't that bad. The skin had a nasty slice, but her abdominal wall was not penetrated. Cool water helped slow the bleeding, and he told her so, using Greek, holding her discarded shift against the cut.

She said something to him that sounded like Greek, but he could not track it. Deciphering this vocal code would require more exposure, he decided.

He looked up. The two women were staring at them, concerned. The younger woman held the sword, point down and away, so the blood would not drip on her, but she could attack him in the blink of an eye.

"She will be okay," he said again in Greek, "but I have some bandages in my pack that will help."

They looked at him blankly. He repeated, "I think she will be okay."

The older woman spoke to him, but he didn't understand. Then she stepped forward and took his hand, leading him away from the girl to the edge of the pool. Reaching down to the water, she wet three fingers and lifted them to his lips, standing on tiptoe to reach so high. She looked at him quizzically. Then she did it again, and after touching his lips she touched her own and spoke to him. Suddenly he understood what she was saying. How? He did not get it. Bronze swords and flint spears were strange enough, being lost on a jump was so very far out of the ordinary. But this was scary and unreal. Nevertheless, he did not understand her before, and now he did.

"What is your country?" the older woman repeated. "Your language. We have before your language not heard. Us you saved," she continued after a moment to be certain that he understood. "That man be Achaean. Unspeakable things they do to captured women. For us taken had he bad it would be."

Standing at the water's edge, Shelby towered over her, unscrambling her words. The woman could not be as much as five feet tall, maybe four-ten, if that. The little one, with the cut in her side, was barely four feet and couldn't weigh forty pounds. At six-two, he was more than a foot taller and three or four times their weight.

And, he suddenly realized with chagrin, naked.

Completely naked.

By this time, the young woman had joined her mother at the water's edge and they both looked up at him, squinting against the bright sky, then down his body and up at him again, expressionless. Their heads barely reached to his rib cage.

"I do have clothes," he explained, a flush coming to his cheeks, "over there. When I saw these men in the night lying in wait, I did not have time to put them on."

The older woman continued looking him steadily in the face, while the younger woman, very beautiful in her ferocity, looked over at the wounded girl and moved that way to tend to her.

"I, uh, took them off to sleep," he stammered.

The older woman's gaze did not waver. Her dark eyes drilled into him.

"What men?" she asked at last. "Only one man saw we, you besides."

"Another man is over there. I got him first."

He pointed and began walking that way. The woman followed, retying her clothes.

He held up his hand in caution as they approached the bushes where he hid the short man.

He was still there, eyes open, and struggling to release his hands. He snarled when he saw them, thrashing.

The woman reacted immediately. She spat out a name, and reached for a rock. Before Shelby could stop her, she bashed the man's skull multiple times.

"Over," she said, panting, pointing to the man and toeing his senseless body.

Shelby turned the now comatose man onto his back, hating that he was now involved in two deaths, and one of them a murder.

"Give sword," she commanded, taking it from his hand. She plunged it into the man's ribs and midsection a dozen times, then hacked his groin into pulp, splattering her arms and the hem of her dress with his blood.

"Thief!" she said at last. "Him I know. I him banished. Now he does not come back."

Shelby realized that he understands her speech much more clearly. How did that happen?

"Uh," said Shelby, backing away, "I will put my clothes on now, if you will excuse me."

"Oh." She looked at him, still distracted by her fury. "You. Be you a god?"

"I am not a god. If you cut me, I will bleed."

Hmm," she said, studying his face. "Yes." She put the sword down on a rock. "Yours. Go put on clothes, if you are supposed to wear them."

She turned back to the girls, as though he no longer existed.

"If I am supposed to wear them?" he mused. "I wonder what she means by that?"

In fact, he was full of questions. "How can she communicate so effortlessly with me?" he began, mumbling to himself as he recovered his gear. "Where am I? Why did I just fight a battle with bronze weapons? I may have jumped through more than empty air last night," he thought as he pulled on hiking shorts and t-shirt. He decided to leave the still damp pressure suit he had worn for the jump, his helmet, other things but to take his knife. "I need to be careful about my gear. I don't hear a rescue chopper, so maybe the guys don't know where I am either. The biggest question of all: Where the hell am I?"

Back at the wounded child, he clasped the gash together with butterfly bandages, applied an antibacterial salve, and secured the wound with gauze. The gash was not as bad as it could have been, and the young woman had stopped the bleeding by applying pressure with the girl's shift. Just a gash, a glancing slash, not a puncture, but it had bled freely. "It will leave a scar," he thought. "She should be seen by a doctor."

The others silently watched this procedure. Finally, indicating the gauze bandage, the older one asked: "Did your wife weave that for you? What kind of loom does she use?"

He was nonplussed by her question. "What kind of question is that? She's asking about a loom while the girl bleeds?" he thought.

"No," he replied, "these things are made by machines, not by hand. But enough questions; I want to get you to safety before there's another assault."

"You must come back with us," the woman said, introducing herself. "I am Metis. My people call me 'Mother.' My husband is Phorbus. These are my daughters Kalista, the little one, and Melia. You must come with us so we can celebrate your courage."

Shelby glanced over at the dead man on the bank next to the pool, the corpse's blood still draining into the dirt. While he and Metis had been away tending to the other man, this one was rolled over, his nearly severed head only partially following his body, and castrated. Pieces of gore lay exposed in the sunlight. "Melia must have done that," he thought.

"Thank you, Metis," he said aloud. "I accept your offer."

Melia draped clothing gently over the prone and groaning Kalista, then Shelby lifted her as Metis and Melia turned to ascend the path they had come, knotting and securing their own clothes but leaving the baskets.

"If the chopper comes," he thought to himself, "they'll find the chute and other things and hang around. Besides, I'll hear them and come back. Carrying this child to safety is more important than waiting here."

At the top, panting and sweating, he was so tired that he was afraid he might drop the girl, but he managed to let her down gently. "The jump, the long vigil, and the fight have taken more out of me than I thought," he decided. "I need to be in better shape. She doesn't weigh that much. Why am I so tired? I should have recovered faster. The blackout last night during the jump was not a good sign. Maybe it was hypoxia. Now this fight, the adrenaline … Maybe I'm getting old."

Turning, he saw the distant horizon spread out before him, and though he knew they were there, he could not see even a trace of the Gryphon, probably snagged in a treetop somewhere, or of his parachute, now lying on the bottom of the pool with its beacon.

CHAPTER

SIX

At the top of the long hill in the shade of tall ash trees, Metis sent Melia running to alert the guards posted at the edge of the forest, and to bring help and a cart.

"It won't be long before guards get here," she thought. "Melia can run very fast, and before long they will see her."

Metis was full of questions and suspicions about this large stranger, but held her tongue, watching him. He seemed to pose no threat, so she waited and observed him quietly. She allowed her mind to rumble over the Goddess' prophecy about the doom of war upon them and a stranger coming to deliver the city, wondering whether this was the man.

"This giant," she mused. "This is deep mystery. He is not like any warrior I have seen before. He moved silently, quickly, thoughtfully. He caught the Achaean off guard. I don't recognize his language or his manners. It's as though he appeared out of nowhere, like a god. Yet, he did not kill, only incapacitate. Why not? He seems kind, but the tilt of his head and look in his eyes show a deep sorrow. What is he?"

Shelby leaned against a tree, obviously tired, sweat pouring off his furrowed brow, watching over Kalista who lay in the shade nearby crying quietly whenever she thought anybody was paying attention.

"I need to watch him," Metis continued thinking. "Melia with her long hair and strong arms made an impression on him, but she makes an impression on all men. Maybe he has made an impression on her, too. If so, he will be the first. It is time for her to get married and to raise a family of her own, but no one has caught her. Yet.

"We need warriors like him in the harvests to come. An army of such giants would reap Achaeans like grain.

"It will be interesting to see what Phorbus knows about the dead scum by the pool. Maybe they came to kidnap Melia. Maybe only that. That could have been enough.

"I should have listened to the jackal's song last night.

"Now, this giant man. He may be what he appears: kind and dangerous. But you never know about strangers.

"He could be a god, even though he denies it. Or at least a demigod. There is something about him besides his size. The Goddess told me she would send someone. Maybe he is the promised one.

"Phorbus may know more about him. Phorbus sees deeply into men."

While Metis studied him, Shelby sat with his back against a tree, his eyes closed. The night had been long, and he was unusually tired. It was not like him to be so tired. Kalista wanted to be next to him, and he let her stretch out there, with the back of his hand on her arm to keep her calm. She didn't move, except to whimper a little, but her dark eyes were wide open.

"I think the whimpering is an act so her mother will leave her alone and let her stay next to me," he thought, dozing briefly, his chin against his chest. When he looked up again, Metis was sitting straight on a fallen log, legs together, hands on her knees, watching him with narrowed eyes.

Her black hair, laced with gray, was braided and tied around her head. Mature in beauty and form, time had just begun to etch her face. "She is so beautiful," he thought, "like the statue of Venus in the Louvre, but much shorter. Fierce, too." He glanced at the hem of her dress, red where the man's blood splattered it. "Like a lioness at the kill. She is not a woman to cross."

Shelby nodded off, his body relaxing as his head fell forward onto his chest. Metis watched him collapse into unconsciousness and thought: "Good. While he sleeps he is not dangerous." Moments later, she saw him twitching in his sleep, and heard a deep growl escaping from his chest. His was a troubled sleep, a nightmare, full of anger and fear. His legs tautened, then relaxed, then tautened again. Then, he was still. Kalista, lying next to him, looked up at her mother with widened eyes, but said nothing.

Suddenly, he opened his eyes, startled. His hands went to the ground, and he was up, slipping behind the tree, out of sight. A second later, he moved further off, behind another tree, and she lost sight of him. Briefly she caught a glimpse of him slipping through brush a little way distant, circling. She was amazed that a man so large could move so swiftly, so silently.

"I may have underestimated him," she thought, trying to catch a glimpse of him.

An instant later, two of the armed guards she had left beyond the woods rushed into view on foot, their bronze-tipped spears ready for battle. She did not hear them padding over the soft ground until they were almost on her, but the sleeping man had heard them! He alerted at some noise only he could hear, or some sense of their approach, and disappeared into the surrounding brush without a sound. But to do what? Hide? Surely not.

"What a remarkable man," she thought. "Remarkable. He must be the one sent by the Goddess."

SEVEN

XXXXXXXXXX

Then, there he was! Behind the guards!

"Stop and don't move!" Metis commanded them, holding up her palm. She herself did not stand, though Kalista let out a gasp of surprise. "You, Yiannis, stop! Now. Eumaeus, stop!"

They stopped. It was a good thing, because the man behind them appeared out of nowhere with a strange, long knife in his hand. He was a split second from attacking them.

"Don't look behind you," Metis warned. "Put your spears down. If you value your lives, kneel to me now."

"Now!" she insisted when they hesitated. "Now! Yiannis, down!" The younger guard hesitated, but her tone overcame him. He went down, lowering his spear.

"Melia told us you had been attacked," the older one sputtered, slowly kneeling on one knee, trying to look behind, resting the butt of his spear on the ground. The round, bronze shield on his back clanked against the hilt of his sword.

"What had the giant heard?" Metis wondered. "Their sandals padding on path's soft leaves? Their panting? Amazing vigilance." Metis saw his eyes blazing, the veins standing out on his neck and forehead as he silently closed. She stood slowly.

"These guards are from Phorbus, from my husband," she said speaking over their heads. "They come because Melia alarmed them. Others soon arrive. We are all safe now. Even you," she added, recalling his nightmare. "You are safe too."

At that, the guards looked around, grunting with surprise at the giant man who had approached so closely and so silently from the rear. Yiannis jumped in alarm, rolling, scrambling away to crouch defensively before Kalista, his spear in both hands, a startled snarl on his face.

"Apparently he is more willing to die for Kalista than for me," Metis said to herself.

The giant stood still, not pursuing him. The nearer guard still knelt, looking from the man to Metis and back.

"This man saved us," Metis said. "He downed two armed men. We will treat him as friend and honored guest."

"Yes, Mother," said Eumaeus, obediently.

"Giant," she said, looking up at him, "I realize I do not know your name. This is Eumaeus, head of our guards. Over there is Yiannis, another of our guards. If he is lucky, he may live beyond next harvest." She smiled humorlessly at Yiannis.

A queen's smile can make the blood run cold, and she knew it. She looked at Kalista, who was now trying to stand without bending her stomach. Metis knew Yiannis would help her youngest daughter up if he dared to touch her in front of her mother.

Well, he had touched her before. She knew that now.

"These girls," she thought.

Abruptly, the woods filled with shouts and stamping. Horses, men, Phorbus himself, galloped up, swords drawn. At least 100 men in arms.

"We are safe," Metis said, stepping in front of the stranger. "This man rescued us and defeated two attackers. They are dead on sacred rocks. We welcome him with gratitude."

She looked steadily at Phorbus, until she saw his rage turn to concern.

Shelby also looked at the king. He was broad shouldered, with dark, unruly red hair gone gray at the temples. A full gray-streaked beard accented his large, white teeth. A light-blue cloak draped across his shoulders, and he carried his shield slung over his back. Beside him was his spear bearer, a younger man with a bundle of eight spears. No one carried a gun, only swords and spears, and they wore bronze armor. Everyone wore sandals. The saddles did not have stirrups. "What the hell? Where am I?" he asked himself. "Is this a set for a movie about the ancient world?" He looked around for cameras, lighting, microphone booms but instead saw archers coming through the woods. They took up a semicircle around the scene, arrows notched.

Phorbus stared at Shelby.

"Who are you and why are you in our country? Why were you at Goddess' sacred pool?"

Shelby stared blankly, foolishly, while he deciphered the question, but soon it came to him. All those years living with his Greek aunt helped.

"King," he said, deciding to play along in case it was a movie set, even if it wasn't, "I am Charles Shelby from a land called America over the western ocean."

His words sent a ripple through the assembly. Even Metis was surprised. To be from a land across the distant, rumored ocean was unthinkable. Only the gods traveled so far.

"Where are your wings that you flew so far in one lifetime?" Phorbus demanded. "Also your language. That is not a language spoken by any of the known kingdoms of the world."

"Great king…" he began, now realizing that the language was becoming easier to understand, but Metis rescued him by interrupting.

"Phorbus, enough of this," she said. "We will take him back to palace, and when he is fed and rested we will hear his full story. Tonight we feast. All night we ask him questions and listen to his story. But now, return. The little one is hurt, and he bandaged her and carried her up. I must send Matrons to purify sacred pool and bring dead bodies back here to be examined. Meanwhile, we will learn more with patience."

"Your words are wise as always, Mother," said Phorbus, sheathing his sword. "The stranger is welcome, and he will teach us to pronounce his name. Come stranger, you are welcome. Some of you there," Phorbus pointed to the guards, "go with him to show way."

"He will ride in cart," said Metis, as Melia and a driver plodded into the gathered troops with a creaking mule cart.

Little Kalista now became the focus of attention as Phorbus dismounted and kneeled beside her. He mumbled to her, and she nodded, tears streaming from her face. Then he effortlessly took her up in his arms and carried her to the cart, everyone parting to make way.

"Get up with her, stranger," he said. "We follow behind."

CHAPTER

EIGHT

T he cart driver was poor company. He sat silently holding reins and a short whip, staring ahead with his one eye. The other eye was gone, leaving a gaping empty socket, and he continually chewed on his lower jaw with toothless gums. Every time the cart bumped, which was frequently, his mouth opened and clapped shut with a popping sound. Occasionally, he caught a fly in his mouth, which he swallowed.

He was naked, but for a small bronze band around his neck, and sat dangling his legs over the front edge of the cart, his bare feet just high enough above the dusty road to occasionally hit a rock or scoop up a pile of mule dung. Melia sat in front next to him, her legs folded under her. Shelby leaned against the cart's reed side behind them with Kalista on a pile of blankets next to him.

He stared behind at Phorbus and Metis talking quietly to one another and flanked by a brigade of hard-eyed archers and spearmen. Then he reached forward and touched Melia's arm, calling her name. Behind him, bows with notched arrows raised and the archers' eyes narrowed as they judged their distance. He ignored them. They would not shoot at the queen's daughters, he was sure.

Just as he touched her, however, a shadow passed over them. Looking up, they saw an imperial eagle swooping at tremendous speed, its talons opened wide. The next instant, it thudded into a passing dove, leaving a puff of feathers floating in the air. Then it recovered flight, taking a great beat with its massive seven-foot wings, and flew slowly off toward a walled city in the distance, gaining altitude, the rumpled dove dangling in its claws.

Melia looked at Shelby, then back at her parents. When Shelby followed her look, he saw Phorbus pointing at the eagle and Metis speaking fervently to him.

"Old ones make much of this," Melia said, turning to him as the feathers drifted away on the light breeze, her voice even clearer to him than Metis' was. "Bird hunting for dinner, but they will say that Goddess has given sign." She smiled slyly, her pretty teeth showing, her eyes looking at him steadily. Her speech was a little stilted, lacking the usual English articles, or he did not hear them. In that part of his brain that delighted in decoding verbal signals, he realized that Metis had spoken the same way. They were using some Greek language that was not translated easily into English. "Some will say it is sign from Zeus, but them we frown on."

He left his hand gently on her arm, thrilled by the sense of her skin, a kind of deep organ tone seeming to grow from his fingers into his whole being. She met his gaze openly, turning slightly to him. Did he see the concavity of her back increase a little, thrusting her breasts forward? Perhaps a millimeter of movement, hard to detect in the jostling cart, but he became aware of their gentle movement and her skin's glow.

Through verdant pastures and extensive vineyards, Shelby and Melia passed the time talking, and with every word he felt more in touch with her, better able to understand. He also learned a lot about their civilization, and was surprised to discover that her city had been in this beautiful, fertile valley for at least a thousand years.

"Harvests," Melia called them, instead of "years."

He also learned that she began hurling stones as a child, running through the vineyards to drive away the birds. This was the primary occupation of children from age 3 to 8, she told him. And she discussed Metis slaying the thief at the pool.

"As priestess, she also judges," Melia explained. "She knew that man; banished him as thief. In our country, if good citizen will speak not for criminal and agree from trouble keep him, he is banished. Or executed." She looked at him, her steady eyes like blue crystals brilliant in the morning light. "We keep few prisoners. It
is waste of resources."

Her beauty drew him. She was soft, lithe, smart, but with a ferocity that reminded him of a dangerous animal. A lioness, perhaps. He felt his heart swelling in his chest as he gazed at her,

her full lower lip, her perfect features, feeling some electrical cable thrilling through his body. He awakened to her presence, her scent. Her soft skin, despite the morning's exertions, despite the splatters of blood on her clothing, the little smear of blood on her left elbow, glowed in the rising sun, soft, calling to be touched, caressed.

"Wow," he thought, monitoring his body's desire for her, his awareness completely absorbed by her.

Later, Shelby was surprised to see the city walls. Perhaps five miles north of the forest, across fields full of grain, vineyards, and pasturage, they rose forty feet, with roofed guard towers at the corners and huge gates set midway in the long walls. A large, flat-topped hill, a kind of mesa, rose on the north side of the city, crowned with a white-columned temple on the far side. A thin column of smoke ascended the still air in front of the temple.

"Ah," Shelby thought, "the city's acropolis. But not in ruins. That smoke might be an altar. It's like a living classical town, nothing changed in four thousand years. Bronze weapons, temples, wooden cart wheels. Maybe an altar. Clothing that looks like the chiton, but open down one side and cinched with a belt. Where the hell did I land last night?"

In the green fields surrounding the town, cows and sheep grazed in picturesque content. He saw vineyards full and leafy, and grain shone golden in the morning sun. A winding river, perhaps thirty feet wide, flowed at a gentle pace through a rolling green valley that stretched toward distant mountains on three sides.

"If the Gryphon beacon is working, sooner or later a rescue chopper will be back at the pond," he continued thinking, shifting on the hard deck of the cart to a more comfortable position somewhat closer to Melia. "But who knows whether these short people will let me go back to their sacred pool? Or even, if I go, whether I will be in the same century I just left."

These and other thoughts, and mostly the stunning image of Melia sitting up so easily and erect next to the driver, tumbled through Shelby's brain as the cart bumped along. Kalista put on a good show of being the injured party, whimpering a little whenever he looked away and then trying to force a smile when he looked back. "This is going to get old," Shelby thought.

The silence between Melia and Shelby stretched comfortably

while he gazed about.

Finally, Melia spoke.

"Tell me about your country and your wife who makes these clothes." She reached out and fingered the edge of his t-shirt, looking closely at the fabric and the stitching in the seam. He was conscious of the backs of her fingers brushing his biceps.

He explained he did not have a wife and that he bought his clothing from a shop, or actually from several shops. The cloth came from places far away from where he lived and was made on massive looms that ran night and day.

As he talked, she turned a little more toward him, absorbing his thoughts, facing him finally with her legs folded, her short chiton depressed between her thighs. It was the most innocent pose in the world, but it affected him deeply and his eyes occasionally strayed to the declivity, where her folded hands lay.

Sometimes she asked Kalista if she understood everything, and they talked about it together. Listening to them, Shelby realized that he could no longer be in the twenty-first century A.D. Who had never heard of America? Who thought the ocean was a myth? He might very well be in the twenty-first century B.C. Last night, he went to sleep beside a still mountain pond near the entrance of a cave filled with ancient paintings and drawings, and this morning awakened in the presence of the women whose ancestors may have left those drawings. He had gone to bed a consultant with NATO and awakened a stranger in a land of warriors armed with bronze swords and sharpened flint spear points. He could not wrap his mind around it.

"We are nearly to town," she continued after a few moments, "and I will go with Kalista. I tell you what expect." She frowned at him as she thought over her words. Perhaps she realized that her speech was out of sync with his. She tried again.

"You are stranger in country such as ours," she tried again, listening to how she sounded, attempting to perceive what he heard. Gazing at him steadily, she took both his hands and held them. Though she didn't open her mouth, he suddenly heard her voice, full and sweet, speaking in his mind. "When we arrive, Mother will order that you be bathed and fed, and you will be given a place to rest. Later there will be a feast, and many warriors will come to see you. Father will honor you for what you did at the pool today."

It was perfectly clear, yet not a spoken word passed between them.

"How did you do that?" he asked her.

"How do I speak in your mind?" she smiled, silently.

"That's what I mean. How do you do that?"

"It is a trick some women learn from the Goddess," she laughed aloud. Suddenly the articles of speech were there. "First I listen, then I call, and when you answer then I think of what to say. I'm glad you're here. I need practice."

"Can I do it?"

"Maybe. Can you hear the Goddess when she speaks?"

"I don't think so. Never have."

She cocked an eyebrow at him in disbelief, then rotated her face in a gesture that he took for sympathy.

"Can you hear my thoughts even when I don't speak them?" he asked. It occurred to him that this could be awkward.

"I can hear your body speaking before even your mind," she said, crinkling her eyes in mirth. "Most women can hear a man's body, which is always bellowing in its way. It is very clear to most women. Some get so accustomed to the noise that they ignore it. Perhaps after so many years, most women." She lapsed into silence, but he did not perceive her speaking to him.

"First the Goddess," she finally said aloud, her tone changing from playfulness to seriousness, dropping his hands. "First hear the Goddess, then maybe you will learn to talk."

They drew closer to the massive city gate with its recessed bronze-clad doors.

The furrows of concern on her brow eased away at last as she watched him. Like her mother, she had plenty of questions about this huge man. "How can he be the choice of the Goddess if he cannot hear the Goddess speak?" she wondered.

"Now listen," she said to him. "At least you can hear me. To-night you will be given gifts. I don't know if you have gifts to give back, but an exchange is customary. As the guest, you will present gifts first if you have them. After you think about it, you can send one of the bath girls to me if you need advice."

"Bath girls?"

"Oh yes. In our country, all warriors are bathed by girls. Kalista is still too young for such duty. It is a job for girls of a certain age, for it teaches them about caring for a warrior. Some of the girls are quite beautiful. They will bathe you and then oil your body and rub your muscles. It is an appropriate bath for an important warrior." She looked at him, a blush rising to her face and a smile perking up at the edges of her lips, but a look bordering on, what?, vulnerability? in her eyes. This was the woman he had watched thrusting a sword into a man's back and chopping at his neck just hours ago, and most certainly then castrated the body. He was surprised by her turn to apparent tenderness, this blush, this contradiction.

"I will not be there," she added, her tone softening as she looked away.

Maybe it was the angle of the sun, but he thought perhaps her eyes were changing colors from deep blue to dark gray.

The metamorphosis enchanted him.

NINE

Closer to the city, they left the fields and passed through a village of farmers and artisans occupying small, oval huts built of mud-packed reeds woven around posts. They appeared to have only one entrance, while a hole in the center of the low domed roofs let out smoke. Barefoot farm workers of both genders, some clothed in short linen tunics and some naked, stared at and hailed the procession. Naked children were everywhere. Soon, the broad way through the village opened onto a bare plain lying before the city walls, an area free of cultivation and habitation where no invading army would find shelter from archers on the walls.

At a rough estimate, the city looked to be large enough to house at least twenty thousand residents, maybe more, he thought, a huge metropolis by classical standards. Hundreds, maybe thousands of citizens lined the tops of the walls, watching their approach. When Metis and Phorbus entered the plain behind the lumbering mule cart, the people began cheering and waving.

Melia leaned back to him to speak over the noise. "They are worried about the attack against us. They may also have seen the eagle take the dove and believe your arrival is propitious."

"Is it?" he asked.

She looked at him with gravity for a long moment.

Finally she said simply, "Yes."

Moments later, coming up a low rise they arrived at the city's double gate: a foot-thick outer gate recessed into the rock and bound with bronze, a short courtyard overlooked by a parapet above, and a second somewhat smaller gate also bound by bronze. Tall thresholds crossed each gate, grooved to admit only wagon wheels of a specific width. He had seen something like it in the streets of Pompeii, but that city was built in an advanced iron age. Nothing like this, as far as he knew, had been attempted in any bronze age settlement. He gaped at the massive fortification as they passed underneath, the cart wheels channeling into the grooves and the mules straining to heave up the ramp.

"You're staring," Melia said.

"If your whole city is this well planned, you have a magnificent defense," he said, looking at the parapet overhead where archers would have freedom to shoot down into the small courtyard, a kind of "murder well" that did not begin to appear in medieval European castles until the Fourteenth Century. "I saw nothing like this in the ruins of Nineveh."

"Nineveh is in ruins?" She was shocked.

"It was when I went there during a tour in Iraq," he replied, not thinking. "It is on the east side of the river. The Tigris river. The city of Mosul is on the west side now."

"But we have trade routes with Nineveh," she said, looking at him shrewdly. "They know the Goddess. When was it destroyed?"

He suddenly recollected himself. How much could he tell her? What could she believe?

"We need to talk," he said. "I may have come from a time far in your future, just as you may be far in my past. As for Nineveh, it was destroyed about 2400 years, I mean harvests, before my time."

"I have been suspecting something like this," she said, "that the Goddess chose not just a great warrior, but she chose to break the order of time itself in sending you to us. Mother will be interested in what you tell me, and I expect the Matrons will want to interview you."

By now the cart had rumbled into the town and people crowded the rooftops, pushing to get a glimpse of them. A collection of naked children ran alongside, threatening every moment to fall beneath the large cart wheels and occasionally getting a swipe across the face from a mule's tail when they got too close. Nothing about the driver varied at all. No change of posture, no change of behavior, the whip never twitched at the odiferous rumps of his beasts, but as the streets grew smoother his flopping mouth made fewer popping sounds.

The streets gave way to a large, shady marketplace, an area with neat rows of awnings where women sold vegetables, chickens, cheeses, and clothing. Huge plane trees, five to eight feet in diameter and over ninety feet tall, grew in parallel rows across the square, making an impenetrable barrier to the cart and providing dense, cool shade for the many pedestrians.

Shops were everywhere, with thousands of people moving to and fro, carrying packages and buckets. Most package bearers were naked adults, deeply tanned, with solid metal collars. They followed women wearing robes with colorful patterns woven into the fabric. The air smelled of fresh produce, airy shade, and comfortable wealth.

The peace of the marketplace was stunning when compared to the noisy desperation of marketplaces in Karachi and Kabul that he knew well. Naked children, some with collars, ran and played in the shade. Twenty or so naked boys and girls, jostling and giggling together, had climbed one of the branching trees to watch the scene below them. Their dangling legs lined a yard-thick branch of dusky tan bark.

The cart turned right, moving around the market along a row of houses with shady awnings. They passed women grouped at tables sipping wine and eating, loom workers, men carving wooden figurines, jewelers, and goldsmiths. At the far side of the market, a wide staircase beyond another heavy defensive gate wound up steep rock toward the acropolis. Next to the staircase was a high-walled palace.

Shelby understood at once the strategy of this structure.

During peace, it could be the seat of government, and during war, it could garrison soldiers to defend the staircase. Any invading army that made it as far as the marketplace would still have more than half the battle to fight to gain the acropolis itself.

"How many times has your city been invaded?" he asked Melia, nodding at the superb defenses. "I am amazed at how well planned your defenses are. Even your marketplace could be barricaded to halt an attacking army. A lot of thought and planning has gone into creating these defenses."

As she turned to respond, the sunlight slanted across her face, bringing into sharp relief her small, straight nose and her high cheeks, her full lips in a gentle smile. "We have not retreated to the acropolis for defense since the new gates were built 200 harvests ago," she said. He did not see her lips move, so she must have been speaking in his head. "From time to time, we send young men of military promise to tour the world, and they return with ideas and plans to make us safer. Nineveh is one of the places they go."

It was unnerving to have someone speaking in his mind, but not astonishing.

"I recognize some parallels with Nineveh," he said aloud, not attempting to reply silently, "from what I could tell from the ruins."

"It is important to us to defend our women and children," she said aloud. This time he saw her lips move. "It is how we worship the Goddess and thrive. Surely you will learn more of this as
time passes."

"Meanwhile," she continued a moment later aloud, with a sigh of resignation, "you must meet the brothers." She gestured to four men standing on a low rise between the shady market and the palace.

Shelby wondered at her sudden switch to audible speech. Why did she go back and forth from speaking in his mind to speaking out loud? Just play?

The most prominent of the brothers had wild red hair and a golden red beard, was almost as broad as he was tall, and was in constant motion, laughing. He had no neck at all, his trapezoids reaching to his ears in a pyramid of muscle. The tallest one was slender, like a sinewy male model with dimples, but muscles that rippled in the daylight, a gymnast's physique, with tawny blond hair the color of wheat. Next to these two were a pale, dark-headed one with a slight stoop and deep set, suspicious eyes. His over-done smile with his upper lip curled back over his upper teeth, appeared insincere. The fourth was completely hairless, with a tiny nose and ears and the darker skin sometimes called "olive." Not green, just not tan, either. As far as Shelby could tell, he was completely expressionless and motionless, exactly the opposite of the burly redhead, and had the sleek muscles of a swimmer unlike the redhead's brute bulk.

"These are my brothers," Melia said, speaking loudly so they could also hear her as the cart pulled up. "They will take care of you. They also will want to test you, being men. Why men cannot believe what they see with their own eyes ... " Her voice trailed off. Then, more brightly, but only in his mind: "Please don't kill them. It would make your stay here more difficult."

She winked.

"Brothers," Melia said, once again audible, "here is a stranger who is our honored guest. His name is Shelby. He fought bravely and defeated armed men to rescue Mother and your sisters. Treat him as a brother and see to his needs." Turning back to Shelby, she whispered: "I may not see you again until the feast. Have you been at a feast before? Ask the brothers about it." She placed her hand on his forearm and turned back to the brothers. "Shelby, Kratos is the redheaded one, like father. A warrior. He killed a man with a head butt one time. Iapetus is the oldest, the black-headed one. Eurymedon is the youngest and tallest. The one with no hair is Ophion." Then she took her hand away, leaving Shelby with a distinct feeling of loss, but turned back to him and leaned closer to whisper, smiling, "If they try to test you, beware of Kratos' head."

Kalista whined and fussed as they got her out of the cart, every movement eliciting a string of complaints. Eventually her old nurse and other women managed to do it without making her bend in the middle. The brothers, all of whom offered to help, stood around helplessly watching the no-nonsense women handle the wounded girl. Shelby, towering over the brothers, stood off to one side observing.

Ruddy Kratos had massive shoulders and thick gold hair on his arms and the backs of his hands and fingers. He looked like a serious, dangerous fighter. But then, Shelby saw, three of the brothers had the no-nonsense look of warriors he had seen among his Ranger buddies. Dangerous. Happy. Playful. They reminded him of lions sporting with a ball in the zoo. "I know these guys," he thought. "I have eaten with them and shared barracks and night patrols. We have played together like dangerous beasts. They are tough and reliable. They are warriors."

The fourth brother, the one with the chilling smile, was Iapetus. He differed significantly from the others, apparently lacking their bonhomie. Not so rugged or physical as they, he appeared to be much older and more cunning despite the pallor of his skin and the early stoop of his neck. From Shelby's vantage, looking down on them, he saw this brother's stringy black hair thinning on top, a monk's cap of baldness clearly visible.

"He could be dangerous in his own way," thought Shelby.

"More a politician than a fighter. That smile. I don't know about that smile. Reminds me of a dyspeptic quartermaster with something to hide and nothing to give away."

CHAPTER

TEN

The brothers led Shelby into the long porticoes of the palace, past columned open courtyards with fountains burbling in cooling pools and through labyrinths of corridors and rooms of obscure purpose. Not far into the maze they turned into a quiet courtyard where, at the far end between two columns, was a curtained alcove.

"We leave you here for women," the dyspeptic brother said, "and come back after bath and rest." He managed a grimace resembling a smile, like a constipated colonel with piles or the rictus smile of a corpse.

"We have questions," added the burly Kratos with a laugh. "Many questions, but rest now, if women allow it." They grinned broadly at him, relishing some kind of joke as he scanned his quarters: marble floor piled with pillows and soft fleeces, an unlit brazier on a tripod, some low stools with trays. Someone prepared the place with care.

"Thanks," Shelby said, overwhelmed by his circumstances.

"I look forward to seeing you soon."

Later, Shelby lounged in his alcove, pondering the strange path his life has taken, the odd twists of luck, and the consequences of decisions. He was, overall, pleased with his present circumstances. Beautiful, mostly nude women had thronged around him during the bath, pampering him, apparently ready to satisfy his every whim.

"Not a bad gig for an old army horse," he thought.

Then, as often happens, his mind drifted back to his last battle in Afghanistan. His actions there earned him a Silver Star and another Purple Heart, but they also prompted his superiors to encourage his separation from the Army.

A man cannot dissect twenty-five insurgents with automatic weapons without attracting attention. He had become a public relations risk. He understood that. The political consequences of slaughtering twenty-five native Afghanis single-handedly, even if they were armed, even if they had been firing on his troops and had killed his commanding officer — well, it had been better for him to leave the service quietly before the popular presses found out.

And he really had gone over the edge. He knew that. He knew it at the time, but chose to let his rage take over anyway. Afterward, they said he had fired thousands of rounds. Lying on the cushions in the alcove, Shelby stared at the ancient wooden beams overhead, his eyes fixed, unmoving, as his mind searched through the uncontrolled horror he had roused within himself on that last mountaintop. Images of his cruelty rose to torment him in his reverie: an old, toothless villager kneeling before him, his arms raised in supplication and Shelby, enraged, emptying a clip into the man's scrawny body. Blood mist floated on the hilltop, he tasted it, felt it settling onto his face, the odors of cordite and disemboweled intestines overwhelming the high mountain air.

Rousing, he jumped back to the present.

"Where the hell am I?" he wondered.

"Have I jumped through time? Does that explain it?"

His mind wandered back to the room full of attractive, short women who had scrubbed and toweled him, chattering and laughing all the while. He thought of their naked athletic legs and their vibrating young breasts.

"Why would I want to go back?" he thought, smiling. "But no Melia. She told me she wouldn't be there, and she's not using that mind trick to speak to me. I wonder where she is. I wonder what the bath would have been like with just Melia."

In another room, Melia was carefully inspecting her toes. Sitting in a cushioned chair of gold-plated wood, she propped her feet on the marble ledge of a great window that looked out over the vast, rich valley. She was deep in thought. Around her sat or stood the young women who had tended Shelby in the bath.

She had known these girls her whole life. They were the daughters of important women in the city, or cousins. They, like her, had been raised to be self-determining, independent, and strong-willed. With their muscles rippling beneath their soft, smooth skin, they looked like sculptures carved out of butter. Feminine and commanding, they were beautiful, fearless, and most of all, they were reasonable. They served the priestess and her daughters who, with the council of Matrons, ruled the country. They were politically powerful and knew it, and they were young. None in this group was a fool. None was timid. Despite their laughter and chatter, they had bathed Shelby with appraising, analytical attention, taking the measure of the man with his physique. He passed their scrutiny, and they were amused.

"He's clean," said the old nurse Euphrosyne, finally breaking the silence, speaking for the girls. Her wrinkled, jowly face showed no movement, but her eyes twinkled with suppressed mirth. Behind her back, where the girls could see her but Melia could not, she wiggled the fingers of one hand. Then she made a cupping motion with both hands and bounced her hands up and down, the universal gesture of weighing. A suppressed gasp of giggling rose around the group of girls. They would have laughed out loud if Melia had not looked so blank. Oh, he was clean, their glances told one another. You betcha. Clean as a god.

Melia, seeming not to hear, continued looking at her toes while the others choked back their good humor. She separated each one, slowly pulling it side to side, over and over.

Eventually, she lifted her head and looked blankly at the nurse, who dropped her eyes. Then, she went back to studying her toes.

The girls knew Melia just as she knew them; they knew her temper and respected her intelligence. They knew she thought of things possibly far beyond their understanding, but they suspected she was thinking of the strange giant's physique, as they all were. His huge biceps and pectorals. His perfect skin with its small round scar on the top of his shoulder. His maleness.

They sensed that the big man impressed her, and they had never seen her impressed by a man before. The number of suitors who had shown up and left like scalded dogs could not be counted. Her disdain was legendary. Now, she seemed to see this big man, this giant, in a way she had never seen another. They all saw her eyes turn back to him as they led him into the baths.

He was a good-looking man. Not a boy. Powerful. A fighter. Intense, almost brooding, but chiseled handsome. He had an air of vast experience. He was obviously smart and capable. He had a dimpled chin. Shoulders like boulders. Short, curled black hair. A day's growth of thick, smooth whiskers. Best of all, he was new, different, with an exciting new smell of manhood about him, so unlike all the men they already knew. Of course she thought about him. They all did.

Poor Rhodia had actually wet herself when she started rubbing oil onto his massive shoulders. Poor girl. She was trying so hard to keep from panting, or passing out, and giving herself away. They all had giggled at her, but the stranger completely ignored her. Rhodia was so bright red! They couldn't wait to tell Melia. She would want to know every detail about the stranger, everything they had seen. She had told them so, yet here she sat brooding in her own way, playing with her toes.

The room remained quiet for some time, no one daring to stir.

Finally Melia rose from her chair.

"I won't stand for it," she said. "I will not be victimized by Achaean men. None of us will. This must never happen again!"

She glared around her at the women, who did not know whether to humor her or act stunned. What did this have to do with the big man, they wondered. None of them was a victim. It was a country ruled by women. The women chose their mates, and discarded them if they were not satisfactory. This was the way it had always been in the city.

Melia paced impatiently around the room.

"Only women are allowed at the sacred pool," she raged.

"Now three men have been there in one day. Two of them are dead, and before long we will know their identities. And this Shelby man has also been there." She was the only one who had mastered the pronunciation of his name.

She paced for a while.

"Rhodia!" she said suddenly.

The twenty-year old recoiled with sudden guilt, the pink draining from her face, but then she recovered. Her long, dark lashes flickered. With her left hand, she pulled her red hair up away from her shoulder, tucking it behind her ear. She was a powerful young woman, bold and clever. She also was the closest of all of them to Melia.

"Oh, get over it," Melia said, seeing her discomfort. "You can't have him anyway."

The girl bit her lower lip.

"Don't worry," Melia added. "I'm not angry."

As the eldest daughter of Metis, Melia was the second-most powerful person in the city. She could make life too unpleasant to live if she chose.

"No, I've been thinking about something else entirely," she said. "You know the prophecy. The Goddess was to send someone. This Shelby might be the one, but while we figure that out I want to get this stranger to help us form a group of fighting women to protect the pool. What do you think of that idea, Rhodia? Would you help do that? We all know your temper. You would be perfect to help lead it."

Rhodia was prepared for ridicule and rebuke over the man's bath. That was what she expected, and she hesitated. As she tried to think of an answer, there was a commotion at the door.

ELEVEN

XXXXXXXXXX

"Ah, so there everyone is," said Metis, sweeping into the airy room as the girls leapt to their feet. "Some of you," she said, pointing, "turn that chair around. Melia, I do not know why you are always staring out the window. The life is in here, in the home."

The chair squeaked on the marble floor as naked slave girls rushed to move it.

Metis sat down, the queen's prerogative in a room of standing women.

"Now I suppose you have all heard the report on the stranger," she said, glancing around the room. Her eyes fell on Rhodia, who reddened again. "Really, Rhodia," she admonished. "You should control yourself."

The poor girl blushed beet red, obviously ashamed.

"But . . ." she started.

Metis held up her hand. "I don't want to hear it."

"But . . ." Rhodia began again.

"I said I don't want to hear it. You acted like you had never seen a man before, much less bathed one, and you have. All of you have. Many times. It is one of the hospitality rules of the Goddess. We care for the stranger as one of our own when he has been welcomed into the house."

"Well, within reason," she added after a moment's reflection.

She unwrapped the bundle one of the servants had brought in. Inside were Shelby's clothes, shed before the bath.

"I have been through his clothes," she said. "They are very different from anything we know, but I see nothing here that could be a weapon, other than his remarkable knife. Except for the knife," she held it up for all of them to see, "he is unarmed. He is a magnificent warrior and we're lucky to have him, but until we know him better we should never be alone with him. I do not believe he is a threat to any of us, but you never know with strangers."

"I volunteer to test his threat," said Rhodia, wishing instantly she had kept her mouth shut. The room erupted in merriment and even Metis smiled briefly, before turning an icy glare on Rhodia that silenced them all.

She paused for order, then spread out the bundle of clothing and emptied Shelby's pack onto the floor. "Not much here seems useful" she said. "How did he get food on his journey? What kind of animals can he catch and eat with just a knife? I am bewildered by this man. We have much still to learn."

She mused for a while as Melia watched her.

"The cloth is very different from ours," Melia finally said, rubbing Shelby's t-shirt between her thumb and fingers, "and the seams are double-sewn with great precision. I do not believe there is any cloth like it in any country we have heard of. But I do not believe he is a god for all that he looks like one. A god does not carry any of these items, or dress in this cloth or in this way. He is a man. By and by, we will learn who he is and where he is from. Meanwhile, I think we have learned many new things already today."

"He can certainly fight," she added. "Like some great cat. You should have seen him leap."

"Yes," Metis added after a moment reflecting on her daughter's interest, "but his fighting is not like any I have ever seen. He is quicker and quieter than any man his size ought to be. You didn't see him slip away into the trees when Eumaeus and Yiannis came running up. One moment he was dozing against the tree next to Kalista, the next he vanished behind a tree. The next thing I knew, the guards were running up, and he was many paces away, creeping silently through the brush. He came out on the path behind them, his eyes blazing. He was ready to kill them, too, if I had not commanded them to kneel and not look behind. He is not a common warrior."

Metis watched as the girls took in the report, and saw Rhodia look dreamily down at the floor. "That girl," Metis thought, "will cause trouble."

"So, now that you've all heard the report," Metis finally

continued, "you know as much about him as anyone. We will gauge his boldness by and by, but what do you think of him? He is not one of us, but from a foreign land where they do things very differently. What do you think? Will he be trouble?"

"My lady," said Rhodia, emboldened again, "I don't think he will be any trouble at all." She could not help breaking into another smile, and the girls set to giggling again.

"Oh grow up," scolded Metis. "There are plenty of men in this world, and no matter how strongly you feel about one, sooner or later he will go off and get himself killed or you will choose another. It's the advantage women have over men, that we survive and they cannot live without us."

Then, Metis, too, allowed herself a smile, which broke the dam and released the excited chattering and giggling that the girls had been holding in so long. Their high-pitched voices and laughter echoed around the chamber and spilled out into the hallway beyond. "Ah, that civilizing force, the laughter of women," Metis thought.

For a while, she let them go, watching Melia, even Melia, smiling. "Now that is a rare thing," she thought. "A good thing. Maybe this giant has breached some wall inside the princess. The whole world will be pleased, if that has happened. The Goddess, all the women, have been wary of her disdain, her pride. How can she follow me as priestess if she remains a virgin? The Goddess is not interested in virginity, but in fecundity. Already Melia has missed some good harvests for bearing children, but it is not too late."

While the girls chattered and giggled to one another, Metis sent one of the slaves out for food. Soon, trays of figs and honey, bread, grapes, and wine came in.

She helped herself, offered some to Melia, then to the other girls, and the tension in the room eased into the companionable drone of women's happy voices.

"Now girls," she said, once they had settled down and the big man was no longer the only thing in their thoughts, "as you know, Phorbus will be feasting our guest tonight. I believe the king has sent the sons to talk to him, but our duty is to provide the hospitality for the feast."

"Oh, Mother," started Melia, "don't tell me you want us to dance for them. You know how it stirs them up."

"Well, of course you will dance for them. What else do you

expect? You will dance, and you will sing. Ilexa will play the lyre.

I will oversee the sacrifice, and Phorbus will preside over the men. That is how it is done."

"But Mother, it will put thoughts into their heads. You know what happens."

"My dear," she said, raising her voice a little to indicate that her mind was made up, "you will all dance, and you will lead the dancing. I expect you to dance as perfectly as you do everything else, and, yes, of course it stirs the men up. That is why we do it. We remind them of their youth and their power. It is how we honor the Goddess."

"Oh, Mother," Melia sulked. "What happens if they start to kill one another? What happens if Shelby, who is not used to our ways, cannot control himself, and the brothers have to kill him? Or worse, if he kills them? The room will be full of men, and no women after we leave. Who would calm them down? Surely we should be cautious around the stranger, until we know . . . ."

Metis held up her hand, and Melia fell silent.

"Moreover," Metis continued in a somewhat sterner tone,

"I expect all of you to smile at him. Yes, Melia. Especially you.

I expect you to smile at all the men. Don't give me that look. I know what I am doing."

She thought for a minute.

"Rhodia," she said, half turning in the chair, "you will not dance. Tonight you will sit against the wall and play the drums."

"But," the crestfallen girl pouted, "everyone will think I am a slave girl. I should dance, too."

"You have had enough fun already today. Tonight you will play the drums, and you will think about what you are doing and do it right, or tomorrow you will be learning how to knead bread in the kitchen."

"Again," she added sternly, "and this time, I will take away your clothes." The room was shocked by her words, but then they all saw a twinkle in her eye and the ghost of a grin on her lips. Everyone knew she was, almost, not serious. She was almost teasing Rhodia.

Almost.

"Now," she continued, standing up, "prepare yourselves. You all know what to do. Darken your eyes a little. Redden your lips.

Practice so you do it right. We will not have the house embarrassed by your clumsiness, girls. I am going to oversee the sacrifice, and Melia will join me when the sun reaches the far hill. The stranger deserves the best we can give, and the men of the city need to be reminded of their duty to us.

"Get ready," she concluded. Looking around her, she was pleased with what she saw, and she strode proudly from the room.

TWELVE

XXXXXXXXX

S ilent, naked women wearing only gold bands around their slim necks brought in his freshly washed clothes and his pack, along with refreshments of wine, cheese, and bread, and then withdrew without a look or a sound. Shelby was not sure what to make of it, but decided to accept what the house had to offer. It was turning into a pleasant place, so much nicer than twenty-first century Germany.

He was thinking about abandoning the twenty-first century altogether, if he had the chance, when the angular face of the oldest brother, Iapetus, poked through the folds in the hanging linen curtains and smiled that smile.

"Hello, friend," he said. "Want company?"

Iapetus' pallid complexion and apparent dyspepsia belonged to a much older, care-worn man. His eyelids telegraphed a life of uncommon boredom.

"Sure," Shelby said with an answering smile, rising. "Come and talk." He hoped his skill with the language was up to it. He quickly had no trouble at all with Melia, but some difficulty with the women during his bath. Of course, being surrounded by so many naked women had interfered with his concentration.

"I brought brothers," dyspeptic said, coming around the corner. Two of the others followed with grins, pushing and bumping.

They were a jocular pair, despite the scarred arms and the legs showing beneath their short tunics. The fourth brother was more somber, but well muscled though completely hairless.

"Their sandals are very fine," thought Shelby, admiring the gold decorations. Each brother had a gold hilted dagger in a sheath strapped to his shin. Their short tunics appeared to be woven from fine, sky-blue wool and trimmed with gold thread. A pattern of dark reds and blues was woven into the hems.

Shelby clasped forearms with each brother in turn, looking him in the eye, and tried to recall their names. He remembered Iapetus and ruddy Kratos right away, but needed some correction with Ophion's name, and had totally forgotten jocular Eurymedon's name.

"We come from counsel," Iapetus said sitting down, "with information on men. Bodies were here brought."

Lanky Ophion, the hairless one, nodded his bald oval head slightly, not removing his eyes from Shelby. His small ears lay close to his head, and his eyes seemed unusually bright, set deeply into the shadow of his hairless brow. He did not have a beard or any hair anywhere: bare arms, bare legs, no eyelashes even. His preternaturally immobile face was exacerbated by eyes that did not blink. The sense of self-possession and of absolute stillness in his demeanor suggested that he could be a dangerous opponent, missing nothing.

Now with a chance to appraise his physique, Shelby decided that Kratos looked every inch like a powerful fighter. His square body was topped with a neck so broad it was almost no neck at all. Redheaded and ruddy, his massive forearms and huge calves telegraphed dangerous, furious strength. His face bore a distinct resemblance to Phorbus, the king, and his wide-set teeth were perpetually on show behind meaty, smiling lips. Even his fingers, with their thick fur of golden red hair, looked short and pudgy with muscle.

The youngest brother, Eurymedon, in his mid-twenties, was more willowy and lithe than massive, like an Olympic gymnast instead of a fighter. Each sinewy muscle clearly showed as he moved his arms. Shelby noted that he looked more like a masculine version of Melia than like any of his brothers. His gray-green eyes favored Metis, though his lips curled in an almost-sneer. It was an expression of haughtiness, not of disdain.

Despite the men's physical differences, however, Shelby could tell the brothers were all members of the same family. Even hairless, small-nosed Ophion was similar to the others in noticeable ways.

"One man was thief from this city," Iapetus continued, "as Metis told. With sword she wounded him, but she killed him with rock when she hit cranium. His hands and legs bound were."

"Right," said Shelby, "When it all started, I didn't know what was going on. That man was closest to me and he was armed. I had seen the women coming down the hill. When they went into the cave where the water comes out, he dropped down from the wall onto the grass near the pool. He almost landed on me. I was not sure what to do, but I knew the women were not armed and both this man and the other were. I thought it would be best to subdue him, then come back to question him later."

Iapetus and the others nodded. They had already heard the accounts from the women. Shelby noticed that he was not hearing the articles in their spoken language and their word order was off, just as with Melia until he became accustomed to her speech.

"We are by other man mystified," Eurymedon broke in. "We not before him have seen. His right arm, the wound, we question. It is enigmatic."

"Women say you spear dodged and cut with sword his arm in your left hand, slashing underneath," Iapetus said. "We examined wound. More damage, perhaps arm cut off, done could you."

"My thought" Kratos said, turning serious. "Why you not cut off arm and him kill?"

"Well," said Shelby, thinking back, "it's not my habit to kill."

"If they only knew," he thought to himself.

"This was not a clear case in my mind," Shelby continued. "I mean, the women were unarmed and should have been defended, and the men were armed and obviously dangerous, but I prefer to leave men alive while I think through the situation. It is always easier to ask questions of the living than of the dead. The women, of course, had other ideas."

"Every day not is," Iapetus said, "that man naked two fully armed men subdues and two princesses and queen saves." He grinned unpleasantly. Shelby decided he did not like Iapetus.

Kratos nodded slowly, his eyes on Shelby.

"I still do not understand how slashed you his artery and disabled arm, yet not kill." Kratos was watching Shelby closely.

"I was trying to disarm and disable him, not kill him," Shelby said.

They looked at him blankly.

"My intent is to solve problems, to employ reason where possible."

"Are you saying that even though attacked they two princesses and queen you would leave men alive?" Eurymedon struggled to understand, the pattern of his language becoming clearer to Shelby.

"Well, all of you said that you didn't know where the man was from. Or even what his motives were. If he intended to assassinate the women, he brought enough backup to kill three unarmed women swiftly. If he intended to kidnap them, he could have killed one of them and bound the others. He might have been able to carry off all three."

Shelby stopped for a minute to think.

"If he were acting on his own, then I would be led to one kind of conclusion. If someone else sent him, I would be led to a different conclusion. I wanted to know whether I was dealing with the isolated action of a criminal, or with the design of a much larger force."

"Larger force," Kratos stated with certainty. "This man and his criminal companion were to women's pool sent to carry off women and steal gold treasure. They expected to strike blow at city to soften us for war."

"That may be," Shelby said. He paused to think about the consequences. "So you are saying that the disappearance of Metis would soften the city and make it vulnerable for war?"

"Yes. City mother is she," said Iapetus. "She is priestess of Goddess who gives life. To lose her and Melia at same time is catastrophe. People completely disheartened, worthless, by that. They would have no fight in them, no resistance."

All sat silent for a few minutes, and Shelby felt that his empathy with the brothers was growing.

Finally, Eurymedon spoke up.

"So you rescued not only our mother and our queen, but you also rescued the living presence of the Goddess. This is great accomplishment. At the feast tonight, you will be honored for it."

"Thanks," said Shelby, falling silent and waiting, but glad to notice that Eurymedon's speech was sounding more and more normal.

"Feast before" said Iapetus a moment later, unfolding that grin again, "we have few matters talk of. First, you need name we pronounce. Only Melia your name can say."

"And that's Melia," added Eurymedon, "so it doesn't count."

"Suggest name do you, or give you one?" Iapetus asked.

"My mother called me Icarus," said Shelby, "because she said she didn't know where I had come from, like I had just dropped out of the sky. That was her joke." His smile was not quite convincing, but he thought it would do fine for a name. Surely they would know the name.

"You Icarus are," said Iapetus, "if approve Metis and Matrons. Because we do not know where you come from, like legend. Icarus is for you good name. Metis will approve. When she you calls Icarus, that is you." Iapetus nodded and blinked as he spoke of Metis.

"That's a curious gesture," thought Shelby.

"Now, Icarus," Kratos said, "we need to know how you came to be at pool of women."

They all looked steadily at Shelby without a flicker of eyelid or muscle. Waiting.

"I will tell you everything just as it happened," Shelby said, returning their steady look. "I don't expect you to understand, though, because I don't understand."

Kratos frowned. The others just stared.

"You already know that I am a stranger. Probably you already know that I am not like any other stranger you have ever seen."

"Not exactly true," said Kratos. "You are man. Women reported your impressive physical condition." He smirked as he said this.

The other brothers remained rigidly attentive, concentrating on Shelby.

"We know you fight can and warrior respect deserve," Kratos continued, "but we know not where you learned to fight or why you fight the way you do, so we don't know if you can join us as warrior. We know about you little, and this makes us uncomfortable. The city is not open. We allow no strangers. You are here only because Metis brought you, and she has her own reasons. So we need to know who you are and how you came to be here, and then perhaps we will learn your ways and you will learn ours."

Now Shelby realized that Kratos' speech was also clearing up for him.

"Usually we kill strangers," added Eurymedon.

"I am a man. Your mother thought I might be a god, but I'm not. I believe that I am from a different time than you, from a time in the future, but how I got here I do not know." Shelby knew they did not believe him. He could see the doubt in their eyes, even brooding anger.

He waited while they digested this.

"What you future mean?" asked Iapetus.

"Look at my clothes, my boots," said Shelby, retrieving the stack from the floor. "Here, let me show you my knife." He rummaged around in his pack and pulled out the SOG knife.

In unison, Kratos and Eurymedon reached down to the hilts of their own daggers. Ophion narrowed his eyes. Suddenly, with a gesture too fast to follow with the eye, a piece of knotted cord appeared in his hand. Iapetus recoiled, but then moved forward again as his eyes focused on the weapon.

"What is?" he asked. "I not these materials recognize."

"No," said Shelby. "This is a knife of course, but it is made from a metal that is very strong and does not rust. Possibly it could break, but probably not." He handed it hilt-first to Iapetus. "See, it is lightweight, but the blade will cut a bronze sword."

Iapetus tested the weight, the edge.

"Sharp," he said.

"Yes," said Shelby. "I shave with it, and I keep it sharp. What good is a dull knife?"

"To cut yourself," smiled Kratos, now on familiar territory.

Kratos knew about weapons. He held out his hand for the knife, which Iapetus passed to him, blade first.

"This is excellent weapon," Kratos pronounced. "We need swords like this. Spear points. This metal would change warfare."

"And you can use the metal for other things, too," said Shelby, "like axles, horse bits, gates."

"If you stay with us, could you teach us this metal to make?" asked Kratos.

"I don't know. I could teach you how to get started, but I am not trained at making metal. The trick is making a hot enough fire. But, you would have to learn to mine the metal and refine it, and even then you might not get it quite hot enough. Still, it would be a start."

They passed the knife between them. Then, Ophion, whose knotted cord had disappeared again, handed the knife back to him, hilt first. "Ophion is uncommonly observant," thought Shelby.

"The knife does not prove to us that you are from future, only that you are from place we do not know," Kratos finally said. "And it does not tell us how you came to the pool."

"I will tell you what you will not believe, but it is the truth," said Shelby, knowing that the hard part of the interview was coming up.

"I jumped from a flying machine, and I flew through the air until I landed in the pool."

THIRTEEN

XXXXXXXXXX

Eurymedon leapt to his feet, sputtering.

"That cannot be true," he said fiercely, "no man can fly. Tell us truth."

"I . . ." began Shelby.

"Icarus," began Iapetus, but Kratos interrupted them all, pulling Eurymedon back into a sitting position.

"You cannot fly. If you could fly, you would not have climbed the cliff with Kalista." Kratos was not pleased.

"You are right, Kratos," Shelby said. "I cannot fly the way you think of it. I can drop from heights and float down."

"Through the air." Kratos said it like a statement.

"Yes, through the air."

"If I throw you off acropolis, will you float down?"

"No, I will fall, just like you. I need a special device to be able to float. It's called a parachute."

"What height from did you jump?" Kratos' concern was re-mixing his syntax to Shelby's ears.

"That part might be harder to explain," Shelby said.

"From cloud? Did Olympians throw you down?"

"It will be difficult for you to understand, but no. Men made a machine that flies, I flew in it, and I jumped out of it to float down."

"I do not understand," said Kratos, "and not happy am I when I understand not. But finish story. Tell how you got to pool."

"I did not land in the pool because I wanted to, Kratos, but because when I was coming down there was no other place open enough to land. The device I used to float through the air, the parachute, is at the bottom of the pool. We can go there to pull it up, if you want."

"Why not tree?" Kratos had turned dark in the face. "Like a bird?"

"Birds do not weigh what a man weighs. The branches would break, and I would fall."

Shelby paused while the brothers processed this, nodding.

"Look," he said, "I know this is confusing but it is also confusing to me."

He told them about spending the night at the pool, the song of jackals, then seeing the man hiding in the woods above the pool.

"If you were submerged in the pool, you may be impotent," Eurymedon grinned. "That is what the women say. I don't know if it is true, but the women like to bathe in it, and the story keeps the men away."

"Perhaps you find out," said Iapetus, breaking the tension, and they laughed. All except Ophion, whose facial expression never varied.

Kratos, however, was still not satisfied.

"I have heard you say how you came to pool," he said. "I don't believe it, but I wait to make final judgment. I think you say truth, and I you want to believe, but I am still unsettled. I do not care for subtlety and disguise."

Shelby nodded.

"I don't know what flying machine is, and I don't know why you would leap from one. What happened to it when you leaped out, and where were you? Where is it now? I am more interested in flying machine than in some device that helps you float down. Flying machine might be important in war."

"Last night, if the flying machine did what it was supposed to do, it landed near Mount Ararat north of the land between the two rivers, far north of Nineveh. At least five other men and a woman were on board the machine, and they were delivering medicine to friends near the mountain."

Kratos made an exclamation that sounded like "bullshit."

"These things are hard to explain, Kratos."

"Then how know we you lie not?"

A vein over Kratos' left eye bulged on his forehead, and sinews at his temple showed the clinch of his jaw. Shelby recognized the inherent intimidation in these displays.

"I told you that I came from a different time, a time in the future. In my time, we have flying machines, and soldiers are trained to float from them as one form of warfare. In that way, soldiers get behind the enemy to destroy his supply and pin him between two forces. I was one of those soldiers."

"I know you fight. Were you trained to fight?"

"Yes. I am a warrior in my own time."

"We may learn more about your training soon. Meanwhile, stop talking about 'your own time.' I don't care about your own time, whatever you mean by time. You are here now, and I want to know why."

"Kratos, my friend, I want to know why, too. I do not understand it any more than you do. When I woke up yesterday morning, I was far away from here. When I leapt from that flying machine last night, I was still far away, and I was living in an age that had flying machines, exotic clothing, strange metals, and other tools you have never seen. I can tell you of these things at length, but unless you believe me when I say that I don't know why I am here or how I got here, then nothing else matters."

Kratos stared at Shelby for a few moments. No one dared to move. Shelby held Kratos' gaze without flinching, but with his chin down a little, hoping that his demeanor would be interpreted as honesty and not as belligerence.

Finally, Kratos spoke again.

"Metis said her first impression was that you were the god Hermes, who is both great benefactor and great trickster. He delights in disguises and tricks. I do not believe that you are Hermes, but I think Metis may have sensed something about you that is disguised. I want you to tell me what it is."

He leaned back, folding his arms across his chest. All of them shifted a little on their cushions.

Shelby did not take his eyes from Kratos.

"My friend Kratos," he began, "you have put your finger on the very thing that disturbs me also. Something is hidden here, but it is hidden also from me. I will tell you what I think has happened to me, but I don't expect you to believe me because I don't know that I believe it myself."

Shelby was aware that Kratos likely had killed more men in hand-to-hand combat than anyone he had ever known. Kratos had that air. His mobile face was like a storm cloud, furrowed with concentration and danger.

"What I think happened," Shelby said, "is that sometime during the night, while I was asleep by the pool, or maybe before that when I leapt from the flying machine to float down, I was moved backward through time from my own age to yours. It is a difficult thing to understand, but it is the only explanation. I see no iron or steel in your culture. I see no bits on your horses or stirrups on your saddles. I see only bronze tools and weapons. This tells me that I have moved backward in time almost four thousand years. I mean, harvests."

Kratos was not satisfied, but finally, he sighed with resignation.

"I don't believe the hidden thing has been revealed," he said, "but I don't believe you are lying either. I think you are telling the truth, as you understand it. What do the rest of you think?" Now, Shelby realized with relief, the syntax of Kratos' speech was normal. In a corner of his mind he wondered why the progression was Eurymedon first, now Kratos. Ophion had spoken hardly at all, but Iapetus' speech remained dense, as though shrouded.

"Is truth-teller," said Iapetus, "but truth hard understand is. I him like. He tell us if different he thought."

"There was the eagle," reminded Eurymedon.

"Yes," nodded Iapetus. "Eagle that caught dove. Good omen. It is symbol that gods favor us."

"Also, the eagle can fly," added Kratos sternly, looking at Shelby, "but Icarus cannot fly." Then, he smiled.

"Oh, I can't fly," Shelby said. "I can stand, walk, run, jump, roll on the ground, and climb, but I can't fly."

"He rescued the women and he tended very skillfully to Kalista," said Eurymedon. "We don't know how he got here, but he has already been a blessing to us."

"I agree," said Kratos. "It would be wrong to kill him. Metis invited him in, so we accept him as a guest. I remain mystified. Part of my mind suggests that he might have been in with the other two men."

Kratos spoke to the other brothers now, as though Shelby were not there.

"He could have killed both of those men, but he didn't. One he merely subdued. The other might have recovered. His actions made him look heroic, but other interpretations are possible. He could have hired them. If he did, he could only have one of two motives: One, he intended to take the women himself, and then did not do it. Maybe he changed his mind. Maybe they were too fierce for him, and he realized he could not take them alone, but I doubt it. From that may come his second motive, which he has accomplished. He has entered our city, and even our palace."

Kratos paused while his words sank in. "If he is spy sent here to examine our defenses and seek out weakness, then he is very dangerous man indeed." Shifting on his cushion, he gazed at each of his brothers in turn. Coming to rest on Iapetus, he said, "If he is traitor, we must kill him."

Then, turning to Shelby: "I have one more question."

"I think you are suspicious of me," said Shelby, smiling.

"It is my nature," Kratos responded. "I am forthright man, but many men are not." He let that sink in. "If you three were together, then you have succeeded in one thing because you have entered city as a spy. If you were not with them, however, perhaps another motive. Perhaps you went to pool to win approval of Melia. Many men have tried to win Melia's approval, and all have failed. We think you may have succeeded."

Eurymedon broke in with a wide grin. "Of course, none of the others first appeared before her naked, so you may have given yourself an advantage the others had not thought of."

They all laughed, and the tension eased amid the questions and suspicions, which did not go away.

"So," Kratos continued, "if you are an enemy, then you are here as spy on the city. If you are suitor, then you are here to woo Melia, and we need to know even more about you. You are dangerous man."

"Friend Kratos," Shelby said, "I understand your concern and also your very thoughtful analysis of this situation. I assure you that I mean no harm to anyone, and I will answer all questions you may ask. I am here only because Metis invited me, and I am not a spy."

"The eagle could not have been a plan," said Eurymedon, after a bit of reflection. "That was a divine sign. I do not believe he is a spy. And if he is here for Melia," he added with a wistful grin, "I think we brothers will have little luck affecting her opinion of him."

Ophion agreed, speaking for the first time. "You are right about Melia," he said in a low voice. Shelby was surprised at the nasal, deep-toned sound of Ophion's voice.

"Brothers," said Shelby, "I hope you will not kill me and that you will allow me to show my gratitude in your service. If Melia wishes to know more about me, I will welcome that. If she does not, I would still like to be of what use I can be to you and the city."

"Noble Icarus," said Iapetus, his upper teeth showing. "We your words to counsel report, we will. At feast, to meet you many elders want, though your story puzzle will."

"If you want a bit of fun afterwards," said Kratos rising with the others and his speech resuming its familiar pattern as he became more comfortable with Shelby, "and you can still stand from all the wine we will make you drink, I hear of a lion prowling the southern farmlands. Maybe we can go and hunt him, eh? What do you think?"

"Never hunted lion," Shelby said, "but it sounds like fun. Will we bait him or track him?"

"If he's there, he will be tracking us," said Kratos, his face breaking into a wide grin that showed the gaps between his teeth. "That's the fun of it." With a chuckle he led the way out.

Iapetus lingered.

"It time is feast for prepare. Sacrifice tending Metis and other women are. I want about you know more, what you do, what you know. Maybe time we have?" He reached up to clap Shelby on the shoulder in a gesture of familiarity that Shelby found unwelcoming, then disappeared through the curtains.

FOURTEEN

XXXXXXXXX

"Oh hurry up!" exclaimed Melia crossly. The girls braiding her hair looked at one another knowingly over the top of her head, and pretended to hurry.

"This is taking much too long. Get on with it. I have things to do."

Though she was not yet dressed, the sunlight angling into her second floor chamber was already turning a deep gold. She had only minutes to prepare for the sacrifice. After that, she would have no time to tend to herself.

"I need to see Shelby before I leave for the sacrifice," she said, for the, perhaps, twentieth time. "He has no idea what is going on, and somebody needs to tell him."

"I'll tell him," offered Rhodia, emboldened now that her indiscretion at the bath was common knowledge.

"You will do no such thing," snapped Melia. "I will have you stripped and flogged and tied to a mule cart if I catch you talking to him again today. Believe me, I'll be watching."

A quick turn of her head to emphasize her point yanked against one of the girls braiding her hair.

"Ouch!" she cried.

"We will be done in a moment, if you don't pull it all out and make us start over," said one of the girls, snippily.

"Besides, Melia," said Ilexa, who was already dressed and never understood why it took others so long to get ready, "it is just a feast. We've been to thousands of feasts, and this isn't even a big one. No one new will be there. Except Icarus, of course."

Ilexa was teasing, but Melia did not appear amused.

"Arrrgh!" she growled. "Hurry up!"

The braiders were nearly done anyway. They had taken her long auburn hair and wrapped it in tight braids around her head, with the merest fluff of a ponytail at the back. They expected the ponytail to captivate the men.

"Are you done yet?" Melia complained.

"Melia, settle down," said Rhodia. "This agitation is not a good sign."

"Oh sure," said Melia. "You're the one who bathed him."

Suddenly, she quieted, blushing a little.

All the girls exchanged looks. Maybe love had finally made a successful assault on Melia's cold heart after all. This was going to be a very interesting evening. Very interesting.

"Kratos wants to take Shelby lion hunting after the feast," Melia continued. "One of the slave girls told me. You know I hear everything. That's what she said. Lion hunting. After the feast! After the day he has already had!"

"Does this worry you?" asked one of the braiders, finishing up.

"Of course it worries me. You know Kratos. Big bully. Always wants to test wits and strength against everyone. He won't rest until he's gone against Shelby."

She paused.

"I already told Shelby not to kill them, but what if he forgets? What if they trap him so he gets killed? What then?"

No one answered.

"Melia! Melia!" cried a voice from the hallway. Little Kalista appeared in the doorway, holding her side. "Mother says I am too young to go to the feast and that I have to stay in my bed all night. It's not fair."

"Kalista, what are you doing up?" Melia asked. "You will start bleeding again, and then the whole day's healing will be wasted." Turning to some of the others: "Take her back to her room, and stay with her until she calms down. Get her some wine."

They all understood. Some wine, and perhaps something a little stronger to help her sleep.

"Kalista," she continued, "you will not miss anything, but you are wounded, dear one, and you can't go to the feast. How would you stand or sit? You would have to lie down the whole time. Go with these girls back to your room, and I promise you we will send you lots of treats."

"But I want to know what's going on, too!"

"You will. I promise." Melia tried to look like a kind older sister. With nearly eight harvests difference in age between them, Kalista had always been like a little doll to her.

"I will come and talk to you when I can and tell you everything that happens. Everything that is said, all the funny stories, everything. Some of the girls will bring you sweet things from the feast all along, so it will be the same as being there."

"I want them to carry my bed down to the portico where I can hear it all," pouted Kalista. "If I have to stay in my bed, then I want my bed moved!"

"Kalista, I promise. I will send my own nurse, Euphrosyne, to see that you don't feel left out. Now go back to your room. You are not a fit spectacle for the feast."

"Do it," added Metis, coming in from her adjoining room. "Off with you. Some of you, go with her. Make her comfortable, but make her lie down and be still."

To Melia: "Are you ready? It's time. We must go fast if we are to catch Helios on the rim of the hills."

"Yes, Mother," Melia answered, rising and fastening her gowns together one more time. The short dancing gown, which reached only to mid thigh and fastened over her shoulders with golden brooches, was easy to put on. Over the fine pleated linen, she draped an indigo robe with gold thread tracing the birds of wisdom: the owls who watch through the night, the ravens who scent death, the eagles who are the divine will.

In her hair, the girls fastened the silver disc of the moon, and from her perfect ears dangled stars set with glittering crystals from the cave of the Goddess. Her long bare neck was unadorned, making an important statement in a culture where nakedness and a band on the neck denoted slavery. On each arm she wore silver bracelets set with the same glittering crystals, each bracelet representing the fish from the sacred pond.

Down her right side where the two halves of the robe came together, her body could be seen from armpit all the way down her long leg to her foot. The robe was clasped closed at hip and breast with spun silver woven into cords and tied with ingenious knots set with glittering crystals. She was completely covered, but the glimpses of her beautiful body as it peeked through the strategic openings of the gown would drive many men — men who were not familiar with the costume — to distraction.

This was why she was dressed this way.

It was not a costume she liked, but it was what was expected of the rising queen — to weave the female spell, to draw forth the power of men, to summon and command them and bend them to the will of the Goddess: to procreate, to protect, to bring peace. In the dress and in the manner of wearing it, she symbolized everything that made life. The crops, the animals, the burgeoning vineyards and the ripening grain, the smell of bread in the morning, the laughter of women and the noisy play of children, the golden age of humankind. The people believed how she moved in it predicted the rainfall and the harvest, the increase of flocks, and easy births.

Tonight she was to wear it for Shelby, even though he was an ignorant foreigner and a dangerous man.

"Mother," she said as they walked out into the gathering gold of the falling day, "Mother, I really wish you would think about this dance tonight. We can have the sacrifice, and the Goddess will be pleased whether I dance or not."

"Hush, child. I have decided."

"But Mother, what of the stranger. We need to think of him. I know already that he has seen me."

"You have seen him, too, my dear. He is the first man you have looked at and seen. This is an important night for both of you."

"What do you mean?"

"I mean that how he responds tonight will tell us more about him than anything he can say or any question we can ask. We will measure the man tonight."

Displeasure passed quickly across Melia's face, and then was gone.

"Mother, it's not fair to test a stranger like this on his first night. He won't know how to respond. What if he does something stupid? What if Kratos attacks him, or one of the others provokes him? What if one of the boys from the city tries to test him?"

"What boys?"

"You know, Iros, Athanasios, Noemon. The boys who want me. Surely you know who I mean. Do you think it will be good for them to see that I continue to reject them now that this strange man has appeared? What if he provokes them? What if their jealousy causes them to provoke him? I watched him this morning. He is not a man to play with. He is a warrior in his own way, though different from ours, and that makes him more dangerous than a bear."

"Kratos has invited him lion hunting after the feast."

"I know, Mother, I know. I'm not nearly as worried about Shelby meeting the lion as I am about Shelby meeting the boys from the city. The boys are so, so foolish. They will think they can impress me if they fight with him. Oh!" She stamped her foot in frustration. "Men are so predictable! Don't you see?"

"I do see, dear, and that's why we are doing this. Everybody is predictable, except your Icarus. He is the mystery we do not understand. We don't know who he is, where he came from, who his parents are, how he got here, or how he will act. Tonight, we will find out."

"Does it have to be like this? Do I have to provoke him?"

"Can you provoke him?"

"Mother, I know it. He touched me at the pool, and it was like lightning struck both of us. I don't want to lose that feeling in something so, so, I don't know, something so put up, so calculated."

"You have a lot to learn about men, my dear," smiled Metis, and spoke no more for they were drawing near to the site of the sacrifice.

FIFTEEN

✗✗✗✗✗✗✗✗✗✗

S helby drummed his fingers across his thighs, tensed and released his muscles. He hated waiting. He wanted to explore the palace and learn more about his surroundings, but after meeting the brothers, he knew he must wait for an invitation. Now that he understood the nature of their suspicions, it would be dangerous for him to be loose in the house.

"Relax," he told himself, and lay back on the cushion of thick sheepskins and stuffed pillows, looking upward.

Massive marble columns rose into the air, supporting the carved roof. Around the walls ran a frieze of dark blue stone, probably lapis lazuli. Sconces set into the columns held torches ready to be lit at night. The second floor of the palace completely encircled the courtyard as well, and he had the sense that most of the women were on the second floor. Sconces made of pure gold were set into the columns at the second floor level. "They will look very cheery in the dark," he thought.

Closing his eyes, he focused all his attention on his other senses. He heard the pet quail in the courtyard scratching at the tamped gravel, and the constant splashing of a spring-fed fountain.

Though filled with activity, the house was almost silent. People hurriedly passing from one place to another, their clothing breezing and their light sandals or bare feet made the only other sound. He did not yet understand how the house functioned. He knew he was in an alcove off the portico around a central courtyard, or around one of the courtyards. He assumed the house contained other courtyards and was larger than it appeared from the outside.

"I wonder where Melia is," he thought. He longed to see her again. The hours they had been apart seemed like days.

His thoughts stalled. "Melia," he said. "Melia."

Nothing. No response from the magical girl.

"Where is Melia? When can I see her again? If I touch her arm again, will I get the same buzz in my chest?" He summoned every detail of her to his mind's eye.

"She is so beautiful. That skin, those flexing muscles, that flush of rage. Touching her was like touching the innermost part of myself."

"I wonder if she felt the same way. Probably not. I have no standing with her. She lives here. She has thousands of other men to choose from. She could choose any one."

"I am just a stranger," he thought. "Maybe one to be treated with patience and civility. Perhaps, in her mind, that is all I am."

He heard a slight patter, like the sound of naked feet on tile, and sensed the room change. It was warmer now, and smelled of fresh bread and milk, the smell of women. He opened his eyes.

Three naked girls stood quietly at a distance, looking at him. When they saw him open his eyes, they slipped behind the linen curtains. Moments later, they returned with several other women.

The oldest one, the wrinkled old woman who had supervised his bath, spoke first.

"Hello, Icarus. We hope you are rested."

"Thank you, Old Mother," he replied, hoping it was the proper term of address.

Her face showed nothing, but he thought he saw her eyes twinkle. His first foray into formal speech might have been a success. He had not been with these people a full day yet, but he felt growing confidence in his ability to communicate. He had little difficulty talking to the brothers, and now he felt that he fully understood their speech. Remarkable. One of many remarkable things to happen today, and as he realized that he the image of Melia floated like a ghost in his mind's eye.

"We were told to dress you for feast and to explain what to expect," the old woman said.

"Thank you," he said again.

"Melia insisted on proper instruction. That is why she sent me, her nurse. I am called Euphrosyne."

"I am pleased to meet you, Euphrosyne," he said.

She nodded gravely. "What I say will be proper. What brothers told you maybe not, for they are jokers. So sit, and I tell you."

He sat quietly while she told him about the upcoming feast, the sacrifice, the arrival of Metis with the meat, the way the meat of the sacrifice would be served, and the dance.

"All of the girls will be dancing?" he asked.

"All girls who are worthy," she replied, taking him by the hand and urging him to stand. "Melia leads them."

Melia.

Well, then. That was all right. He could look forward to that.

"At feast," the old woman continued as she and the naked girls draped him in the native costume, "herald goes around room and welcomes each guest by name. Last, he comes to you. This herald tells what he knows of you, and all say welcome. Then all eat. Meat is big ritual. After eating, wine. Wine is next big ritual.

Wine steward brings wine and fills wine cup for Phorbus. "Phorbus speaks, probably to praise you," she continued. "He passes the cup to you, and you drink. You may speak at that time. Then you pass cup to man next to you, probably one brother for they have all met you. Or may be one of our important warriors. I think it is Amphinomus, our general after Phorbus. Each guest may speak, but most will not. It is bad form to slow the cup with words. At some point, maybe right after the first circuit of the cup or maybe later, Phorbus will invite you to tell your story. Phorbus decides for all men when to slow down drinking. More likely, he will ask for reports from Amphinomus and others about actions at sacred pool. When all is open, then you tell your story. Then the gifts and more wine. Much more wine. Men enjoy these feasts. Women not so much, for they make men noisy and bad sleepers." She clucked with disapproval at the thought.

She made him turn around in front of her, inspecting his clothes, re-tying a cord to provide better draping. "You will do well, Icarus," she said at last, smiling at him. "You have already convinced women, and when they are convinced, then everyone is convinced." Her nearly toothless smile was broad and reassuring. "Wise men trust women's instincts about men in the same way they trust hunting dog instincts about game. We women like you."

"I am honored," he said. "Your words give me courage for the evening."

He hoisted his rucksack, prepared to go. Euphrosyne had explained that he must carry something into the feast to give away. Everything except the gear he left behind at the pool was in the rucksack. He would empty it before the king tonight. It was all he had, and he was convinced that it contained no secrets. Someone had been through everything in it, but had taken nothing. Tonight, he would just give it all away and see what happened.

SIXTEEN

XXXXXXXXX

Iapetus joined Shelby as Euphrosyne led him to the andron, the gathering room for men.

"Icarus, you look like tall citizen," he said with his unnerving smile.

"I think I would like very much to be a citizen," Shelby replied, "if I can serve the city and your mother. It is not at all clear to me that I will be able to return to my own time and country, and fate has put me here. I wish to make the most of the time fate has given me."

"About that," Iapetus said, a thoughtful look on his face, "you must tell us your ethnos tonight, your country, and your genos, your family. We all desire knowledge where come you and your country."

"I will hide nothing from you," Shelby said, "but I hesitate to add to the confusion of my appearance here. I don't understand it, I don't expect anyone else to understand it, and I don't know how it happened. What of this story do you think the other men will want to hear?"

"Tell everything," Iapetus said. "Old men will respect your story, and everyone joys for saved women today. You have no idea how important that drasis, that act."

"I understand," Shelby replied, "but remain confused. I feel as though I don't know anything right now." Perhaps it was his disliking for Iapetus, but Shelby noticed that he accommodated to Iapetus' speech patterns more slowly than to the others.

"You know some things," said Eurymedon, joining them. "You know Melia, and everyone is talking about how you have changed her. Has she changed you?"

"That's a personal question, Eurymedon," Shelby said with a smile, "but I will tell you. Yes, I am a different person since meeting her this morning." He paused. "I can't explain that either."

"Metis can explain it, but she probably won't," Eurymedon said, his youthful face breaking into a grin. "Good luck to you, little giant."

"I hear nothing little about this man," said Iapetus, attempting to be jocular.

"He's a giant in every way, according to the women," Eurymedon chuckled, "but we are all little when it comes to Melia. We will see if he can grow." He made a gesture with his hand that caused Iapetus to burst into laughter.

The andron was a sumptuous room, large enough for 200 guests, lined with wide, padded benches covered with bolsters and pillows. Columns soared to the high ceiling, which was open to the evening sky above. Brilliant gold sconces on the columns held bright oil lamps. Faint smoke rose from them and dissipated through the open roof. The central floor of the room was covered with a thick woolen rug of pale blue.

"The full moon after this one coming bring traders," said Iapetus, following Shelby's upward gaze. "One moon and half a moon. Last full moon of summer. We trade much with surrounding countries at that time. Our sheep produce fine, silky wool that turns pale blue when brushed and spun. It looks dingy and gray on sheep, but after sheared them and washed, wool makes fine cloth and has a color traders prize much. We are wealthy city, and that is source of comfort to us, but also woe." He led Shelby to his place as other men began filling the room through various doors.

"Why woe?" asked Shelby.

"Because others envy. We keep constant guard on sheep, or they stolen be. Our sheep in world only have soft blue wool. Very rare. We also have every kind of metal: gold, silver, tin, copper, lead. Great mines have we in northern and eastern hills."

Iapetus paused to nod at some younger acquaintances. They nodded back, but their faces telegraphed displeasure.

"Our women also very beautiful," he continued, "and our fields abundant and rich. For these reasons, our neighbors jealous, and we fight always."

"I understand," said Shelby. "In my country we have a saying, 'peace through strength.' It means we can only be at peace when we are better at war than our neighbors."

"Yes, us that is. If you fight cannot, then fight must. If fight you can, then not. Sometimes fight because fool can beat you thinks."

"I've had some fights like that," agreed Shelby.

"So all we have. So all we have."

Despite Iapetus' statement, Shelby seriously doubted that Iapetus had ever been in a fight. The man's narrow shoulders, thin arms, and chin-forward posture all suggested he was the kind who talked big, then hid. Shelby thought less and less of Iapetus.

A large retinue of musty smelling, gray-headed old men entered with Phorbus at their head. The king spotted Shelby standing with Iapetus and signaled him to come and sit at his side. Iapetus nodded at Shelby and patted him on the back to send him on his way, then turned aside and sought his own seat with Ophion and Eurymedon several places down from Phorbus. Shelby noticed that the sour youths Iapetus had greeted earlier had seated themselves nearby, behind Iapetus.

Men in double rank spread around the rectangular room on cushions and low benches. The elders gathered toward the front of the room, sitting on either side of Phorbus. Younger men, warriors in their prime, men needing to be tested and ranked, some already leaders and some merely city boys with ambition, occupied the lower end of the rectangle.

Kratos dropped his solid bulk onto the bench to Phorbus' right, landing with a grunt. It was his favorite spot, the one that typically ensured he got the lion's share of the wine.

"Flying yet, Icarus?" he called, smiling.

"The wine has not yet started," replied Shelby with an answering smile. "We will see."

Kratos enjoyed the joke, and some of the elders smiled as well, looking from one to the other.

As the feast began, Phorbus went out of his way to be attentive to his guest. He sat him at his left hand, a place of great honor, and steered the conversation away from any questions of importance. Instead, he made sure every man in his corner of the room had a chance to greet Shelby.

A little later, a hush fell over the andron and all the men rose as Metis entered, ushering slaves bearing the sacrificial meat. She looked fatigued and moved slowly to her seat a little above and between Kratos and his father. When she sat, the rest of the room sat also and a pleasant murmuring began, unlike the almost belligerent raucousness of moments before. She was there as an observer, not a participant, but the change in the room at her presence was obvious to Shelby.

Several female attendants followed her and stood behind the royal pair at the head of the room as the vast platters of freshly roasted meat made their way around and everyone ate their fill. Then, a pair of muscular naked servants brought in a large golden bowl. More servants, supervised by a wine steward, carried in large wineskins and urns of water. A pleased murmur went up around the room at the number of wineskins.

The wine, perhaps four gallons, was mixed with water in the large bowl. Stirring the mixture with a short golden rod, the wine steward tasted it, smacked his lips, and added more wine. All of the men broke into smiles and begin jostling one another. They could tell from the generous portions of wine being poured out that this would be a night to remember. Truly the guest was honored.

When the wine steward was satisfied, the naked servants hoisted the heavy two-handed bowl, carefully pouring the mixed wine into a large golden goblet of about half a gallon. Then, falling on one knee, the steward presented the cup to Phorbus.

The king stood to receive the cup and turned to Metis. He spoke of her graces and understanding, and then thanked the Goddess through her for the gift of the sacrificial meat, the abundance of wine and grain, the sweet cheeses of the flocks. Raising the golden wine goblet, he knelt, tipped a few drops of wine on the floor as a gift to the Goddess, and presented the cup to her.

She took it to her lips and drank, saying nothing. The faraway look in her eyes indicated that she was in a kind of trance, or at the tail end of one. Phorbus took the cup again, tipped again, and then drank himself. He handed the cup back to the steward, who refilled it and handed the cup to Shelby.

As elegantly as possible, Shelby stood and lifted the cup over his head with both hands. It seemed the right thing to do. He thanked Phorbus for the gifts of shelter, food, and wine, tipped some of the wine from the cup, and then turned to Metis.

"My lady," he said, "I raise this cup to you, to your good health and long life, and to the blessings you bestow upon all who are fortunate to know you." Then, he drank, and passed the cup back to the beaming steward.

A murmur of approval filled the room.

The steward then presented the cup to the man sitting to Shelby's left, and so the circuit of the wine began. Each man tipped a few drops out, drank, and passed it on. When it got to

Kratos, the bowl was almost empty though the cup had been refilled many times. Had the man before him emptied it, it would have been refilled with wine and water and Kratos would have had the opportunity by the rules to drink it all. The men suspect the wine steward planned not to let that happen, given Kratos' reputation, and may have planted Kratos' companion to ensure it.

"Come now, friends," Kratos cried. "You have left me precious little here. Let us fill again, and look, you, move it along a little faster."

He drained the cup and held it out, but the wine steward smiled broadly, and stepped on to Phorbus, where he refilled the cup.

The cup went around the room four more times, each man drinking his fill. On the fourth circuit, it still had at least a quart of wine in it when it got to Kratos.

"This is more like it," he roared and drained the remainder of the wine in a single breath, exhaling loudly at the end and smiling broadly at the company. "Now, that's a draft that will prepare a man to hunt a lion!"

"Guess I'm in for a lion hunt," Shelby murmured to himself.

As the cup started around the room once more, the elders conferred with one another about the stranger. The general consensus was that he was not practiced enough in the arts of good manners to be anything other than what he said he was. He was a little clumsy and it was obvious that he was trying to understand how to fit in. He was not one of them, but more importantly, he was not one of the enemy either. Perhaps he really had just dropped into their midst out of nowhere.

Still, they were unwilling to come to a conclusion. They had not yet heard his story. They would know more after that, and they would know what to believe after they heard from the women. The Matrons would confer at dawn, and then the city would know. Meanwhile, he seemed to be a kindred spirit to Kratos, and that was a good thing. Perhaps he could help Kratos govern himself and keep him safe. Kratos was too important to the city to be wasted on foolish games. Maybe this stranger could help as he did with Metis, and Melia, and little Kalista. Physically, he seemed a match, the only man they knew who might match Kratos' strength.

During the cup's sixth circuit, drumming began in the outer corridor, and the men began to cheer. The dancers were arriving!

The timing was perfect. The food had been eaten, the wine had been shared and its effects felt, and now the evening's entertainment could begin.

The girls snaked into the room, their arms raised, twirling in unison. Altogether, they stamped their right feet. Then the sinuous line reversed with twirling and waving of arms. They danced in a line around and behind the men, sometimes leaning over them to breathe in their ears or lightly stroke their hairy chests. Sometimes they danced to one another.

The drumming was loud, varied, and insistent. Once they circled the room, the girls wove their way into the center, dancing on the woolen carpet. Then with a clash of cymbals, they stopped, raising their arms slowly to the passage where they entered. Everything was silent, except, of course, for the hushed breathing of the men. Attendants had carried away some of the lamps, and the light in the room, glinting off the golden objects on the walls and guests, dimmed.

"It's like a little galaxy of gold stars," thought Shelby.

The cymbals crashed again, and the drumming resumed, slow and soft this time. A lyre strummed, and a single moaning flute began to weave a hauntingly seductive tune.

Everyone looked toward the door. Suppressed gasps gave dimension to the darkened room.

Melia appeared in the passageway, arrayed in silver like an angel of the moon, her indigo shawl spread between her hands, her taut body caught in the rhythm of the dance.

She lifted her arms above her head and turned, slowly at first, then faster and faster. Every turn brought her closer to the center of the room. The indigo shawl spread from her hands like the wings of night, golden images of birds seeming to rise from it in the twinkling light. Her feet barely touched the ground, her clothes barely touched her body. With every turn, the long line of her sinuous body was exposed, the lifting flesh of her breasts, the concavity of her belly, the inward curve of her thighs. Now only her toes connected with the earth, moving faster and faster. The other girls surrounded her, all moving to the beat, stamping their feet together in rhythm.

Swirling around the waving form of Melia, the girls became more and more sensuous in their movements. The men saw nothing but hips, breasts, softly sculptured arms. Suddenly, the girls stopped, poised, and the drums stopped with them. Everything was silent. Then a new, slower cadence began on the drum, and the girls moved again, this time singing.

Shelby could not take his eyes off Melia. She rotated in his head, and his mind whirled. The movement of her hips dictated the beating of his heart, his breathing. She had entered entirely into him.

"I will never be myself again," he thought. "I will always and forever be partly me and partly Melia. My heart and my body move only because she moves."

He stared after her as she and the other women danced slowly in intertwining lines from the room, their singing voices fading with the drumming and flute into distant hallways. Stunned silence followed them, then the andron erupted in cheers and clapping, every man on his feet, every voice raised in the ebullience of joy and the promise of conquest.

Every voice except Shelby's, who remained transfixed by the apparition of Melia, unable to tell if he were dreaming or awake.

SEVENTEEN

XXXXXXXXX

Metis sat, chin propped on the back of her hand, her exhausted eyes dull beneath her drawn brows. Despite her trancelike appearance, she missed nothing. Shelby's complete submission to Melia was as evident to her as if he had stood up before the Goddess and the city and declared it out loud.

"He is no enemy now," she thought. "No matter what he may have been, he is no enemy now."

She turned her gaze to the stunned men around the room, watching how the sheer beauty of the withdrawing dancers entranced them. "Though he is no enemy, he may still be trouble as a friend. Time will tell," she thought.

During the eruption of applause and cheering from the men, attendants began bringing lamps back into the room, and the light grew, gradually restoring order. When the andron was lit and sufficiently quiet again, the speaking began.

Old Phemius, one of the city's senior elders, rose first. For decades, he had been the first to speak. He bowed to Metis, who in her reverie briefly lifted her drained eyes to him before sinking back into her thoughts. She did not need to attend to Phemius, who only said what everyone already knew.

Before Phemis finished recounting the story of the eagle and the dove, Metis saw Melia standing at the doorway. Stripped of her shawl and her silver ornaments, she caught Metis' eye. Metis raised one finger and beckoned her into the room. "The girl will rule here after me," she thought. "Though she knows much, she needs to know more about how these men think, the depths of their minds, their probing intelligences, the interplay of their anxieties and their jealousies. She will bend them to her will through her beauty, but they will follow her because she understands. Understanding is a lifelong process."

Melia slipped behind her father, touching him on his shoulder as she passed, and settled on the floor at her mother's feet, her right arm resting on her mother's knees, her legs folded beneath her, her head perfectly erect on her beautiful unadorned neck.

Phemius finished, but no one noticed. They had all been watching Melia. She turned her expressionless gaze on them all, and remained still. She had mastered the art of stillness and it drew them all to her.

Metis watched from beneath hooded eyes as her daughter manipulated the crowded room of leaders and warriors without stirring a finger, with perhaps only a glance and a tilt of her chin.

"I will let her rule now, if she can," Metis thought. "Let's see how she governs this crisis." Then, she, too, became still.

Phemius turned and asked Metis if his telling of the incidents of the morning was accurate. Metis remained still, allowing Melia to nod, to assume the power of the room. Phemius sat down, and Melia turned her gaze to Amphinomus, the commander of the warriors. She did not need to speak. Her look was her command. The general rose immediately, shaking his curly white hair as he stood.

"We examined the two men killed at the pool," he said to her, in a voice heard clearly across the silenced room. "Every part of the myth, the story, Phemius told is accurate."

Shelby realized that now he understood every speaker's vernacular. Is that because Melia entered the room? All the stilted-sounding language had vanished.

"It appears Icarus has told us the truth," Amphinomus continued. "The two intruders spent time on the rock above the pool, probably several hours judging from the compression of leaves and earth. We found footprints of one man embedded in soft earth where he leapt down. This coincides with the story Icarus told the women. So far as we are able to determine, everything happened exactly as it has been told. A fight, a spear point thrust deep into the ground, and two men destroyed.

"We know one. One was kleptos, a thief and fugitive from this city. He may have beguiled the other with tales of wealth and power. Or he may have been a guide. We know about him, his family, his friends, and his background. The world is a better place today because he is dead."

He paused and shifted on his feet, gazing steadily at Melia.

"We questioned his acquaintances and family and now know that he communicated with them. They told me his contact shocked them, as they never thought to hear from him again. However, they did not report the contact to us. This is suspicious. His mother and father both confessed that they missed their son and would like to see him again. We believe this is a natural desire.

But he may have contacted former acquaintances, as well, and thus we suspect he was motivated in his contact by more than a simple desire to perform his maternal respects."

Phemius rose again to speak, holding up a single finger as though to signal for attention. Thinking better of it, he sat back down.

"The other man is an Achaean," Amphinomus continued.

"We have watched them spread out of the north for many harvests. They lust after our sheep and our land. I think they also lust after our women and our gold." He swallowed, looked away from Melia, took in Shelby and then some others with his gaze, then looked back at Melia. "They take many wives and have many children, and over time they must expand their territory. Considering the damage to us if Mother and Melia had been taken, we must believe that this assault is part of a plan for war."

He paused to let his words soak in, and again looked around the room, letting his gaze linger on the younger warriors at the bottom of the andron.

"We are strengthening our watch on the northern border, at the passes through the mountains, and on the west where the hills are more difficult to defend. If an army is marching against us, we will know it." Finished now, Amphinomus nodded to Phemius and sat down.

Phemius rose and turned to Metis, then to Melia. "At this juncture, Mother, I think it would be useful for the assembly to hear the explanation of Icarus." He looked at Shelby and smiled in a kind, fatherly way, a look that did nothing to settle Shelby's nerves.

EIGHTEEN

XXXXXXXXXX

S helby's first reaction was to look at Melia, and he heard her voice saying, "You will do well." Swallowing, he stood as though floating, aware of the adrenaline surging through his body. He would rather face a firing squad than make a public speech, but all evening he had been remembering the many scenes of feasting and speaking written by Homer. He would try to imitate Homer's examples, but knew to keep it simple. He had nothing to gain as a stranger by attempting to speak elaborately, especially as language might still be a barrier.

"Queen," he began, shifting his eyes to Metis, who continued to sit quietly, eyes glazed, "and King, beautiful dancer Melia, and honored assembly." He paused and looked around the room. "I know I speak a language that differs from yours, and I hope it does not add to the confusion about why I am here. First let me thank all of you and this great city, and especially your queen and others, for the courtesy you have shown me this day." He paused again to let his words be unraveled. When he saw that they were following him, he went on.

"You have heard the story, from the moment that the women were attacked. The question you have of me is where I came from, who I am, and why I am here. I can only answer two of those questions. I can tell you who I am, and I can tell you where I come from and how I happened to be at the pool. I cannot tell you why I am here."

He looked around the room silently, his eyes peering into each man's face.

"I am a stranger here, as you know," he continued, "and I am here through no wish of my own. I come from a far country called

'America,' a very powerful country that lies far to the west over the great ocean beyond the pillars of Herakles."

His statement caused consternation and a subdued murmuring erupted as men whispered to one another. They had only heard myths of a distant ocean, and could not conceive of anything beyond it.

"In my country, we have developed weapons and items of daily use of which you have never heard. I will show some of these things to you in a few moments." He gestured to his rucksack on the floor next to Phorbus.

"From my youth, I have been a warrior like some of you here. I trained in warfare and I have seen much combat. After a dozen years of warfare, I was wounded and sent home to rest. I no longer go to battle, but I help my army develop new weapons and methods of delivery. Specifically, I work on a project to allow warriors to jump from great heights to the ground below without injury."

Iapetus spoke up.

"Icarus, tell how you came to our country."

"Certainly, friend Iapetus," he replied. "I flew."

A gasp went around the room.

"How did you fly, Icarus?" roared Kratos. "Can you fly now?"

"No, Kratos, my brother," said Shelby with a smile. "We have had this discussion. I cannot fly now. I have explained that in my country there are large machines that can sail upon the air as a ship sails upon the water."

"What kind of machine can sail upon the air?" asked Phorbus, sitting up in his throne and speaking in a voice that commanded respect and silence.

"You know how the wind feels in your face when you gallop your horse," said Shelby. "The faster you go, the more solid the air seems. We have machines that go very fast, much faster than the fastest horse. These machines are winged, and when they reach a certain speed, they lift from the ground."

"I'm confused," said Phorbus. "I really do not like to be confused. Yet the fact remains that you are here. We will listen to your story, and we will be entertained even if we do not believe it."

"Let me show you what I have brought with me," Shelby said, picking up his rucksack, "and then you will understand that I come from a different time and place. I am a man just like you. If you cut me, I will bleed. I cannot fly by myself, but I have been on machines that can fly. I hurt when I fall. I can become sick. I can fight and I know how to kill, but I don't like it. I desire to protect those who are weak from those who are stronger. I am devoted to a life of readiness and defense. I have led men in battle. I have carried my fallen comrades home for burial. I have tended the wounded. I am only a man like you."

He opened the pack.

"First, you will see that I am from a different time and place if you look at the construction of this pack. These devices are called zippers." He pointed them out and showed how they work. "Very useful," he added.

"These are my clothes, of a fabric you have never seen and woven and stitched in ways you have not seen."

He unpacked his backup shorts, socks, his windbreaker.

"Now we get to the items you might be more interested in. This is my coil of rope. Usually I would carry it on the outside of my pack, but yesterday when I packed I thought it would ride easier inside. Phorbus, I make you a present of my rope."

He presented the coiled rope to the king, who took it, fingering it.

Phorbus was amazed. "It seems to be an ideal rope," he said, "soft, smooth, and light. How strong is it?"

"It could lift one of those columns," said Shelby, pointing at the two-foot stone pillars that surrounded the hall.

Men around the room exclaimed and craned closer to get a better look.

Phorbus held up the blue striped rope for all to see, then uncoiled it. "It is a strong rope," Phorbus said. "It has no give. It does not stretch, yet is very light. This is a worthy gift."

Shelby took the rest of his items out of the pack, leaving only the flask of whisky in the bottom. He explained each one in turn, and then passed the items to Phorbus, who distributed them among the sons. They, in turn, allowed their neighbors to examine them.

When nearly everything was out, he pulled out the knife, holding it up.

"This is a knife from my country," he said. He drew it from its sheath. Another gasp went around the room, and Amphinomus reached for the dagger on his shin.

"This knife is made from a metal that is very hard. It cuts

bronze. It could penetrate a bronze shield. It can be damaged, but not easily, and it will hold its sharp edge for many cuttings." He shaved the hair from his left arm to demonstrate.

"I present this knife to the city, and offer it to our queen Metis as a token of my allegiance to her, to this city, to her family, and to all of you."

He sheathed the knife and turned, kneeling before Metis, placing the knife in her lap with both hands.

"Good so far, Shelby," breathed Melia in words only he could hear as he bent to place the knife. The scent of her made him dizzy.

Metis stirred as though she had been slumbering. She was clearly exhausted.

"Icarus, friend," she said, "thank you for this gift." She lifted the sheathed knife above her head.

"Children," she said, addressing the audience, including even men who were decades older, "Icarus is our friend. Treat him with respect and regard his power." She paused, exhausted with her effort to speak, but gathering fresh will to go on. "Do not provoke him, for his ways are not ours, and you do so at your peril. I have seen him fight, and I have seen his strength. He is like a god, though he denies it. And now I have something to tell you that I hoped I would not need to say."

She struggled to stand, Melia springing up to help her.

"The Goddess has revealed to me that the most dangerous war of our long history is upon us. Many in this room will die for the city in the coming trials. We cannot triumph if we do things the same way we always have. The Goddess forecast the coming troubles, but she also said she would send someone to help us."

Her face became more animated and strength seemed to flow into her. Her lungs swelled and her eyes brightened. "We will prevail," she said, "the Goddess promises us this, and the life we know will continue beyond the lifetimes of any here tonight. Possibly even beyond the life of Icarus himself. Icarus may be the one the Goddess has sent. Or we may expect another." She smiled at him, then looked back at the andron. "The ways of the gods are not clear, and when and whether we will be tested before all of you have forgotten this prophecy we cannot know. Know only this, that the Goddess forecasts war and destruction. I believe the war will also be fought in the heavens, as well as between men, and its outcome is not known nor the age when peace returns. Worship the Goddess, my brave children, and pray for her protection, for you will need it."

She looked at Shelby. "You have not emptied your pack," she said, smiling, "but I wish you to keep this knife for me. You may need it." With both hands she handed the SOG back to him.

"You are right," he said. "There remain two more items." And he pulled out his LED flashlight.

"Before I show you this item," he said, "I want to warn you not to be alarmed. I will not use it much, because it has a limited life. If I leave it turned on, it will spend its life in a day. But while it has life, it is very useful."

He turned on the flashlight, almost completely hidden in his large hand.

The crowd gasped and surged in surprise. Men leapt to their feet, pointing.

"Yes," he said, as they quietened. "It's not magic but it is a wonderful thing. In my country we call it a flashlight." He shone the beam around the room and up one of the tall columns toward the clear night. Then he turned to Melia.

"I present this flashlight to you, as a token of my love and appreciation. Today you have brought light into my heart that will live much longer than this little thing."

On one knee before her, he held the flashlight up to her in two hands.

"We misnamed you," said Phorbus, smiling at him. "We should have named you 'Phosphor,' the light bringer."

"No," said Melia smiling and holding out both her hands to Shelby. "We named this man Icarus because he dropped upon us without warning. But the Goddess be blessed that he came today! Here, sir, hold this little light for me," she said smiling as she handed it back to him, "as a token of that inward light."

The room filled with laughter and applause, and there was a lusty cheer from the back ranks.

When the men settled again, Shelby turned and smiled at them all, and then said, "One item yet remains in my pack to give out, and this one is for Kratos."

"Friend Kratos," he said to the square man with the wild red hair and wide-set teeth, "friend Kratos, I have saved a precious gift for you. I hope you like it."

Kratos rose and stepped forward.

Shelby pulled out the flask, and the whole assembly erupted into laughter when they realized it was filled with a liquid. They guessed what Kratos would be given.

He let them have their fun, and when they subsided, he spoke loudly. "This is a flask of wine, as you can see, but the wine is not like the wine you have drunk tonight. Will you share it with me? Perhaps others will share it?"

Kratos broke into a broad grin, and lifted a golden cup, draining the last of the wine from it.

"Icarus, I can drink anything you can drink," he said, puffing up his chest, "but I can't fly, and neither can you!"

"Let's drink to that," said Shelby, looking around to see if others were willing to try his "wine," the 124 proof whiskey.

Eurymedon held up a cup, remembered it had wine in it and drained it. Iapetus started to hold up his cup, but stopped.

Shelby reached over and poured whisky into the cup held by Eurymedon, who sniffed at it suspiciously. Then, he turned to Kratos, who lifted his cup.

"I will drink from the flask itself," said Shelby, "which is my custom. Let me fill your cup."

Kratos took the cup and tossed back the whisky while Shelby leaned his head back and drank deeply. A full swallow's worth.

Kratos looked up at him with a broad grin, and Eurymedon began lifting the cup to his lips to join them.

"That is great wine," said Kratos in a loud voice, and then, just as Eurymedon was about to taste it, he suddenly grabbed his throat with both hands and turned red in the face. He jerked. His eyes bulged out, and he fell to his knees.

Shelby was shocked. "What? What is this?" he exclaimed to himself.

Kratos fell over backward and went rigid with his legs straight out, trembling.

"He's playing, Shelby," said Melia's voice in his head, but he was too alarmed to pay attention.

He dropped the hastily-capped flask and bent down over Kratos, whose eyes were closed. He was not breathing. Eurymedon quietly put his untouched cup down. Phorbus and Metis were both alert now, watching, and Amphinomus rose to his feet, his dagger out. The men at the rear of the andron surged forward in alarm. Shelby bent over him, listening for breathing, put his hand on his chest to feel the heart pulse.

"It can't be poisoning," he thought. "Is it an allergic reaction? A stroke? A heart attack? Good God, what have I done?"

Beneath his hand was a strong, steady pulse.

With a loud laugh, Kratos sprang up, grabbing Shelby around the head. It was a wrestling hold, and Kratos was trying to throw him, laughing loudly. "It's a joke," Shelby thought with relief. "A practical joke by Kratos!

"Oh, well, let's see how he fights."

Without warning, Shelby scooted out from under Kratos, reversing the hold. Now he was above the shorter man, trying to bend his arm behind his back. Instantly, Kratos fell to the floor, sweeping his legs against Shelby's, trying to trip him, but Shelby evaded, twisting but holding on.

The crowd cheered on the fight. Out of the corner of his eye, Shelby saw Melia and Metis smiling, and Phorbus slapped his knees with pleasure. As sweat broke out on both men, Kratos became more slippery.

The shorter man was very fast and very strong, but he could not break away from Shelby. They pulled one another to the ground, part of Shelby's mind telling him that he should not embarrass his opponent in a friendly fight, part of him wondering if he could.

At last, he and Kratos were locked faced to face, each breathing hard. Kratos reared back his head. Sensing the blow, Shelby jerked sideways, but still caught the head butt glancing on the side of his face. Kratos reared back again, but Shelby was ready.

Changing holds, Shelby pulled the shorter man into his chest and rolled with him to the ground. He was so much taller that he lifted Kratos completely off the ground, and they hit full and hard. Shelby continued the roll, Kratos still held tightly against his torso, and then wrapped his legs around him. He held on. Kratos was pinned, and his head butting was through.

"One, two, three," seconds counted Shelby silently. Then, looking up at Melia and smiling, he rolled, letting Kratos go. The short warrior broke free, kipped away, and came up crouched for a lunge. Shelby somersaulted backward to give them some distance, and hand-sprung into a similar crouch.

"Friend Kratos," he called, "I didn't know you would like my wine so much!"

The other laughed and stood straight. "You are a fighting dog, Icarus. That was a good match."

"Kratos, I think you beat me," Shelby said, breathing heavily. "Your head is too hard for an old man like me. Come," he said, straightening up and smiling, "let's drink some more of this wine."

Phorbus rose with a broad smile on his face and called in servants. As Shelby stood with his arm over Kratos' shoulder and Kratos' arm around his waist, servant after servant, all naked, entered with gifts: bronze armor, a gold-chased bronze shield, robes, gold goblets and chains, swords, and spears. Ophion offered his own gift, a rope woven from human hair, and Iapetus placed an intricate dagger with a jewel-encrusted hilt on the heap. Kratos clapped Shelby on the back and dropped his own sword into the pile, and Eurymedon added a magnificent bow and a quiver of arrows. Melia brought him a javelin, handing it to him rather than placing it on the pile, a smile in her eyes.

Finally, when the heap of treasure was mounded in front of him, Metis stood, and the whole room stood with her.

"Icarus, welcome to the city at the center of the world," she proclaimed. "Honored guest and friend, you have here a home for as long as you remain."

NINETEEN

✕✕✕✕✕✕✕✕✕

The party was over, and Kratos and Shelby set out for the lion. As they neared the city's southern gate, they saw the last of the partygoers entering their homes. Now the streets were deserted, except for the sentries on the walls and at the gate.

"We're going out to kill that lion," Kratos called to the guards, his words slurring. "Open up!"

"But Kratos," said one of the gate guards, dismayed. "We are not allowed to open the gates. Orders."

"We'll kill some guards first if we need to," Kratos said, shifting his long spear from his right hand to his left and absentmindedly scratching his balls.

They heard the unhappy guards discussing this. Then, they grumblingly assented, and the postern gate — the small gate next to the main gates — opened. It was big enough for a man, but not a horse, and they passed through a narrow passage and slipped outside the walls.

"Now, friend Icarus," said Kratos, as they padded along the dirt road further and further from the city. "I have heard that the lion comes up in the night from the south."

"That's the direction of the sacred pool," Shelby said. "Isn't it?"

"Yes," answered Kratos, "mostly. The pool is further to the west. Maybe the lion beds down in the hills to the south, near the pool, but not too near." Kratos belched. "The Goddess keeps almost all the wicked and unworthy away from the pool." He paused. "That's another reason why I question how you got there."

"Are you saying I'm wicked and unworthy?" Shelby grinned.

"Almost all, I said," replied Kratos. "Not just you. Two others were at the pool also." He grinned mischievously back.

They carried long spears, and Kratos also had a short bronze sword at his side. Shelby had his SOG knife, which, with its nine-inch blade, he doubted would be much help against a lion. Neither of them thought the encumbrance of a shield would be much use. If they met a lion, stealth and rapidity of movement and cunning would be their only hope.

"About 20 percent stealth and about 80 percent being able to outrun the lion," Shelby decided as he thought about it a little longer. "Maybe 100 percent being able to outrun the lion."

"If a lion stalks you," he wondered, "what do you do? You can't climb a tree, because lions climb trees. You can't run, because they can run maybe three times faster. They can hit sixty miles per hour in short bursts. They aren't long distance runners, though. If you can get, say, a mile or two ahead of him, you might avoid being eaten."

"Hey Kratos," he said after a moment, as they ambled along the road kicking up dust. "I understand there are two rules for hunting lions."

"Oh?"

"Yeah. Rule One: Hunt in the daylight when your eyesight gives you an even chance against his nose."

"That makes sense, but remember, he hunts with his ears, too. A blind lion can still eat."

"Right, which leads to Rule Two."

"What?" The toe of Kratos' sandal caught on a hard spot in the path, and he stumbled a little, righting himself with his spear.

"Rule Two: Don't do it at all."

"You are a funny man, Icarus. Now then, answer me this question." He burped. They were well beyond the city walls now, and the burp seemed to disturb the quiet countryside. Shelby thought that maybe the shorter man was enjoying his large quantities of wine a little more than necessary. "Answer this: If we do not hunt the lion, who will hunt him?"

Shelby looked at the stars, recognized the constellations. Leo was still unseen, below the horizon.

"That's why I'm here," he said at last. "Also, because I think I may need to keep you alive tonight."

"Ha! Good man." Kratos clapped him on the back. "We may live to hunt many lions after tonight. But, tonight, we hunt this one."

Their spears were not the crude flint affairs he had seen earlier in what was turning out to be an incredibly long day. These spears were outfitted with long, bronze four-bladed heads, tapering to an exceptionally sharp point. Each edge was razor sharp.

A puncture made by one of the points would cut simultaneously both up and down and side to side, leaving a star-shaped hole. The shaft of each spear was about nine feet. They were too long, and too heavy, to throw. They were thrusting weapons. Deadly, but not designed for precision. This bothered Shelby. Rangers like precision weapons.

Kratos broke in on his thoughts.

"The peasants report that the lion comes every night to carry off a sheep or a cow," he said. "I doubt that this is true, because a lion does not need to eat every night. Maybe he just enjoys killing." He paused for a moment to pull his chiton, or tunic, out of the crack of his ass, hiking a leg. With his huge muscles, clothes were just in the way.

"He seems to be moving up from the southern slopes, but he has a wide range. Two men on foot will not do much, so I have already sent a mounted troop to ride behind us and funnel him toward us. The lion will not attack a group of men, even though he might enjoy a horse. He will slink away and look for easier prey."

Kratos gave his famous smile, scattering the moonlight with his teeth.

"That means, he will eat us if he can."

"Sua sponte," Shelby muttered to himself. "The trouble I can get myself into."

The Latin motto was drilled into every Ranger. It had been the Ranger motto for half a century. You slept with it. You woke with it. You remembered it. You were reminded of it. For Shelby, he admitted to himself, the worst part about being out of the Army was the sense that he no longer had a place to be, no place where he belonged, no danger to volunteer for, and so, no honor.

"Sua Sponte," he thought again. "I am because I am willing. I am the one who volunteers."

"You see, Icarus," Kratos continued, "the way you hunt a lion is you let the lion hunt you."

"I thought it was more dangerous if you did that."

"Icarus, you have much to learn about the world. Tell me what you know about the lion."

"I only know a little, and most of that is about the lions in Africa. I know nothing about the lions here."

They strolled for a few more steps along the broad path through fields of standing grain. "For example," Shelby continued, "I know that the male lions usually don't do much of the hunting. They let the females do that."

"Wise males," said Kratos. He was sobering up quickly.

Shelby thought that Kratos' metabolism must be incredible.

"The females hunt in a pack. They coordinate with one another. One will act as a decoy to set the prey in motion, but the others are in ambush waiting for it."

"Our lions do not hunt in a pack," said Kratos. "We have only one lion. I think this one is a male because he eats what he kills, and he doesn't carry away the remains. The female will carry her kill back to her cubs. Still, we lose more livestock than one lion would eat, so I am suspicious. But I have seen his tracks and they are much larger than the usual female."

The wind rippled gently through the grain, which seemed to stretch out before them like a shallow sea. At every step, they stirred living things from the sweet smelling plants: whirring grasshoppers, white winged fluttering moths. Elsewhere, the field, lit almost entirely by the stars and a hint of moon behind the far eastern mountains, was still except for the occasional stirrings made by the gentle air. The insects there were undisturbed. The jagged outline of hills bordering the valley loomed in the distance. Behind them, like so many stars drawn to earth, glowed torches carried by sentries on the city walls, now several miles away. And Shelby saw a light in the white temple on the acropolis, very faint, very far away.

"But," continued Kratos, "tell me why we let the lion hunt us."

Calm pervaded the fields, as though nothing dangerous could be lurking there. Shelby pondered the question in silence but kept scanning the fields, uneasy. He was beginning to find Kratos' nonchalance disturbing, and it occurred to him to wonder how many lions Kratos had hunted, and killed.

"Will he hunt us?" Shelby finally asked in response. "I thought wild animals generally tried to avoid humans."

"Icarus, you cannot hunt a hunter. The hunter will hunt you. If there are two hunters, they will hunt one another. When it is a lion and a man, the lion hunts the man because he is the greater hunter. He has a better nose, better eyesight, better hearing, and he is stronger and faster and less fearful."

Kratos acted a little put out and took on a patronizing tone.

"Two of us only are here. You are meatier and taller, so he may see you first. I am shorter, so he may think I am an easier target." He chuckled. "Either way, before this night is done, one of us will smell lion and know his own fear." He paused and pulled up his short fighting tunic, or chiton, splashing urine onto the dirt road. "In case he misses us the first time, I will leave a trail to follow."

Shelby turned away and surveyed the fields again. In the far distance he heard the whinny of a horse, borne down from the north by a light air. Suddenly, he felt a funny yet familiar sensation in his hands and lower arms, the kind of feeling he had the first time he jumped out of an airplane.

The fear washed over him suddenly and he almost dropped the spear. Behind his eyes, the mind's theater began projecting scenes of war and slaughter. The barrel of an AK-47 looked down at him from only feet away. He closed his eyes for a moment, fighting to regain control, hoping to hide the shudder from Kratos, that involuntary twitch, the sudden tightening of abdominals and pecs, the goose bumps, the hollowness.

"Come back, Shelby," he heard the voice saying. Her voice.

He heard it in his head, not his ears. "Come back."

When he snapped out of it, Kratos was looking out across the field.

"I think he will find us soon. Let us stroll and talk quietly together, but stay alert. Already I think he may be stalking us."

Shelby looked around, the fear lifting his feet from the ground. At Landschul, the hospital next to Ramstein where they took him after Afghanistan, the medics told him that he probably would have some Post Traumatic Stress Syndrome, to be aware of it. "Nobody gets shot and doesn't remember it," they said. "Don't be surprised. It may crop up when you don't need it to." "No," he told himself, "settle down. Focus. This is now. Look, the moon is about to show over the hill. Keep your night vision by not looking at it."

He swallowed, but his throat was dry.

"If we hear him, that means he has scented us," Kratos continued. "He may roar. He likes to scare his prey into running, because they are so easy to track. They make so much noise. He can catch anything that runs, and I think he has more fun that way."

Shelby glanced behind at the trail winding back to the city, lengthening in visibility as the rim of the moon breached the far hills, deliberately slowing his breathing, getting himself under control again.

"We will not hear him on the attack until he is upon us. Possibly you will hear his breath just before you feel it on the back of your neck. Possibly he will growl as he is lunging at us, but then he will already be in the air. We can only kill him if we are better prepared for his attack, and anticipate his charge. Otherwise, one of us is his dinner tonight."

"I will not allow him to enjoy much of you, Kratos," Shelby said, trying to make a joke, hoping that he had put down the weightless fear that gripped him.

"I am sorry you did not bring more of that wine," Kratos replied. "Wine with his dinner. That's what the lion needs."

"Well, if he eats you, he'll get plenty," Shelby said with a laugh.

"Funny, Icarus. Funny." But Kratos enjoyed the comment.

They walked along in silence, surrounded by the profound peace of the fields and the hills. Shelby found it hard to believe that anything as dangerous as an 800-pound lion could be creeping through the fields on their trail.

Fifteen minutes passed. Once the moon was clearly up, Kratos proposed to retrace their footsteps along the road.

"Maybe we have not left a good enough scent," he said.

The nimbleness of fear loosened everything in Shelby's body. His limbs grew supple, and he knew he would lose attentiveness now that all his glycogen had been used. He struggled to confront the irregular patterns of his body, to find that happy medium that means survival.

"You've done this thousands of times," he reminded himself. "You have faced death often. Get over it."

"Kratos," he began, thinking to change the subject and relax a little, but the shorter man held up his hand.

"Look," Kratos said.

They were back at the place where Kratos urinated on the road. In the damp dirt was the imprint of a huge lion's paw, wider than a man's boot, bigger than a man's hand with the fingers spread.

"He has found us."

For the first time, Shelby saw anxiety in Kratos' face, but it quickly turned to glee in the moonlight.

"We will have our lion tonight, Icarus," Kratos whispered harshly. "Maybe in the next instant, maybe in an hour. When he thinks the time is right and we are relaxed, that is when he will spring."

In an odd way, Shelby was relieved. Knowing that a real menace was lurking in the dark was better than phantoms. Real things he could deal with, even things like the lion. The phantoms were much more powerful, because they did not terminate. They had no dimension, and could not be killed. The lion was real, here and now. He sighed.

"Ah, Icarus," said Kratos, "if I live, I may come to love you for that sigh. Now I know you are here to hunt the lion."

"Bring him on," Shelby growled, grinding his teeth. "It will be the perfect end to a very interesting day."

CHAPTER

TWENTY

I n the pale light of the moon, Shelby noticed the lion's paw
prints almost overlapped. The hind paws were almost directly
behind or on top of the forepaws. A meter or so ahead, the
prints appeared again. Each step covered a lot of ground. This lion
was huge.

The lion's fur absorbed the sound of its feet striking the
ground and dampened the rush of air around its body. The prickling on the back of his neck told him that even now they were being watched. Scanned. The inhuman brain behind those eyes and
teeth was calculating distances and attack velocities.

Kratos, who had moved ahead several paces, paused to look
back at Shelby squatting in the road, examining the prints.

"He has been tracking us this whole time, friend Icarus," he
whispered. "We are already marked men." The sense of urgency
was clear in his voice. "He could have attacked us at moonrise
without warning. Now he is somewhere in the darkness watching us. It is my scent he carries on his paw, but he may take
either of us."

Shelby rose slowly to standing, glancing over his shoulder
down the road behind. He saw it clearly in the moonlight. No
shadows, no movement. Either the lion was behind them on the
road, or, more likely, off to their right, moving with great stealth
through the standing grain. The light air, not really a breeze, came
down from the north, and the lion would prefer to hunt with their
scent always in his nose, borne along by the air. The lion was
downwind.

Shelby nodded his head to the right, and Kratos glanced that
way.

"Maybe," he whispered. "You may be right, Icarus, but a lion is not predictable. He is a very skilled hunter."

He moved up to join Kratos, though he worried about the limited range of motion with the spear, with Kratos to one side. Still, it was comforting to have a fighter standing nearby. "The paradox of war," he thought. "You want your friends next to you, but that might reduce their effectiveness while also making them targets." For a moment, his eyes began to glaze with a scene of smoke and explosion, but he grabbed himself before he slipped away into unreality.

"If we are alert to our right, he will attack from our left," said Kratos. "If he is threatened, he will attack from the front. I don't think he feels threatened, though, because he has not warned us with a growl. This lion is hungry, not angry." He paused and stepped ahead. "Be alert. Be ready." Again the powerful man's face showed mad grinning. "Be ready!"

Nothing.

Nothing happened.

Nothing moved in the grain. The light air died away, and the world became still. The whirring and buzzing of insects subsided, then came alive again. From the far edge of the field where the shadows deepened under the native stands of olive and ash trees, a night bird sang a plaintive call. Behind them, the moving torches on the city walls were very far away, winking on and off with a promise of safety.

To run would mean to die. Anything that moved would attract the lion. Anything that ran would be killed in his massive jaws, his ferocious legs and claws.

The waiting always got to Shelby. Again he blinked away the vision of war, the fear, the stench of death.

Kratos whispered that they should move along the road, separate a little, be casual, perhaps talk in a loud voice to indicate a lack of alarm. It might cause the lion to betray himself as he moved with them, stalking them.

"Maybe not, friend Icarus," he said, suddenly aloud.

Shelby started at the sudden sound of the voice. It seemed to carry in the dark. He forced a laugh.

"Okay, Kratos, my drinking friend. Let us call out to one another while we watch," but he wondered whether he heard a sound behind his voice, a low growl from somewhere. On the left?

On the right?

A dozen insects leapt into the air on the left, perhaps twenty feet away, but he saw nothing. A moment later, another batch of insects leapt up, whirring away on the right toward the distant trees, perhaps sixty feet. Is that where the lion was? Which of those was the random act of insects, which caused by the lion?

His breath came faster.

"Did you notice the insects?" he called out to Kratos.

"Oh yes. Both sides. And the growl? You heard him?"

"I did," he said, taking another step toward the rising moon, casting the moon's shadow behind onto the quiet road. They were retracing the steps they had taken earlier and soon would be on a stretch of road they had not yet walked. The ground undulated to the right, rising on a gentle slope perhaps ten feet or less, but enough to cast a shadow against the moon. "If I were a lion," he thought, "stalking prey, I might choose that dark patch to hide in."

"He is playing with us," Kratos said again. "He is playing with his dinner. I think he wants the sport of killing, not the food. Watch!" Kratos took off running, about twenty steps, and stopped suddenly, turning back to Shelby.

There! A movement on the right! A growl!

"Oh yes, Icarus, yes, he's here. He wants to play before he kills!" He turned to the spot where the grain had rustled. "But you —" His voice was cut off by a gasp and a jerk.

The lion charged. The grain buzzed as it thrashed against his pounding legs, catching Shelby's attention. He whirled. The lion was coming from the right, attacking on his quarter.

Shelby saw the lion's fierce eyes and heard the giant paws striking the ground. Bam! It was gaining speed. One more stroke and it would leap. Bam! The lion was airborne, forearms spread, claws wide, huge teeth catching the moonlight.

The instant he saw the lion, Shelby dropped to one knee, his spear at his side. Facing the charging beast, he waited for its leap, and raised the point of the spear.

The world stopped as the lion floated in midair. The pounding of Shelby's heart was the only sound, the keening of fear pitched high out of the primordial depths of his being.

The lion hit the spear, directly in the chest. Shelby leaned against the massive weight, letting the beast's momentum carry it deeper onto the spear, pulling it overhead, where it was suspended briefly like a pole-vaulter at the height of his leap. He felt the spear go home, but the monster was not dead.

Landing on all four paws, the animal let out a roar of anger and leapt again at Kratos. The spear broke when he collided with the road. Maddened by pain, he clawed the road as he attacked, throwing up plumes of dust.

But the beast's heart was pierced. He staggered. The spear point emerged between his shoulders, and he fell on his side mere inches from stunned Kratos' feet. Another heave of the lungs, a twitch, a paw extended towards Kratos, and the massive lion died, its terrible fangs exposed, its brilliant amber eyes still glowing in the quiet moonlight.

"Great Goddess!" exclaimed Kratos. "Oh Goddess, Goddess, Goddess!" He yelled in delight something that sounded like "Geronimo," three or four times. The yell rebounded across the fields. Jumping up and down, he slapped his thighs.

As Shelby walked toward him, he noticed the collar.

The lion was wearing a collar!

TWENTY ONE

XXXXXXXXXX

The sight of the collar alarmed Shelby and he hurled himself at Kratos, knocking the ruddy warrior down just as a spear whizzed overhead. Kratos did not see the spear, and thought that Shelby was playing, letting off steam. Grasping him in a bear hug, Kratos rolled over with him on the ground, laughing loudly.

"Spear!" Shelby whispered harshly. "Somebody threw a spear at us."

He rolled away from Kratos to the edge of the road and heard steps fleeing through the standing grain. Shelby leapt to his feet, but could not see in the dark. Drifting clouds dimmed the moonlight, and the shadows in the field were deep and impenetrable.

A group of insects rose on the right side of the road, but he heard no other movement.

"Kratos, it was a trap!" he whispered. "The lion was trained to attack us. Look at this collar."

The thick leather collar with brass or bronze studs was tight about the dead lion's neck.

"His manager was over there with him, watching the attack."

Kratos sobered up completely, bending down to finger the collar, holding his own spear in one hand. He felt around the lion's neck for the collar buckle and removed it.

"Let's keep this out of sight," suggested Kratos. "We may want to look more closely at it tomorrow." Musing, he added: "This is a bad day for the city, Icarus. Thank the Goddess you were here. Between the lion and the assassin, I would have had no chance."

"It sure looks like an ambush to me," Shelby said.

In the distance, they heard hooves beat against the earth.

"Hurry," said Kratos, "let us start skinning the animal. You will wear its pelt as a token of your power. Let us keep this attack to ourselves, though, until we uncover the truth. Someone wanted to kill us. Or me, anyway, because only late tonight during the feast did anyone else but the brothers know we would go on this hunt."

By the time the horses thundered up the road, they had partially skinned the animal. All except for one of the horses whinnied and shied when they caught scent of the lion. Ophion's horse, as his master leapt from the saddle to the road, was still, calm, unafraid of the huge lion.

"Brother?" Ophion asked anxiously, grasping Kratos with both arms. "We heard the yell. Everyone is terrified." He looked at the blood smeared over Kratos' clothes, his hands and legs, spots of blood on his face.

"Hello brother," said Kratos grinning. "Icarus killed the lion. It was a magnificent kill! I have never seen anything like it."

They turned to Shelby kneeling at the corpse, using his SOG to slice the tawny skin away from the beast's bulging muscles. As he worked, Shelby looked for any sign on the lion's hide that it might have been marked or branded, but found none.

Ophion watched with his hairless, expressionless face. "Funny how the man's words never seem to match his expression," Shelby thought, seeing the bald man scan the fields as though looking for something. "It is a furtive glance, but he cannot hide his body language. The stiffness in his posture doesn't match his concern."

As Kratos recounted the story to the riders, Shelby realized with a start that he recognized one of them.

"Where have I seen this man before? Ah, yes. It is Yiannis, the young guard who was so taken by Kalista earlier today. What is he doing riding around with Ophion? Is he a member of the house guard? He was on foot earlier in the day. Why is he on horseback now?" Shelby wondered, his mind working it over like a terrier with a bone.

As Shelby worked at slicing through the tough hide from the lion's neck to his pelvis, some of the riders dismounted and came over to gape at the beast. "How accurate am I in this assumption," he asked himself. "Is it a plot? Was this an assassination attempt? If so, is Ophion implicated? Why? Because he heard the yell and came to investigate, or is it because he was the first on the scene?"

Continuing to mull these ideas over as he worked at the skinning, Shelby thought, "It would take a lot of work and planning to train a lion to hunt a specific person, but it could be done. You associate discarded clothing of the target with the lion's meal. Drag bloody meat along a trail and reward the beast with it only when he mauls a figure wearing the clothing. Maybe hide the chunks of meat inside a mannequin. Later, maybe dress a condemned prisoner in the clothing."

His knife sliced along the lion's breastbone and entered the soft, white fur of its belly. He wanted to take great care not to puncture the abdominal cavity and spill the predator's guts into the open air. The rank smell of digesting meat would be overwhelming, so he slipped the fingers of one hand under the skin on both sides of the blade and worked carefully, lifting the flesh with a kind of tearing sound from the abdominal wall then slicing it with an upward stroke.

"A lion could be trained," he thought. "It would require a small but steady supply of fairly fresh clothing from the target and at least a year's worth of time, but it is possible."

By now, the whole party was standing around him, jabbering away about the lion and the kill, though they kept their distance. It was Shelby's kill, and they were not going to crowd him, an attitude he understood and appreciated.

Finally the slice was finished and the beast's huge genitals cut free from the belly. He pulled the skin in both directions from the chest and stomach, finally freeing it from the carcass. Then he sliced up the length of each leg and peeled the skin from them as well, cutting through the ankle joints to preserve the claws. Turning the beast over to skin his back took a lot of muscle, and he needed help. The lion's joints were too flexible to make his limbs of any use as levers against his bulk. Finally, he came to a decision.

"Ophion, friend," he said, "come and lend a hand. Feel these teeth!" He tugged open the lion's massive jaw to expose the fangs and heard an intake of breath from the riders. "I think friend Kratos may need more wine now," he added, seeing that Kratos had strolled over to the side of the road to relieve himself again.

That broke the tension and general laughter began. Wise cracks. Surprised Kratos could hold it so long. Teasing. Exclamations of wonder. Praise for the kill. And finally, when Shelby bent again to roll the beast over, a dozen hands helped.

Sure enough, some of the riders had wineskins on their horses and soon the whole party was refreshed, Kratos included. But his furrowed brow showed that he was holding back a godlike fury now that the first rush of adrenaline had died away, and he was struggling to control his hands so no one saw them tremble.

"He stood his ground. I can say that for him," Shelby thought. "Kratos had been prepared to take the lion face on and at full charge. He had been prepared to die. He had been caught by surprise and his own spear had barely risen as the beast clawed at him. It had all happened too fast for him, but he stood his ground. Now his body language is as pronounced as Ophion's, but different. In contrast to the stiffness of an unseen fear that seems to ooze from Ophion, Kratos is almost levitating. He is a bit too loud. A bit too jerky in his movements."

"Back to work," Shelby said aloud to the men. "The sooner the skin is off this lion, the sooner we can go back to the city."

He almost said, "Back home."

TWENTY TWO

✕✕✕✕✕✕✕✕✕✕

K ratos and Shelby re-entered the city well before dawn. Shelby saw hooded figures ghosting through the streets and looked questioningly at Kratos.

"Matrons," Kratos said quietly, "and their attendants. They have a council with Metis every morning."

"Who are Matrons?" Shelby asked, recalling that Metis said something about them earlier.

"Matrons run the city. The men fight, but the Matrons govern," Kratos said. "They start early each day checking on every home in their district, for no door can be closed to them and no secrets kept. Their duty is to keep the city happy, which they do by keeping the women happy and by teaching the women how to care for their men."

Shelby had questions and Kratos sensed it.

"They go into every house in their district every morning, expecting the women to be awake and preparing for the day, helped by their daughters, starting their ovens, making up fires in the hearths, drawing water, feeding babies."

"Sounds like a good plan," Shelby said.

"It helps. Of course, people can be troublesome. Some women cannot handle the home, and for such women the Matrons assign an attendant. Sometimes the woman is removed from the home for a time to rest and the attendant takes over her duties. Sometimes, the woman is not returned to the home and other occupations are given her."

They were nearly back to the palace through the sleeping streets, and more hooded figures were approaching, in twos and threes.

"Understand your men and you will be happy," Kratos said. "This is the teaching of the Goddess. But men, like cattle, must be tended, domesticated. It requires a certain skill, and the whole city's effort."

"Men don't seem like cattle to me," Shelby said. "They seem a lot more dangerous. More like lions."

"But even lions can be trained," Kratos grinned, patting his forearm.

"Home and hearth, whatever is best for mothers and babies, these are the creeds of our city," Kratos continued. "It solves problems, but not all of them. Men can still be feral. So can women. Metis executes any man who attacks a woman, part of her duty as the priestess. The rule is inviolable. The duty of the priestess is to enforce obedience to the Goddess's rule. The chore of managing the happiness of the city is never finished."

He led the way through the darkened passages of the palace back to Shelby's alcove, where he sat down heavily on one of the cushions, leaning back and yawning.

"The Matrons know everything," he finally said, resting his head. "Nothing can be hidden from them."

"Then they know who trained the lion," Shelby said.

"Maybe," he said. "Maybe Metis knows already. Or Melia.

If they don't know now, they will. No thing can hide from the Goddess."

And he was asleep, snoring. Shelby soon followed his example, dreaming of Melia.

TWENTY THREE

XXXXXXXXXX

A bout four hours later, Kratos and Shelby exited once more through the city's gates, leaving one of the guards with the lion's pelt to take to the city's talented craftswomen for tanning. Now, they were eager to learn what they could about the lion, his handler, and that spear.

While they walked along the mostly empty dirt road from the city, Kratos told him more about the city's government. It was entirely in the hands of the women, specifically supervised by the Matrons who enforced the Goddess' rule of whatever was best for mothers and children.

"Whatever is best for mothers and children," Shelby repeated. "I do not find much of that in the world I come from. It is a very wise principle." He thought how it would affect American politics and culture, amazed that such a simple idea was not already in force. "So simple, so profound," he said.

"It works for us," Kratos said. "The Achaeans are more brutal, and I think they do not care about women and children. It is one reason they are such dangerous enemies to us. Who would thrust a spear at little Kalista?" he asked, angrily. "Who does such things? Animals." He spit.

"I want to see the footprints of the man who threw that spear at you and follow his trail if we can," Shelby replied. He was right, Shelby thought. The Achaeans were a serious, cunning threat.

In stark contrast to the previous night, the fields in the dawn light were peaceful beyond measure. Already workers were among the crops, and the lowing of cows, the bleating of sheep, and the sounds of human activity drifted toward them. Soon, the sun would top the eastern ridge where the moon had risen hours earlier.

Over his shoulder Shelby saw the pale crescent of the moon lingering above the western hills, lazily dipping toward oblivion. But as his eye wandered over the western hills, he caught a glint of metal in the morning sun, near the topmost rocks of the hills.

"Do you have sentries posted in the western hills?" he asked Kratos, gazing at the sunlight slowly easing down the ridges.

Kratos, a few steps ahead, turned back questioningly. "It is possible, but not likely. Usually we do not patrol the hilltops, unless there is pasture to protect. Why do you ask?"

"I saw a glint of metal from the top of one of those hills just as the sunlight touched it, but I haven't seen it again."

"Could have been metal. Could have been water on the face of a rock. I've seen that happen."

Shelby nodded, continuing to look out over the fields and into the distance. It was an Edenic place. Rich soil, productive and apparently happy people, peaceful. He had never seen a place ruled by women until now. Women bosses were not in great supply in the Rangers. So far as he could tell, this country looked like it was working out just fine.

The men he saw the previous night at the feast were warlike and dangerous, neither slackers nor loafers. They had purpose and could work together. They had bonded as a fighting unit under Phorbus and his sons. Yet they did not call the shots. Metis, ordained by the Goddess, was the power of the city, and through her the Matrons ruled.

The ideal city-state, he realized, is not the one ruled by the philosopher king but the one ruled in favor of the greatest good for mothers and babies. "The whole history of the human species comes down to it. Nothing else can be more important. Yet men in their pride and strength continually batter away at the notion.

It is so simple, yet we forget. How? How can we ignore something so obvious?" he thought.

The spot where they killed the lion was easy to find. Men had already dragged the skinned carcass off the road, burying it in the neighboring field, destroying some of this year's crop in the process. But the lion would be fertilizer for next year's crop, and a year from now, the lion's rage would be patted out into harmless grain cakes and baked flat against the sides of mud ovens to feed babies and their mothers.

"I hope that will be the end of the story of the lion," he said quietly to himself, "but I doubt it."

Kicking around in the standing grain some yards from the scene, Kratos recovered the assassin's spear and closely examined it. Meanwhile, Shelby searched through the field and found the assassin's footprints. Lying near where the footprints disappeared into the field he also found a short, white shirt. A chiton. He held it up.

"Recognize this?" he asked Kratos.

"It's a chiton. It's something everyone wears under their robes."

"Is it yours?"

"Why?"

"Because if it's yours, then it was used to lure the lion here."

Kratos walked over and looked at it.

"Let's take it back to the palace and ask Metis. She will recognize the handwork and be able to say who made it, even if she doesn't know who wore it."

"She can do that?" Shelby asked.

"Certainly. The weaving and stitching is individual to each weaver. Metis will know which of the city's thousand weavers made this cloth, and which woman sewed it. Melia would know, also. You and I, we would not be able to tell maybe ever, but they would have no doubt."

"The big question is whether you ever wore it."

"Why would the trainer, if the lion was trained to hunt me, carry the shirt with him?"

"I don't know. Maybe he carried the shirt because the lion would track it, and that way the trainer would always be able to get the lion to come to him. Maybe the lion was also trained not to attack the trainer? I don't know. Can lions be trained like that?"

Kratos pondered the question as they looked over the chiton. He idly rotated the spear's shaft in his right hand, testing the balance, while he thought.

"The lion would have associated my scent with raw meat. The trainer would have carried the chiton to lead the lion to meat, but how he could train the lion to attack me without attacking him,

I don't know." He paused, then turned his almost demented bright smile on Shelby. "I need to tell you again that you made a magnificent kill last night. Unbelievable. I would never have thought to let the lion impale himself."

"Sometimes," Shelby said, squeezing Kratos on the shoulder, "it's best to wait."

The camaraderie unnerved him. It re-awakened feelings Shelby had not felt since combat, with team members who were like brothers. Or closer than brothers. With men he could depend on with his life. Men who walked in valor and honor, the fraternity of war, trust, and a fellowship only felt when huddled together against a dangerous enemy, shivering through the night under fire, back to back in a foxhole.

Looking at the grinning man beside him, he realized that last night's attack had bonded them. They shared a deadly secret — the collar, the chiton, the spear, the running footsteps. Who would have known that the lion wore a collar? Who could have furnished the chiton? Kratos' life was in danger, and so was his own.

"Can I stand to lose Kratos?" he asked himself. "That is the question. Can I take another crushing blow like the one in Afghanistan, the one that led to the slaughter? Can I endure my heart breaking again?"

This time, the flashback was longer. For an instant, who knows how long, the mountain top battle in Afghanistan was overlaid on the open fields of grain glowing in the morning sun, like a painted celluloid template dropped in front of a window. He saw both the pleasant fields and the deadly night battle. The sounds of automatic weapons filled the air. Then, the template receded.

He came around to find Kratos shaking him and calling his name. He was still gripping Kratos' shoulder, and it must have hurt. His fist was cramped. He struggled back to the present, "If it is the present," he thought. "If I am where I seem to be. If this short man is real, is someone I know."

"You were gone, Icarus," said Kratos slowly, earnestly. "I am beginning to think perhaps you can fly after all."

"Oh, man, Kratos," Shelby said, "oh man. Listen to me." Shelby took him by both shoulders, rubbing the one he must have bruised. "I was fighting a war a long way away. On a mountaintop. I lost many of my men, and I was wounded, but I killed 26 of the bastards. Some of that was luck, because they were bunched up, but I also chopped them into pieces with my weapons. It was a bad rage. Now sometimes I cannot get it out of my head."

"I understand, Icarus," said Kratos, his face clouded, but his eyes showed new confidence in Shelby. "All warriors have visions.

When mine become too much, Metis gives me a potion to calm my spirit and let me sleep. It is healing to sleep. We all have visions. Today under the sun you tell me yours, and I tell you mine so we can share as brothers, better brothers perhaps than the real ones."

"It is hard for me to go there, my friend. Sometimes it feels like a weakness, to have a vision I cannot turn from. It's like being possessed."

"Yes," said Kratos, as they turned back to search the ground for footprints. "Yes, it is like being chained. Like a wild animal suddenly chained."

He bent over to point at the ground, straightened up and turned to Shelby, his finger still extended toward the ground. "Remember, friend Icarus, a horse that is not broken is of no use. The vision is training you. When you accept that you are trained, then you will find a new life and a new freedom. That's the way Metis explained it to me. She said it is frightening to give up what we know, but that the new way will be better than the old.

I still struggle, but now when my mind rebels I know that it is the trainer's rope around my neck."

"Never an easy time for the horse," Shelby said.

"No," Kratos agreed. "Here are the footprints. Let's follow them. They may lead somewhere."

TWENTY FOUR

XXXXXXXXXX

Kratos and Shelby set off across the field, hardly needing the imprints of the fleeing feet on the ground because of the clear path of broken plants. After a while, they topped a small ridge and had a better angle on the trail. The spot where the assassin lay was clearly visible. Apparently he had crawled over the ridge to avoid revealing himself against the moonlit sky, and paused to make sure he was not being followed. When he wasn't, he took more leisurely steps across the field toward a road leading south.

They followed the trail until they lost it in the many footprints on the road, then continued toward the ancient ash trees descending the distant southern slopes. Shelby studied the roadside, looking for further evidence of either the lion or the assassin. Kratos, searching on the opposite side of the road, came across the remains of a slaughtered calf, its flesh almost obliterated by birds and jackals. He called Shelby over.

"We are near the spot where I first saw the lion's paw prints in the road," he said. "I do not remember seeing this calf before. It has been well gnawed."

Shelby inspected the carcass, looking carefully at the torn flesh. Resisting the smell of the rotting flesh, he brushed aside the buzzing flies. Overhead in the trees, large black birds congregated, waiting noisily for them to leave. Dog prints, or perhaps jackal prints, imprinted the dirt on all sides.

Finally, Shelby found what he was looking for: a star-shaped puncture wound. An animal slashing at the meat with its incisors would make slits, but a star-shaped wound could mean only one thing. The calf had been killed by a spear. Sure enough, looking more closely at the exposed bones Shelby saw what could be slash marks from a knife.

He pointed this out to Kratos, who hung back. Despite his jovial demeanor earlier, the shorter man's stomach did not seem up to deep whiffs of rotting calf. When Shelby called him over, however, he came.

"This calf was killed and butchered, and left here to look like a lion kill," Kratos said, after inspecting the wound.

Not far from there, Shelby found the lion's paw prints in the road. "Had the lion been fed on the killed calf while it lay next to the road?" he wondered. "Had the meat been cut from the calf and taken to the lion, and later the sated lion led back by his collar to the site of the kill? Had the raw meat been wrapped in one of

Kratos' chitons?" As they strolled upwind from the kill, they debated the procedure.

"Surely we need to figure out what they were doing before the attack," Shelby said, "because now I think we know for certain that it was planned. It was an assassination attempt on you or on both of us. The failure of their first attempt only means they will try again. The more we understand their methods, the more likely we will identify who is doing it, and how."

"If the chiton belonged to me and was taken from the stack of cleaning before being washed, then probably a slave was involved," said Kratos.

Shelby recoiled at his casual mention of slavery, but suddenly he realized that the only people he had seen wearing collars and nothing else must be slaves. Shelby asked him about it.

"We don't clothe the slaves," Kratos replied. "What naked person runs away? And you're right, you will not see many naked people except slaves."

"Good point. Naked people usually return to the place where they have their clothes. I did, yesterday."

"Yes, that's right. Naked people do not run far. If you see a naked person running across a field, you know it is a slave escaping. Everyone gives chase. However, this is not the only reason. Naked people are also reminded every waking moment that they survive only because their masters allow them to. This is the real reason to keep the slaves naked. It reminds them that they are not their own masters."

"Does that never change for them?"

"No. Never. With a trained horse, you sometimes remove the saddle and the ropes. With a human, you cannot give them clothing. It changes them."

"So the theft of the chiton is a much more serious crime than I had imagined."

Kratos smiled at him. "Yes, it is. If a slave stole it, then it is an act of rebellion that may get the slave punished or sold to the traders when they come in a few weeks. Or executed."

"Are all your slaves purchased, then?"

"No, many are captured in war. The more valuable ones are captured, but the more valuable ones are also the ones with more to gain from escape. They are usually smarter and better trained. Most of the weavers in the city are women captured in war, women whose men failed to protect them."

"You keep them naked even though they spend their time weaving cloth to make clothes for you?"

"It is not so bad as that. They have quiet, sheltered places to work. They are allowed covering during cold weather. The Matrons oversee the treatment of slaves, just as they do the treatment of women and babies. Mothers, babies, and slaves are fed and cared for and valued by the city. Slaves are neither abused nor chained, but to be naked in the city means to be owned by someone else. The collar says clearly who the owner is. The slaves in the palace work hard to remain in the palace, where they have a better life than most. To be a slave is not the same as to be free, but everyone must work all the same whether slave or free. It is the Mother's will that all be busy. Thus owners work alongside their slaves, and over time there is trust and even friendship. It is not so bad."

He paused.

"You do not have slaves in your country, Icarus?"

"We had slaves once, but we set them free."

"Are your people happy now?"

"I'm not sure. We are all free, and that is a kind of happiness. We have some serious social issues. Poverty, ignorance. It is a very large country and so we have large problems."

Shelby was not going to discuss the random wars, the global economy, the unemployment, weapons of mass destruction, medical techniques that prolonged pain in those who were dying, or the general failure of the educational system. Kratos would never understand these things. He would never understand gunpowder, and gunpowder had been part of western civilization for a thousand years. Airplanes. The Internet. An electoral process open to abuse and corruption.

"My country has come very far from a society devoted to the protection and honor of mothers and babies," thought Shelby, "yet very good at protecting the interests of the very rich."

"I may not understand your country, Icarus," Kratos finally said with a rueful smile, "but I think I will understand you. For me, that is enough." He turned his gap-toothed grin up to him. "Even if you nearly tear my shoulder off."

Shelby gave Kratos' shoulder a friendly rub. "Sorry I gripped so hard."

"Bah," said Kratos.

They walked on together side by side, looking for more signs of last night's lion, the road dwindling to a mere path.

TWENTY FIVE

✕✕✕✕✕✕✕✕✕✕

From the palace's upper floor gynaeceum, where the Matrons gathered for their morning counsel, Melia watched Shelby and Kratos set out before dawn. Perched in the high window at the back of the quiet room, she saw them walk together down the road and followed them in the distance even after the Matrons began to gather. She saw them uncover the spear and find the chiton, and she watched as they followed the trail through the standing grain up and over the little rise. She saw them disappear from view, only to gradually re-emerge much further away, still following the trail.

One by one, the older women came to her as they entered and looked at her, resting their hands on her gently with sympathy, or kissing her lightly on the hair in greeting. Many followed her gaze out the window, though most lost the ability to see clearly long ago. They had insight, however, that traveled very far indeed.

Without speaking, they knew who Melia was watching. They knew the scene of the lion attack could be seen clearly in the distance from her perch in the window, and they all knew the details of the events the previous night: the feast, the introduction of the strange man, the exchange of gifts, the wrestling match with Kratos, the lion hunt.

They were suspicious of the lion. It was the wrong time of year for a lion to appear. Lions were most dangerous at foaling time, in early spring, when the scent of birthing blood of the newly born drifted down the southern slopes into the dark forests. All were uneasy about yesterday: the attack on Metis and the girls; the appearance of the huge, god-like man, naked like a slave; the eagle with the dove; and the lion.

It would be a busy morning. Too many things changed in one day. Metis became so gloomy after the sacrifice. What had the Mother Goddess told her?

Whatever it was, Melia and the new man were at the center of it.

"Imagine, just dropping out of nowhere like Icarus," they thought in their silent way, agreeing with one another through glances and nods. "A man of no standing, no family, no history. Is he the right mate for her, or is she just overwhelmed by him? She's not a silly girl, like Rhodia, but then she is very much a girl. Young woman. No doubt her brooding in the window has something to do with balancing her feelings for the new man, a hero really, with her perception of him. She has never been one to be foolish, but ah, what is love if not foolishness?"

Metis entered at last, attended by a few slave girls. One of them helped her walk. Her pace was slow and labored. All the women rose in honor of her, some of them almost twice her age, and she nodded to them. It was obvious she was in pain, and she seemed to have aged overnight. The playful woman who set out with her daughters to worship at the sacred pool yesterday appeared old and worn out today.

Finally seated, she dismissed the slaves with a wave of her hand and smiled weakly at the assembly, nodding to them to take their seats.

"Mothers, I am very tired this morning," she began, "as you know. By and by, I will tell you all that is on my heart, but as we always do, let us first discuss our business. Tell me how the city lives today."

One by one the Matrons reported on their neighborhoods — the troubled homes, the happy homes, the children, the nourishment and care of the men, the happiness of the women. Although little changed, day after day, these were important reports. If a child was sick, it was reported and monitored. Fevers, stomachaches, spotty faces all came up in the daily report. The health of the city was as large a concern as its happiness, its supply of water and food.

A healthy city was best for mothers and babies. Some illnesses, like some people, needed to be isolated. Some illnesses ran their course. Some ill people never became whole again. The Matrons were not severe, but neither were they living some kind of illusion. Some warriors, and women and children, suffered and died. The ways of the Goddess were clear and easily observed. Her ways included sickness, aging, and death. Her reasons were mysterious and opaque, but under her guidance, the city continued and thrived.

"Matrons, thank you for the reports," said Metis at last. "At the current time, we believe the city to be as healthy as it can be. Now let me tell you about the sacrifice and deliver the prophecy that has weighed so heavily on me all night."

At her Mother's words, Melia turned. The two men had disappeared anyway, even from her view, and the daylight was full upon the valley. She listened.

"If the man we call Icarus had not appeared at the pool, today would be very different for the city," Metis continued. "We know one of the men, of course, and we should have executed him before now. The other man is Achaean. This is the beginning of a great war. The Goddess has let me see the bloodshed to come and how we are to cope."

She stopped and closed her eyes to let her words sink in. "Oh, Goddess! Oh, Goddess!" Metis cried to herself, her heart rending inside her as she remembered the familiar and eager faces of the men, saw them torn in the coming war. "If only they knew. Oh, the grief of foresight. Oh, Icarus, you fallen man. Can you save us from the calamity that is coming? Is that why you are here?"

The Matrons looked at one another while Metis was lost in her inner thoughts, but they were not surprised by her words. Metis only confirmed their suspicions: a war had begun with subterfuge instead of attack, but it had begun. They knew too well how crippled the city would be if Metis and Melia were gone and Kratos dead. It would be a stunning loss. The other brothers did not have the commanding presence of Kratos. Iapetus was an administrator, not a fighter, and Eurymedon was immature. Both of them lacked imagination. Ophion was not trusted: he had no women in his life. He was cold, unpleasant, odd, and distant. The Matrons knew he could never lead the warriors.

"How does Phorbus feel about the stranger?" asked one of the Matrons. "He sees deeply into men."

"Phorbus approves," replied Metis. "Like all of us he has questions. He is willing to accept the stranger as a gift from the Goddess, but like the rest of us he doesn't know the purpose of the gift. Perhaps the ambush at the pool was the only excuse the Goddess needed. Killing the lion that threatened Kratos may be an added benefit."

"His coming saved the city," breathed another Matron. Though nearly ninety and bent almost double, her dark eyes gleamed. "But the Goddess is not fond of miracles."

All the Matrons understood the time-honored methods of the Goddess: to continue, to endure, to flower again, to give birth and renew. She did not interfere like the drunken, vicious, and capricious male gods of the Achaeans. Though the Zeus of the Achaeans had influence among the people of the city, few saw a need to worship him. What, after all, could Zeus offer in the way of life and renewal?

The Matrons knew this disturbance in the pattern of life had come in some way from the Achaeans and their brutish gods. Metis and the Matrons did not need to argue the point. They all knew it. Their thoughts flew around the room wordlessly, communicated by gesture or eye contact. The coming of the strange giant looked like an episode in a battle between gods. He was here because the Goddess had been driven to bring him.

They could almost feel the trembling shock as divine wills clashed.

"It is agreed then," said Metis after a few minutes, though few words had been spoken. "We are threatened by the Achaeans, and by their gods. We will move the army to preparation and reinforce our supplies against a siege. We cannot fight against gods, but we can fight against men. Choose three among you to accompany me to Phorbus, who will want to prepare Amphinomus for our meeting. I think we do not need to await the return of Kratos and Icarus, for they will only find evidence to support what we already know. Melia, do you agree?"

Metis turned to her daughter, who had listened to the silent dialogue of the Matrons without participating, as was her place.

"I think Kratos and Shelby will find something of great interest to us," Melia answered. "I also think they are hiding something from us now, but I don't know what. When they return, they will tell us. I believe that they will show us evidence of a more extensive threat. Perhaps we should spread the word to watch our Achaean slaves more closely. Especially the newer ones."

The Matrons nodded gravely.

"One more thing," Melia added, "I think it is time for the unmarried women in the city to prepare to fight. This time, the Achaeans may be more cunning than they have been in the past. We may lose many men in the coming war, and the defense of the city may fall ultimately to those of us who do not wish to go into slavery or die in their brutish onslaught. I will accompany Metis to the meeting with Phorbus and consult directly with Amphinomus about supplying women with weapons."

"The walls can be defended by archers," said Agala, a wizened Matron whose stooped figure had walked the city streets daily for more than eighty harvests. "Women can be good archers, perhaps better than men. You must choose women whose eyesight is good. Also, my dear, if you have never shot a bow, you will learn that you need to bind your breasts and protect your forearm from the snap of the string." She smiled toothlessly, her wrinkled face cracking in a million crazy ways. "It is appropriate for women to defend the men's backs while they fight outside the walls."

Metis nodded, and the silent assent spread around the room. The sun had risen fully now, and the gynaeceum brightened. The rich carpets on the floor picked up the warm radiance of the light and spread it glowing around the marble room, the dust motes dancing in the air as the women moved. Against the wall, draperies of sky-blue wool glistened in the morning, and the dark ash wood of the bronze-fitted doors came alive, the wood's grain seeming to deepen and to somehow strengthen in the early light. It was a comfortable, airy room with a high ceiling supported by marble pillars. Bronze statues of indomitable women stood between the pillars against the wall. Gold sconces for light and bronze braziers for warmth stood ready for the changes of the day or of the season.

"When the assault comes against the walls, then women will be even more vital for supplying the men with arms, binding their wounds," Agala continued. "I have seen this several times. Once I went with our army when we besieged Tereon, and I watched the battle and the conquest of that city." She paused, catching her breath, remembering the ancient time so many years ago: her youth, and her husband, and the beautiful young men who were destroyed. "Our men have preserved us from slavery. Many women within our own walls had men who failed them. Ours have not failed, thanks to the Goddess and her wisdom, but a regiment of trained women at their backs will give them courage, I believe."

"You have spoken wisely, as ever, Mother Agala," said Metis. "Melia had this idea yesterday as she was thinking over the attack at the pool, and it is a good one. We have many women in the city who do not wish to go naked as slaves to be raped and murdered by the Achaean beasts. We may need to fashion a new stock of weapons better suited to the strengths of women, but I am certain we can be effective if we train. Let us pray to the Goddess that we have the time to train."

Nothing more needed to be said. Every Matron and assistant understood the meeting's full import. It was time to move their neighborhoods into preparation for war. A trained group of women as an adjunct force in the overall preparation for war was a good idea, and Melia would begin choosing her fighting troops today.

As the others left the room, Metis took Melia aside and looked at her questioningly.

"I don't know, Mother," Melia said quietly. "I think so, but something is hidden. Perhaps he will help me with the training, and then we will spend time together. I like him, you know."

Metis nodded. "Yes, I know. I think he has knowledge we have not yet seen. He may help us save the city, this time."

"This time," Melia echoed. "Maybe."

TWENTY
SIX

✕✕✕✕✕✕✕✕✕✕

The lion's prints became less evident as the trail diminished toward the forest of towering ash trees. The grassy verge of the forest, where the trees shaded the ground and the cultivated grain did not grow, was a kind of general highway for wildlife and was frequently used by shepherds driving their sheep to pasture, or boys grazing their cows. In recent weeks, though, the reports of the lion kept shepherds and herders away from the long, verdant way, and grass that had been clipped short by the browsing animals had lengthened. Except for the indentations of animal hooves after the last rain, the dirt was too carpeted with grass to leave much trace of passing footsteps or of the lion.

The day was still young and strong sun glittered through the high branches. Here and there, birds decorated the golden light, their gay chatter in turn punctuating the morning silence. In places, a ray of sunlight slanted across the massive tree trunks, occasionally but rarely reaching the ground.

In the distance, six or seven miles away, rose the walls of the city, their gray bulk glowing in the morning sun. The polished bronze weapons carried by the patrol along the parapets twinkled like so many tiny golden stars in the morning light.

Kratos noticed Shelby's admiring gaze. "It is a noble sight, is it not?" he said. "The envy of surrounding tribes is easy to understand, for they live in squalid mud huts low to the ground and wallow in filth at the mercy of their neighbors."

"Sometimes those with the least to lose can be the most deadly enemies," Shelby replied. "I've seen that in many places of the world. Deadly, and illogical in their hatred."

They scoured the edges of the forest, looking for evidence

of the lion's path that might lead into the dark trees. As the sun warmed the fields behind them, cooler air on the forest floor rippled with convection, bringing the scents of deep foliage, rotting vegetation, the dense oxygen of the trees.

"Ah, the ash trees breathe upon us," said Kratos. "I wish they could speak."

"Perhaps they have a language of their own that we do not listen for. The birds seem to listen, however, and I notice that they have become quiet. What do you suppose they hear?"

"Men?" asked Kratos. "I suppose it depends on which birds. Some birds flee from men, some complain. The hoopoe complains loudly, but it is more common to the north of us. The smaller songbirds just become silent when they are bothered, and fly away."

In the low screen of vegetation bordering the grassy verge, they finally found a path leading down the slope into the trees.

"A woodcutter's path," whispered Kratos. "Shall we explore it?"

Shelby nodded, and almost immediately they spotted the print of the half-ton lion in soft leaf litter. Ahead, the path wound down through the trees into a darkness that was only half-lit even with the sun directly overhead.

Not far into the shadows, perhaps 150 yards from the verge, Shelby sniffed human funk on the air and held up his hand to signal Kratos to stop, not speak. The hand gestures that were common to the Rangers were not wasted on Kratos. He, too, smelled the camp — the thin scent of acrid smoke and the fetid odor of human waste fouling the clean air of the forest.

"If they are still there, they may have lookouts," Shelby whispered. "I will scout ahead. You wait here out of sight, and I will come back for you. Understand?"

Kratos nodded.

"I may need to kill someone, and I don't want it to be you by accident. Stay here, out of sight, until I come for you."

Kratos nodded, but whispered back: "I am not happy to be missing any of the fun, Icarus. Because of the lion last night I will let you go ahead as you wish this time, but next time we kill together."

Then Shelby heard something moving not far away. He clapped his hand over Kratos' mouth and urged him to the ground. Together they crept deeper into the brush, and Shelby left him there.

Moments later, moving away and low to the ground so he

could not be seen, Shelby saw a man creeping along with a spear. Behind him was another man, scanning side to side, just coming into view in the dim forest light. Then in the distance he heard the clank of metal and the urgent muttering of many voices mixed with laughter rising and falling, perhaps a woman's sobbing, a shriek cut off. It had to be a camp.

"I'm always pleased at how effective a sleeper hold is in an ambush. It's mostly quiet, especially if you can get the other guy's feet off the ground, and they go out quickly. True, it can be deadly, but I've had a lot of practice," he thought grimly as he lowered the limp body to the ground.

With one man out, a quick knot to hold his wrists together, Shelby went for the second one, the one in the lead. The guy should have seen Shelby coming, but he thought it was his partner. Before he reacted, Shelby had his forearm under the man's chin. He startled and gasped, but Shelby had already hauled him into the air by the hold on his windpipe and kicked his feet out. He let him drop, jerking upward near the bottom and his neck gave. Shelby did it again, and heard the reassuring snap of his cervical vertebrae. The man was dead.

"So far, a good morning's work. Now for the camp, but first to get Kratos to mind the prisoner," he thought.

Shelby dragged the body over to Kratos and whispered to him to cover it with leaves. "I've bound and gagged the other one, but you need to guard him while I scout ahead. Don't let him make a sound. If he moves, kill him."

Kratos' face was blank.

"Understand?" Shelby whispered urgently.

"Yes sir," said Kratos in a wondering tone. "I see now why Metis suspects you of being a god. Tell me what to do, and I will do it."

"Good. Until we return to the city, let me be in charge. Guard the other man."

Shelby showed Kratos where he hid the unconscious soldier and then crept off.

TWENTY SEVEN

✕✕✕✕✕✕✕✕✕✕

T he familiar reverie of battle rose in him again. Nothing existed but the mission. No physical agony, no exertion. "Sua sponte!" rose to his lips silently and filled him with an extra degree of tension, with more strength.

He was back in his own clothes after the night's excursions. His boots, his shorts, his dark t-shirt. Unlike just twenty-four hours earlier, he was clothed and had his SOG knife. Nothing rustled or rattled as he moved quickly and silently. The "appropriate" clothing he had worn to the feast and the lion hunt waved in the air when he moved, sending out little disturbed air currents that a seasoned predator would sense. He was much happier with his own close-fitting, silent gear.

Finding two guards suggested to him that a large contingent was nearby. If the contingent had been small, two men would not have been assigned in a pair to the patrol. Instead, one man would have been posted to give an alarm. The human smell he caught in the forest air would lead in the direction of lookouts before he found the camp. Better-trained men would be kept closer to the core of the camp; more expendable troops would be sent to patrol the perimeter and raise a cry. His next concern, therefore, was to see the lookouts on the perimeter before they saw him, and to remove them.

The ground continued its gentle downward slope, but ahead he guessed that it dropped more precipitously. Then, through dense foliage below a bluff he caught a glimpse of an encampment. He also heard a soft but steady rasping sound off to his right that he took for a birdcall.

Rasp-rasp-rasp, pause, rasp-rasp, pause.

Moving quietly along the bluff, he spotted an elbow moving behind a tree some thirty yards away. It was a lookout, and he was on the opposite side of the tree.

Timing his steps to the rasping to mask the sound of his feet in the leaves, he eased closer.

It was the man's right elbow.

Shelby recognized the repetitive motion as the lookout sharpening a blade with a stone. He was not paying attention because he expected the perimeter patrol to alert him, so he was unprepared and distracted. Nevertheless, he was probably a trained fighter holding two potential weapons.

Shelby considered his options. They always make noise when you hit them in the chest, even when you puncture the heart. The lookout was too awkwardly placed for a sleeper hold without a struggle. Again, too much noise.

Throat was the only solution, and that was messy. Force with precision, take out one or both carotids through tough side neck muscle. It was not an easy way to kill a man, but it was his best option.

At the back of the tree now, Shelby paused when the rasping noise stopped. He waited, listening for the man to move, second by second, hardly breathing. Then there was another rasp. "Ah, that explains it. The man was testing the edge for sharpness," he thought.

The lookout cleared his throat and then rubbed his back against the bark of the tree, making a harsh scraping but revealing to Shelby that he was wearing nothing metal on his torso.

That was a good sign.

On the third rub, Shelby leapt around the tree slashing with the SOG. It caught the Achaean under his left ear and his eyes widened, but he was dead, his head nearly severed from his body, blood fountaining from his carotid. Sidestepping the gushing blood, Shelby let the man fall toward the ground, holding him by the hair as he collapsed, his eyes blinking in shock, his breathless mouth opening, his blood pouring into the darkening earth and gnarled roots of the ash tree. A clean kill. His spear with its brightly sharpened bronze blade went down with him, and Shelby retrieved it from the spreading pool of blood. The foul odor of the man's bowels emptying in death overcame the sweet smells of the forest, and then gradually, oh so gradually as they always do, he stopped twitching.

Shelby sliced the leather jerkin off the man's back and cut away a section of the cloth shirt beneath, using it to wipe the blood off the SOG and to clean away the spatter of blood that hit his leg when he stepped around the man's severed head. He was too close to the camp to waste time hiding the body, and doubted there would be another lookout. "If it were my camp," he reasoned, "I would have one patrol of two men and two lookouts stationed within shouting distance. So there could be another lookout, but I can observe the camp without running into him."

He crept carefully toward the slope and looked over. It was a small camp of twenty to thirty men. A fire burning in the middle fueled by dried ash produced almost no smoke. Crude lean-to shelters surrounded the fire. Off to one side was a large wheeled cage, stoutly built. The lion's cage.

A woman was tied to a stake in the middle of the camp. Men taunted her. Some urinated on her. Despite her gag, he heard her muffled screams and cries. A golden band around her throat suggested she was a slave, possibly from the palace. Was this the slave who provided the clothing worn by Kratos? Was it another woman captured from the city? He could not tell, but he did not like what he saw. The woman had been brutalized, her face bruised and swollen, her swollen hands tied above her head were purple, almost black.

He doubted that he could save her with the few weapons he had. He scanned the area. Here and there along the ridge were fist-sized rocks.

The Achaeans were hitting and slapping her, but at a sharp rebuke they backed away and a burly man with a whip took over, and began flaying her naked body.

"Enough," thought Shelby. "This stops."

He returned to the body of the lookout and made a quick downward slice through the man's cervical spine, cutting the cord. The man's head came loose from his torso.

He picked it up by the blood-soaked hair and returned to the overlook above the camp.

It would be a long throw, but the man's hair was easy to grip.

Whirling, not caring if he was spotted, throwing a wide arc of blood from the severed neck, he lofted the head high into the air and watched its path.

Yes, long enough.

It fell short of the man with the whip, but rolled between his legs as he reared back for another blow at the bleeding woman. The head came to rest at her feet, but her eyes were closed against a pending blow, and she did not see it.

The camp sprang into uproar, and Shelby circled away and downhill. They recognized their lookout's head and stormed up the hill in his direction, but Shelby was already around the camp, coming up behind the woman, ready to cut her loose.

A commotion above the camp signaled that the Achaeans had found the sentry. Harsh orders barked out and the sounds of frantic men scrambling through the brush, shouting, rose in pitch. Despite the noise, he heard the whinny of horses coming from an obscure thicket some distance away. "Aha," he thought. "Horses had pulled the lion cart, and they were penned away from the lion."

Passing behind the woman, he noted how she was tied at the stake but he did not stop to cut her down. He had more to do first. Securing three horses was one thing. Setting the other horses loose was another. He expected at any moment for the woman to become aware of him, but she remained unconscious. Her sagging body weight pulled her shoulders from their sockets, and she bled from blows to the head. Her face was a mass of bruises and broken teeth, and she stank from the urine. She might already be dying, he thought, but the men beating her seemed intent on killing her anyway. Meanwhile, he had work to do to counter the return of the soldiers.

The calls of the Achaeans up on the hill assured him that he still had time. He cut all but three of the horses loose, and then took a burning piece of wood from the fire and whirled it to strengthen the flame, setting fire to a few of the lean-tos and leaf litter. Then he rushed to cut the woman down.

In the smoke, he could tell that she was dead. He cut the gold slave band off her neck instead and put it in his pocket.

Achaeans appeared at the top of the ridge above the camp and saw him. Screaming, they rushed toward him, but Shelby leapt on one of the horses, towing the other horses behind. He circled the back of the camp, giving himself distance and a dense screen of smoke for escape, and urged the horses up the steep hill away from the Achaeans.

In moments he was near Kratos, who must have heard the ruckus in the camp and the scrambling of the soldiers.

"Everything okay?" Shelby asked urgently.

"Yes, Icarus, but I think you got here just in time to save this man's life."

The gagged sentry looked at both of them.

Shelby turned the man over and knelt on him to loosen the knots. In a moment, he re-tied the man to make a more convenient bundle. A second later, he slung him over a horse's back.

"Hold him," he told Kratos. "Tie his feet to his hands beneath the horse."

Movement nearby meant Achaeans coming their way.

"Let's get out of here," he said.

C H A P T E R

TWENTY EIGHT

XXXXXXXXXX

"How many were there?" asked Kratos once they slowed the horses.

"Twenty or thirty, maybe a few more," Shelby answered. "I killed a sentry and then threw his head into the camp. You probably heard the commotion."

"So that's what happened. Yes, I heard quite an uproar. Why did you do that?"

"They had a woman, a slave, tied to a stake. They were urinating on her. When they started to whip her, I decided to divert their attention." Shelby clenched his jaw. "So I tossed the sentry's head into the camp. I also set fire to the camp. You probably smelled the smoke."

Kratos smiled at him. "Icarus, you amaze me."

They rode in silence for a moment, the bound soldier bouncing painfully on the horse's back with each jolting step.

"I know she was a slave because she had a gold band around her throat," Shelby added, taking the band from my pocket and handing it to Kratos. "Maybe you will recognize the ownership."

Kratos turned the band over in his hand. "Well certainly. This is a palace slave. Her name was Danae and she had been in service for, oh, about six or seven harvests. She was purchased from the traders seven harvests ago."

"What else does her band tell you?" Shelby asked.

"Not much, but we can find out more. Metis or Melia will know where she worked or will know who to ask. The women employ the domestic help. The men do not interfere." Kratos looked down at the bound and gagged soldier. "I think," he added, "that the women will find out a good deal from this man."

As they approached the city, Shelby described the details of the camp to Kratos — the cage for the lion, the lean-to shelters, the supplies.

"This has been a well-thought-out plot," Shelby said. "It took time to train the lion. The attack at the pool yesterday was just the first blow, obviously, but it has been planned for many months, perhaps years. I expect we have not heard the last. We need to meet with your warriors when we return."

"I expect the meeting is already set," said Kratos, looking up at the distant city. "The Matrons will have sensed the danger, and I know we have been seen from the walls. I expect Melia has seen us, also, returning with this enemy on strange horses. You will hear the clanging of the smiths as they hammer out new weapons before we get to the gates."

"Tell me about the traders you are expecting," Shelby said. "I wonder if they are part of the plot also."

"That's a good question," said Kratos. "They come once in the summer to buy our wool, grain, crafts, and gold, and to sell us slaves and spices. The farmers buy and sell livestock at the same time. It is something everyone looks forward to. A lot of drinking happens." He smiled.

"More than last night?" Shelby asked in mock amazement.

"This time, probably not as much."

"How long have the traders been coming? I mean, has it been forever, or is it a new thing in the last few years, I mean harvests?"

"Oh," said Kratos, "for time out of mind. They come from all over. Sometimes from the land between the rivers, sometimes from Persia, even more distant lands. Some ride on camels, but most are in carts drawn by short ponies or asses. Some are dark skinned, some lighter shades, all manner of dress and customs. It was the traders who brought the worship of Zeus and the Olympian gods, and to them our customs of worshipping the Goddess must seem ancient and wrong. Of course, Metis knows better."

He paused to think. "The men we saw today, they are probably Zeus worshippers."

"How widespread is the new religion in the city?" Shelby wondered if a religious war was brewing.

"In the palace we do not hear about the religion at all," replied Kratos. "However, when the people cheered yesterday after the eagle took the dove, it was because they saw it as an omen from

Zeus welcoming you to the city. The eagle is the bird of Zeus. The Goddess is the mother of Zeus, so she tolerates her son, and Metis tolerates him also. It may have been a good omen, but the rising influence of Zeus among the citizens can be a problem. He is a man's god."

Shelby dropped into deep thought.

"The motives of human behavior are simple, really," he mused. "Religion or ideology is a big one. Ego is another. Sex. Need. Some wars are fought to capture scarce resources for survival, but not many. Mostly it comes down to power or ego, and to religion or ideology. If you excavate the human soul far enough, you always get to ego. Enforcing your own religion on others is just ego. Warring for wealth or resources, usually just ego. Sex always comes with conquest. Women are enslaved, not killed.

"So," he thought at last, "Zeus versus Goddess religious conflict is a son versus mother problem. Repressed son seeks freedom from domineering mother. There's sexual reverberation to that. The son feels inadequate until the mother is dominated or controlled. That's an ego plus sex problem, a powerful combination. But personal. I wonder if these religious conflicts are just an idealized version of an actual mother-son conflict. Can that be a source of the plot we are seeing, with the lion and the ambush? Who else but a son would seek that kind of power? Can a mother-son conflict influence a whole culture? Can it promote a war?

"I guess that depends on the son," he thought with a glance at Kratos.

"What?" asked Kratos.

"Oh, nothing. Just thinking. About sons and their mothers. I didn't have a mother, really. My mother hated being a mother and I always felt like she dumped me when she could. I grew up in boys' schools and camps and hardly ever saw my parents. Then they died before I was twelve harvests."

"Icarus, that sounds ideal to me," said Kratos with a smile. "I get really tired of women bossing everybody."

"Especially you," Shelby said.

"Especially me," said Kratos.

The strapped Achaean began to struggle against his bindings.

"Careful friend," Shelby said to him, "we are almost there. Then we will see what you know."

"Mmmph!" said the guard.

"Well, yes, we could talk to you now, but we want the women to see you first. After all, your group has been plotting against the women, and I think they deserve the first go at you." Shelby assumed that the guard had heard something about the city's women. If not, he would soon learn that there are some women in the world you cannot tie up to a stake and urinate on.

Or beat to death for sport.

"I think we should get our information out of him before Metis sees him," said Kratos, a warning tone creeping into his voice. "Metis is not a patient person. If she learns about the fate of the slave woman . . ." His voice trailed off and he winced.

"Yeah," thought Shelby, "I saw what she did to that guy at the pool yesterday. She is not a woman to mess with." Then another thought occurred to him and he signaled Kratos to continue, using the rotating motion that implies pouring more from the mouth.

"You're right," Shelby said, continuing the thread of Kratos' statement. "I think so. Nobody could expect her to be patient if she learned what this Achaean was doing to that poor slave woman. I watched Metis chopping a man's balls off just yesterday. She seemed enthusiastic about it."

"Enthusiastic is not the half of it," replied Kratos, catching on when Shelby made a significant glance at the bound soldier. "Oh no, let me tell you about the women of the city. They eat the balls of slaves for breakfast."

"No!" Shelby exclaimed in a disbelieving tone. "You mean every day?"

"They'd do it every day if they could, but usually it's just the balls of men who do something wrong. You know, steal, or lie."

"What about planning an attack on the city?" Shelby asked, noticing the sweat dripping from the back of the soldier's neck and his involuntary twitching.

"Oh, that would be bad," Kratos grinned. "In a city where the women rule, men are kept under strict control."

"You mean, like being tied to the stake and whipped to death?"

"Worse than that. Much worse than that. Although tying to the stake is part of it." Kratos obviously enjoyed this. His teeth glittered through his thick red beard and his eyes crinkled with delight. "You cannot believe what they think of to do to a man they are mad at. Besides, you know women. They never get over it. When they are mad, they stay mad forever. I watched Metis sacrificing one of the men to the Goddess. It was not a pretty sight."

"Tell me about it," Shelby said, trying to keep a shocked tone in his voice but grinning along with Kratos.

"They tied him up in front of the altar, you know, hanging from his hands, with his legs tied spread-eagled."

"Was he naked?" Shelby asked.

"Of course he was naked. The first punishment is always to take away the clothes. What they did then was not pretty."

"What had he done?"

"A woman accused him of raping her. He was only fifteen."

"Was there a trial?"

"It doesn't matter. When a woman makes a charge against a man, it's always the man's fault in this city."

Shelby wondered if this was an actual the case.

"I wonder if we should wait to take this one to the city," Kratos continued, "until we are ready to dispose of him. I think we should question him out here, and if he cooperates then maybe we can find a way to keep him off the altar."

"Off the altar!?" Shelby exclaimed, and the Achaean let out "Mmmmph!" at the same time.

Kratos watched the prisoner twitching, then continued spinning his tale.

"This fifteen year old, he was strung up between two poles, hanging by his wrists. All the women came to look at him and decided he was guilty."

"Just like that?"

"Icarus, you amaze me. Who can follow the logic of women? Of course just like that." He grinned again. "So Metis started with his toes. First she cut off the little toe of his right foot, and then cauterized the wound with a brand from the altar."

"There was a fire in the altar, then," Shelby said.

"Fire always burns in the altar," Kratos replied. "Metis threw the toe onto the altar and apologized to the Goddess for such a meager offering. But, she promised, there would be more. Then, when the toe burned to ash, she cut the little toe off the other foot, and she kept on cutting off parts of him until he passed out."

"No!" Shelby exclaimed again.

"Oh yes. Justice is swift, but punishment is long in the city. Our prisoner will learn how swift when he meets the council."

Kratos was savoring this description a little too much,

Shelby thought. Unless he had seen it.

"They kept him alive during the night. You could hear him screaming all over the city all night long. I won't tell you what they did to him on the second day, but you can imagine."

Kratos paused and it was obvious from the grim set of his face that his enjoyment in the tale had faded. Perhaps Kratos had been recalling a memory after all. "It must be hard to have a mother with that kind of power," Shelby thought. "Could Metis torture a young criminal? How does the brutal exercise of that kind of power mix with motherly compassion and domesticity? I bet psychoanalysts have a field day with questions like that. I have seen men deliberately torture other men and women and I thought it cruel and unwarranted and unjust, but it is not the same as a mother of six doing it. How does it affect her children?"

Shelby's mind drifted from Metis to Melia. He remembered the way she plunged the sword into the Achaean at the pool, then hacked at his neck. She was not one to hold back. Now it occurred to him to wonder whether her exercise of power was constrained in any way. Had she stopped only because he told her to, or had her submission to his command been only apparent? Could she submit to any man? Now that he considered it, he thought not.

"The Rangers drove submission out of my own mind," he thought. "We were taught to be fearless, cocky, indomitable, persistent, and completely obedient. We did not think about orders, we just did them. For us, conquest was a way of life. Have I come upon a city ruled by women with the same attitudes — fearless, indomitable, and unyielding?"

Kratos had fallen silent, and Shelby lapsed deeper into his own thoughts.

"I wonder what shaped the culture of these women," he asked himself. "Did they learn to be indomitable as a result of their history, or is their unyielding spirit something they inherited from the earliest days of human civilization? Do they, like me, like so many Rangers, confuse vengeance with justice, until vengeance conquers them? Do they too have their hilltop experience in Afghanistan? Does everyone? If revenge and killing do not make the pain go away, then what does? Have these women found an answer to that question, or are they still climbing that hill in the dark, assaulting the ambush, as I am?"

He shuddered.

"Come back, Icarus," Kratos said presently, quietly, looking over with sympathy. "You were gone again."

Shelby cleared the vision with a shake of his head. The visions always came back to that last battle. Why did everything always come back to that? He looked up at the city walls, now close enough to distinguish the joints between the stones, and realized that here, in this bright daylight, some things are not always about a firefight in the dark.

"Kratos, I think you have given me and this fellow here food for thought."

He noticed that the man jerked at the name "Kratos." Thinking back, Shelby realized that it was the first time Kratos' name had been spoken. "That's interesting," he thought.

"You know, we may have come far enough toward the city already," Shelby said. "Maybe we don't need to take this fellow in right away. He might be valuable to us, and we might want to let him earn his freedom by talking. Why don't you ride on to the city and have some men bring us a tent and better rope."

Kratos spurred on ahead, and Shelby dismounted. With the SOG, he sliced the man's bonds, making sure to pass the knife close enough to his face for him to get a good look at it. Then, Shelby lifted him off the horse as though he were a child and set him on his feet. Reaching up with his knife to the Achaean's cheek, he slid the blade under the gag. A quick flick cut the cloth binding, and he pulled the gag from the man's mouth.

TWENTY NINE

✕✕✕✕✕✕✕✕✕✕

"**I**s there anything you want to tell me before Kratos returns with the men?" Shelby asked.

"A man named Kratos is the one we were after," the Achaean spit out. "They said we would be paid a lot gold if we got him."

"Who said that?"

"The ones in charge. You know. The leaders. Those kind."

"Friend," Shelby said, "we may have a lot to talk about today. If you cooperate, I will keep you away from the women."

He fell to his knees. "Oh thank you, thank you," he shuddered. "We have been told about the women. They are harpies and eat male babies. What I was listening to just now makes them even worse than that."

"You may speak freely in my presence," Shelby replied, "and I will treat you with kindness. Do you understand? I'm not sure the others will feel that way about you, so you must speak all that you know. You must tell me everything."

"Yes, yes," said the man eagerly.

He might be acting, but he seemed genuinely frightened by his prospects. However, that did not mean he would tell the truth, only that he was scared. Then again, only men who cared about their lives got scared.

"How are your bands?" Shelby asked. "I want to be sure they are not too tight." He fussed over them, giving the man a sense that he cared about him.

It worked. The Achaean visibly relaxed a little.

"What happened to Gorgas?" he asked.

"Who?"

"Gorgas. The other man I was on patrol with."

"I'd rather not say," Shelby said, "but I will if you want."

"Yes," said the man, "he was very close to me, and I worry about him. Tell me."

"I think he will be okay. I left him tied up just as I did you, but he was unconscious. The others will find him eventually, or I will go back and find him tomorrow."

"Tomorrow? You will leave him tied up in the forest all night? In the dark? What about the animals? He is very afraid of the dark."

"Yep," Shelby thought, "not the sharpest knife in drawer. That's what I thought. That's why he was leading the patrol, and why this one was with him."

"Well, the lion is dead now," Shelby said. "I think the lion's presence scared off the lesser animals. Probably even the bears. Although the jackals are still around, I don't think the jackals will bother a living man. So he ought to make it through the night."

"Can we go back to him when we are through here?" The Achaean was earnest, but Shelby wondered about his motives. Probably lovers, was his guess.

"If you tell me everything I want to know, and I believe you have told me the truth, then I will carry you back to the place and let you find Gorgas. Right now, I do not feel much compassion. I will ask the questions, and you will answer them, and then we will see. So, once more, before Kratos returns with the men, what do you want to tell me? Start with your name."

The Achaean talked. His name was Bren. He left his father and mother to join the Achaeans when he was just ten winters. After spending several winters as the lover and servant of one of the older soldiers, he was released from bondage and made a full soldier. He was seventeen when he met Gorgas. Gorgas was five winters younger, just twelve. Gorgas asked Bren to take care of him.

It was the way things were done in the Achaean army. An older boy slept with a younger boy and they went to battle together. It was a very close relationship. "Tonight will be our first night apart in more than ten winters," Bren said, his eyes watering.

"Why are you in the valley?" asked Shelby. "Why the lion?"

"We have a great army and will invade this wealthy land with its short people," Bren said. "We want the gold, but not the women. No. Nobody lusts for those harpies. We intend to kill the women as we rape them."

Bren poured out words like someone opened a tap. Shelby had difficulty following because it was disjointed and he stumbled and repeated himself. But eventually Shelby got it all, he thought.

"You say the lion was brought to trap Kratos?" Shelby asked at last.

"The lion was brought to eat Kratos."

"Why Kratos?"

"Everyone knows he is the commander of the army. Others give the orders, but he leads the men. Without him, the army would be in confusion, leaderless. They could not resist us."

He said that with a hint of pride. Apparently the lower echelons of the Achaean army believed a city run by women was defenseless. It was not possible for them to conceive of an army that was not led by a single heroic male. "This is one of the shortcomings of a patriarchal society," Shelby guessed. "In a patriarchy, there can only be one boss, and he is the toughest guy around. The silverback. The alpha baboon. The commander-in-chief. Was it treasonous to equate the commander-in-chief with an alpha baboon?"

"So the plan was to disable the fighting ability of the army and then invade, is that it?"

The Achaean looked a little taken aback.

"Yes. Certainly. That's all we have talked about for five winters. We have been planning a long time for this, training, gathering forces. It has been very expensive," Bren said. "Rations were cut because of all the new men. Lots of promises were made."

"Tell me about the lion."

"The lion was with the traders. He was huge, and a man we called Leonidas was his trainer. I first saw him when Gorgas and I were going with the traders, then a soldier named Timon recruited us. Lots of Achaeans mix with the traders to get a look at the city."

"How did they train the lion?" Shelby continued.

"At first a man from the city came to talk to us about it," said Bren. "I don't know his name. It was more than three winters ago"

"A man. Did you ever see him?"

"He came to our camp in the forest the first night we got there. He was wrapped up, but I heard him speak and saw his face in the firelight."

"You know he was from the city, then?"

"Oh yes. The accent, his height, everything. He seemed to be a very angry person, but very cultured. He kept everything under control. He didn't speak to me. He only spoke to Timon the leader. He put his arm around Timon's shoulder, and they went off together to the lion's cage. No one heard what was said. The next we knew, he was gone, and Timon was posting guards around the camp and tamping the fire down. Getting that huge lion up the slopes in that cage was hard, I can tell you. We nearly dropped him off a cliff several times, and I wish we had."

In the distance Shelby saw Kratos leading a group of mounted soldiers out of the city gates. Perhaps Phorbus was among them.

"It's possible that he's lying," thought Shelby. "It's also possible that he isn't lying and that the city has a traitor. Who has motive for treason? Usually, the motive for treason is money, but the man Bren described doesn't sound like someone who needs money. Then what? Ego? Sex? Ideology?"

"What else can you tell me about this man?" Shelby asked.

"What do you mean?"

"I mean, was he tall or short? Was he fat or thin? Did he have a beard? Was he bald? Tell me everything you remember."

"He was one of the short people. Like from the city. He did not have a beard, but I didn't see the top of his head. I thought I saw hair beneath his hood."

"Was he wearing sandals?"

"Everyone wears sandals. Except you," Bren added.

"Tell me about the sandals. Were they rich looking?"

"What do you mean?"

"Did they have gold or silver ornaments on them? Were they new? Were they good?"

"They had silver ornaments on them I think."

"Fat or thin?" Shelby asked.

"Sort of medium. Not fat really, but not skinny. He looked slim rather than fat, but short like all the short people in this valley."

Shelby knew he was being strung along, so he changed the subject. In just moments, the city's troops would arrive.

"Tell me about the lion training."

CHAPTER

THIRTY

XXXXXXXXXX

T he Achaean did not get a chance to answer before Kratos arrived with thirty men on horseback, accompanied by Phorbus and Ophion. Behind them, another seventy or so mounted men thundered from the city gates. Shelby was not surprised. Kratos had alerted the whole army.

Phorbus dismounted first and walked over.

"Icarus, I have not had the opportunity to praise you for killing the lion last night. Magnificent accomplishment." The king's deep voice resonated, even in the open space before the walls. "I can't wait to see you wrapped in its skin. What a trophy! I looked at it this morning. Those claws! Enormous! Congratulations."

Shelby had almost forgotten about killing the lion. That was a long time ago, and he had killed several men since then.

"Thank you, sir," replied Shelby. "I'm glad I was able to do it. Mostly, it was luck."

"Nonsense," beamed Phorbus, clapping him on the arm. "The Goddess has blessed you, and us. That is not luck. That is fate." He punched out the word "fate," and then repeated it, with a finger to Shelby's chest. "Fate!" He smiled again.

Shelby was more aware than ever of the relationship between Kratos and his father. They had the same smile, the same chin and nose line, the same red hair. They had some of the same bluster. Here was a true general. A leader.

"Who is this?" Phorbus scowled at the prisoner.

"He says his name is Bren, one of the soldiers I captured from the camp."

"Bren, uh? Look at me, scum," Phorbus demanded. "Bren? Bren from where?"

"Orous, your honor. I am Bren from Orous."

"Who was your father, Bren from Orous?" Phorbus was impatient with the man. He seemed to be swelling with rage, growing taller and louder as he took the measure of the captured man.

"My father was Agiou. Agiou of Orous. I am his only son."

Phorbus looked at Shelby. "I knew this man, Agiou of Orous. He was a liar and a thief. An enormous fat man. This son of his will be no better. We should kill him now and save ourselves the trouble of him."

Shelby had feared that Phorbus would skew the interrogation this way. Brutality is the last resort, and usually unsuccessful. It was much easier to get the truth from a cooperating witness, one who bartered his life or comfort for his knowledge. Still, now that Phorbus had spoken, Shelby saw that a change in tactic might also be effective.

He turned to Bren.

"What do you say to that, Bren? The king says your father was a liar and a thief and that you are too. Have you been wasting my time?"

The prisoner, still on his knees and sweating profusely since the arrival of Phorbus, began begging for his life.

"Oh, shut up," demanded Phorbus. "One of you there, come over here and kill this dog. We don't have time to waste on him."

"With all due respect, sir," interrupted Shelby, "if you would let me work with him a little, I think we can get some valuable information."

"I think you're wasting your time. The truth is not in him. I can tell by his eyes," said Phorbus angrily, "but I'll give you a few moments." Turning to Bren he said: "You hear me scum? I will listen to what you tell this man, and if I think you are lying then I will kill you." He gestured to Ophion, who strode over to the man and struck him with the back of his hand, a stinging blow.

The Achaean trembled. Tears began down his cheeks.

"Look at me, Bren." Shelby squatted in front of the prisoner to put himself on eye level. "Look at me and tell me the truth, and I will help you."

Bren looked through frightened, reddened eyes.

"Tell me why your men were beating that poor slave woman." Phorbus interrupted, his ears growing purple. "What slave woman?"

"It was Danae, Father," Kratos said, holding out the gold slave band. "She was one of the palace slaves."

"I know who she was," Phorbus replied angrily. "I know who all of them are. A king knows everyone. Tell me what happened to her."

"Icarus says they beat her to death, while I was guarding this one," Kratos said, pointing at the weeping prisoner.

"Did you have a hand in beating her?" Phorbus demanded, his hand on the hilt of his sword.

"No, no, no! It wasn't me," pled Bren. "Tell them," he begged Shelby, "it couldn't have been me. I was on patrol."

"It's true," Shelby said. "I saw her tied up in the camp after I subdued him. She was hanging by her wrists from a pole with her feet tied. Her body and face were covered in bruises, and the men were urinating on her. Then, they started to flog her. It was an ugly scene. That's when I threw the head into the camp to distract them."

Shelby's story got the king's attention.

"Threw a head in? Whose head did you throw in?"

"Oh, I don't know. Some sentry going to sleep on duty. His hair was long enough that I got good momentum for the lob and it rolled right between the legs of the one doing the flogging. The camp came alive like a hornet's nest after that."

"So I would imagine," said Phorbus, the purple glow receding from his ears as his face widened in a smile. "Well done again, Icarus. You are proving to be a very interesting man. Proceed with your questioning."

Bren had not heard about the head, and it caused him to break out blubbering again.

"Bren, listen to me," Shelby resumed. "Tell me why the slave woman was being tortured."

"Timon thought she had lied to us," he said. "Kratos was supposed to be hunting alone, but you were with him. When Leonidos returned and he told us how the lion was killed and skinned, Timon decided that she had betrayed us."

"When did she come to the camp?" Shelby asked.

"About sunset during a feast at the palace, and she was not observed. She often came in the evening to bring the clothes and the lion's food, and would go back to the city before first light to be about her duties in the palace."

Shelby looked at Phorbus, who was looking with concentration at Bren.

"This part is true," Phorbus said at last.

"Tell me how many men were in the camp," said Shelby.

"All my fingers and toes plus another hand and two fingers. We had four on patrol and two sentries. Leonidos was the trainer, not really a soldier. The rest were soldiers. Timon was the leader."

"Where were the sentries posted?" Shelby asked.

"They were posted on the ridge above the camp. The patrol was between the ridge and the fields."

"You were not expecting any trouble from the south, then, from the other side of the camp?"

"No, only our own people are south of us."

Phorbus watched the man intently. He nodded slightly.

"How many of your own people are south of the camp?" asked Shelby.

"I can't count that high. Many. More than all my fingers and toes twice."

"How did you get the lion's cage into the camp?"

Phorbus interrupted. "The lion was in a cage?"

"Yes sir," said Shelby. "It was wearing a collar when we killed it." He nodded to Kratos, who took the collar from a bag slung over his shoulder and handed it to his father.

"So you killed a tame lion, then," said Phorbus with a scowl on his face. "That's not the same thing as killing a wild lion."

"I agree. However, I killed him while he was leaping at us to kill us, so there is that to say for it."

"It was a magnificent kill anyway," said Kratos. "Collar or no collar, I don't think it was tame."

"That lion was a man-eater," said Bren. "The woman would bring prisoners from the city for it to eat. I think they were drugged."

"Did you see the lion eating these men?" asked Phorbus, the purple glow now in full bloom across his ears and forehead.

He looked even more fearsome than before, thought Shelby.

"Not just men," said Bren. "Usually children. Some women. The slave woman brought different people at different times."

Shelby, too, was angered. He found it difficult to focus and began to drop into a reverie of rage. Kratos, standing behind him, put a hand on his shoulder and Shelby shuddered. Then, swallowing hard, he asked, "How often was this done?"

"Every few nights, maybe every third or fourth night."

"Were you ever on patrol on the nights she brought the victims?"

"Yes," Bren said.

Phorbus started to butt into the questioning, but Shelby put up his hand, focusing intently on the prisoner.

"Did you ever see anyone with her besides the victims?"

"Yes. Sometimes the man came, but he stayed near the fields while she came down to the camp. I don't think he wanted to be seen. Sometimes Timon would meet them at the edge of the fields and take the victim and they would go back. Often the woman came and spent the night. She and Timon would make love against the cage while the lion ate the victim."

"How was the victim presented to the lion?" asked Shelby.

"The victim was dressed in special clothing. I don't know anything about it, but the woman would bring the clothing. Then the victim was gagged and tossed into the cage."

"Was the victim alive? Awake?"

"Oh yes. That's what made it fun to watch." He caught sight of Phorbus and swallowed. "I mean for the others to watch. Gorgas and I were always on patrol. They wanted to keep us out of the camp, and Gorgas is afraid of the dark, so we always were close together."

Kratos and Ophion moved to stand by their father, who seemed about to explode. Kratos held his father's hand from drawing his sword, and Ophion hugged him, whispering to him. It was clear that Phorbus' sons loved him. They also respected Shelby's interrogation. This prisoner would never walk away from the interview, but the time of his death had not yet arrived.

"You are lying," hissed Phorbus. "What are you lying about? Suddenly you told a lie."

"He is trying to excuse himself and Gorgas," said Shelby, "but not even a fool like Timon would assign a night patrol to a soldier known to be afraid of the dark. Bren lied about being on patrol, didn't you Bren?"

Struggling against his bonds, Bren whined desperately, "What more do you want from me? I've told you everything I know. I've told you the truth!" He started blubbering again.

"Kill him," muttered Phorbus through clenched teeth. "We have work to do." He turned away, his mind made up, his order given.

Kratos glanced at Shelby, but before either could move, Ophion garroted the prisoner. A slight movement, and then the knotted cord was around the prisoner's neck. A sudden choking sound rang out. The man's face swelled and reddened, and his eyes bulged. A sickening crack from his neck, and he was dead. Shelby had not fully respected Ophion's speed before. Now he did. Here was a silent assassin you never wanted behind you, he thought. Or very close at all.

"Bury him," Ophion hissed in the general direction of the cavalry. Then, he walked after the king. Shelby followed.

"Sir," Shelby said, "We should send troops to the southern border, but there may be a threat in the west as well."

Phorbus looked at him, an expression of disgust still on his face.

"Oh?" he asked.

"According to this man, the Achaeans have raised a very large army. Probably the key period of attack will be the night when the traders arrive. I guess that many of the traders this time may be Achaean warriors in disguise, intent on infiltrating the city. Also I believe I saw armed men moving on the western hills this morning."

"Thank you for your observation, Icarus," said Phorbus. "We will attend to it." He turned away to confer with his sons.

Kratos looked over his father's shoulder at Shelby. His expression was blank, but his eyes seemed to say, "The old man is in charge." Shelby understood. This part of the city's story was now out of his hands. Kratos had been saved and the plot revealed. The city contained a traitor, the mysterious man who came with the woman and conferred with Timon. It all seemed to fit a unified and well-informed plan: the attack at the pool yesterday and last night's attempt against Kratos.

"Who is next," Shelby wondered. "Iapetus? Ophion? Kratos again? Eurymedon? Phorbus? Any plot that doesn't include Phorbus will be a failure. How powerful is Phorbus without Metis? All members of the ruling house are potential victims. What lines of succession do they have? Who governs the city and the defenses if one or more of these people is killed?"

He turned away from the knot of warriors, his eyes sweeping over the ruts made by Bren's heels as he was dragged into the grain for burial.

"More to the point," he thought, "what motive could a traitor have in destroying the city? Greed? Revenge? Power? All of these? Probably. Wipe out the ruling family and the whole place could be yours.

"Except for the Council of Matrons.

"The hierarchy of power in the city might not be that easy to manage after all," Shelby thought, "but to a mind accustomed to a society ruled by one alpha male baboon like mine, that might not be apparent."

Phorbus clearly had no more need for him. Events would unfold without him, and Shelby decided that he needed rest. Rest, ah rest. What a long day and a half. He was exhausted.

Phorbus turned from his counsel to look at him.

"Icarus, thank you for your work these two days. You have done great things for us and revealed much that was hidden." He mounted and sat easily on his restless horse. "You, Eumaeus," he said, speaking to the grizzled guard who had been one of the first to see Shelby yesterday, "I know the love you have for Metis and our city. You will remain here to continue your loyal protection of her. Take a few guards with you and accompany Icarus safely back to the city. He is our honored guest and we wish for every good thing to come to him for his service. I have preparations to make and a conference with Amphinomus."

To Shelby he added, "Eumaeus, whom you know, will escort you back to the city gates. Thank you for your service."

With that Phorbus wheeled his horse, and the troop thundered off toward the city.

Shelby gazed out over the peaceful valley filled with farm-hands busy in their fields. Now, though the sun was high, the maturing day was still fresh and cool. Crops were turning golden in the late summer; the grapes were plump and frosty, ready for wine. Fruit was ripening on the trees — figs, apples, pears. Honey-bees, industrious as ever, were cramming their cells with sweet-ness. With Eumaeus and a small group of soldiers following along as he strolled toward the gate, Shelby ruminated on this vision of harmony and sweetness. Despite the apparent calm, he felt an odd, hard pulse knocking below the surface, where gorgons of evil contested for the earth, striving to be born in hatred and murder and the stain of blood.

C H A P T E R

THIRTY
ONE

✕✕✕✕✕✕✕✕✕✕

etis already knew that Danae was missing, and women of the palace who oversaw domestic slaves were searching for her. Before Shelby re-entered the city, therefore, the Matrons had begun inquiries and interviewed her known acquaintances.

If the woman were seen, she would be picked up.

The tracking hounds were the next step, but the Matrons had not gone that far yet. Perhaps she had not fled but was only hiding with a lover. Perhaps she would reappear, but Metis doubted it. Males were predictable, but not as predictable as slaves.

Unless she was not really a slave, thought Metis. "What if she has been a spy all along? An Achaean woman sold into slavery by her husband, but no broken teeth, no bruised limbs. . . ." Metis wondered about her from the start.

Over time, Danae gravitated toward work in the palace laundry and her supervisors were satisfied. She earned more freedom as trust developed, so she could have found a way out of the city without arousing suspicion. In peace it was done all the time. Metis knew that some guards could be bought off easily, and some passages through the walls might not be sufficiently guarded. "A slave wanting to escape could get away from the city," she thought, "but how far could she go in the fields? Not far."

None of the likely passages were on the south side of the city, where the lion had been killed. "Probably the lion did not kill her," Metis thought, "but the picture is murky just now. In time, everything is revealed."

Metis wondered if she should probe this disappearance as she had others. Normally, she talked to everyone who worked with the runaway if she were not found right away. But Melia was good at this sort of thing and her abilities grew day by day. Finding Danae should be her duty.

"She will make a wise priestess," Metis mused, "perhaps the wisest of all time. Her intuition is unmatched, and lately she seems to be developing another skill, a kind of projection of herself, that she was working on Icarus last night during the wrestling match. This sudden connection with the giant Icarus has accelerated her empathic skills, connecting her to others, drawing them to her. Him most of all."

As Shelby paced the short distance back to the city from the interrogation with Bren, Melia and Rhodia were strolling through the market with some other companions discussing the slave's disappearance. The city was roiled by the events of the previous morning, and now the disappearance of Danae, the lion, Shelby and Kratos out before dawn, and the noise and dust of troops riding out: it was all connected.

"What do you think Danae had to do with the lion attack last night, Rhodia?" Melia asked.

"I think the slave has been hiding something for a long time," Rhodia replied.

"You can always tell when a slave is hiding something," added Ilexa. Though Ilexa was a slight, pale young woman with narrow shoulders and long, thin fingers, she was uncommonly observant and reflective. "Danae had an unsteadiness in her eyes and a deadened expression; she was unwilling to engage."

"Yes," said Melia. "I noticed the same thing. She was trying to hide her mind, too."

"You can expect that from men, who always want one thing," said Rhodia. "What a shame it is that so often when you get men to open their minds, nothing is inside."

The girls giggled. Not one of them made fun of Rhodia this day, but their eyes brightened a little as though they were inwardly grinning whenever they looked at her. Their knowledge of her short temper and of the plentiful teasing she got about the incident during Icarus' bath are the only things that kept their amusement hidden.

"You're probably right, Rhodia," Melia continued a moment

later, herself amused at how her companions honored Rhodia. "With a woman it is different. Every woman is a connection to the universe, to the Goddess, and the Goddess speaks through every woman. When I seek the presence of the Goddess in a woman and she is not there, then the woman is hiding something."

She looked significantly at Rhodia, then looked away. "With patience, in time the hidden thing is revealed."

THIRTY TWO

XXXXXXXXXX

S helby approached the massive, bronze-bound gates of the
city feeling that he was returning home. In only twenty four
hours, he seemed to have found a place, a way of belonging,
a family he never had.

Eumaeus and the four soldiers who had accompanied him
said goodbye and went off looking for their unit at the palace,
leaving him alone to find his way back to his alcove.

On his way through the double-gate system, he noticed five
elderly men of the city, all gray haired and balding, cackling at one
another over a game played with smooth black stones and speaking to passersby. It was clear that these elders provided amusement for the guards. But they also scrutinized every person entering or leaving the city. They might be enjoying a harmless game of
chance, but they were also the watchers. The old gentlemen kept
their beady eyes on the guards just as they did on the rest of the
busy traffic.

He was looking down to avoid stepping into one of the ruts
cut into the innermost sill, when the air pressure changed.

"Hello Shelby," said Melia.

He looked up, startled, to see her standing there, smiling up at
him. The afternoon sun gave her long auburn hair a golden sheen,
her fine skin and features were radiant. Her hair was down, falling
in thick waves over her shoulders to her breasts. She was a vision
of beauty and sweetness, and his heart almost stopped. "She is so
beautiful," he thought.

"Thank you," she said, although he had not spoken. The five
girls with her hung back, smiling shyly at him. He thought he
recognized one or two of them from the bath yesterday, but it

was Melia alone he cared about.

"Brother Kratos has had you busy this morning," she said, taking his arm just above his left wrist and turning to walk with him. "Kratos never sleeps. He has too much energy. If you play with Kratos, you will be exhausted." She waited for his reply, but he was quiet. Her presence disrupted his ability to think. "You might also be dead," she added, joking with him. "Kratos is the dangerous one."

"I thought maybe Ophion was the dangerous one," said Shelby. "I saw him in action a minute ago. He has the fastest hands on the planet."

"Ophion," said Melia, and paused. "He seems odd to many people. He has mastered stillness."

"Yes, I think that's it," Shelby replied. "He seems almost supernaturally still."

Ophion is fast, and he is lethal," Melia said. "He is also a good friend and loyal. You may never be able to talk to him, though. Almost no one can, except Metis. Phorbus and he have a close bond, but I don't think they talk. Not the way normal people talk. Ophion is one of the world's hidden beings. He knows things no one else knows, and he moves in ways that no one else can."

They paused while a cart passed, its tall wheels squealing. Shelby was conscious of her small hand on his bare skin. It felt natural for her to hold his arm this way, leading him like a wayward child. Perhaps he was a wayward child.

"When we get to the palace you can tell me what happened this morning with Kratos," she said. "I think Metis will also want to hear what you say, though she may already know more than you imagine. But first, hero, I want you to rest. Sleep."

They turned left along an intersecting thoroughfare winding toward the plateau over the city, the acropolis with the temple on top.

Passing through, he noticed that the streets could be barricaded at either end by gates set into the walls. Some gates slid into place, some swung, but the effect was the same. The city could be sectioned and quarantined. "Such planning," he marveled, "as though a master plan had been drawn up before the city began construction. So many cities worldwide just accidentally grow, like Houston or Tehran, with no planning and no control. Here, it was different. Every structure, every pathway, had a defensive reason. All the buildings had porches out over the street to provide shade and commercial spaces below, but also they could be used for defense. The many twists and turns made the city a maze of intersections, odd angles, and blind alleys. The city could only be conquered on the rooftops, bit by dangerous bit."

Yet the city was flourishing. It was a happy, busy place, and it smelled healthy. He knew the aromas of Mumbai, Kabul, Calcutta, and their squalor. This city seemed like heaven by comparison.

"What are you thinking, Shelby?" Melia asked.

"I'm marveling at this city's planning. Everything seems to go together, unlike other cities I have seen. It looks easy to defend, but the defenses are not built at the sacrifice of the population. I wonder, what happens when the population increases? Can the city be expanded?"

"You know by now that the city is governed by women," Melia replied. "It was also planned by women with defense in mind. That applies to our population also. We think about the number of children and slaves we need inside the city. Obviously, provision must also be made for the population of farmers and herders outside the city gates. When war comes, we must have provision for those who will shelter inside the city. That means the women and children, because the men will be fighting."

"Of course," he said.

"The city will function almost without noticing that the men are gone, because the women do the city's work already, or over-see it being done."

"But what about population control?" he asked. "The more people you have, the more you must provide and protect. How do you manage that?"

"So far we have not had to worry about population," she replied. "When we have surplus population, we sell slaves to the traders. When we need workers, we buy slaves."

"Do you control how many children a woman can have?" He was curious. Famine and disease controlled population in other cities, but not here.

"We have not had to do that," she smiled, "because we love children so much, but yes, I think there is a limit to how many children a reasonable woman wants to have. Metis had six, but the first four were males so she continued. Then she had me. I think Kalista was an afterthought, but a welcome one. Most women do not have more than three. Three children is plenty, and sometimes they die."

"So now I have another question of a slightly different nature." He paused.

She looked at him as they passed around a cart where a woman supervised two naked male slaves unloading crates of noisy ducks at a vendor stall. The street was crowded, though everyone recognized Melia and liked getting a closer look at the giant who killed the lion. Naked children danced along behind them, watching everything they did and discussing it in shrill voices with other children on the porches over the street.

"My question is how hard would it be for someone to disappear from the city?"

"What do you mean?" she asked.

"I mean, if someone were kidnapped from the city, would it be known? Could someone be captured in the city and taken out of the gates at night and no one know about it?"

"I don't think so." Melia frowned. "I think all the citizens would be known. It might be possible for slaves to go missing, but then it is the owner's responsibility to govern her slaves."

"Who checks up on the owners? Is there a system for monitoring the health of the slaves that requires the owners to account for them?"

"How do you mean 'account'?" she asked. "Do you mean, how do we know how many slaves are in the city?"

"Well, yes, that's part of the question."

"The slave owners tell us. They purchase the slaves. The slaves belong to them. They are property. They can be sold. They must be fed and given work or they become difficult to control. Otherwise, it is up to the slave owner to manage her slaves."

"Do men own slaves?"

"Women and men own property in this city. When a man marries a woman, whatever he owns becomes also the property of the woman. If a man owns slaves and marries, then his wife takes over care of the slaves, even if they are artisans employed in the man's business, like a brick mason or a woodworker. It becomes the woman's business, and she manages it. Mostly, slaves are used to provide labor. Outside the city, slaves are used in the fields as well as in the homes."

They passed through a portico and out into the open street

again, the din of the neighborhood market gradually receding.

"Why are you asking these questions?" she asked, dropping his arm. She seemed to be glowing in the midday sun, floating, and he fell into her deep eyes.

"What?" she asked in his mind, reaching for his arm, bringing him back.

"I heard a report this morning that persons have been kidnapped from the city and taken to the camp where the Achaeans kept the lion. Men, women, and children, but mostly children according to the report. One at a time, several days apart. I wonder if that is possible."

He did not want to tell her the complete story. He wanted to preserve her from it, from the horror of it, from the image of gagged children, terrified, thrown into a cage with a hungry lion, trying to flee, caught on the bars, dragged in its hungry maw, shaken, torn apart. He shuddered again as he tried to suppress the image himself, and she turned pale as she felt his surge of fury and disgust.

Then she let her hand glide down to his hand, which she clasped, her face draining of color as the horror of his words sunk home.

"Shelby, this is something we will discuss with Metis," she said aloud, shuddering at the images that swarmed into her mind from his. "Now, I think you need to rest. I did not know the lion was kept by Achaeans. This is very troubling." Still holding his hand, she led him on toward the palace in silence.

He knew now, looking down at her radiant head in this morning light, that he loved her. He was in deep, profound love for the first time in his life.

More importantly, she understood.

CHAPTER

THIRTY THREE

XXXXXXXXXX

W hile Shelby and Melia walked through the city, Phorbus and Kratos met with Amphinomus inside one of the guardrooms at the city gates. Ophion stood at the door, his silent presence assuring that the men would not be interrupted. The troop waited outside.

"Let's scour the southern forest," Kratos suggested. "The attack on the women at the pool and a camp of armed Achaeans in the south make me uneasy."

"I'm confident in the protection of the southern terrain," said Amphinomus. "Despite a few armed Achaeans, it would be difficult or impossible to move enough men up the rocky southern slopes for an invading army to pose a threat to the city. The informer was just boasting."

Phorbus considered.

"Getting the lion and twenty or so troops up through the cliffs and dense vegetation took a great deal of planning and energy," he said. "Even at that, they had no large hidden place where they could gather undetected. If they can't mass, then at best they will be merely harassment."

"I don't like it," said Kratos. "The fact that we found one camp only suggests the possibility of others. I think we should reconnoiter the whole slope."

"We need our troops stationed where they are most needed," Amphinomus replied. "You can't move an army up the southern slope, and the eastern ridges and hillsides are too exposed for one to move undetected. Our sentries on the walls can see any movement there. The main threat time and again is from the west and north. The citadel on the north is strong, so the west is our weak spot and where we will have the biggest problem with invasion. Let's position scouts within view of one another as a picket line to alert us to movement in the south and concentrate on the west."

"The pass and citadel have prevented invasion from the north since it was erected over 100 harvests ago," agreed Phorbus. "With archers on the walls overhead, no army can move easily through that pass. I am not concerned about a threat against the citadel from outside. If it falls, it will be because of the treachery within."

Amphinomus became very still, his deeply carved face rigid.

"Do you suspect treachery?" he asked.

"The lion was trained to assassinate Kratos," Phorbus replied. Under the heavy brush of his eyebrows, his eyes narrowed at Amphinomus. "The attack at the pool was treachery. Yes, there is treason. What are you doing to uncover it?"

Kratos took a step back, watching the two powerful men. The warm and long-standing camaraderie between the two had suddenly turned frigid. It had not occurred to him that Amphinomus might be treacherous, but the suggestion was before him. Phorbus was almost never wrong about men. But Amphinomus? "He is Phorbus' oldest friend," Kratos thought. "Still, he did ask to wed Melia five harvests ago, and Metis refused. Is that enough? No. It is unthinkable. Not Amphinomus."

Ophion, never far from Phorbus, drifted silently closer, noiseless.

"Father," Kratos interjected, "we know Amphinomus."

The shadow passed from Phorbus' face, and he relaxed a little. "Yes, yes," he sighed, "we do know him. Our old friend. But, you understand my concern, Amphinomus."

"Of course. Your wife, your two daughters, your son, a slave from your house. Of course. But never think it was me!" He breathed heavily.

"No, I don't. Forgive me. Let it pass. I am deeply disturbed, as you well know. This war has begun with treachery. Let us work together to root it out before it destroys us."

"We have our best fighters in the west with Arktos, at the garrison and the hill forts," said Amphinomus. "The supply lines are well protected. We don't have walls or gates, but we have visual contact along the entire length of the western border. Still, perhaps Kratos should take command there, leading forays into the armed Achaeans on the western slopes. He might be able to take the war to them."

"I would like nothing better, Father," Kratos said.

Phorbus nodded. "Amphinomus, I will ride to the west with Kratos to oversee our arrangements there, counsel with our old friend Arktos, and make sure of our preparations. Ophion will accompany us. You put the city on war footing. Begin collecting the women and children, and recruiting the farmers and herders. Post additional sentries. We are at war now, even if arrows are not flying. Prepare the city for siege, though we may quell the threat. You know what to do."

"Yes," said Amphinomus. "I have already thought of many ways to improve our defense and will begin today. Tonight we will double our watch on the walls, and our crafters have increased the production of weapons. All our resources are going into spears and swords, shields, and the like."

"I like the idea of riding west," said Kratos. "Let me say farewell to mother, and I will be ready to set out." He turned to go.

"I will set out from here as soon as the troops assemble," Phorbus said. "Give her my love."

"And mine," said Amphinomus.

Ophion, still watching Amphinomus with reptilian stillness, said nothing.

CHAPTER

THIRTY
FOUR

✕✕✕✕✕✕✕✕✕

Melia led Shelby into his alcove and urged him down, bending over him. Her hair fell around him and her breasts brushed against his face as she kissed him, pushing him backward onto his fleece.

"Sleep now," she said gently, placing her hand over his tired eyes. "Sleep. I will be back later."

She vanished through the linen curtains without a backward glance, and Shelby was asleep almost instantly. He had no idea how long he slept, but he was vaguely aware of persons coming and going, of distant stirrings beyond the courtyard, of tumult. He dreamed troubled dreams, again, in which he was half awake, climbing an unending rock wall to face an enemy. He could not find a handhold; a rope slipped; the men below him were worried; the enemy discovered them; he climbed toward them anyway.

Then, those dreams passed, and he floated over fields of grain, free in the sunshine. In the distance stood Melia, alone. She was in danger, but he could not get there to help. His legs would not move him, no matter how hard he tried to run. She smiled at him. She did not perceive the danger.

What is the danger? It was hidden in the grain, it was moving with the wind over the grain, there! The grain trampled under its foot! There! Again! It stalked her! He must go. He must save her!

He awoke in a sweat. Possibly he cried out. Kneeling at the end of his pallet was Metis, sitting quietly, waiting for him to awaken. The light had fallen outside, and night was coming on, the glow of lamps began to filter into his alcove through the draperies.

"Yes," said Metis. "She is in danger. We are all in danger, but the danger is hidden at this time. You have been sleeping badly but deeply. If you like, I can give you something that will help you sleep more soundly."

He was suddenly awake. No one had ever gotten that close to him while he slept. "I guess I'm getting old," he thought. "Letting my guard down. It's a good way to get killed."

"Go ahead and take a few minutes to awaken fully," Metis continued. "I need some information from you and some advice. Then I think Melia would like to talk to you. Do you need some refreshment? I understand you have had a very trying day."

Her kindness warmed him as he came more fully alert, and something wound too tightly inside of him relaxed a little at the sound of her words. Then, he remembered the story Kratos told about the slow torture of the boy, and he wondered. Was it a fiction, or was it factual? "This woman is a priestess, a mother, a queen. She can probe my mind," he warned himself, a sense of exposure now overcoming his sense of her geniality.

"The Goddess teaches us how to perceive her world," Metis continued. "The Matrons knew something was wrong about the lion. Now we know it was a trap. Everyone knows Kratos' character, so it was clear the trap was set for him. In killing the lion and uncovering the plot against Kratos, you have performed another great service. The city thanks you again. As the mother of Kratos, I also thank you. You have now saved three of my children as well as me."

She spoke kindly and compassionately, and he heard sincerity in her voice.

"What the Matrons know extends beyond the capacity of most males to understand," she said at last, returning his gaze. "Women connect to a universe that flourishes and dies, that creates and destroys. Men are necessary to us, but their understanding is limited by those things in which they are most interested. They seek to destroy but not create, or to create but not destroy, to live and not to die, or to die and not to live. Men are not chosen by the Goddess to be witnesses to the truth or beauties of the world because they cannot cross the boundaries of their own minds. For a man, everything is about his status with other men." Then: "Tell me about your dream of Melia."

The abrupt change of topic caught him unaware. He stumbled mentally for a moment, recalling the vision. Then, he told her.

"It was awful," he said at last, shuddering.

"Yes, that would be awful if it were true," said Metis. "In reality you should know that there is little in this world of which Melia is unaware. She is in danger, and she knows it. She is always in danger, but now more than ever for she is also in danger from you. You have opened a door in her heart that has always been closed, and the door leads into an unknown place where she longs to go. This is a good thing, we think, for it will mature her in ways that cannot happen otherwise, but it also has the possibility of confusing her. We do not need a confused Melia at this time."

"I have also been affected by Melia," Shelby said quietly, glad to talk about her even if it's with her mother. "I have never known a woman so beautiful, so graceful, so smart. I would throw myself at her feet forever."

"I know that," Metis replied with a small smile. "We all know that. The Matrons knew it before either you or Melia. These are not hidden things, even if they are private. However, I do not think the Goddess sent you to us for you to grovel on the ground at my daughter's feet. I don't know why the Goddess sent you, though several possibilities occur to me. Perhaps she will let you stay. I am afraid though, Icarus, that one night you will go to sleep and when you awaken you will be back in your own time."

So she believed him. She understood that he was out of his own time. She should have believed him, but he wasn't sure until that moment.

Would he return to his own time? Would he awaken from some long dream and find himself next to the pool, a rescue helicopter thumping overhead?

"Therefore," Metis continued "because we don't know how much time we will have you with us, it is imperative that we know all we can about this gift from the Goddess. She has blessed us already with your presence, but that must not be the end of it or she would have taken you away already. So we think there is more for you here. I trust you have also felt blessed here. I sense that you have."

"I have," he said, "yes. I do feel blessed. I have a chance to use my training, I have a chance to see in actuality the living history I studied so long, and of course, I have met you and Melia. If this is a dream, it is rich beyond measure. If it is reality, it is a blessing I cannot comprehend."

"I'm glad we agree, then," she said. "With your permission, I would like to invite two of the Matrons to meet you and listen to us talk. Would that be permissible?"

"Yes, ma'am," Shelby replied, rising to his feet.

Metis did not rise from where she sat upon feet tucked beneath her. A moment later, the draperies parted and two old women, white haired and wrinkled, dressed in dark robes, glided into the alcove. They nodded at him and then sank to the ground next to Metis, kneeling in the same manner, their hands folded in their laps. Their withered lips were no more than wisps in their wrinkled faces, and the tendons of their necks were pronounced where the skin shrank away long ago with age.

"These are two of the Matrons," Metis said, addressing Shelby. "We do not need to speak much between ourselves because our understanding runs in channels other than words. This may be unnerving to you, but know that they want what is best for the city and for you. You can relax in their presence and speak freely for there is no hidden thing when we are gathered. Sit down, then." She gestured at him.

He sank to the floor, sitting cross-legged. "Hello Matrons," he smiled, looking at each one. Their eyes twinkled, and they nodded at him.

"We have heard about the lion, the camp, the slave woman, the clothes, and the prisoner," Metis said. "Now we want to hear from you what you saw and what you did. It is not necessary to tell us why you did it, though if it makes the telling the easier, then do so."

"You see much," said one of the Matrons, her voice creaking but her tone kind, "you see what we do not see. If we can see as you see, then we better understand the purpose of the Goddess in bringing you here."

He began with the lion hunt: leaving with Kratos in the dark, wondering about the spears, the leaping lion, the lion impaling himself on his spear, the spear breaking, the dying beast crawling toward Kratos, the collar. He told them all of it down to the death of the Achaean from the camp.

They were riveted throughout. None of them spoke or interrupted until he finished.

"Go on," she said, when he finally stopped. "Tell us what happened then."

To him, the biggest news was that he met Melia. So that's what he said.

"What else happened?" asked Metis. "What did you see? What did you think about when you entered the city?"

"Oh," said Shelby, "I thought about the wisdom of the city's defenses, of how the streets are laid out to confuse an invading army. The use of porches over the streets to provide shade and as a vantage point for fighting. It is a very intelligently designed city."

"What else?" she asked.

"I wondered who was responsible for the design, for the master plan. I have not seen a city like this so intelligently designed elsewhere in the world. The conquest of this city can only occur on the roofs, because the streets are too well defended."

"Then you thought about Melia."

"Yes, my thoughts after that were completely taken up with Melia. It is true. I don't think I noticed anything else."

"Thank you, Icarus. This is a very complete retelling of your day. It does not explain your troubled dreams, although it is interesting that Melia substitutes for Kratos in the grain field, and the daytime substitutes for the night. We will counsel over these matters."

"I did wonder whether there is a way to keep track of the slaves," he added, remembering. "I know the slave woman was from the palace, but how did she gather the victims for the lion? It is hardly possible that she was working alone."

"No, you are right," Metis said. "It is not possible that she was alone. The unknown man who appeared with her once or twice also plays a role. Even he might have been serving someone else. We believe this plot is deep and the intrigue complex. What most disturbs us is that it is hidden from us, just as the reason for your coming to us is hidden. We shall ponder these things."

She rose gracefully to a standing position, followed by the Matrons. Shelby scrambled to his feet with a good deal less grace.

"I would like to assign a slave to you to help you and care for you," Metis said. "Do you prefer a girl or a boy? Perhaps two girls?"

"Thank you, gracious queen," Shelby said bowing his head. "But I have never had slaves before, and I would not know what to do with them."

"It is necessary for you to have someone to help you bathe,

clean your clothes, and bring you food and drink," she said. "Also, of course, as a resident in this house, it is important for someone to watch you as well as to watch out for you. This may be more important than ever now that we see the scope of the plot against us. It is for your own good, as well as for ours."

"In that case," he said, bowing his head again, "I yield to your superior wisdom. Please provide me with whomever you think will suit me best."

"Would you like me to present you with a group of possibilities?" she asked.

"Again, no," he said. "I bow to your discretion. Choose whomever you think best suited."

She looked him full in the face, her dark eyes penetrating once more into his mind, and then she turned and left through the draperies. The Matrons whisked away behind her without a backward glance, leaving him standing there alone.

CHAPTER

THIRTY
FIVE

✗✗✗✗✗✗✗✗✗✗

While Metis was interviewing Shelby, Phorbus was riding with Kratos and Ophion to the western defenses. On the six-hour journey, Phorbus pondered his sudden flare-up at Amphinomus. "Is something there?" he wondered. "What can it be? Am I just worked up over the two plots interrupted by the stranger Icarus?"

He decided that after a few days with Arktos he would travel north to the citadel to inspect its preparations and to assess Achaean strength. It could take weeks to close the western border adequately, and every day that passed was a day of danger from the north. "But what treachery am I leaving behind in the city? Is there equal treachery in the citadel?" he asked himself.

A good bit of his mind wondered about Amphinomus, too. Phorbus had not felt completely at ease with Amphinomus since Metis denied him marriage to Melia. That had opened a rift between them he had not felt before in the sixty years of their friendship as they warred shoulder to shoulder against foes all over the world. With an only son Melia's age, it would have been a bad match. Metis had been right to refuse. But was the rift enough to drive treason? And if not Amphinomus, then who? Who else would have motive and ability?

"Someone," he decided, backing away from an accusation against Amphinomus, "someone with contacts among the Achaeans. Who is that?"

Gradually, under the monotony of the jogging horse, his thoughts drifted back over his last four decades as consort to Metis, the duties of kingship, the constant threat of invasion by heathen Achaeans. Riding into the sun, Phorbus went further back in his mind, remembering his time with Arktos and Amphinomus on their world tour, all those decades ago, the sights they had seen, the strange places and people they had encountered.

The city sent the three young men on a tour of the world, but not for pleasure. That trip was meant to teach them about the best practices of war and defense, to expose them to knowledge, and to hone their understanding of basic military principles. Phorbus' time was not wasted. He made careful sketches of Nineveh, Babylon, Knossos, Memphis, and the hill forts of Libya before returning home.

They traveled through seven harvests on horseback and camel, constantly moving. Sometimes they traveled with caravans for safety from bandits. Other times the three of them dared the road on their own, secure in their sense of strength. It was a hard journey, the way long, and the people interesting and deceptive. However naive they had been when they left, they were no longer so by the time they returned home, browned and dusty and wiser.

Courting Metis had been easy, he remembered as they began the gradual ascent up the western slopes through the rich vineyards. She chose him the day he returned from his journey, entering the citadel with the traders on their annual visit. He would never forget that first adult sight of her. When he had gone on the tour, she had been a pudgy girl child. Seven years later, she was beautiful. He saw her standing on the parapet of the citadel overlooking the noisy procession, the morning sun giving her a golden halo against the sky. They locked eyes, and in that instant whatever had been strange or unknown about his future evaporated.

She had been Melia's age, maybe a year or two younger, but her look changed his world, and the rest was easy. Now, he rode westward with two of his mature sons, one on either side, into a setting sun with peaceful fields turning to lavender and gold in the growing shadow of the hills. The country looked well managed, the crops properly attended. He was proud of his role in protecting the country, helping to keep it prosperous.

"All of that is threatened now, by barbarians gathering on the borders in their stinking, feral gangs," he thought. "Our whole way of life."

THIRTY SIX

✕✕✕✕✕✕✕✕✕✕

Shelby had just settled down with his SOG to sharpen it —
a lion and a man's neck can dull a good blade — when the
curtains parted. A naked female slave, tall and slender with
close-cropped curly blonde hair and large blue eyes, entered and
knelt in front of him. She was possibly 20, beautifully shaped
and lithe, in full maturity, her breasts just hand-sized perfect. Her
high cheekbones suggested a trace of Slavic or Nordic ancestry.
Following her was a naked slave boy of 13 or 14. He was shoulder
height to the girl, with full lips and a head of black curls. He knelt
beside her.

Shelby stared at them, wondering what to do next, when
Melia entered.

"Hello," she said brightly, beaming at him. "I see Metis has left
it up to you after all to choose a slave." She giggled, something he
had not seen her do. "Of course you can keep both of them if you
wish," she added, amused at his consternation, gazing at the
naked pair.

"What am I supposed to do with them?" he asked.

"Anything you like," she replied, sitting down on the covers of
his bed and tucking her legs under her. "Anything at all. If you say,
'Go and bring me food,' then one of them will do that. If you say,
'I need wine,' one of them will run to get it."

"What if I say, 'Bring me Melia'? Will they do that?"

"They will come to find me, but I might not come." She
dimpled with a mock pout. "I'm not used to being told what to
do." She paused. "Except by Metis, and that's so often that there's
hardly time for anyone else."

"Also," she said, sparkling again, "if you say to them, 'Get into bed with me,' then they will do that too."

"Can I teach them to be free?" he asked.

"In time we might allow you to buy them, then you can set them free if you want. We might give them to you for services rendered. Remember, Shelby, there is no such thing as a free slave. If you set them free, you will lose their service."

"I understand that," he said. He had been so lighthearted when she came in, but now he became grim again. "I told Kratos that we used to have slaves in my country, but we set them all free."

"We will explore that at another time," she said. "Here, slavery is sometimes a choice. These two chose slavery because otherwise they might have starved to death, or worse. Well, actually, their parents chose slavery for them. They have been with us for several harvests. The girl is called Ino and the boy is Dolios. We trust them."

She smiled at the two, who looked down but were obviously pleased. "They will also tell me every little thing you do." She smiled at him. "Although I will already know."

Then, Melia sent the two slaves away, Dolios to bring bread and wine and Ino to prepare Shelby's bath.

"Now we are alone," she said. "For a few minutes. Perhaps tonight we will have more time together. Right now, I need your knowledge."

She reached out her hand to his arm, lightly, barely touching it, and gazed into his eyes.

He leaned forward toward her, thinking to kiss her. Her nearness made him dizzy, the scent of her. She smelled like fresh bread and flowers and whisky's amber danger, like all of the good things in the earth, and he felt himself dropping, dropping, free falling into her deep eyes.

"Shelby," she whispered, leaning in to him, her breath gentle on his lips. Her hand moved up his arm as he reached for her, and he breathed in, as though to entirely inhale her, become one with her.

"Who are you?" she whispered. "Who are you?"

His eyes had been closing as he concentrated on her nearness, but now he opened them at her question and saw her. She had moved away perhaps only a millimeter, but it was far enough for their eyes to lock.

He heard her voice in his head, speaking to him, low and urgently.

"Yes," he said aloud. "Oh, yes."

She dropped her hand from his arm and leaned back as Dolios came in with cheese, olives, bread, and wine. Putting them down, he knelt in the corner next to the pile of treasure from the feast and looked away from the pair. He was motionless.

"I don't think I'm going to get used to this," Shelby said at last.

"Think of them as servants and guards," Melia replied with a smile, her composure regained. "Their welfare depends upon yours, so it is in their own best interests to keep an eye out for you. They will stay awake while you sleep, warn you if you are needed, carry your messages. They will guard your gifts," she nodded toward the golden pile. "You really need them. Besides, both Metis and I want you to have them. Most of all to keep you safe and allow you rest."

Shifting a little where she knelt in front of him, she continued, both her hands resting on her thighs showing beneath her chiton. "Now, I will talk to you about the things that are most on my mind." She took a deep breath through her nose, lifting her head slightly to his scent.

"The ambush at the pool yesterday morning could not have happened without prior knowledge that we would be there. The attackers had to be in place long before we arrived. Now we learn of the lion and Danae."

"It looks that way," he said.

"Your arrival here interrupted a well-developed and clever plan. It took many harvests to put Danae into place in the palace, and probably many harvests to train the lion."

"Yes," he said.

"The lion's diet was expensive, unless the victims were stolen. We think the victims were purchased for the purpose, otherwise we would have heard about people and slaves missing. The theft of Kratos' clothes was also carefully thought out. This city is under attack from within."

"That's the conclusion I came to as well," Shelby said. "I thought I saw troops moving on the hills to the west when Kratos and I were out this morning. It was a long way away, though, so I could not be sure."

"Phorbus will already have troops stationed at the frontiers around our land," Melia said. "This is not the first time we have been attacked. For more than a thousand harvests the Mother-Goddess has sheltered her people in this valley, and for almost as many harvests barbarians and pagans have tried to overrun it. This is not a new story. It has been conquered before, but our people were able to recapture it."

"The story does not end in your time," he said grimly. "I have fought enemies with different weapons in the same kind of strife, in wars started by them for the same purpose: to rape and pillage, to capture, to murder, to control. It makes you think that some things never change."

"Yes," she said sadly. "Over and over, always the same story. Fight, destroy, kill, burn, rape, steal, and always by men. The women follow behind their male scum and kill or enslave the survivors. Many of our slaves are captured in this way," she glanced at Dolios, "but not Dolios. His parents brought him to the palace. It is likely that he will eventually be freed to join our troops, especially if you teach him."

Dolios did not acknowledge her comment, but Shelby was sure he heard it. "We have survived through planning and through anticipation," she continued. "We have learned to keep a trained army, to be vigilant. For centuries now, the men have done all the fighting. The women follow the men into battle, killing the wounded enemy and caring for our own wounded men. We supply our men with food and help to make the weapons. Some of our women are very skillful at the forge, and every woman is trained from youth to manage her house, her slaves, and her business."

"I see," he said, as she paused. Ino came in and stood by the curtains waiting to be seen and called on.

"Ino, is Shelby's bath ready?" Melia asked.

"Yes, mistress. Shall I attend him?" Her alto voice was smooth, resonant, and soothing.

"We will both attend him," said Melia, rising. "He and I have more to discuss." Turning to Shelby: "Come, sir. I will go with you to see that you are properly cared for."

Shelby felt heat rising to his face. He would disrobe before her, and she would talk to him as he sat in the bath, just as he had sat yesterday surrounded by all those women and girls. He would need to teach himself to get accustomed to their ways, but for a man raised among men it was hard to get comfortable with the constant presence of so many females.

Melia reached a hand out for him, and he rose to follow her. He was conscious that he had been rising in more ways than one in her presence, but maybe that was a good thing. It would be interesting when he finally dropped his shorts at the bath.

Melia, who might be aware of Shelby's predicament but was showing no sign of it, signaled Dolios to remain. She told Ino to bring the tray of refreshments, and then led the way through the courtyard and down the hallway to the baths, holding Shelby by his sweaty palm.

THIRTY SEVEN

✕✕✕✕✕✕✕✕✕✕

"The palace is quieter tonight," Shelby said to Melia as she walked with him toward his bath.

"Father took a lot of troops with him when he rode out this morning," she said. "Maybe that's why."

"So, Kratos told me that it is a full day's hard ride to the northern frontier, and more than a half-day's ride from the city to the hills on the west," he said. "I guess that means the city is much closer to the southern rim. It took less than two hours to ride up to the palace from the pool."

"That's true," she said, not really listening. She seemed distracted, a sudden change from their intimacy of just minutes ago in the alcove.

"I guess you have garrisons along the way, then," he continued, searching for her attention again.

"Of course. We have fresh horses, food, and soldiers stationed at regular intervals. It's the only way to guard the valley." She spoke as though she were not listening to the conversation.

Moments passed in silence as they walked through marble columned courtyards. "While you are relaxing in your bath," Melia finally said, "you and I can discuss the few things that I want your help with." She spoke no more for some time, and he did not bother her.

Although the palace was quiet, it was not vacant. He saw people talking in small groups or moving about their business. It was late evening and darkness filled the corridors. Overhead through the open canopy of a courtyard he saw bright stars in their fierce remoteness. In the peaks of the Hindu Kush, those same stars had looked very cold to him. The whole world was very cold then. Tonight, they were every bit as sharp, but not so cold. No, not so cold by far, he thought.

They were at the baths. Turning through a passage and then off to the side, they entered a domed room with a large raised round tub about ten feet across and three broad steps up from the floor. Benches lined the sides of the room, and thick draperies hung across the entrance. Ino set the tray down on one of the benches and loosened the draperies to close off the area while Melia sat on the edge of the tub. Cushions stacked on one of the benches waited to be arrayed around the tub on the top step for kneeling or sitting. On one wall of the room, a hot fire burned. Large clay pots of water hung over the fire, and the heat and steam from the water filled the room.

"Ino, help Shelby undress and get into the tub," Melia said, "and Shelby stop looking so shy. To live among us, you must become accustomed to our ways."

As he looked at her, he pried his shoes off his feet. She looked vulnerable, available, sitting there primly on the tub's edge, her legs together and her hands resting on her bare knees. He could scoop her into his arms and make love to her right then. Instead, he pulled his t-shirt over his head. He had worn the shirt all day, crawled on the forest floor in it, fought in it, killed several men in it, narrowly avoided being soaked in blood, and ridden a horse bareback. The shirt was not clean. Nor were his shorts, which he loosened. Gripping a horse with his bare legs had not done him any favors, either, in the way of cleanliness. Even he smelled the odor of these exertions. Ino came up behind him and took his shorts, pulling them down. Both women were amused to see that he was wearing underpants, which they did not expect.

"What are those?" Melia giggled, pointing at them.

"We call them underpants," said Shelby, knowing from this point on all possibility of dignity on his part was forever gone. "You wear a kind of undergarment called a chiton. It's the same principle."

But yours are closed at the bottom," she said. "What good is that?"

"Oh," she said in a small voice when she saw how easily they came down.

His ego would have been more pleased if her little round "oh" had been for his anatomy, he thought, but alas.

Shelby stepped to the tub and tested the water with his hand. It was very warm. In fact, it was perfect.

Will you join me?" he asked Melia.

"Not tonight," she said, "we have things to discuss. Ino, come here and bathe your new master while I watch you. I want him taken very good care of." She smiled sweetly at him, never taking her eyes from his.

He slid into the water and scooted over to where she sat.

"Now," he said, "tell me what you want."

Ino pushed his head forward and poured a bucket of water over him. He did not expect it, and sputtered.

"Not too vigorously at first, Ino," Melia said. "Let him get used to it. Then, you can pound on him."

"Oh, don't pound too hard," he said, "I'm pretty sore in some places. It's been an active two days."

When she saw him settled into the water and Ino massaging his huge neck muscles, Melia said, "The attack at the pool yesterday. I want to talk about that."

"And here I am without my clothes on again," he said, smiling up at her.

She acted as though she had not heard him.

"We must continue going to the pool to worship the Goddess," she said instead. "It is where Metis receives many of the prophecies. Sometimes we hear voices, the voices of the Goddess."

"The Goddess has more than one voice?"

"The Goddess has a thousand voices, both female and male, both young and old, and many of them are not human."

"How do you know what you are hearing is not an echo?" he asked.

"It's not an echo," Melia replied. "An echo only repeats what you say. These voices issue from the honeycomb of passages leading into the inner caves, and Metis says that sometimes in the dark recesses of the passages you can see the people who are speaking. They shimmer like mirages, but grow more substantial when you listen to them."

"No," she continued, "we know that what we are hearing are not echoes from our singing. So it is necessary for us to continue this practice. Even if war comes, it will be necessary. After yesterday, I also see that I must take an armed guard to protect us."

"I see that," he said. "What's the problem with that?"

"We are afraid that if the guard is composed of men, then the Goddess will hold back from us. For many centuries, men have not been acceptable in that place. We can send them there to do certain things, but they do not belong, and they are forbidden to be there when Metis is speaking with the Goddess. When Metis goes, the armed escort waits in the trees at the top of the hill out of sight of the pool with their backs turned. Yesterday, she told them to wait in the fields before we got as far as the trees. She often does."

"So you weren't worried yesterday when you came down the path to the pool because there had never been an attack there before. Is that it?" he asked.

Ino used a narrow piece of wood to scrape the dead skin and oil from his back, and pushed him forward so she could reach lower. When he spoke, he was inches from the water and unable to look up at Melia.

"Yes, that's part of it. Also Metis had been told at the last changing of the moon to come with her daughters and no other escort. That's why she stationed the escort so far away. We wonder whether the Goddess planned the ambush, but dismissed that thought because she also provided your presence. Through how many harvests did she have to search to find the right person to bring to us? It is beyond understanding." Melia's eyes dropped now, and she looked at her hands, turning them palm upward on her tanned knees. "If she is capable of bringing a man such as you into our time and so far from his own, then why did she allow the ambush to occur? We don't understand."

"I don't understand either," he said. "I am happy to be here and to serve you and your mother. I am glad I was able to do the things I've done, but most of it was because I surprised them. I might not be so lucky the next time."

"No," she said, "I'm not worried about your ability. I'm worried about you being here. You could disappear again as suddenly as you appeared, and we might never know what happened to you."

Her eyes clouded, and he thought, hoped, he saw them tearing a little. On the other hand, her face had flushed in the warmth of the room. Her perspiration showed among the tiny gold hairs of her forearm.

"Shelby, I will be blunt. Here is what we need from you while you are here. We need you to help us form the women into a fighting force, partly to protect our worship of the Goddess and the holy place. We know war is coming, and we fear the enemy will invade the city this time. We know we have a traitor, one who has taken time and gone to great expense. We don't know if this is man or woman, one person or a group. Regardless, an unknown enemy inside the city compromises our safety. All of our warriors are on duty and busy. When an emergency such as this occurs, no one has time for innovations. But we need to know what you know about fighting, about weapons, and about preparing for an invasion. We want your advanced knowledge, your knowledge from the future to help us, and I want you to help me build a fighting force of women who knows what you know. The men will never innovate, but untrained women can be taught by you from the beginning and it will be no innovation. It will be training."

Her eyes took on a glittery quality, a star-like sharpness.

"We will not lose the city. For a thousand harvests, we have defended the Goddess and her valley, and we will not be overrun by Zeus-worshipping heathen. We will not be beaten!"

"God, she's pretty," Shelby thought. "And dangerous. This is the girl who butchered that Achaean yesterday."

"Stand up," said Ino, "and turn around."

Tall as she was, Ino rose on tiptoe to reach his shoulders when he stood, and she vigorously scraped his back and legs, casually tapping him on the inner thigh to make him spread his leg further. She lifted his genitals, moving them side to side to ply the scrapper, then lowered them as the sensation of her touch and the look on Melia's face began working on him again. "Whew," he thought.

"Melia," he said, returning to the thread of their conversation, "of course I will help you. Why are your women not practicing archery now?"

"The bows that are strong enough to kill a man at any distance through armor are too stout for us to bend," she said. "It takes a man's muscles to string them and shoot them, and not many women have that strength. Bronze armor cannot be penetrated, even with our strongest bows, so only a lucky shot at an exposed area, like a face or knee, can bring down an armored enemy. Most Achaeans do not own bronze armor, however, and come to war dressed in thick leather or leather lined with cork. When we make bows that are suited to our strength, they are not deadly enough and they have a limited range. Our strengths are in hand work, weaving, the loom, crafting." She paused. "Planning, management," she added as an afterthought.

"To keep the city from conquest," he said, conscious of standing before her, "you need strong bows on the rooftops. You must keep control of the rooftops. To keep control of the rooftops, you must keep the enemy in the streets and shoot down upon him. They will fight back with fire, hoping to burn down your advantage, so you will need to act quickly if the wall is breached."

She thought about that.

"Yes," she said, "that was the original plan for the porches overlooking the streets. Archers on the porches could control the crowd below, but you would need archers on both sides to shoot under the porches from opposite sides of the streets."

Ino urged him into the water again, pushing his head under and vigorously scrubbing it with her hands. He had a glimpse of her short blonde pubic hair and thin vaginal lips as he went down, holding his breath, bracing himself with his hands on the floor of the tub, feeling her bare legs moving against his arm, his shoulder.

Finally she let him raise his head and he came out of the water staring into Melia's steady gaze, her eyes penetrating him.

"I know we can teach the women to shoot," she said at last, "at least at close range, but with what? This time I fear that we are vastly outnumbered and will lose a lot of our men before the enemy breaches the walls."

"That becomes a question of design and materials," he said. "I will think about it overnight."

Ino allowed him to scoot back to the wall of the tub just inches from Melia and began massaging his right foot.

Shelby continued, "New bows would be good. I wonder if we have other tools at our disposal. And we need to find the traitor. If nothing is hidden from the Matrons, why don't they already know who it is?"

Melia did not reply for a time, merely looking down at him. Then she stood up from the tub rim and fetched a cushion from the bench. She brought it back and placed it on the top step, sitting sideways with her arm on the tub's rim. They were face to face.

"Ino," he said, "bring us some wine."

Ino stepped from the tub and dripped over to the bench to bring goblets, a stream of bathwater sparkling from her pubis. Shelby's attention was momentarily distracted by it.

Melia smiled at Shelby and said, without moving her eyes

from his face, "Ino, you may go and dry yourself by the stove while Shelby and I talk."

"Now," she asked him in a quieter voice, "will you help me form the women into a fighting force, and will you help us develop weapons that will be effective against the Achaeans? Everyone else is too busy, has too much to do."

"Of course I will," he said. "As long as I am with you, for whatever reason I am here, I will try to be useful. Apparently Phorbus doesn't need me."

"Phorbus and his men have worked and trained together for decades," she said. "They have their way of doing things. You may be useful to them, but not until they know you much better."

"So I guessed" he said. "Tonight, I will think about what sorts of weapons would be suitable for women. The real worry will be fire spread by the Achaeans. We need a defensive strategy to protect the rooftops from fire, perhaps water cisterns stored on the roofs. With buckets and enough water, even children can keep down fire. Fireproof roof covering is also important, such as stone or pottery." He mused for a moment. "Will you come back to the alcove with me?"

"No," she said softly. "Not tonight."

"When will I see you?"

"I shall come for you at dawn," Melia said with a gentle smile. "Don't kill me when I wake you up."

"I promise," he said.

"And it may be that I will know the answer to your question by then."

He looked at her quizzically.

"About the Matrons," she said. She stood and looked steadily down at him stretched out in the cooling water, her eyes traveling slowly down his long body. "Ino, finish him up and put him to bed," she said, without looking at the slave girl. "Do whatever else he tells you to do, but most of all help him sleep. He will have a busy day tomorrow." She looked back to his eyes and smiled. "Sleep well, Shelby. No lions tonight."

Then, she was gone.

THIRTY EIGHT

XXXXXXXXXX

Phorbus felt the warmth of the fields breathing on his back. The evening air near the high hilltops was cooling rapidly, and stars winked in the darkening sky. Ahead he saw troops of soldiers on either side of the road, and more off to the sides, and was pleased that they were alert. On the other hand, they had seen him coming for at least three hours. No reason they should look less than alert.

"Arktos!" he called out as they rode in. "Show yourself."

A dark man more like a bear than a human stepped out between two of the huts and lifted an arm in greeting.

"Phorbus, my King! Welcome. Let us take your horses. Get some refreshment."

"I will, and bring me riders for the citadel. Two riders to go by separate routes. We have war and glory upon us, old friend," Phorbus said, slipping easily from the horse and clapping Arktos on the back. "The Achaeans mean to try us again. I am certain of it."

"At last," grinned Arktos. "Keeping watch is boring, Phorbus, even for an old friend. I would rather be slaughtering the heathen."

"Idle, were you?" Phorbus smiled in return and looked around. "You seem to have kept the camp well-prepared. How are your stocks of food and water? How are the men?"

"The men are as bored as I am, for these many months. Fighters do not survive without fighting. So we have games and I give trophies to keep their interest up. War will be better for them. Nothing inspires a fighter like blood on the ground and the screams of dying men. We both know that well."

Phorbus liked visiting with Arktos, his old comrade. When they were young, Arktos' shaggy hair had been glossy black. Now it was turning gray, like his own, but he heard no weakness in the warrior's words.

"Achaeans are buzzing over the hills like flies around rotting meat," Arktos added, as they strolled into the commander's hut.

Two roughhewn logs supported the roof of the hut, which was covered with dried skins and branches. The walls were mud and stone. A fire burned in the center of the hut and its smoke escaped through vent holes near the center of the roof. In this summer heat, the fire did little to help the ambience of the place. Phorbus was already warm from the hard ride, but he appreciated the chance to recline and refresh. As this long day waned, the low fire would keep off the chill of the night.

While they rested and drank Arktos' thick, fermented honey wine, Phorbus told his old friend about the events of the last few days, the ambush at the pool, the lion, the Achaean camp, the giant stranger, the evidence of treason.

"We have seen many countries, old friend," Arktos said, tilting the bowl to his mouth and passing it back, "but this is something we have never seen. What is the giant doing now while you are here?"

"Melia wants to use him."

"I bet she does."

"Good one, Arktos," Phorbus said mirthlessly. "Melia wants to learn what he knows. She has an idea for a troop of fighting women."

"Women do many things very well," Arktos said, taking another large gulp from the bowl and beckoning to a slave in the corner to bring food. "They should know how to fight and defend themselves. Especially now. We may find more Achaeans than we can kill this time. We may need them."

"I left it with Amphinomus to activate the city defenses and prepare for war," Phorbus said, giving no hint of his earlier suspicion. "The plot suggests that the times have changed. The Achaean threat is different now. Always before, the Achaeans lacked leadership and strategy. If this plot is any indication, that has changed. If they have changed by adding leadership and strategy, forethought, to their warfare, then we must change too. The Achaeans are taller and heavier and more numerous than we are, so we must be smarter. You and I will discuss how that affects the western border during my time here. In a few days, I will continue to the citadel in the north where we will have similar talks. This is a critical time, Arktos. We have not faced this kind of treachery before, and it has been brewing directly beneath our noses."

"This is disturbing news. You are right. Times have changed and we must consider our tactics. If they come at us with discipline and order, they may be more difficult to kill. The worst thing is, they know where we are. Still, we have strong defenses. I just wish our western border was not so long. They might break through so strongly we would not be able to stop them. Effective reconnoitering and response will be most critical."

"Those are my thoughts," said Phorbus. "We need additional sentries to alert us to their movements. We need a way to communicate quickly, perhaps even in the dark. Most of all, we need to be able to reposition troops quickly to meet their advance, without leaving ourselves unmanned elsewhere. This will no longer be a war of small skirmishes. I think the citadel can hold, but the west may be key."

"Does this Icarus stranger have any ideas? From what you say he is a good fighter."

"He may be a warrior in his own country, but I have not seen him in battle so I do not know how he thinks or fights. The women say that he does not fight the way we do. He is very quick; he killed the lion as it was leaping at him, and beheaded a sentry with his remarkable knife without alerting the Achaeans. I don't know much more about him. He did warn me that he suspected the traders would be Achaeans in disguise and advised me to consider keeping the gates closed this season."

"It would be a blow to us all, but we have reason enough with the attacks on the women and Kratos," Arktos said. "What does Amphinomus say?"

"He thinks our problem is in the west. Like all of us, he does not want to miss the fun of the traders, but this year it may be a fun we cannot afford."

"No, I would send emissaries to the traders to tell them they may not enter this year. Will the city rebel if we do that?"

"We can leave the Matrons to deal with the attitudes of the city," Phorbus said, "thank the Goddess. We have enough to worry about. The Matrons should be the ones to decide about the citadel gates, too. The people trust their wisdom and will accept their judgment."

"Indeed," muttered Arktos draining the bowl and turning to refill it. "Indeed."

Phorbus reclined on the cushioned skins. His clothes were still wet with sweat, his own and the horse's, but the rank odor could hardly compete with the male stench of Arktos' home. In a strange way, that made Phorbus comfortable. "One can have too much of women," he thought. "Sometimes a man just needs to be with other men."

Arktos left him with the almost invisible Ophion and his thoughts while he went to give instructions for their dinner. The sounds of the soldiers stirring around the campfires outside made a pleasing rattle to Phorbus' ears. He was sorry about denying the traders. That was one thing everyone looked forward to. Sometimes a thousand traders, sometimes more, came from all corners of the world to barter for the city's sky-blue wool and the gold handiwork of the crafters. They brought weapons, armor, slaves, spices, salt, horses, cattle, and other treasures hard to come by in the fertile valley. He also had seen some weapons made of a new, heavy metal, but they seemed brittle and unwieldy. "And chariots", Phorbus thought. "The traders would bring chariots – one, two and three horse chariots. Is it time to invest in them?" This was another thing to talk over with Arktos.

Ophion shifted on the floor, spreading himself out with his ear to the ground in his curious way of listening to the earth. Phorbus watched his strange son for a while.

"With war upon us," he thought, "it might be too late to change the way we fight. A cavalry of mounted archers has always worked. Swiftly moving wagons to convey troops from one part of the field to another would be better than chariots carrying two or three lancers.

"Still," he reasoned, "one must not discount the power of stallions charging a line of men on foot. The Achaeans have many horses. If they have chariots, it will be difficult to hold the field against them, and a retreat to the city walls might be our only choice."

Leaving Phorbus and Arktos to talk, Kratos rode a half-mile up to the top of the hill to check on the garrison. He found it well stocked and alert and sensed nothing amiss.

From the high vantage of a twenty-foot tall tower, he looked down the outer slopes of their border to the lands far away on the horizon to the west. They looked peaceful at first glance, but as he searched in the swiftly fading twilight he saw spots of movement. Men, lots of men, were moving about slowly, deliberately.

"Garanus, do you see the movement down there?" he asked the garrison lieutenant standing nearby.

"Yes, sir. We have been watching them for months. They seem to be moving around, but we cannot determine a purpose. They do not appear to be massing for an attack, yet the number of sorties up our slopes has increased to two or three a week instead of two or three a month."

"I see. You know they had a camp in the southern woods?"

"Yes, sir. We heard."

Kratos squinted into the dusk, trying to determine what was happening on the slopes and the plains beyond. "Are they building fires at night? Can you see an encampment? Could they be settling the country to farm it? What have you gathered from your prisoners?"

Garanus thought for a minute.

"The few I questioned all say the same — that the Achaeans are led by five kings and are more numerous than stars. Also, they are hungry. Apparently they do not have enough food to feed them all, so the raids have been mostly for food."

"Do they have women with them?" Kratos asked.

"Not with any of the parties we've captured," the lieutenant said.

"Then they are not starving," said Kratos. "They are pirates. If they were starving, the women would be leading the search for food or coming alone. I don't believe them about the lack of food. That is just an excuse." He turned and smiled at the tall, thin soldier. "They are coming because they want to fight, and they want to know about our strength. They want our food and our women and our city. Be prepared, Garanus. Soon their raiding parties will number in the hundreds or more."

"We can stop any size party, sir. Would you care to inspect the storehouses and the weapons?"

"How many arrows do you have per man? I know we have always kept 100, but I would feel much better if we had a stock of 2,000," he said as they walked along the top of the high wall and disappeared down a set of stone steps at the end of the parapet, "and a relay system to keep them supplied during an attack."

Phorbus looked up as two men entered Arktos' hut.

"You two messengers will ride for the citadel at full speed," he said. "Tell Pausanias to seal the valley. As of now, no one may pass. If we allow the traders into the valley this year, I will send him notice. Until he gets it, he must keep the gates shut and the walls manned. We are under attack. If the Matrons decide differently, then we will send instructions.

"Tell him also to light a signal fire when you arrive. If I see two signal fires, I will know that both of you have arrived and that the gates have been closed."

The messengers thundered off on their horses, each taking a different route to the citadel. They would change horses three times before they reached the distant citadel, and would arrive before dawn.

He sent a third rider with a message to Amphinomus relating the instructions he sent to the citadel, and a request to Metis to refer the question of the traders to the Matrons. He expected a reply from Amphinomus before noon the next day. He also expected the Matrons to reject the traders. They never put the population at risk.

Messages sent, Phorbus and Arktos settled down to a dinner of wild boar and Arktos' invigorating honey wine to discuss strategies that worked in the past, those that did not, and what the future war might bring. They talked long into the night, waiting for the signals, Ophion silent along the ground like a long snake.

THIRTY NINE

✕✕✕✕✕✕✕✕✕✕

The urgency with which Phorbus and his two sons rode to see Arktos eased when none of their sentries reported any new movements by the Achaean forces in the hills. Scouting parties, usually led by Kratos, went further and further afield harassing the Achaeans and estimating troop strength, but doing little beside killing a few Achaean soldiers every day. Still, the Achaean presence loomed and was the steady topic of conversation every evening.

"I do not know what they are waiting on," Kratos said one evening after an hour of staring at the fire in Arktos' hut. "Why don't they come on? They seem to be making no arrangements of any kind to attack."

"My guess," said Arktos, "is the dogs want to wait until we've taken in the harvest. Then they hope to swoop in and kill us, and take the food. It's two months until we begin gathering the grain."

"We could start harvesting the grapes now, though," said Phorbus. "The wine would not be as sweet, but at least we would have it in the jars. I'll send an inquiry to Metis tomorrow about that. She is the one who sends out the order to harvest. I hope she doesn't wait too long."

"Like that time twenty or so harvests ago when the weather turned bad and we lost half our food and all our grapes," said Arktos.

"Fair weather, and peace are both needed for harvest," Phorbus said. "I don't think she waited too long on that occasion, but the timing was bad. We felt that the Goddess was disciplining us, that we had done something wrong, and for a whole year the city population went around like scolded children."

Ophion, who rarely participated in conversations at any time, perked up at the mention of Metis, but remained silent. He sat with his hands flat on the ground, his legs crossed, and his dark, deep-set eyes darting from one to the other. But he did not speak.

"I wonder," continued Kratos after some time, "about the friezes I saw in Nineveh. Do you remember them?" He directed his question at both the older men, who had toured the world just as he had done and had gone to many of the same cities.

"Along the main thoroughfare, or the ones in the palace?" asked Arktos.

"The ones showing the victories of the kings. Most of them were on the walls around the marketplace, but there were some very interesting ones down near the temple of their male god, what's his name?"

"Was that Baal?" Phorbus asked. "I had a hard time remembering all their gods."

"Baal doesn't sound right, but maybe it was."

"What about them?" asked Arktos, combing his beard with his spread fingers.

"Remember how the soldiers had curved shields and it looked like they were marching with shields linked?"

"I didn't think about it at the time," said Arktos, "but I seem to remember something like that."

"It was different from the way we fight," said Phorbus. "I remember that."

"I've been thinking about it a lot," said Kratos. "The combined effect of a whole mass of men moving together behind an impenetrable wall of shields must be much greater than all those same men fighting as individuals. Instead of man to man, you have twenty or thirty to five. It multiplies the impetus of your charge and you have much more weight to throw against their front."

"War is certainly changing," Arktos responded. "I've heard that they have chariots."

"I believe our mounted archers are more effective than their chariots," said Phorbus.

"But not if the chariots attack our foot soldiers," said Kratos.

"Why not?" asked Phorbus.

"Because they are armored, and they charge with the weight of horses as well as men, and their spear throwers are very deadly. They move from place to place quickly, and their spear warriors are not tired out with running to the fight. But the main thing is the weight. All that weight concentrated in one place is hard to resist. Horses are faster than men, so when they hit the front they hit harder."

"They're bigger, too," said Arktos.

"I don't follow you," said Phorbus. "What are you saying?"

"I'm saying that it looks like the way to win a battle is through weight and speed."

"It's through ability and training and coordination," said Phorbus.

"That too, but we need to innovate to stay ahead of the Achaeans. They have chariots. We don't. We need a tactic that is just as effective as chariots."

"Do you think your linked shields will be a defense against chariots?" Phorbus asked, testily. He knew how long it could take to change the way men did things.

"Stop the horses, stop the chariots," said Ophion suddenly. When they all looked at him in astonishment, he returned their gaze, and then looked away, his garrote suddenly in his hand, flicking out, flicking back, now in one hand, now in the other.

"I don't know what we do about a chariot charge," said Kratos finally. "Ophion is right, but how do you stop a horse? Men kneeling with spears in front of them will still be run down by the horses, even if they kill the horses. And who wants to kill horses?"

Arktos looked from one to the other of the powerful men. He wanted to speak, but he also did not want to interfere between a man and his son.

"Besides," Kratos said, "how do they fight with those chariots? Arktos, have you seen them in battle?"

"I have not seen many battles with chariots, because we have not had many wars. We have had skirmishes, but no pitched warfare for many harvests. I discussed chariot tactics with a man I got drunk in Nineveh, and I can tell you what he said, but I don't know that we can trust it. He was a braggart, but the more he drank the more he talked."

"Go on," said Phorbus.

"What I understand is that nobody wants to kill the horses, those simple creatures. So what they do is drive the chariot into the first ranks of the enemy, the hero and his spear bearer jump off and fight, and the chariot retreats out of reach of the enemy.

If the hero gets wounded or needs help, the chariot comes to pick him up. If the hero needs to be on another part of the field, the chariot takes him there."

"So you think they are mostly just transports," said Kratos.

"Yes and no," Arktos replied. "The charge of the horses into the enemy ranks usually drives the enemy aside, then the hero kills them from behind. Sometimes the hero gets off the chariot, sometimes he does not and the driver just urges the horses after the fleeing enemy, killing them in their backs."

"So what stops a horse?" asked Phorbus, knowing that it was a rhetorical question.

"Only ditches, breastworks, spikes in the ground, that kind of thing will stop a horse," said Kratos.

"You can tell it to stop," said Ophion. Everyone looked at him again. "I tell them to stop," he said defiantly, and turned away, practicing with his garrote, flinging it around his foot and catching it as it completed a loop. After a bit, he looked at Kratos and signaled to Kratos's neck.

"No, Ophion, you cannot practice on my neck," Kratos grinned.

Arktos looked away and would not meet Ophion's eye.

"I have never spoken to a horse and had it understand me," Kratos said to Phorbus. "But Ophion knows how to do this. If we had ten thousand Ophions in the front line, we could stop all their chariots, I suppose, and save the horses too."

His conciliatory tone and good humor restored the equanimity to the discussion, and Phorbus finally asked, "So, my brave son, what does this have to do with linked shields?"

"Chariots are expensive and difficult to move from battlefield to battlefield," Kratos said, "whereas foot soldiers are the opposite. We will always face more foot soldiers than chariots, and all manner of things can hinder a chariot. Horses might not run through fire, for example, or be able to cross a stream. I think our chief threat is from foot soldiers."

"So?" prompted Phorbus.

"So that means that improving the way foot soldiers fight might offset the advantage of chariots."

Phorbus and Arktos looked at one another. Now Arktos kept his mouth shut. He knew from long instinct and native wisdom that the leadership of the army was changing from Phorbus to Kratos. It had not happened yet, but it was coming. So he said nothing.

"What do you propose?" asked Phorbus.

"Let's think about this together and then I will tell you. What I think is that it comes down to weight and speed. A chariot tramples over a single man fighting by himself, because the weight of the horse is much greater, and you combine with that the weight of chariot and of its occupants. A single man cannot stand up to a chariot."

"Of course," said Phorbus. "This is obvious."

"But how many men equal the weight of a horse. Of our men, I mean, for the Achaeans are larger."

"What difference does that make?" asked Phorbus.

"If we have more men massed as a single unit in front of the chariot, the chariot will be halted."

"Why?"

"Because it would be like running into a wall. The wall does not move, and therefore the wall wins."

"I don't think it can be done," said Phorbus.

"I watched Icarus kill a lion the size of a horse, by himself. He was not heavier than the horse, but his spear was planted on the earth, which is."

"Is what?"

"Heavier than the lion. Or the horse. Here is what I imagine," Kratos went on, "I see a unit of 144 men, twelve across the front and twelve men deep, all standing as a single unit, the front rank kneeling with their spears planted in the ground and the second rank leaning against them with their spears also planted. Behind them are ten more ranks of men leaning against the men in front to support them, and to absorb the shock. Then a chariot could run full onto the group, and the group could take it."

Phorbus and Arktos exchanged looks. Ophion, bored again, edged closer to Kratos.

Kratos whirled around at him and muttered, "Not now, Ophion. Not now!"

Ophion rose silently and went outside.

"I want to start training the troops up here to fight in these dodecas, these 144 man units, these twelve by twelves. I want them to eat together, sleep together, and walk in step everywhere. I want them to learn to run, each man's chest pressed against the back of the man in front. That's how we start the training. What do you think?"

"I'm not sure how effective it could be, since all a chariot needs to do is turn aside to avoid the group," said Phorbus.

"But if it turns aside, then the dodeca turns with it, pinning it between itself and the next dodeca. Suddenly the chariot is trapped, the hero killed, and the horses and chariot captured."

It was Phorbus' turn to pull on his beard as he mulled this over.

"Go on," he said at last.

"I want to make sure each garrison has a trained dodeca," Kratos said. "We can have contests, give prizes. The men might find it fun, and I think it would allow us to slaughter the Achaeans on the field, for all their height and weight. I tell you, 144 city troops moving as a unit, as a single man, will carry all Achaeans before it. And we could have 100 or more of them by the time the Achaeans in their sloth decide to invade."

Arktos looked between the two. Finally he asked, "What about the shields?"

"What do you mean?" asked Kratos.

"If the men are running chest to back, where are their shields?"

"If they are on the front rank, the shields are before them, shielding them from the enemy. If they are on the sides, the shields are on the sides, to protect their flanks. If they are in the middle, the shields are overhead, to protect them from rocks and arrows and spears. In fact they are completely armored and protected."

"In the back?" asked Arktos.

"The men in the back could place their shields on their backs," Kratos said, "and move forward. Or we could train them to run backwards."

"Running backwards would slow the whole unit," said Phorbus.

"Yes," said Kratos. "I'm not sure about the back rank. Perhaps they carry their shields on their backs when they are running, but once they smash into enemy, they revert."

"A man pushing backward is stronger than a man pushing forward," observed Arktos.

"Yes," said Kratos. "Whatever we decide, the back rank will require the most skill and the most training. But I believe it will work. What do you think, father?"

"It will work in one place on the battlefield," said Phorbus.

"It remains to be seen whether it will work everywhere."

"I like the plan," said Arktos. "The men have been sadly bored. We have far too many soldiers up here for the work there is to do, and training them in a new system is perfect." He rose to go outside for a moment, and Phorbus reached over and put his hand on Kratos' knee.

"This is a very thoughtful plan, my son," he said. "It is an innovation, but your reasoning is thorough and sound. Let us begin with a single unit and see how it goes. If one dodeca works, then we will expand the training to include all the garrisons. We should have twenty dodecas by the fall, if the Achaeans do not strike before then"

"Thank you father."

"First Icarus, then the lion, and now you and your new ideas," Phorbus replied. "The world is changing before my eyes."

Arktos came back in, leading Ophion, who was holding his garrote loosely around Arktos' neck.

"I like the plan," he said, shaking Ophion gently loose from the garrote and unwinding it from his neck. "Especially since we have this lull from the enemy. I'm like you, Kratos, I cannot fathom what he is waiting for, unless it's for the harvest."

"It's the harvest," said Phorbus, a tired resignation in his voice. "It's always the harvest. No matter how the world changes, it always comes back to the harvest."

CHAPTER
FORTY

The midnight sacrifice ended and Melia helped Metis to her feet.

"Going to bed, mother?" asked Melia. Lately Metis had been so tired.

"Not yet, daughter, but you go on. I can find my way down from here."

"I don't like leaving you alone on the acropolis," said Melia. "Something hidden is moving, and I feel that it threatens all of us."

"You are right," said Metis. "But I can only see if I move between the Goddess' knees and let the voices and odors of the earth enter my mind. You don't need to stay. I may be here the rest of the night. Go now, you have a lot to do tomorrow."

"I will wait out here and sleep on the step," said Melia.

"As you wish," said Metis, climbing the broad steps to the huge idol of the Goddess. "Call Icarus if you can," she added, "to come and keep you company. Or send one of the Matrons to fetch him."

They both glanced over at the pair of Matrons resting comfortably in the shadows where they had been observing Metis' trance, then she was between the Goddess' broad legs and heading for the secret chamber. The small bronze door squeaked open with a weary sound, and Metis entered a small square room, a perfect cube, under the throne of the seated idol. On the surrounding walls were twelve small idols of the Goddess in the same seated position, hands resting on knees. In the center of the room was a cross-legged stool beside the low stone wall of a well, and a blue wool robe thrown over it. She seated herself on the stool, took a deep breath to compose herself, then leaned over the well pulling robe over her head, staring into the darkness of the earth and inhaling her odor.

She remained for several hours, vision after vision flowing into her brain. She saw Phorbus asleep in Arktos' hut, and Kratos explaining a new shield design to the garrison's armorer. She had a pleasant chat with Ophion, the only way in which the two ever spoke. He told her about Kratos' plans for the army, a new way of fighting, and it pleased her. Talking to Ophion always made her happy. She delighted in his child-like simplicity which so contrasted with his deadly abilities. Ophion was one of the hidden creatures of the world, deep in wisdom and the secrets of the earth, but shut off from others. She never understood that about him, but at least they talked when she was in her trance over the well.

Eurymedon was sleeping, as usual. Her young son was so easy to please. She saw him curled between his slave girls, those twin Persian beauties she bought when the traders came last year.

Where was Iapetus? She never found Iapetus during these trances. Perhaps, she thought, it was because he would not die. Maybe only those whose lives were normal, who were on the road to death, could be seen in the well. Certainly that child Kalista was floating in the well, also asleep and, what is she dreaming of? oh, butterflies. Just like her.

She couldn't find Icarus, either. But that did not bother her. She was not sure that Icarus was real. He was certainly real enough to Melia, and perhaps that would be enough, but he did not seem to have a place in the well.

Everyone else was easy to find. She enjoyed seeing her mother again, catching her up with what was going on, and her father. She saw them every time, though.

And right after them all came the Goddess.

She could not really see the Goddess. She saw a place where the Goddess would be if she could be seen, not an emptiness exactly, but more of a fullness in a place where there was nothing. It was hard to describe, but the experience was always the same. The sense of terror mixed with love, the hair rising on her neck and the goosebumps on her arms, the blankness of her mind, until, finally, she summoned the magic words from her stunned mind.

"Oh Goddess," she cried, "tell me what I must know for your people."

But the Goddess did not speak. She never spoke. Instead, she flooded Metis' mind with images: images of fire and war, of blood on the ground, of the Achaean camps spread out toward the west like pools of rain shining in the setting sun, blood red, of the city aflame and smoke rising into the sky, drifting to the north, of violent shaking and stones falling from buildings, of darkness, of choking dust. And that passed and was replaced by the image of a single grape, frosty with its native yeast and ripening in the sun, of a bunch of grapes, of a vineyard, the vision drawing back until a happy people were once again seen gathering the grapes through fields of standing grain and the gentle lowing of cattle filled the air.

Metis woke with a start, her head on the edge of the thirty-inch wide well, the robe fallen to the floor at her feet. Outside the bronze door she heard the calls of early birds and smelled the fresh morning air.

She rose from the chair, her stiff bones creaking, and made her way thankfully through the door, down between the idol's broad legs, to the step where Melia lay curled and asleep, wrapped in a shawl and her head resting on a bundled fleece. Someone had brought her these things in the night, for she was sure the young woman had not stirred from the spot.

"Wake child," she said gently, touching her shoulder, "and let us go to bed for an hour. It will be a beautiful day."

FORTY
ONE

XXXXXXXXXX

From Shelby's perspective, the next few weeks were idyllic. But his first night with Ino and Dolios was not what he expected. He was exhausted after his bath, and wanted nothing so much as to fall into his bed when he and Ino finally arrived at his alcove. But no, the two insisted on an elaborate ritual of disrobing him, of easing him down, of arranging his legs just so, his arms, his head, of covering his naked body, stroking his head, cooing gently to him.

"Oh for God's sake cut it out!" he finally snapped, flinging their hands aside.

They looked at him reproachfully, but withdrew their hands. Dolios' big, brown, almond-shaped eyes actually teared up, and Ino turned her slender, shapely back on him, and moved away toward the foot of his bed without a word.

He could tell he had hurt their feelings, and after a minute he patted the bed and spoke to them, "Come here, both of you, and sleep with me. I mean, sleep. Just lie down, close your eyes, and sleep. If you get cold in the night, wrap some of these fleeces around you, though how anyone could get cold in this climate is beyond me. But let me tell you," he continued, as they obeyed his commands with dubious, halting movements, "I don't care to have people touching me. Well, not all people, but people I don't know. And I don't know either of you yet. So sleep, and we'll try to get along better tomorrow."

And with that, he rolled over and went to sleep, kicking off the overbearingly warm fleece and luxuriating with the cool air on his bare skin.

Thus began several weeks of idyllic existence for Shelby,

and he sank deeper and deeper into the fabric of the city's life, absorbing its pleasures and his heart lightening in its happiness.

True to her word, Melia appeared at his bed every morning, silently moving in like a ghost and sitting next to him, sometimes causing Ino or Dolios to move out of the way. Sometimes Dolios, or more rarely Ino, would pull cover up over his bare legs and torso when she entered. Sometimes she was too early for them, and was already kneeling next to him before they awoke. She spoke softly to him and occasionally put her hand on his chest, smiling at him in the dim dawn light. The slaves took to sleeping on the far side of him to give her room, and slipped quietly out of bed and padded away on their bare feet when she appeared, returning after a decent interval with breakfast of fresh bread, fruit, cheese, and wine. They acted as though Melia's appearance was the most natural thing in the world. Indeed, maybe it was.

Shelby cherished these times. Inhaling her scent in the dawn stirred him in ways he had never been stirred before. Her eyes, her hair, the fine shape of her nose and chin, the bend of her elbow, the translucence of her skin dizzied him.

But when he reached for her, she drew away. Once he caught her arm and tugged at her to pull her nearer, and she smiled at him but restrained him. She would not make love to him simply because he desired it. No. This was not about him. Not yet. There were too many questions still.

She never teased him. She made him understand how deeply she cared for him and desired him. She was the promise, the future, the universe ahead of him, unexplored country, the challenge. Under her taming hand, he gradually found his memories of war receding. "Maybe," he thought to himself, "Kratos was right. The visions were taming me for her."

Through her steady calming presence he worked steadily at training young women to be warriors. Her idea was perfectly logical. The cult of the Goddess needed armed women capable of taking on the much larger Achaean male warriors, and they needed weapons.

As word of the Achaean plot against Metis and her daughters, and then against Kratos, spread around the countryside, women began moving into the city with their children. Those who could be spared in the fields came with the youngsters to supervise. No one questioned their right to seek safety and protection.

Males stayed behind to do the work, to tend the cattle and shear the sheep, and to gather in the crops; women brought the next generation to the city for protection.

Later, unless they were summoned to war, the males too would be sequestered in the city, bringing with them their arms and prepared to fight. Meanwhile, they began slaughtering the less useful animals and preserving the meat, tanning the hides, and preparing thick leather shields and body coverings for themselves. The walls of the city were useful for drying strips of the meat in the sunlight, and soon fresh blood was streaming down its sun-bleached walls, gradually turning dark in the bright sun and attracting legions of those damned flies.

Overall productivity increased, and hundreds of supply wagons streamed into the city to the warehouses where Iapetus supervised unloading and storage. No one had any illusions about the onset of war. They had been fighting the north men for centuries. They would do it again. They would protect their women and children, and the Goddess would help them as she always had. In the great scheme of things, everyone knew, the males were expendable. The mothers and their young were not. The whole culture served that principle. It did not take many males to breed a culture; but it did take fertile women.

During the day, Shelby, Melia, and Rhodia stood near the city gates watching women enter from the outlying farms. When they saw a strong, straight-backed girl in her late teens or early twenties, they pulled her from the throng and talked to her. If she had children, they encouraged her to take care of them and sent her on, but from time to time they found a woman who met the physical criteria and was not a mother yet. These they recruited. Melia, often accompanied by Rhodia, talked to each one earnestly. Some they sent away because they were too silly, or too slow. The rest were chosen for the Meliae.

Eventually they recruited fifty young women, strong, straight-backed, serious. Not one of them was five feet tall, but they were agile, young, and accustomed to the physical life of the countryside. It was a start.

Meanwhile, Shelby planned his training. He intended to introduce these women warriors to the compound crossbow, if he could find the right materials. It was an innovation that would dramatically improve the women's firepower.

He also discovered how talented the city's craftspeople were. In two days they hit on a design for cambered wheels, essential to a functioning compound bow. Then they searched for the trickier thing, axles for these wheels, and sufficiently flexible materials for the crosspiece. No matter how powerful the weapon, if it weighed twenty or more pounds then it would be too heavy for the women to use. What he wanted was something that required minimal effort, was light enough to use defensively to parry a spear or sword or use as a club, and was durable and dependable. These were significant design problems.

Fearing he might wake one day to find himself back in the twenty-first century, Shelby wondered what he should do for Melia first. He had so much to do, and – possibly – so little time.

Meanwhile, he had fifty young women to train. He would not think about anything else. He would not. He would not anticipate being separated from Melia. He would control his mind. He would. It was his mind, after all. Who else could be in control of it? Just a simple act of willpower.

He told himself this over and over during his waking moments.

CHAPTER

FORTY
TWO

✕✕✕✕✕✕✕✕✕✕

T he first day with the Meliae was not completely satisfactory. The young women clustered in an isolated courtyard, regarding Shelby with suspicion and caution. They wore full-length robes, and their faces were like masks, without any change in expression. They were silent. Melia had told them what they were to do, but they did not expect to receive instruction from a man.

True, he was a very large man. Also, he was not wearing clothes typical of other men, so he was not one of their men. He was clearly not an Achaean, nor did he smell like one, so he was not an enemy. Still, he was a man and they were not sure about that. Men did not tell women what to do.

On the balcony overlooking the courtyard, Metis and three of the Matrons watched. Their presence was important on this first day, for it gave Shelby an authority with the young women he would not otherwise have. Nevertheless, it took cajoling from Melia and Rhodia to persuade them to cooperate, and some were obviously still making their own decisions about that.

"Playing to a tough crowd," thought Shelby.

With Melia next to him, he explained what he needed the women to do.

"You must improve the strength in your arms and upper body," he told them. "You must improve your stamina. You may be required to kill heavily armed men, and you must know how to do that without hesitation, but strength is first. You must be as strong as you can be. Acquiring deadly weapons and the skill to use them won't do you any good if you are not strong enough."

He paused to see if he was getting through, but met only stony silence and immobile faces.

"Actually," he thought, "the women look like they are physically fit enough already. One or two could brutalize horses, big broad-shouldered women with tough looking faces and square jaws, eyes glaring like steel marbles. Others look like they could easily, and willingly, kick someone's teeth out. A few are gazelle-like, the runners and leapers of the crowd. These are not limp-wristed pampered women with slender necks and powdered noses. These women are strong." He had seen platoons of Army recruits who were wimps by comparison.

Still, acquiring and keeping strength was an everyday thing. A daily habit. He would set them a routine to make the most of what they already had.

"You made some good choices, Melia," he said to her quietly. "You have chosen some tough looking women."

He raised his voice to speak to the recruits. "You must be able to fight well enough that you do not lose these weapons to your enemy. No other warriors anywhere in the world will have weapons like them. Only the Meliae will hold them and learn to use them."

At that he got a glimmer of interest.

"Until your weapons are ready, I will teach you some arts of self defense. An honor guard of the Goddess needs those skills."

For more than a week prior, Shelby had worked with Ino in the evenings on self-defense. He taught her basic judo, the art of using your opponent's weight and velocity against him. Now he called her out in front of the women.

They gasped when they saw her. She was a slave. They did not expect to take direction from a man, but taking direction from a slave was unthinkable. Insulting.

"I know what you are thinking," he said. "But, I have been training Ino for several days, and I want you to see what she can do. This is for demonstration purposes. After Ino performs the two or three moves I want her to demonstrate, I will train Melia to do the same and you will watch and practice on one another."

He and Ino squared off on the newly raked dirt of the courtyard.

She eyed him sharply, ready for him.

Suddenly he rushed at her. She deftly stepped sideways under his arm, and he thudded to the ground on his back. He rolled forward, sprang up, and rushed her again. She flipped him again. He rushed again, and this time she flipped him and kept his arm, bending his wrist and rotating his body as he fell. He landed with a thud on his stomach, his arm pinned helplessly behind him, her foot in the middle of his back.

Though it knocked the breath out of him, he had gotten the women's interest.

He also stirred their anger. To see a slave treating her master in this way was offensive, and they all looked up at Metis to judge her reaction. It was also dangerous. What if other slaves tried to do it?

Metis looked down with interest, but without emotion. The women took the cue and swallowed the first flush of their fury.

Shelby rolled away from Ino and stood up, dusting off his shorts. "Thank you, Ino," he said. "You are dismissed. Go and tend to your business in my alcove."

She inclined her head toward him and walked away. Everyone saw the twitch in her naked hips as she went. She was extremely pleased with herself.

"You next, Melia," he said.

She did not blink, but stepped forward to be instructed.

He walked her through the paces, first slowly, bit by bit. As he expected, she learned quickly. In minutes, she learned to flip him, a tight little smile on her lips.

"Okay, Rhodia. You next."

The girl had avoided him since the day he arrived, the memory of her indiscretion in the bath still burning in her cheeks whenever she thought of it. To be suddenly near him again was disconcerting. The smell of him. The strength of him. She fought it off and approached. A quiet snigger ran among the young women, despite their rigid faces. She heard them muttering and turned bright red, adding to her consternation and their amusement. Was there anybody in the entire world who had not heard about the incident?

As he had with Melia, Shelby walked her through the paces, gradually increasing the speed. Within moments, she flipped him, resisting the strong urge to follow him to the ground, to fall upon him.

That broke the spell on the young women. Now they understood. If Rhodia could do it, they could do it. It did not count if

Melia did it. Everyone knew that Melia was special, extraordinary, but Rhodia was one of them, even if she blushed. They understood.

He paired them for practice and Melia and Rhodia circulated among the group. The girls quickly saw that their long robes, called himations, hindered them, and soon these were discarded. The women stood in their chitons, grappling with one another. Minutes later, they shortened their chitons, halving the length to expose their legs and give them more maneuverability.

With zest they took to throwing one another to the ground, laughing when they hit the loose earth of the courtyard, then bounding up to repay the favor. It was a general melee before long, but he had cleared the first big hurdle. He had awakened their enthusiasm.

Thankfully, no one broke bones. These women grew up knowing how to roughhouse, and they took to the physical training with zeal. "These are the best recruits I have ever seen," Shelby thought. "They may learn enough to stay alive."

The next morning during Melia's visit, he discussed uniforms.

"I don't think uniforms mean the same thing to women that they mean to men," she observed. "Men are visual creatures who need to sense togetherness through symbols. Women will never belong to one another in the same way, and they probably won't take orders either. The important thing for women is for them to know the rules. They will follow the rules."

"You may be right," he said, pondering this. "Still, I think it will be important for them to appear different from the other women. We want to make this an exclusive club, to make them feel important, to belong."

"Perhaps we should ask them how they wish to distinguish themselves in the city," she said. "They are the ones who are most concerned about it. Really, I think it would be a mistake for a man to tell these fighting women how to dress."

"I think it is important for them to have an identity, however," he said.

"They are guardians of the Goddess. That will be sufficient for them. Let them choose how to present themselves in that role. And be prepared: each one will present herself a little differently."

He detected a sense of resolve in her. He knew it would be useless to argue, just as it was useless for him to reach for her. He assumed she would come to him when it was time, if they had time. She would cooperate in her own way, when time did not matter.

The second day they began vigorous calisthenics, especially upper body exercise, and they reviewed the basic judo moves. Shelby introduced new moves he learned in close combat drills and used frequently. The women left the morning session covered in dust, their hair filthy and sweat streaming down their faces. When they began, gradually, to smile, he saw that as significant progress.

By afternoon, they were clean again, but they had changed their clothes. Under their loose chitons they now wore sashes around their breasts and pubic areas, like bikinis. When he started the afternoon session, the chitons came off and they grappled with one another with much more freedom. Throughout, they worked hard and remained serious, but when the afternoon session broke up, they wandered out together giggling.

That evening, Melia brought Shelby to join them at supper where she introduced the idea of a uniform.

The idea circulated around the room as the women ate and talked among themselves.

"What are they thinking?" Shelby whispered to Melia.

"Hush," she said, "be patient."

The next morning, all the young women appeared in the courtyard wearing red sashes over their heads to protect their hair. They had also cinched their white chitons with red sashes. The bikini-like sashes they wore underneath were also red. The contrast between the chitons and the sashes was becoming, and Shelby approved. Not that his approval much mattered.

The third day he began physical training in earnest. He ordered them to gather at dawn, and they did half an hour of calisthenics to warm up. Then they set out on a slow run around the top of the city walls. Over time he hoped to build them up to a daily 15K run, about the circumference of the city, but at first he thought the more secluded path around the walls would work for conditioning. They ran up and down stairs from the street to the top of the wall, and leaped gaps, but overall the route was not too taxing. Running the circumference of the city outside the walls would be more challenging, but also more exhilarating, with the open fields, the stream beds, here and there a copse, rocky obstacles. It would be a good training ground, he thought.

That first run around the city walls, however, made him move the runs outside the walls immediately. He was leading them, Rhodia and Melia cruising along easily behind, when he heard a commotion behind. Turning around, he watched as the young women ran past a group of armed guards at their station. Each woman casually reached out and flicked or grabbed the crotches of the men as they jogged past, laughing at them. The poor guards, backed up against the wall by the throng and gripping their spears, could not get out of they way. And some of the women were a little more dexterous than the others, laughing at the consternation they caused.

"I better change the route," Shelby thought. "This kind of distraction could get out of hand."

By week's end, young women who started out reserved and suspicious had become enthusiastic, involved, and happy. Training was going well. He was surprised by how rapidly they acquired strength, as they climbed ropes, leapt obstacles, and practiced their self-defense with knives, swords, and spears. He began with a modified program of martial arts, but saw that soon he would have no need to worry about scaling back the training. These women were coming along better than any class of recruits he had seen. Their motivation and morale was extraordinary.

The first crossbow arrived at the end of the second week, but it was too hard to load and cock, and it lacked any way to hold the bolt in place when shooting downward. Melia could barely cock it using both hands while leaning over it, resting it on the ground and bracing it against her stomach. Shelby regretted the reddened area on her bare abs when she stood again. Also, it was too heavy to carry all day. It would not do.

That evening he discussed the problem with Melia as they rested.

"Let's put the problem to some of the craft masters," she suggested. "Dolios will show you where to go."

FORTY
THREE

XXXXXXXXXX

Dolios led the way carrying a small lamp, holding it high over his head so the light would not blind him as they traversed the quieting city, now quite dark but for the occasional gleam of a lamp through an open door or window. The murmur of families and rattle of crockery drifted into the street from the houses, and gypsy cats appeared here and there, all of them gray in the dim light. Doves cooed in their monotonous single-note song from the eaves. A baby squalled briefly and then gurgled.

They turned down a stone street several blocks from the marketplace and found a thick oaken door propped open. Just inside at a low table, an elderly woman lounged on cushions, an equally aged man opposite her. They talked quietly over a low lamp, chuckling. The man was carving an intricate design on a wooden goblet as they chatted.

They looked up as Shelby stooped at the doorway, which was much too short for him.

"Ah, Icarus!" exclaimed the woman. "Come in. Join us. We have wine, and Arcas has made some excellent sweet bread."

"Thank you, Hestia," he said, entering the small comfortable room, signaling to Dolios to wait for him outside.

"No, no, bring Dolios in also," she said, half rising on one arm. "The slave of Icarus is welcome here." She grinned, a pleasant sight in her long, wrinkled face, and with a muscular hand beckoned the boy in.

"I have brought the crossbow," Shelby said. "It is exactly right, but the women cannot use it. For me, it is perfect, but the women cannot cock it." He held it out to her and sat down at the table.

Arcas poured wine for him into a two-handled bowl carved

from dense ash wood and scooted over a platter with a pile of warm, sweet-smelling bread.

"He flavors his bread with fig blossoms," Hestia said, a happy smile spreading on her face as she looked at Arcas. "He is a very clever man. I'm glad I have him."

Arcas cast his eyes down, a mere hint of a blush on his cheeks.

"He picks the fig blossoms in the spring and puts them in jars of olive oil to preserve them. Then he has plenty for all summer. Sometimes he uses berries or other flowers. Arcas is very creative." She beamed at him again.

"Now," she said, turning to Shelby, "your problem. I worried about the string. Getting the little wheels right was our first problem, but it meant we could make a stronger bow. Now it is too strong for them to bend. Do you have a solution?"

"I think so," Shelby said. He used a piece of sharpened wood to draw out his design on a wooden tablet with a surface of malleable clay that Dolios carried for him.

"If we install a lever here," he showed Hestia the design, "we can hinge it here at the front with a sliding block down a groove here. The block can catch the string and pull it back into the cocked position." He showed her how it works.

"Would it be better to put it on the bottom of the crossbow?" she asked, seeing the rationale for the design.

"That would also work," Shelby said, "but if we put it on the top, then we can make the lever a kind of pipe that the bolt flies through. I call that pipe a barrel."

"Oh, I see," she said, visualizing the innovation, her face breaking into an excited grin. "That also means you get rid of the notch at the end of the bolt, which speeds loading and saves production time."

"Right," he said. "It just rests inside the barrel. The string passes through these slots down both sides. If we angle the fletching, the bolt rotates in flight, and the fletching holds it in the barrel if we shoot down from the wall at the enemy."

"Fascinating" she said. "Hmmm…" She was lost in thought. Arcas signaled to Dolios and the two of them carried away the bread and wine. A moment later he came back with another lamp, but without Dolios, who was probably in the kitchen enjoying some refreshment of his own.

"Why do you want to angle the fletching?" she finally asked.

"Because it will make the bolt more stable in flight. Arrows lose much of their force by wobbling in flight. An arrow shaft undulates or flexes as it moves through the air. Making the bolt rotate will conserve the force from the string and improve accuracy."

She nodded, but looked at him quizzically. "Can you really see an arrow wobble in flight?" she asked. "Are your eyes that quick?"

"Yes," he said. "You need to know what to look for, but it oscillates. It is one of the things archers compensate for, if they are any good. But that oscillation requires energy that could go into the thrust of the bolt instead, if we converted it from an up-and-down motion to a rotating motion."

"Could we perhaps cast the bolt with angled fins instead of feathers?" she asked. "That would make more of a hole in a body. Also, We should put grooves on the sides of the shaft to promote bleeding."

"Excellent!" exclaimed Shelby. "Genius! Yes, you are absolutely right. If the bolt has fins that cast at the same time, then production is more efficient. Wise, Hestia. Very wise."

"We may not have much time, I fear," Hestia replied sagely. "Already I hear that we need to increase production of the other weapons. These new weapons may not always be priority, if there's war, so anything we can do to make it simpler to produce will be good. The old men despise new things."

She studied his design for a moment, then re-focussed her attention on the crossbow. Her deeply lined face furrowed in concentration.

"Our problem is getting the right hinge and pins," she said. "If we make a track for the rolling block, we can have it rise up here and fall back here," pointing to the stock, "and reposition the trigger so." She continued staring at the crossbow and the drawing.

"Yes," she said finally. "We can do this. Maybe day after tomorrow. Come back then and see if we are doing it right."

"Thank you, Hestia." Shelby rose and extended his hand to her. "Thank you. I hope this will be an important weapon for the women."

"It will, Icarus. Nobody ever thought of anything like this before. I think we can make it work. There is already a groove in the top of the stock, but this half-pipe lever, this, what do you call it, 'barrel' will make a huge difference. Maybe faster than a regular bow, since you don't have to notch the bolt. And the bolt will be too short to shoot back. The fins could be razors and cut the enemy feet. But the razors might also cut the bowstring. I see some disadvantages but also many advantages here. The biggest advantage is that we can cast the bolts instead of carving wood, fitting feathers, attaching arrowheads, and all the other labor of making an arrow. This is a more efficient design, and it uses less metal. "

"Right, and a shooter doesn't take her eyes off her enemy while she reloads. Thanks Hestia," he said again, calling to Dolios. "I'll see you in two days."

CHAPTER

FORTY FOUR

A week passed, ten days, and finally the Meliae had several crossbows, enough to begin training. For practice, Shelby set up a straw-stuffed chiton with a gourd on top. He painted a beard and a fierce face on the gourd, and told the Meliae to shoot it.

Every woman took a turn with the new crossbow design, learning to cock the bow, to place the bolt, to aim, to pull steadily on the trigger. They picked up the technique quickly, and before the afternoon was out they had torn the chiton and gourd to pieces. Melia beamed.

"Should we set up the target again and invite Metis to watch?" he asked.

"Yes," she said, "but let me ask them."

The question posed, the Meliae looked at one another, serious expressions on their faces. Shelby could not read them at all.

"What's happening?" he whispered to Melia.

"Hush," she said. "Leave them alone. They will do what you ask, but they will do it their way. Wait and see."

Shelby sighed inwardly. "Imagine a company of Army recruits thinking for themselves, 'doing things their own way,'" he thought. "Ouch. Could be fatal on a battlefield. Without the kind of training the Rangers shared, they would be murdered where they stand."

"Will they never take orders?" Shelby asked Melia later that evening.

"Probably not. They are now female lions." She looked at him, her eyes clear and shining. "You cannot tell a pride of lions how to hunt."

"We had an experience with one that was trained," he reminded her.

"Special case," she replied. "It was a male, and it was alone." She turned from him with a smirk.

"Damn," he thought later when he was back in his alcove. "What the hell kind of a problem have I created here? The better the women become with weapons and self-confidence, the less likely they will survive their first encounter with the enemy. Envisioning yourself being brave under fire and actually being under fire are remarkably different things. Intimidation is as powerful as bullets."

It rained that night, an uncommonly hard rain. Thunderheads piled high in the north and roared down over the growing valley, lashing the standing grain and swelling the creeks. The streets of the city streamed. Weeks of dirt and manure brought in from the countryside washed into puddles and filled the cart ruts to over-flowing, illuminated only by lightning flashes for no light came through open doors or windows into the dark streets. Jarring thunder rolled over the city like cannon fire.

Ino was frightened, her nipples rigid in the pale light of the alcove's small oil lamp, and goose bumps on her arms. The color drained from her lips and her eyes stared. At every thunderclap she jumped and looked frantically around. Dolios laughed at her.

"It is not raining on us, you silly woman," he sneered. "It is raining on the roof over our heads. If you were outside during this storm, then you would have reason to be afraid."

"Oh shut up," she replied, jumping again. "Just shut up."

"Both of you shut up," said Shelby, "and come wrap yourselves in the blankets. I'm tired of listening to your fears. It's just rain. Rain is a good thing."

"It's not the rain," she said, "it's the anger of Zeus. He hurls his lightning at someone, and it seems to be the city."

"If he is," asked Shelby, "what would you do about it?"

"Pray. Make a sacrifice. Ask for forgiveness. Give money. I'd hide, but you can't hide from a god."

"That's right," said Dolios. "If he wants to get you, he'll send Apollo to strike you with arrows of pestilence."

"Not if Apollo doesn't agree with him," she replied.

"Wait, wait," Shelby interrupted. "I thought this city belonged to the Goddess. Why are you talking about these other gods?"

"The earth belongs to the Goddess," said Ino. "The sky belongs to Zeus, and the sky is trying to kill us." She shrieked at a close lightning strike.

"This can't be reasoned with," thought Shelby. "Their world-view does not allow them to reason about this."

"Master, you must let me go," she pleaded.

"Go? Go where?"

"To the temple. I must go to the temple to pray. You must let me go!"

Shelby was visibly confused and his brow furrowed. Was she thinking of climbing up the acropolis in this thunderstorm?

"I thought you said that you were afraid of Zeus. Now you say you want to go to the temple on the acropolis. That's where the Goddess is. I don't understand."

He hoped that by making her talk, she would recover from her fear and calm down. But she was wild-eyed in her panic. He understood about panic.

"Not the Goddess. Zeus! Zeus will kill me if I don't run to pray to him. He will kill us all! You must let me go!"

It was beyond reason. He knew he could not reach her, but now he was intrigued. Zeus had a temple in the city? Where was it?

"Go," he said, thoughtfully. "When the storm is over, return directly here."

She was gone, scurrying like a frantic rat, crying and holding her hands over her head as the rain pelted down on her through the open roof of the courtyard. He followed her as best he could and saw her disappear through a gate near the warehouses.

The rain came down in thick sheets like a tropical monsoon, hail bounding off the ground, and Ino ran pell-mell through it, from awning to awning, splashing mud up her legs. Shelby stayed out of sight, but he need not have worried. In her panic, she never looked behind to see him following her. Finally, he turned a corner and she was gone, but he saw dozens of other figures hurrying in the same direction, some hooded, some naked slaves with cloth held over their heads. They ignored him.

Shelby stepped into deep shadow and watched. A dozen or more people had taken to the streets in the storm, hurrying into the same passage from different directions. He did not recognize any of them, but he smelled smoke in the air. Following a small group of hooded figures, he saw that they paused at a nondescript doorway.

A bolt of lightning flashed overhead and they scanned the street, then went through the door and it closed behind them. When he got to it, he saw that hundreds of feet had churned the muddy street into a deep puddle and mud had been tracked on the steps up to the door.

The streets were suddenly empty except for the rain. He tried the door, and it opened slightly. Through the crack, Shelby saw hundreds of silent people staring intently ahead at something out of sight. He heard a moaning incantation. He could shove his way inside, but it would draw attention, so he withdrew.

"This is strange," he thought. Then he smelled smoke again, this time with the distinctive smell of roasting flesh.

"Strange time for a barbecue," he thought. "Likely a sacrifice."

The storm thundered on, but soon the lightning moved off toward the south. Rain fell steadily but less fiercely, and Shelby found his way back to the alcove. "Maybe tomorrow I will look at that place in the daylight," he decided, "if I have time."

Dolios was a lump under the covers, even his head covered.

"Get up and go get me some wine, you lazy bum," said Shelby with good humor, giving the lump a shove with his foot, "and get me some dry clothing."

"Did you see anything?" asked Dolios crawling out, a worried expression on his face.

"Lots of rain. Lots of mud. Why do you ask?"

"I just wondered. You know. Whether you saw anything."

"I smelled smoke, but did not see a fire. Nothing else."

Dolios nodded and disappeared through the draperies, trying to appear nonchalant.

"Oh you little shrimp," thought Shelby, "you need to be taught a lesson about telling me the truth. Soon."

Ino returned an hour later, after the rain stopped. Shelby had drifted off to sleep, but awakened when she moved silently into the alcove.

"Bring a light, Ino," he said.

When she returned with a lamp, he looked at her. The mud was gone from her legs and her short hair was toweled dry.

"Are you okay now?" he asked.

She nodded, not looking at him.

"That was strange behavior," he said. "I will not accept that in the future. Do you understand?"

She looked at him, no expression in her face or eyes.

"In the future, you will understand that the safest place in the universe for you is with me. I will protect you."

"You would fight the gods for me?" she asked, a slight sneer in her voice.

"The gods will not contend with me over you," he replied, leaning forward and snuffing the lamp with his thumb. "Now go to sleep and no more childishness."

FORTY FIVE

XXXXXXXXXX

"Shelby? Are you still here?"

It was Melia's standard greeting in the dawn, whispered in a tone that suggested anxiety, wonder, hope. One day, they both feared, she might whisper through the curtain and he would be gone, as mysteriously as he had appeared at the pool.

Shelby often wondered himself. Had he permanently jumped through time, or only temporarily? Was the Goddess really behind it, or had he stumbled into some kind of wormhole, some random warp in space and time? He mulled these questions daily, hourly, more often. He hoped he would be allowed to stay with Melia, that he would not unknowingly or unintentionally anger some female god and be expelled.

"Metis wants to watch the Meliae with their weapons today," Melia said, interrupting his thoughts. "We have set up fifty hay targets for them."

"Painted gourds for heads?"

"We thought about using actual heads from dead Achaeans. What would you say?"

"You have fifty of them?"

"No, not at the moment, but we can get them. Or should we use live prisoners? What do you think?" She grinned at him and he suspected she was teasing him.

"You have fifty prisoners? Where are they?"

"We can get fifty prisoners. We do not keep prisoners. It is a waste of resources."

"You could go out and order up fifty Achaean prisoners and have them here by noon?"

"Probably by mid-afternoon. It is fairly easy to find Achaeans along the borders. They are more numerous than crows and much less intelligent."

"So the twenty or so in the camp with the lion were nothing unusual, then. You're telling me that your people have been in a continual standoff with these invaders all along and twenty here and fifty there don't make that much difference."

"Not all of them have a lion with them, Shelby," she smiled, "and they aren't soldiers with weapons. Most of them are just raiding the crops. They would rather take the fruits of someone else's labor than exert their own. So they are always hanging around, but getting into the city has always been very difficult for them. They cannot enter through the gates, and the other passages are closely watched for intruders."

He was fully awake now. This sudden revelation forced him to reconsider everything he thought about the valley and its defense. If their border was already so porous, then the city really was the only safe place.

"So at any one time there might be hundreds, maybe thousands of Achaeans lurking in the farmlands, stealing crops and cattle, destroying homes, carrying off women and children? Is that what you are saying?"

"Oh Shelby, of course not. Vagabonds are everywhere in the world. They come and go. We sweep through the lands every day capturing some, driving others into hiding. Those who create a problem or seem to be a threat are rounded up and killed. They know they don't belong. Others sell themselves into slavery. Some we capture. If they are armed, they are executed. Any kind of weapon is a death sentence. They all know that. A knife, a club, a pointed stick. Any kind of armor. The safest thing for an Achaean in this valley is to be completely naked, like a slave, without even a bag to carry food in. They are usually taken and put to work, but we have rules for working too. A lazy or unproductive slave does not live here. These rules have evolved over centuries."

He had risen by now and Dolios was helping him dress, holding up his clothes to him. Ino came in with a tray of cheese and fresh bread. "But no coffee," he thought. "Sometimes I would kill for a cup of coffee. How far is it to Ethiopia from here?"

"We have placed dry straw in the courtyard and we already have straw targets," Melia continued after a moment. "I take it you would prefer not to use live Achaeans."

"No, not this time," Shelby said. "The Meliae need to learn to kill, but I would rather not use them as executioners."

"Oh, it wouldn't make any difference to them," she responded. "They know what they will be doing. Killing does not mean the same thing to a woman that it means to a man. It is not about triumph or victory, as it is for a man. It is about survival and the elimination of a threat. They will do the job and not think twice, because it doesn't matter to a woman." She looked at him curiously. "Didn't you know that?"

"I never thought of it."

"No, I guess not. In some ways you are very childish, Shelby. Very childish about women. This is not unusual among men, I find," she added almost as an afterthought. "Killing a threat is a woman's nature. Men are the ones who worry about it."

From there they went on to discuss the coming day, sharing the breakfast. The Meliae were excited to be exhibiting their talents, and had been up before dawn preparing themselves for the day.

"They are very serious, these women," said Melia. "We can be proud of them."

"They've learned well so far," Shelby said. "Now we must begin the war games. I hope we have time to teach them everything they need to know."

"Teach me, Shelby. Then, I teach them. We speak the same language, we have an intuitive understanding you do not have." She withdrew her hand from his arm and also stood. "It is time for me to lead them. Today."

"You need to know very clearly what you want to do with them. They must have a clear mission. So far, I've been thinking of them as an honor guard to go with you to the pool for protection and as archers on the rooftops, but I think they can do more than that."

"I agree," Melia said. "They need to be able to contribute significantly to the defense of the city. Their weapons already will make a great difference, but they need to do more than shoot."

"So what do you think of this?" He paused to look at her and almost lost himself in her deeply intelligent eyes, her full lips. He snapped out of it with a jerk, but caught her look of amusement.

"Go on, Shelby," she urged.

"I think they need to be a small, mobile strike force. They need to learn to fight in the shadows and hidden places, to move quietly and swiftly, to observe and gather information and to report it. You already have a competent army for the big stuff. The Meliae need to have small but important tasks, and they need to be able to carry out those tasks when a large and obvious force cannot. They need to be able to move quickly, to remain hidden, and to strike hard. That's what I think."

She let his words sink in, and he heard her speaking in his mind: "That's what you were. That's why you learned to fall from the sky. That's why you fight the way you do. So show me. Open your memories and share them with me."

"I will try," he said aloud. "It is very painful, and I am afraid to summon some memories."

"But now you have me," she replied in her soft, alto voice. "You have me, Shelby. When the time is right and the Goddess approves, you will have all of me."

He looked at her lovely face, at the graceful way she stood, effortlessly, at the soft curve of her in the dim light. He thought his heart would break at her loveliness.

Then she turned and was gone through the whispering curtains, leaving him alone to start his day.

Outside in the streets, two of the hooded Matrons were walking together toward the morning council.

"An interesting storm last night," whispered one.

"Zeus is becoming stronger in the city," whispered the other.

XXXXXXXXXX

Later that morning, as they were preparing for the exhibition, Shelby decided it was time to share with the Meliae his vision for how they would be employed. He stood on the newly spread hay of the courtyard, the 50 targets behind him and the women sat before him in a semicircle, their legs beneath them. Melia and Rhodia sat side by side in front of the semicircle.

He towered above them, and they craned their necks to see him, squinting against the morning light.

"You have done well so far," Shelby said. "You have mastered the crossbow, and today you will demonstrate your accuracy and rate of fire to Metis and others. I think Phorbus or one of the representatives of the army will be here to watch as well. I am proud of the progress you have made."

He scanned their faces to see if they understood. Their faces did not change expression. He had the distinct impression that they were tolerating him and his noise only because Melia was there.

"Later today you will move into the second phase of your training. This involves learning the skills to climb rocks, to slip through brush and forests without making a sound, and to kill silently. I have worried about your physical strength before, but I am now satisfied that you are in very good condition. Probably you will not add much more muscle and certainly you will never be as heavy as men. So from this day on you will learn how to use your physical assets of speed, flexibility, and endurance to overcome whatever physical disadvantage you may be at with a male opponent."

He paced in front of them and their heads followed him,

tracking him.

"You will learn to fight like hornets. Individually, you will be quick and lethal, but you will only be a major threat when you fight together. Remember, a thousand tiny holes from a thousand tiny angry hornets can do as much damage as a single kick from a horse. You will swarm, and you will avoid being hit. Your power will be in your determination. You must be determined like hornets, and pursue like hornets, and be as difficult to hit as hornets. You will carry weapons that can kill much faster than they and will hurt much more. You will be the Meliae."

His enthusiasm had grown as he spoke, and by the end of his little speech he felt good about what he was saying, pumping his fist. Frankly, he thought the metaphor with the hornets was a good touch.

Melia rose as he finished and turned to the women.

"Icarus has brought us a long way," she said. "He means well. He does not mean that you are insects, but that when you fight with men you should swarm all over them, hurt them, and move too quickly for them to see you."

She turned, smiled sweetly at him, and sat down again.

"This afternoon," he stammered, regaining his thoughts, "I will begin teaching you rock climbing. We will use the acropolis. Over the next few days, you will learn techniques that may be useful if we need to scale a cliff to fight. It will not be easy, but you should learn it swiftly."

Melia rose again and turned to them.

"When Metis sees what you can do today, she will approve putting you on duty. There are fifty of you. We will divide you into two squads, one squad led by Rhodia and another by me. Rhodia's squad will be on duty during the night. My squad will be on duty during the day. If either squad needs help, then we will all go to help. Later today, I will appoint rallying places around the palace. When your squad is summoned, you must go to the point as quickly as possible, with your weapons, and be ready to fight. The fields are already infested with Achaeans pretending to look for food. It won't be long before we see their armies coming against us. If they get into the city, we will defend the rooftops while our men drive them out."

She looked at Shelby as though waiting for him to say something, but he left her with the floor. He decided, wisely he thought, to stop trying to talk to the Meliae.

"Also, the traders are coming," she continued. "This has always been a time of celebration, but we think the Achaeans will use it as a time to slip through our defenses. In the coming days, Icarus will be teaching you how to spot an Achaean and what to do. Remember the rule. Any Achaean in this valley is an enemy, unless the Achaean is a female and a slave. You will kill any Achaean male you see."

The women whispered among themselves.

"Yes," Melia nodded in agreement, "the distinctions are not always clear. Some of the traders look like Achaeans. Some are Achaeans. They must be closely observed. You must watch them, but also I do not want you to be watched in return. Icarus will teach you how to move in shadows and to stay hidden. With your weapons, you can kill an Achaean from a distance and no one will know. That will be your duty."

She paused to look again at Icarus.

"Shelby," she said quietly, "you should leave us alone now. I have things to say to these warriors that you should not be present for."

He was surprised. He was being excluded from the group and was out of place. It was unexpected, but he nodded to her and left the courtyard, pulling his SOG from his belt as he crossed the threshold. "Might as well check the blade," he said to himself, "while I'm cooling my heels."

FORTY
SEVEN

XXXXXXXXXX

The exhibition went smoothly, and Shelby was impressed by the performance. He expected the women to shoot well, but he did not anticipate how well. On Melia's command, each woman cocked her crossbow, loaded the bolt, aimed, and fired. Each woman struck the right eye of her target's head, the melons exploding almost simultaneously from the impact. The bolts penetrated into the limestone wall behind, sticking there.

Shelby heard the intake of breath from the gallery overhead, though he could not see the spectators. Then, he heard Kratos' voice:

"Icarus! Icarus! Are you down there?"

Shelby stepped out into the open, and Kratos leaned over the railing. He was about to speak when Metis touched his shoulder, and he leaned back, closing his mouth. Shelby had seen the wonder on his face, though, and that was enough.

On the next command, the Meliae loaded their weapons and fired again, shredding the shields and breast armor of the targets. Then, they fired three more rounds each, somewhat less coordinated, but the point had been made.

The Meliae had become a deadly force.

Metis stepped to the railing and looked down at the women and at the lone, gigantic man standing nearby.

She nodded, then turned and left.

Kratos returned to the gallery a moment later and signaled Shelby to meet him outside.

"Well done, Icarus, well done!" Kratos said, clapping his brawny hand on Shelby's shoulder. "I've never seen anything like it. We'd heard about the crossbows, but you solved a great problem by making them easier to cock. Well done!"

"Thanks, Kratos. How have you been?"

"Life on the frontier, Icarus. I love it! Any day I choose, I go out and kill twenty or so Achaeans. I don't know how many thousands of Achaeans are waiting in the hills, but I have many targets and will never run out of them. I also don't know why they are waiting, but while they wait I go in the night and kill them where they sleep. I enjoy killing their sentries most of all. I believe it frightens them to awake and find their sentries were all killed while they slept. But more Achaeans come all the time. It won't be long before we are overrun in the west and retreat to the city. They seem encouraged, as though they know that this time they will take the city."

"So war is certain then."

"Like the rising of the sun, friend," Kratos beamed. "We will have a war of tens of thousands! Maneuvering of armies in the field, great battles. It will be a glorious time!" He seemed genuinely glad of the coming conflict. "The more Achaeans, the more to kill." His wide-spaced teeth glistened in the part-gloom of the shaded passageway. "Just like the carving on the walls of Nineveh. And I'm going to use tactics I saw there, too. I'm training the garrisons to provide squares of soldiers twelve across and twelve deep who move and fight as a unit. The Achaeans have nothing like it. The slaughter will be great!"

"Melia is better and better at leading the women," Shelby said. "She will be a fine commander. So will Rhodia, her second in command."

"Imagine that," laughed Kratos. "Women taking orders from anyone! Ha! Are they taking orders from you? If they are, you are a more remarkable man than you appear, and you appear to be very remarkable."

"They take instruction from me. Melia gives the orders."

"Even so. Nothing like it has ever been seen," he grinned. "Now tell me Icarus, those weapons. They could make a difference on the western hills. How far do they shoot?"

"I don't think you will get them, but they shoot at least as far as a regular recurve bow if not further. They penetrate the Achaean armor. If it comes to a siege, I think they will be very effective from the walls. Right now we only have fifty of them. I'm trying to get the crafters to construct more as backups, in case some are damaged. And the bolts must be cast from bronze, so they are not like arrows. Getting a proper supply of bolts is critical and slow. Metis told the crafters to make them when they can, but now that each woman has a crossbow, the urgency is gone. The crafters are very busy preparing for war."

"How do you think they will do against chariots?"

"I don't know. They will kill a horse and they will probably penetrate the front of the chariot, but I think the front is just wicker anyway, right? The best thing is their accuracy. Surely you don't think there will be chariots in this war?"

"Oh yes. Our spies report more than 2,000 chariots, and the armies in the west have many. I don't think they can get the chariots over the hills, but then no one thought they could bring a caged lion up through the southern slopes either. With horses. We thought horses could not travel through that country, so they may have been building roads while we slept. If we see chariots, it will be when they come through the gates of the citadel, and that is something we hope will not happen."

"How long do you think we have before we are invaded?"

"I don't know, Icarus. They could move at any time. I think they are waiting for all the traders to gather, but maybe not. It would be foolish of them to attack the caravans, which are so well protected and so popular with the people. Arktos and Phorbus think they will strike after the harvest."

"When they come, do the traders bring their own protection with them into the valley?"

"They never have. We have never permitted it. Because they have never been assaulted here, they comply, but times have changed, Icarus. Nothing signifies that more than your presence here. We may not allow the traders to enter at all this year. Once the gate of the citadel opens, it could be difficult to close it again if the Achaeans are massed. A large crowd always travels with the traders and it is possible that Achaean soldiers are mixed with them. The caravan is so much fun every year that the temptation is to trust our luck and open. Song, dance, wares from around the world, acrobats, slaves, fortune tellers, camels, and elephants. It is the highpoint of the year for the population, and they waste almost their full year's production on trinkets and strong drink. Closing out the traders would be very unpopular."

"How will you decide?"

"I won't. Metis and the Matrons will make that decision."

"Have you placed spies among the caravans to report back?"

"Icarus, sometimes I think we are the shortest people in the world. All our spies would be known. We have no tall spies, and we can't trust our Achaean slaves." He paused. "We can't send you because you are too big. Also, Melia would not let you go." He grinned again.

They came to the end of the courtyard and were lingering in the passage, about to go separate ways.

"Kratos, friend, I must return to the females, but perhaps they will be useful. I already have them running the circuit of the city every morning, and I am teaching them close quarter combat skills. They are strong and flexible, even if they are not large, and they are dangerous. I will soon teach them to hide in the brush and fields and to shoot from cover. They can be useful in the fields for harassment, and they will be lethal on the rooftops, if it comes to that."

"You don't have enough of them, Icarus, to take them to the field in any capacity. They better stay here to protect Metis and Melia if it comes to a siege. The Achaeans have bred like flies on dead meat, beyond counting, and once the gates of the citadel open, they may swarm through from the north and assault in force from the west at the same time, splitting our defense. Then we will have war on the plains in front of the city gates. We will give them precious little cover there, but we will have none either except for the walls at our back. It will all be open ground and I foresee a long siege. Even so, it will be glory for the fighters! Glory! And fame! They may overwhelm us with their numbers, but far fewer of them will be left! Stories will be told of the coming war for a thousand harvests."

"Keep up your spirits, friend. You are an incredible warrior. Be alert. We will fight side by side when the time comes."

"As for that, Icarus, I have seen you fight. I would prefer for you to be in front." He laughed his big laugh as he left. "In front, Icarus, in front!" and he was gone.

CHAPTER

FORTY EIGHT

XXXXXXXXXX

After thinking it through, Shelby decided the training in rock climbing would be faster and smoother if he instructed Melia and Rhodia first, privately. So back in the courtyard, he told them his plan.

"Icarus says he wants to show us some things before he shows them to you," Melia said to the women gathered close to them. "You have done well. Play with the balls for a while until we get back. Practice throwing with both hands, because you never know when that will be useful. When we return with Icarus, we can start climbing lessons."

The three did not head to the acropolis right away, however. Instead, Shelby walked them out of the city, explaining that they needed to discuss covert reconnaissance and ambush tactics before heading to the rocks.

They passed through the gates and out into the fields until they were about half a mile away standing in a field of ripening grain. He sat down.

"If we camouflage the Meliae in the grain, then they can ambush a passing enemy. Help me think how we can hide them."

Rhodia sat behind Melia, so she would not be closer to Shelby. She would not get closer to the male than Melia. She was still deeply moved by his presence, and a little angered that he stirred her stomach so much. She wanted to be critical of him, to find something to dislike, but could not. Generally, the biggest problem was that he just seemed to ignore her, and no one had ever ignored her before. If she did not feel so strongly about him, it would be enough to make her furious.

It did not help that the other girls kept kidding her about him, talking about him, discussing the size of his biceps or his thighs. His smell. That was what got her. His smell. He did not smell like the other males. He smelled like a man. All the others smelled like boys. Surely Melia felt the same way, yet Melia was so reserved, so private. "Oh Melia," she thought, "you don't know how lucky you are."

By mid-afternoon, Shelby had demonstrated to Rhodia and Melia how to crawl through standing grain with barely a ripple, to weave their bodies around, to wait for the breezes to play over them before they started a movement, and to move with the breeze. They had never in their lives been told to move without being seen, so he was pleased that they acquired stealth so quickly. Besides, it was fun watching them scoot along the ground, their cute little behinds wiggling, trying to keep from making noise in the grain. It would be a shame to cover those lovely figures with ghillie suits, but that would be the next step. If they needed to fight in the fields, they needed to be invisible.

Melia circled around and approached him from his rear. He was pleased at how well she had done it. Of course, he had suspected she would try that, but he turned in his sitting position when she was only a yard or two away, her eyes blazing out of the shadow of the waving stalks.

"Well done," he said, breaking into a big smile.

Then Rhodia poked the back of his neck with a stalk of grain.

He jumped, rising from his sitting position in a single startled motion.

Amazing. No one had snuck that close to him since he was eight years old and hiding during a game at Cub Scout camp.

"Oh!" he exclaimed. "Well done, you two. Well done! If you can teach the Meliae to creep like that, you will be dangerous warriors indeed!"

He looked at the young women, whose sweaty bodies were covered with dust and bits of grain stalks and leaves, then suggested they go back to the city before taking a look at the cliff walls of the acropolis.

The girls washed at the city gate in a vacated room, provided with large bowls of fresh water and linen towels by the guards. When they exited, pulling their hair into ponytails and rearranging their chitons, they were ready for business.

"What do you think Metis and the Matrons will say when they learn that we are climbing on the acropolis?" Shelby asked the girls.

"I think they will resent it, but after this morning's demonstrations I don't think they will object," Melia replied. Rhodia kept her mouth shut and stayed a few steps away.

"Will it be offensive to them?" Shelby asked.

"It is a holy place, Shelby," Melia said. "It is not a place to play. Still, if you think it is necessary, they will say nothing."

FORTY NINE

XXXXXXXXXX

The side of the acropolis plateau projected beyond the city walls with a sheer drop of at least 150 feet. Jagged boulders like broken teeth menaced at the bottom, and if one looked closely and poked around, the skeletons of many city dwellers could be found. Some had been driven off the high place by war centuries earlier, others had leaped from despair, but most had been executed. A quick shove off the acropolis was a fast and certain death, a free-fall with a shattering landing. Over the centuries, jackals and ravens found it advantageous to frequent the base, poking around for rotting flesh or fresh kills, and mothers scared their children with stories of ghosts of the dead wandering in the night, looking for little ones who were not in their beds where they belonged.

Every settled society has a place like this.

Other sides of the acropolis plateau rose more gently, and Shelby found several areas that looked good for beginning classes in climbing. He knew well that almost everything about climbing rocks could be taught on ten feet of rock face, depending on the angles of the rock. Ultimately, he hoped to teach them how to scale the back side of the acropolis, the steep side, but doubted that they would need to know that before battle broke out.

"I think we should wear black, wrapped closely around us and covering our heads," Rhodia said, interrupting his thoughts. She had wrestled with herself for a long time before speaking, and even now she spoke to Melia, not to him. "If my squad is to fight at night, that would be best for them."

"You're right, Rhodia," Shelby said, smiling at her. "They can wear the red sashes and the white chitons when they are on display, but when they are working I think you are right. They should be in black."

"I'll make that happen tonight," Rhodia replied.

"Yes," Melia said. "We should all have black clothes for fighting."

Shelby saw a good-sized boulder lying at the base of the acropolis, near the steps where people went up from the market to the plateau for ceremonies. Flat on one side, not too high, with some cracks for handholds, it looked right to him.

"We'll start here," he said.

The ever-present ragtag bunch of children who followed them through the city sat on the ground to watch while Melia and Rhodia took off their chitons, stripping to their exercise "bikinis." The children giggled at the unusual attire.

"Watch me," said Shelby.

He scrambled up the face of the boulder.

From on top he asked, "Did you see how that was done?"

"You want us to do it?" asked Melia.

"Of course."

She had memorized his movements and within seconds was standing next to him on the boulder top. Rhodia had more trouble, but she made it. Then the children all ran to the boulder and started climbing it. Some made it, some did not. Some fell and started wailing. Their noise attracted others, adults mostly and older girls, and soon a crowd surrounded them.

"What are you doing up there, Melia?" called a voice.

"Why are you dressed that funny way?" called another.

"Why is the giant standing on the rock with you?" shouted another voice.

Dozens, maybe a hundred people milled around in the growing crowd, shouting questions. Shoppers in the market, already prepared to enjoy the unusual spectacle of the traders in a week or so, swarmed to the boulder with the others. The more people who arrived, the less friendly the questions became. The mood was shifting.

"What kind of example are you setting for the children?" asked a new voice.

"Why are you showing so much skin? You are not slaves," commented another.

"What are you trying to prove?"

Meanwhile, the smaller children still leapt at the rock, trying to climb up and crying. Others who made it taunted them and ran around.

Melia looked at Shelby.

"We are training," called Rhodia to the crowd. "Leave us alone."

"Training for what?" they wanted to know.

"How to fight," she shouted back.

The crowd now numbered over 100, and was still growing. At one mood extreme was a rollicking, carnival atmosphere but at the other an angry group of mothers quickly becoming more vocal.

"Looks like you are learning how to run away," some laughed.

"Trying to fight like Achaeans?" laughed another.

"Why are you letting the children hurt themselves?" shouted an angry mother.

"You asked for this Shelby," said Melia.

"We will go down the backside of the rock and leave it to the children," he replied heading down.

"We have to go back for our chitons," said Rhodia to his back.

But he signaled the two women to come with him, not turning around.

Everyone who saw the gesture was offended by it.

A male did not make such a gesture to a woman in the city, especially in the holy precinct of the acropolis. He did not turn his back on a woman and walk away. Not here.

The crowd waited for the Goddess to flare out at him, to send a serpent snapping out of the rock. When nothing happened, some of them whispered: "He's from Zeus after all. Metis was right to wonder about him."

A Matron, who was observing her people from a rooftop nearby, also saw the dismissive gesture.

"He's angry and frustrated, but Melia needs to teach him manners," she muttered to herself, "before the people kill him."

CHAPTER

FIFTY

When Melia, still in her bikini, caught up with him, she was furious.

"What do you mean turning your back on us and walking off?" she demanded.

Shelby was surprised by her sudden anger, but kept moving ahead, automatically, unconsciously.

She grabbed his arm and turned him around, glaring at him.

"What?" he asked. "What's the matter?"

"You . . ." she sputtered. "You, you, you . . ." she faltered, "heathen! How dare you! Like a savage! An Achaean!"

When she finally spit it out, he was assaulted both in his ears and in his mind simultaneously. The pain drove him to his knees and he grabbed his head, trying to keep it from exploding. It was like a concussion grenade going off inside his skull. His eyes blurred.

Kneeling, he was only slightly below eye level with her. He was vaguely conscious through the throbbing pain in his head that Rhodia had come up behind him.

"Melia, stop it," Rhodia said. "You're hurting him."

"So?" snarled Melia.

Then she slapped him. He felt every bit of that, and so did she. She wrung her hand. His left eye teared up, but then he recovered. The violence made him angry, and he felt himself preparing to explode. "Get a grip, get a grip," he thought, as the pain from the slap overrode the pain in his head and his eyes gradually cleared.

"Don't ever turn your back on me and walk off again, Shelby," hissed Melia. "When we call to you, do not just gesture at us.

Who raised you to be so contemptuous of women? What makes you think you can act that way? With me especially? Me!" She paused, breathing heavily. "What do have to say for yourself?"

"I'm sorry?" he mumbled.

"Is that a question, Shelby?"

She looked clothed in fire, brilliant with shining light. The red of her face spread down her torso, and he saw the flushing skin of her taut belly.

"No," he muttered, his brain beginning to work again. "No, not a question. I'm sorry. I wasn't thinking. I will never walk off from you again. Ever."

"Stay out of this, Rhodia," he heard her say. "Just go over there and turn around. I have something to say to Shelby I don't want to share."

He did not look around. He could not take his eyes off of her.

She looked down at him, and then reached out one hand for his hair, grown longer after the weeks he had spent there. She took a firm hold of it, jerked his head back, and stared into his eyes. Her other hand came up to the cheek she had smacked and traced the outline of her fingers through the rough stubble on his face. Then she bent over him and kissed him, deeply and fully, her free hand going to his throat to feel his carotid pulse, to hold his windpipe, resting there while his heart pounded.

She quit and backed away when he reached up for her, but only inches. Nose to nose she whispered, "Don't you ever leave me, Shelby. Never leave me. Never. Do you understand?"

"Never," he tried to say, but his throat was stuck. He tried again. "Never," he croaked. "I love you so much, Melia."

"I know," she said, straightening. Then, her tone hardened as she said aloud, "Act like it."

She let him go.

Some of the children thronged around the boulder and peeked at them. They giggled and pointed. One of them held their chitons.

"Time to go Rhodia," Melia said, beckoning at the little girl by the boulder to bring their clothes.

Shelby's strength surged back. He rose effortlessly as though floating and followed Melia and Rhodia as they passed in front and headed back down to the palace, hoping that his enormous erection was not too obvious. The smell of the two women made his heart flutter, and he could have drifted after them drawn by their scent alone, like a bee to a flower.

"Well," he said to himself, "maybe rock climbing is not so important after all."

On the distant rooftop, the Matron smiled grimly. "Nicely done, Melia, nicely done," she said. "Just what the brute needed."

FIFTY ONE

XXXXXXXXXX

L ater that evening, Shelby stepped from the bath, and Ino led him to the fireplace, where she rubbed him down with a thick linen towel. When he bowed his head so she could dry his hair, he looked straight into her eyes, her face only inches from his own. Her breath smelled husky and sweet, and he felt himself stirring. Her eyes, however, never left her task, and she never returned his look. She was all business, which was a relief to him.

Of sorts.

This world was complicated. He needed to be very careful around these lovely creatures, or he would make it even more complicated. Possibly fatal.

He lay on a couch while she rubbed his muscles and oiled his skin with olive oil, then wrapped him in a dry robe. They were about to return to the alcove when the curtains parted, and Iapetus walked in, deep in conversation with Eurymedon.

Shelby heard something about Crete and he thought he heard the name "Timon," but the conversation stopped when Iapetus saw Shelby and Ino.

"Aha, Ino, my lovely," Iapetus said cheerfully, his long face breaking into his curious smile, his upper lip curled above his front teeth. He continued to smile as he glanced at Shelby. "I wondered what had become of you. Where did Metis take you? Don't tell me she gave you to Icarus."

Shelby felt the man's jolly tone was forced. "What is he hiding?" he wondered.

"Icarus," Iapetus continued, "good it is to see you again." He strode forward. "My brother and I were about to discuss in bath.

I try persuade him leave on tour to Crete and other centers of learning now before passes sealed by war."

He smiled again, taking Shelby by the forearms and holding him. "What a difference you make here, my friend." He continued smiling at him, fully in control. "You killed lion, you found camp, you captured one scum and squeezed information out. An accomplishment!" He gave Shelby's forearms a sincere squeeze and let go.

"Accomplishment," he said again. "Imagine, killing charging lion like that, and what brute! I saw pelt. Only someone as large as you could fit. It be much too large for me."

Shelby had forgotten that Iapetus' speech was less fluent in his ears than others, and hoped that he would improve his ability to understand the dyspeptic brother. Continued exposure to other people in the city had gradually brought him to a high level of fluency himself. But he had not seen Iapetus since the first day, since the feast actually. Maybe that was why Iapetus' speech sounded stilted, muddy: lack of exposure.

"Too big for me, too," added Eurymedon, also smiling broadly. "Why, Iapetus and I together would be lost under it. You will have quite a trophy, and of course everyone will expect you to wear it."

"Thank you both," smiled Shelby, "and I may wear it in cooler weather. I'm not sure it would be very comfortable in this summer heat."

"Oh, but you must," said Iapetus. "It is symbol of your warrior might. The whole city praises you for killing that lion."

"Thank you," said Shelby, hoping his lack of enthusiasm did not show. "Now we are trading insincerities," he thought. "Did Iapetus really mention Timon, or am I making that up?"

He began moving toward the curtains.

"Not going, Icarus?" Iapetus asked. "Stay. Talk. We want opinion for Eurymedon's travels, suggestions. Phorbus wants him see Nineveh and Babylon, but I think he must go first Crete and then Egypt. Memphis. What think?"

The two brothers disrobed as Iapetus talked, and Eurymedon signaled Ino to bring more hot water for the bath. "We hear you train company of women. You must tell us how," Iapetus continued, loosening his sandals.

"I really don't want to leave the city right now," Eurymedon said, stepping into the bath. His muscular body was beautiful.

The great Greek sculptor Praxiteles might have chosen such a warrior as a model for any of his statues. He had the muscles of a fighter rippling in his shoulders and carved across his abdomen, yet the grace of youth.

Iapetus, shorter and years older, showed a body whitened by indoor work. His pasty legs were covered in sparse but coarse black hair, and his toes seemed to stick off the ends of his blue-veined feet like awkward reptiles.

"Great Zeus!" cried Iapetus as he stepped into the bath. "Water is hot! Don't tell me you boiled self in this, Icarus." He obviously hoped that Shelby would stay to chat.

Ino and Iapetus had exchanged glances when he cried out the god's name, but he quickly returned his gaze to Eurymedon. Shelby pretended he did not see that, but his mind awakened to the idea of an allegiance between Ino and Iapetus.

"It is Ino he wants," thought Shelby. "As long as I stay in the room, then she will remain also."

He looked over at her long shapely legs glistening in the water and pinked from the heat, the smooth curve of her butt, the way drops of water or sweat hung from her nipples as she bent forward.

"She might be worth scheming for," he thought.

"Brother," Iapetus said, "I sit here on tub side until cooler. Is it not too hot?"

"If it was not too hot for Icarus, it's not too hot for me," said Eurymedon, sliding into the water with an involuntary intake of breath. Shelby was aware of the difference in the speech patterns he heard in the two men. Eurymedon's speech was perfectly clear, vernacular. He could not figure out Iapetus'. It wasn't awkward Greek, it was just awkward. He wondered whether everyone heard Iapetus speak that way.

"I suppose I can visit for a while," said Shelby. "I have been to some of the places you mention, though they are quite different in my own time. I spent a good deal of time working with the local population in Mosul, which is across the Tigris River from Nineveh."

"Then you saw great walls of city," said Iapetus. "Our city models Nineveh. Our city smaller but better designed. Walls are similar, however. You noticed?"

"I did. I particularly admired this city's gate and defenses.

I think this would be a very difficult city to take by force," Shelby replied. He studied Iapetus for any evidence of duplicity, but did not see any. Nevertheless, he was convinced that Iapetus held secrets of some kind beneath his open-faced exterior with its weird lip-curling grin.

"Sit and talk, Icarus," Eurymedon said looking up at him.

He agreed although with some reluctance. He did not trust himself to revisit his own past. The visions were easier to avoid if he remained steadfastly in the present. "Ha!" he thought. "Present! As though I am in the present now!"

He placed a cushion on the top step, where Melia sat that first night. Ino reentered the water at a careless gesture from Eurymedon and began the scraping routine.

All through the next hour, Iapetus and Eurymedon kept Shelby busy reminiscing about his travels. He described the pyramids of Egypt, the ziggurats of Babylon, the chariots of the Assyrians. Shelby had not been to Crete, so Iapetus took over to talk about the wonders of that magnificent civilization, their distant cousins. Throughout, Iapetus kept returning to the notion that it was time for Eurymedon to leave the city for his tour. And as he talked, Shelby became more accustomed to his speech and some of the stilted verbal construction faded.

"He has passed twenty-three harvests," Iapetus explained to Shelby, "and as royal son he should leave now and search world. He can return with wife, or Metis will give one if he wants."

"She gave me those two Persian slaves," Eurymedon added dreamily. "The dark-eyed ones. They're pretty, and nice for slaves. I don't think I want a wife right now."

"You haven't seen world yet, brother," said Iapetus. "How can you know what you want? Main thing, leave now before frontier closes with war or you never get chance."

Eurymedon sank under the warm water and blew bubbles out his nose. "Don't hesitate," Iapetus continued when Eurymedon surfaced. "I tell you for own good. Choose small party go with you, perhaps only one, two others, so you travel fast and light and avoid heathens. Day or two will carry you beyond them, and whole world will spread before you." He smiled, a faraway look in his eye. Then, his face hardened and he added, "Do not get trapped as I during last war. Harvests and harvests passed before frontiers opened. You really do not want miss this chance and you will if you do not now go."

"I'm not sure how I feel about leaving the city just now," said Eurymedon. "What if I'm needed? What if Phorbus needs me to lead troops?"

"We have plenty troops, and plenty leaders. Remember, this not our first war," replied Iapetus. "This is your time. Do not waste your time trapped. You are royal son. Do not self be trapped like rat in city when siege comes."

"Do you think there will be a siege?" asked Shelby.

"If they force through passes, or citadel falls, yes," said Iapetus grimly. "All more reason for Eurymedon to be gone."

"If he gets away, he may be safe," added Shelby, his mind speeding. "If he's gone, then at least someone from the royal house will be preserved to start the city again. It's a good plan, Iapetus."

"I did not think that," said Iapetus seriously, "but now you mention, yes, it is also good reason to get away. Decide, brother."

The water finally cooled enough for Iapetus to get in, and poor Ino, her feet turning white and wrinkled, waded over to him to care for him as well. Shelby did not observe any particular body language from Ino that indicated a relationship with Iapetus, but he was not surprised to see Iapetus place his hand on her hip and stroke the back of her leg as she bent over him.

"Status is no barrier to the heart," he thought.

"This lovely girl," said Iapetus sighing, "reminds me ask you about Melia's girls. I hear you train them, Icarus."

"Melia recruited me to do that," Shelby replied. "I don't have much to say. I think they will do well as an honor guard."

"How they fight, do you think?" Iapetus continued, absently stroking the back of Ino's leg.

"I think they will do what is required of them, but I don't know how much experience they will have. In my country, boys grow up fighting with one another so we are used to it and becoming a soldier is not a stretch. We do not encourage our girls to fight or to engage in violent sports, so they have a different cast of mind from the boys by the time they are grown. I don't know what it's like in this country. These young women seem very serious and quite willing to engage."

"How they stand a charge of armed warriors?"

"Again, I can't say until they have had the experience. Right now? Probably not so well. In a few months? Probably the warriors would not get close enough to them to do any damage. I hope it doesn't come to that for them, but then we hope none of our troops come to harm."

"Yes," said Iapetus, shifting away from Shelby and hunching his back even more. Ino moved around him to continue her ministrations.

"Tell about new weapons, Icarus. I heard of them but not seen them."

"Again, I can't say much. I decided to turn a regular bow side-wise and redesigned the arrow. That's all." He felt that Iapetus was prying. The Meliae were not Iapetus' business, and he regretted getting into the conversation. Still, he opened his big mouth. Time to shut it again.

Eurymedon listened intently, then began to chuckle. Finally, he could not contain himself and laughed out loud.

"I bet they will scatter like quail at the first charge," he roared. "Imagine our little short women standing up to a thousand angry Achaeans with spittle in their beards! They'll turn and run, I can tell you that. Run away and hide."

"They will never see battle," said Iapetus. "I think they are decorative."

"You are probably right," said Shelby. "My thought was that Metis would probably take them with her when she went to the sacred pool. Other than that, I have no idea what good they would be." He wanted to play down the significance of the Meliae before Iapetus became more suspicious.

As long as the Meliae practiced in their private courtyard on the women's side of the palace and they stayed in the women's compound, only rumors could circulate. If the truth got out, then the professional warriors could feel threatened. In a country governed by women, the male ego might not have much scope, for ways for men to feel important, he reasoned to himself. So the less said about the Meliae, the better.

He rose to go.

"Abandoning, Icarus?" Iapetus asked.

"Alas, my friends. I am tired. You can imagine what a day spent with angry women is like."

They both smiled.

"Especially when you are not accustomed," Iapetus smiled back. "Rest well."

He looked longingly after Ino as she followed Shelby through the curtains from the bath, then turned to Eurymedon.

"It's time for you to grow up," Iapetus said urgently and quietly when he was sure they were alone. This chance to speak to the young man alone, without an audience, was why he had not brought slaves with them to the bath. And finally, they were alone.

"On this tour, you will become a man at last. As long as you stay here, you will not be allowed to grow. You will always be Mother's little boy, and she will choose everything for you. Your friends and your slaves, your food, your activities. Even your armor and your sword and your horse. Go away, Eurymedon. Grow up," he urged. "Don't end up like me."

The smile spread slowly over Eurymedon's face. "Yes," he replied, "I will go. I will have such adventures! When I return, I will have stories to tell that will impress everyone, even Mother. Who knows? Maybe I will fight monsters, like the heroes!"

Iapetus patted him on the back, smiling to himself.

"I'm ready," Eurymedon said at last. "Whenever Timon is."

"Pack your things," Iapetus said. "I don't know when I can get him into the city, but he will come to you soon. Just be ready."

A slave hurried along the corridor carrying a bundle of clean chitons, heading into the depths of the palace. They waited for her to pass.

"Maybe tonight. Maybe tomorrow. But soon," Iapetus said. "When all is ready. You must move fast and quietly. It is your only hope."

FIFTY TWO

XXXXXXXXXX

The next morning, Metis with Melia, Shelby, and twenty-five of the Meliae rode out to the pool, Metis in front with Melia next to her. The Meliae rode in single file behind them. Shelby brought up the rear, riding bareback on a crotchety old mare. She resented his weight, and he, for his part, resented the lack of a saddle. All he had was a blanket of sorts, tied on with a few wide strips of thickly woven cloth, with a toe loop on one side. She tossed her head and sidestepped in her resentment, snorting at him whenever he tried to govern her.

"Really, bitch," he said at last, speaking English so the women would not understand, "you and I are going to come to an understanding before this ride is done, or you will be eaten tonight. I'm tired of this."

Something in his tone calmed her down, so he kept his mouth shut to keep from breaking the spell. Thankfully, the trip was short. Still, when he dismounted, she tried to step on him, stamping her feet. He shouldered her aside with a grunt and when she reared, he pulled her head down with a jerk.

"Enough," he said quietly but forcefully.

The women were amused. They did not need to understand his odd language to interpret his tone of voice.

"Icarus," said Metis, "you did not bring a sweet apple for your horse?"

"No, I did not," he replied, "but I reminded her that I might eat her tonight if she continues to misbehave."

"Oh, Icarus," she laughed, "you have a lot to learn about females. Harsh words do not compel, Icarus, they do not."

"If you eat her," added Melia, grinning at him, "then you will walk back to the city. Really, Shelby, you should know better." The crowd of women laughed at him, and then laughed again when he reddened from their criticism.

Shelby gave the mare a baleful stare, which she returned with full measure. Then, he turned his back on her.

She bit him. Right on the top of his shoulder.

At this, the crowd roared again.

When she could breathe again, Melia gasped, "What have I told you about turning your back on a female?" and that set them all to laughing again.

Though once he might have flown into a rage, this time he was simply glad she had not taken a hunk of flesh out of him.

"Lesson learned," he thought. "Never deal with females without apples or carrots or something. Diamonds." He glanced at Melia, who dropped her eyes and looked away, wiping away her tears of mirth.

"Okay, women," said Metis at last, gasping for breath after the jollity. "Now to business. We need the Goddess to help us understand what to do. Let's pull our thoughts together. Melia, send some of the guard on to the pool to check for intruders, the rest of you follow with me. Icarus, you will come to the top of the hill, but you do not go down to the pool."

"I am at your command, Mother," he replied, bowing his head, "sore shoulder and all."

He remembered the path through the woods, its gradual descent toward the edge of the steep hill and how the way down turned and zigzagged behind rocks toward the pool. After a month or more, he wondered if his parachute was still on the bottom, and if his helmet and pressure suit were still stowed securely under that pile of rocks.

With five of the Meliae to keep him company, he loitered at the top of the path out of sight of the pool. The others went with Metis.

The women were poor company. They did not talk to him and showed no interest in him at all. Once or twice he tried to engage them in conversation about the training and the crossbows, but they returned only one word answers. It was clear that they were not going to form any kind of camaraderie with him. Their reserve was impenetrable.

After several boring minutes, Shelby decided to reconnoiter the area and told the women what he was doing, warning them not to shoot him. Then he drifted into the woods. He thought he might get a clue about the presence of the Achaeans at the lion camp, which was only a mile or so from the pool. Since the Achaeans got the lion cage up to the southern slope, they might also have a way of getting chariots into the valley the same way, he thought. Maybe they took the lion's cage to pieces and reassembled it, but they also got the horses up. He suspected they had a road of some kind that the city's warriors did not know about, and he wanted to look for it. Overall, he thought the city's leaders took a lot for granted about their natural defenses.

He did not find the camp from that direction, but he knew clearly where to find it from the fields. Later in the day, he decided as he turned back to rejoin the Meliae, they would all go in search of it. That would be a good exercise for them and give them a chance to discuss attack strategies, where to position themselves for most effect, where to look for sentries, how to provide themselves with routes of escape. An actual heathen camp, for he had begun to think of the Achaeans as heathen as Melia did, would be a good practice ground.

As they returned from the pool, Metis was once again exhausted and nearly catatonic. It was clear to both Shelby and Melia that her strength was failing and that she would soon be unable to rule. Secretly Shelby hoped it was a passing condition and that she would recover, but Melia knew that the time was coming when she would rule in her mother's place, and that worried her. She had Shelby in her life now, and the Meliae, and the war: if the Goddess was weakening Metis, then what was Melia to do? She could not keep up everything and rule also, hold the sacrifices, feed the sacrificial meat to the warriors and oversee its distribution to the population, place herself into the trance to hear the Goddess and then decipher what the Goddess said, deal with the Matrons, judge the lawsuits and settle the disputes. No, she could not do all of that and still have Shelby, and the Meliae, and the war. But the Goddess had given her Shelby, and she would cling to him until the Goddess took him away. If Metis failed, would that be when the Goddess took him? The war was insignificant by comparison, as far as she was concerned.

She would talk about it with Shelby, who alone of all her

acquaintance was someone with whom she could discuss such a delicate subject. Thankfully, Metis appeared to revive a little during the slow, very slow ride to the city, and Melia's worries lessened as she watched her mother. But they did not go away.

Shelby's mare had settled down and was more cooperative now, probably because one of the Meliae had found some pomegranates for her at the pool. That bit of pampering was starting to wear
off as they approached the city and Shelby could feel her body tensing beneath his bare legs.

After a while of jogging along in silence, Shelby reined his horse over to Melia. "We still have time in the day," he said, interrupting her deep thoughts. "I would like to take the Meliae to the lion camp. Seeing an actual Achaean camp would give us an opportunity to discuss tactics, attack strategies, and so on. Do you think we could turn back now? I could teach them how to move through the woods silently and give them some practice."

"I think we should change horses before we do that," she said, looking at his mare's ears twitching. "They should never have put you on this mare," she added. "You are so much bigger than she is used to."

She would discuss Metis with him later. Much later, she hoped.

FIFTY THREE

XXXXXXXXXX

With fresh horses and joined by Rhodia's rested contingent, all the Meliae now uniformed in solid black, they rode toward the lion camp. Growing vegetation obscured the path, but Shelby remembered how it turned off near a pair of large ash trees. They dismounted, and he led the women into the forest.

They found the headless remains of the sentry as they descended into the camp, dragged some distance from his tree by animals tearing at his flesh, but the camp was deserted. Danae's desiccated corpse slumped at the foot of the pole, what remained of it. Jackals had torn her body and some of her bones were lying about, crushed, but her head still hung forward with her stringy graying hair splayed around it. A part of one blackened arm still hung from a rope tied to the pole, but the other was gone, fallen from its socket and dragged away. Flies or bees swarming inside the corpse made a buzzing noise. Ants and other insects were finishing the deconstruction of the bodies, and in a year the whole scene would melt into the pastoral calm of the forest.

He gave the Meliae instructions on how to approach a camp, how to remain hidden, how to set up an ambush and afterwards to conduct a search. They practiced approaching the camp several times, moving in unison, preparing to fire their crossbows. When he was satisfied, he had them fan out to look for evidence of more recent Achaean activity, and some distance down the hill from the camp they found a trail with a fresh foot print. He had them stay back and he moved quietly ahead until he thought he detected a hint of smoke on the air. He called the women forward using hand gestures.

"We may be near an Achaean camp," he whispered when they

gathered. "Do you want to try your crossbows on live targets? If we find them, we will need to surprise them, hit fast and hard. You will shoot from cover on my command, so choose your target carefully. Remember, a horse can also be a target, or a mule, or an ox. Shoot the men first, and don't make a sound. No shouting, no calling. Only the sound of arrows in the air. Understand? If I think there are too many of them, we will withdraw and you will move away as silently as you can. I will go first to scout. When I signal to you, Melia will lead her troops to the left and Rhodia to the right. Stay behind trees and bushes, lie on the ground, but try to get clear shots into the camp. Remember, they may have guards posted who will kill you if they see you."

He disappeared into the brush. The women did not hear him go and were astonished at how he seemed to melt away. Nothing prepared them for that.

Time passed and then, without warning, he was back.

"It's what I expected," he whispered. "They constructed a camp similar to the one we found earlier, but further down, with shelters arranged in a circle around an open area. I estimate their strength at seventy or eighty. They are all Achaeans, and they are all armed. I took care of the sentries nearest us, but after the lion camp I expect them to post more, so stay alert. Do not give your-selves away by blundering through the woods. You must fire sev-eral times, but cock your bows behind a tree or rock so you won't be seen, and stay low! Everything depends on surprise!"

"Remember," he added, "they will shoot back if they see you. These are dangerous men, and we must keep the advantage of sur-prise. Choose your target, aim true and steady, fire on my signal all at once, then reload. Wait for my signal, and fire again. After that, fire as quickly as you can at anything in the camp that still moves."

The women were grim, but their eyes gleamed. They were ready.

"One last word. Now this is the most important thing of all, so pay close attention. If we need to retreat, we will need to do so very fast. You must not leave your weapons behind. Bring them with you. If anyone is injured, two of you carry her away along with her weapon."

Then he took Melia and Rhodia aside to explain rendezvous points and fall back positions. Afterwards, he sent the team for-ward, he himself taking the center path.

He stayed visible to the women until they were within shooting distance of the camp, then disappeared while they dispersed to either side on high ground looking down into the camp. When they were positioned, he reemerged from cover and looked them over. They were some thirty or forty yards from the camp, a long distance for a regular bow but well within the killing range of the crossbows. Standing up behind a large ash tree, concealed from the camp, he looked at the ranks on his left and right. They were ready and in position. Behind him in the camp, Achaeans were calmly, lazily moving to and fro, unaware of their presence. The Meliae could see them clearly. Even so, they must drop as many as possible on the first volley, before the heathen could arm themselves and seek cover. He raised his arm, his hand holding his SOG, and then dropped it.

The air filled with a buzz of arrows, the whang of bowstrings, but no other sound. It might have been a flight of hornets, but gasps and cries of shock and pain came from the camp. The Meliae reloaded. Shelby checked both files, and dropped his arm again. Again the air filled with the buzz. More shouts, screaming, more wounded animals, but no returning fire.

Shelby looked around the tree and saw slaughter, bodies littered everywhere. Some were crawling, but most were pinned to the ground. One lone Achaean coming back into camp from the woods, probably returning from the latrine, looked at the devastation in amazement, and then his throat exploded in a mist of pink and he sank, twitching, to the ground. Everything stilled. The Meliae had not uttered a sound: no shouts of triumph, no exaltations. They remained grimly determined and silent, their bows cocked again and ready to fire.

Shelby waited, raising his arm to hold the Meliae from shooting.

Nothing.

Eighty or so bodies on the ground.

"Surely they missed someone," he thought. "Someone is always missed, hiding behind a bush or in a tent."

Nothing.

The crawling Achaeans were dead, shot multiple times, and stillness descended on the camp as the last sobbing died away.

Still Shelby waited.

Five minutes passed. Ten.

Then he heard a sound, a kind of sob, and saw a twitch in the side of a tent. The Meliae heard it too, and they all aimed at it.

The sobbing continued and slowly a figure emerged, a naked boy of perhaps eleven, his buttocks bloodied.

Shelby did not drop his arm, but Melia said aloud, "Shoot," and the boy exploded with fifty bolts in his bruised body.

The Meliae reloaded before Shelby snapped out of it. He was angry, but it wasn't his call. Melia walked over to him, saw his anger, and gave him a significant look while drawing her knife. Then she led the way down the hill to the camp, followed by the silent Meliae. Shelby was left standing alone by the tree.

When he looked again, the women were slowly and deliberately castrating all the corpses, even the horses. They were also picking up their bolts and wiping the blood off. Obviously they intended to use them again.

"So it begins," he thought. "This camp will be found by the next batch of Achaeans, and the rumor will spread. They will know some evil has been unleashed on them."

FIFTY FOUR

XXXXXXXXXX

The Meliae were satisfied with their work, but spoke little on the way back to the city. That suited Shelby fine, because he was not in the mood to talk to any of them. He rode at the rear, letting Rhodia and Melia lead the troops, and gradually fell further and further behind.

"They should not have killed that boy," he muttered to himself, over and over.

He grew angrier as they come closer to the city, and continued to drop further back until he was all alone in the fields, walking his horse slowly under the rising stars. As he did so, the hilltop in Afghanistan reared up once again.

He was climbing into the rifle fire. Boys helped older insurgents load the mortars. Somebody shot him. He threw grenades. He charged them. He cut them to pieces, even as they begged to surrender. He was splattered with their blood. He stared at his hands, dripping blood and gore, the pain in his shoulder growing and growing.

And he blacked out.

When he came to, he was lying on the ground. His horse stood off in the field nearby patiently munching on the grass. He shuddered and he hurt all over, every muscle cramped as he tried to unbend from his fetal position. Even his toes cramped. As he tried to stretch, the shaking set in and he felt himself gasping, struggling to breathe, the vision rising again with its black pall.

But then Melia bent over him, covering him with something heavy and warm, kneeling at his head and stroking his black hair, and the shaking subsided. Finally, he relaxed, stretching out as a languid sensation came over him. He wiped tears from his face.

He felt like he was melting into the fertile earth, becoming one with the grassy smells and the rich dirt. The brilliant stars overhead sparkled through the slits of his damp eyelids, and he sighed. It was over now. Only the physical pain remained, and that too subsided.

He heard the horse shifting its feet and he felt something soft against his cheek, soft but with a tawny smell. A smell that was wild but tamed, spicy but ordinary.

He opened his eyes to look at Melia, her concerned face encouraging him.

"Hello, hero," she smiled. "Welcome back." Her low voice was soft, melodious.

He could not speak yet. His jaw had not unhinged. He shook his head to clear it, to loosen his neck and shoulders, and turned his face to the side.

Straight into the face of a lion.

Shelby jerked away, and Melia laughed at him.

"It's your lion skin," she said. "I had them bring it from the city. I guess your lion has caught up with you at last."

"Cruel joke," he sputtered, but his pounding heart restored its rhythm. He would be all right now.

She slid under the lion skin to be next to him, placing her head on the side of his neck, one hand resting on his throbbing heart.

"Rest, Shelby," she whispered. "I will stay here with you as long as you wish."

"I wish . . ." he began, but she reached up and covered his mouth with her fingers.

"Shhh," she whispered. "I know. Rest."

Later, he awoke under a nearly full moon, his nose buried in her hair where she lay cuddled at his chin. She smelled like every desirable and beautiful thing in the world, like the smell of hidden jungle flowers, startling like the brittle beauty of the Hindu Kush.

He inhaled deeply and she stirred, her hand drifting to his stubble-rough chin.

"Shelby," she said softly, dreamily.

He felt her breathing on him, stirring her body, and he put his hand on the curve of her soft back, stroking down over her rounded butt, resting on the bare skin of her leg, tugging gently at it, separating her legs. He had never felt so rested in his life, so much in dream and yet so awake, so in and so out of time. His erection grew against her belly and she responded with a satisfied sigh. Lifting her head, she pulled herself up his chest, her pubic bone stroking his erection, her eyes fluttering. He cupped her bottom and held her to him as her eyes flickered, her long lashes telegraphing desire, and she smiled. Her face came closer, her breath washing over him, urging him, and her lips drifted down onto his, parting, wet, welcoming his tongue.

There under the bright moon, she pushed herself up, straddled him with her knees, pulled him into a sitting position, hugging him. As she tugged his shirt up and over his strong shoulders, he ran his hands up the back of her legs and she rose to her feet, pulling his head into her stomach, as though to bury it there. His hands reached up to her warmth and pulled her toward him, gently lifting her, probing her, finding her wetness, inhaling her odor, his mouth seeking her taste.

"Shelby," she whispered, "Shelby." Her breath came heavily, and her chiton fell away, her breasts easing over his eyes as she slid slowly down the length of his body, burying his erection in the unknowable mystery of her body.

They were face to face, both her hands holding his head as she peered deeply into his eyes.

"Melia," he whispered, her eyes closing, her lips brushing his. He sank out of time and space into some sweet hidden universe, into the unknown.

FIFTY FIVE

XXXXXXXXX

News of the slaughter at the Achaean camp spread rapidly through the ranks of the Achaeans. Everyone knew that the short valley people killed the men. Ritual castration of fallen males was what their women did. The common soldiers shuddered at the thought. Dying did not bother them anything like the idea of spending eternity castrated. How could they talk to their fathers in the afterlife? Their brothers? Their sons?

A single bronze bolt found at the site was examined by the generals, who were deep in thought. Many of the dead bodies had multiple puncture wounds, some going clean through the bodies, the bolts apparently penetrating both armor and shields.

"This is an interesting weapon," said one general, blowing flies out of his greasy black beard. "It has no notch on the rear, and the metal fletching is set at angles. Why?"

"Perhaps it is only the head and the other part comes off," replied one of his commanders, a tall man with a prominent Adam's apple and a permanent kink in his neck that made him look as though he was tilting his head backwards.

The general mused. "No, I don't think so. This was all we found. We would have found more if there had been more."

One of the junior officers standing near the rear ventured to speak.

"General, sir, I think I know why the fins are at an angle."

"Why?"

"It makes the point spin in flight."

"So?"

"I don't know why making it spin would be a good thing, but that's what happens."

"Find the weapon and keep this to ourselves," the general said at last. "The stupid regulars don't need to know about this. If they can't protect themselves behind their shields, they won't fight, damned cowards. Still, we will win because we are too many for them. When we assault the city, we will put the cheapest troops in the forefront as always. And you!" He turned to the junior officer who spoke of the bolt's fins. "You will lead them. Then you will get to see what good a spinning arrowhead can do!"

Despite the general's orders, rumor flashed among the troops. They knew of the new weapon. Next day, when a survivor was found, he reported that no noise had been made during the ambush. No noise at all. The attackers had all been females, wrapped in black clothing, without armor. They had been completely silent, like the spirits of the trees.

The rumor of the Meliae grew among the ranks.

Sundown was long past when Metis turned from the window. Melia joined her immediately after leaving Shelby at his evening bath, but neither had spoken as the room darkened in the twilight. The slaves did not light the lamps in the room, accustomed as they were to their mistress's lengthy meditations, so they too had remained motionless along the walls in the dark. The room was completely still while Metis gazed out the window, watching first the gathering darkness in the east and the rising of the late summer moon, full at last. It would be a long night, a night of testing, so the Goddess warned, and she wondered if she had the spirit for it.

"Is this my night to die?" Metis wondered. So often when the Goddess spoke of testing that is what she meant — someone died. Some spirit bright like a star went down into the shades never to be seen again. Over the harvests, the Goddess warned of her mother's death, of her father's death in battle, of the many battles fought during the last four decades. Perhaps the Goddess meant that the fates had prepared a different kind of test this time. Perhaps it was a test of one of the boys. Or of Melia. Surely Kalista was too young, but even her death would be a great loss.

Metis spent hours staring out at the eastern mountains thinking about each of the people with whom she was close, the people who touched her heart and for whom she lived. She loved so many, yet some were closer than others. Would the Goddess' ways be secret and closed, as always? She would spend the night in watching, sending her mind's eye through every palace room, every house in the city, out across the pastures and the fields.

When she tried that, her mind's eye kept returning to the eastern mountains with their peaks rising like fangs ahead of the full moon.

"Melia," she said as she turned.

"Mother," replied the girl.

"Tell me of Icarus first."

"He is well and resting with Dolios and Ino. The attack on the Achaeans with the Meliae went well, but he was upset when we killed a boy. On the way back, he blacked out and he and I stayed in the fields all night." She did not need to complete the thought with her mother, who knew how they made love on the fragrant earth. "All day today he spent resting."

"Do you still feel that you know him?"

"Yes, I do. I have not seen any trickery or deception in him. I have confidence in him."

"So I already know. I, too, admire him. I wish others here with us were as easy to see into as that large man." She sighed. "But they are not. I'm glad that he is one who can be easily read, for we need our friends now."

"Are you afraid?" asked Melia.

"Afraid? No, I am not afraid. I was startled by the ambush at the pool, and all that has happened since is very strange, but I am not afraid. What the Goddess allows to happen will happen. It is not up to us to judge what she does."

"Do you think she is in a contest with other gods?" Melia asked. "Does she fight a conspiracy just as we do?"

"The strife of gods is beyond our understanding," replied Metis. "We remain obedient and faithful, and trust them to care for us. Our hope is that they will not forget us amid their own wars. So far, for many thousands of harvests, the Goddess has been faithful to us in her way. We may not live, but the city has endured and will always endure. That is our confidence."

She paused and sighed, then leaned down to speak quietly to the girl. "But we need to get through this night first. Alive, if we can."

"Should we light the lamps?" Melia asked in a normal voice, turning aside the conversation. The slaves had heard what they needed to hear. Now it was time to return to accustomed life, to rest their anxious hearts in the inviolability of routine. The cushion of comfortable spirits generated by the slaves would help to ease Metis, too.

Metis understood her.

"Oh, of course, and bring us wine and some food. Fresh bread, no meat. Bring cheese and fruit and butter." Metis clapped her hands. "Let's get busy!" she said, half scolding.

The relief in the room was palpable. Breaths were released as though they had been held the last six hours. The stillness of the room erupted in scurry and subdued chatter, all the sounds of relieved humans returning to normalcy. It was good when Metis was normal. Everyone knew what to expect.

Melia moved closer to her mother, kneeling at her knees and leaning into her.

"When does it start, Mother?" she whispered, looking around to make sure the slaves could not overhear.

"It has already started," Metis replied quietly. "That's why Icarus is here. I just don't know what it is. A secret like a mighty snake coils in the dark. I cannot see it, but I fear to step too close. You must be prepared, Melia. You could become the voice of the Goddess tonight."

The hair on Melia's forearms rose with the thought and she felt goose bumps. The back of her neck felt as if it had been touched by some cold, toothed creature. Or by Ophion in one of his silent moods.

Do you think it is fated?" she whispered nervously.

"The Goddess doesn't say," replied Metis. "I can't tell. My mind encounters dark areas of the city now. I am afraid we have been less vigilant than we should have. Those who have turned from the Goddess may be our chief enemies, but they may not. I cannot know. At midnight, you and I will sacrifice a bullock to open the hidden places. We do not know what lurks there to be found, or whether the Goddess will allow us understanding."

The two sat in silence for a few moments while the attendants brought in their meal and wine. The whole time Melia looked through the window at the high eastern ridges.

"Will the caves be opened?" Melia asked at last.

"Hush, child," replied Metis. "You may not want to see what lurks in the caves. Terror lives there and can drive you mad. If we go, you will see the skeletons of others who have found an entrance to the underworld. I have no desire to add your body to the collection or to desert the city in this hour."

"Do you think it wise that I do not already know the way?"

"If I am unable to show you, my beautiful straight-backed girl, then you will take Icarus with you. Remember that. I have seen a vision of him in the caves, so the Goddess must be ready for him. Now let us talk of other things, lest these kind attendants overhear and become distressed."

Much later when the house silenced with the night, a quiet figure slipped into the shadows of the courtyard to watch Shelby's draped alcove. It stood for a long while without moving, biting the knuckles of a fist, staring in longing and grief at the still curtains behind which Shelby was attended by Ino.

Eventually, the shadow moved away, keeping to the shadows. No one questioned him, for he belonged to the house.

FIFTY SIX

XXXXXXXXXX

S helby was lying awake on his cushions, the two slaves asleep at his feet, pondering the state of things. He had slept soundly during the afternoon, and needed no more sleep tonight, so he was wide awake when the gasp drifted in from beyond the curtains. Not a gasp, really, but a kind of stifled sob.

At first he thought it was Melia coming to him, but it was not her way to pause before entering. It was someone else.

He woke Dolios gently.

"Come with me," he whispered. "Silently. Make no noise. Do not wake Ino."

The sleepy boy struggled into consciousness. In the dark, Shelby sensed him looking up.

"I need you to tell me who is out there," he whispered. "Come."

He parted the curtains where the shadows were darkest, against the wall farthest from the courtyard. They slipped through, making no noise, Dolios going first.

When he followed he saw a figure moving slowly away, head bowed as though in thought.

"Did you see him?" he asked Dolios quietly.

"I did, but I cannot tell who it is."

"Follow him until you know, then come back to me promptly. Don't let him know you are following him. Stay in the shadows. If anyone asks, you are going for wine or something."

Dolios moved off and Shelby was pleased with how silently he moved. He slipped along unseen, following Dolios at a distance, the unknown figure now out of sight. The main thing was not to lose the quarry. It might amount to nothing, but then it might. No one else was moving about the palace.

Shelby paused to look up through the courtyard roof at the stars. The moon shone brightly into the yard and the trickling spring-fed fountain at the far end was the only sound. Near the fountain, ducks stood on one foot, their heads tucked under their wings, asleep. Nothing disturbed them from that direction.

He padded softly after Dolios but knew it was hopeless. If he wandered too far from his accustomed place, he would be lost in the twisting passages of the palace. Rooms opened off of rooms, passages were bedrooms. The plan of the house was the confusing evolution of a thousand years of occupation. Additions had been made at convenience, without a master plan, unlike the city. Walls were made from huge stones set with or without mortar. The main halls, the places he had been, were dressed and decorated but further into the house where strangers never went, the place was utilitarian and less decorated. Function warred against style, and around a corner it was clear that function was winning.

He returned to his alcove.

When he slipped through the draperies, he found Ino awake in the dark.

"Ino," he said quietly.

"I awoke and you were gone. Dolios was gone also."

"Were you concerned?"

"Of course. If anything happens to you, I will die. Your safety is my life."

"What of your discretion?" he asked. "If I ask you questions, can I trust you not to tell anyone that I asked them?"

"If I am told to be silent, then it is a slave's duty to her master to remain silent," said Ino.

Shelby recognized the evasion of this answer. He would be careful what kind of questions he asked, aware that he was constantly under surveillance. The mission he had just sent Dolios on would likely be reported, perhaps to the wrong people.

"I'm not a detective," he told himself. "I am just a soldier whose buddies died. I'm not Sherlock Holmes. Maybe I shouldn't be starting this game."

Nevertheless, he went on.

"Tell me, Ino, do you remember one of those nights when you bathed me and Iapetus came in with Eurymedon?"

"I do," she said.

"It looked to me that you and Iapetus were familiar with one another. Is that true?"

How do you mean familiar?"

"You knew him."

"The house slaves know everyone in the house, master."

Shelby had run into the slave's brick wall. This was passive-aggressiveness. He needed to build her trust before he could overcome it, but he might not have the time to do it.

"Asking her how long she has known Iapetus will get the same kind of evasive answer," he thought. "Try a different tack."

"How many slaves are normally assigned to one person in the house?" he asked.

"What do you mean?" she responded. He heard her shifting in the dark. He also smelled her and felt the heat of her naked body on his cheek. He would have no problem locating her in the dark, but then, she could probably find him in the dark also, in the same way.

"I mean, you and Dolios have been assigned to me. Is this normal? Do some people get more than two, some less than two? I'm just trying to understand what the customs of the house are."

"Most get two," she said. "The more important you are, the more you have to do, the more slaves you get."

She seemed to be warming, there in the dark.

"I assume that Metis has the most slaves, then," he said.

"No, Melia has the most. She has five slaves who do nothing but take care of her clothes, and three who tend to her hair and face. Then she has many more slaves for other things. Metis does not have so many."

"Interesting," he said. "Who has the fewest slaves of the royal household?"

"Iapetus," she said, and even in the dark her sudden drop in tone suggested that she might be flushing.

"How many does he have?"

"One."

"Who is this slave?"

"It is an old man named Dogbreath or something. I don't know him."

"How long has he served Iapetus? If he's old, it must have been a long time."

"Oh no, it's only been a little longer than a month. I don't think Iapetus is pleased with him, but he has no choice. Metis decided.

He could buy his own slaves, though, if he wanted, because he is wealthy."

"I think he might not be able to buy his own, if Metis is the one who decides," Shelby said. "If he bought his own, then she could take offense. She might want to be in control of the slaves."

"She is a very difficult mistress," Ino said. "The slaves fear her."

"Also," she continued after a moment, "she is in charge of all the slaves, no matter who buys them."

"Tell me how long you have been a slave here, Ino."

"Almost eight harvests. This year will be eight."

"Where did you come from?" He was pleased that she was loosening up. "Talking in the dark always seems to disarm them," he thought. "There is something intimate, conspiratorial, comradely about talking to someone in the dark. You miss all the nonverbal cues, but you build a relationship." If he was going to stay here, he needed a workable trust with Ino.

"I was born far in the north where it snowed much of the time. I don't remember much about it. The nights were very long in the cold weather. I had a large family, and we never had enough to eat. My father sold me to the traders, because he said he could not afford to feed me anymore. That was probably true."

"I see," said Shelby, though he did not. A father's choice to sell a child into slavery was something he did not understand. "Though, I guess, given the choice between seeing that child survive and watching her starve to death, it makes a bit of sense," he thought grudgingly. "Only a bit."

"How old were you?" he asked.

"I was nine or ten cold seasons," she said.

"How long before you were sold to the palace?"

"Only a few months. My father sold me in the darkest part of the winter and by spring I was here."

"So you basically came straight here after leaving home, traveling with the trader."

"Yes," she said.

"Were you assigned to someone right away? What happened when you got here?"

"I was completely untrained when I arrived. They tried to teach me how to make bread and wine, to cook, and so on. I learned laundry, but I was a failure at cooking. I was always being scolded by the cooks."

"So then what happened? You learned these things, and then what?"

"After a while, Metis gave me to Iapetus." He detected an unspoken emotion in her tone.

"They gave you to him?" He was surprised. "But you were just a girl."

"That's true. I was very young. I didn't even have breasts. I couldn't do anything."

"You said a minute ago that Iapetus had only one slave given to him. Was that you?"

"Yes," she said. She fell silent.

"So you have been with Iapetus for seven, almost eight harvests, since you were a little girl?" He had stumbled on the truth at last.

"Yes," she said.

"Until about a month ago, you were his only slave?"

"Yes," she said. "I was." She choked up a little.

"Would you like to go back to him?"

He heard he take a sharp intake of breath, and felt her struggling to master herself.

"Tell me, Ino. I will send you to him if you want to go." He spoke kindly, fatherly to her, this troubled slave girl.

"I don't know if he would like it," she said. "Metis might be furious. It is unwise for a slave to undo what Metis has done."

"Or for a stranger visiting in the house," he added. "You are right, Ino. It might be unwise. If I sent you to him, she might also feel that I didn't appreciate her gift to me." He paused, having established common ground with her. "Let me see if I can get a message to him. The solution for Iapetus is to leave the palace and live somewhere else, away from his mother. Then, perhaps she will let him buy you."

"He can never leave," she struggled to say. "He is trapped here by his mother."

She became silent and he heard her crying softly in the dark. Her irregular breath, her agitation. "This may be a slave," he thought, "but she has a gentle heart. Iapetus must be both a father figure and a lover to her, all in one. Yet, she's a slave. Everything about it is unhealthy, but it is not a remarkable departure for the human heart."

Dolios chose that moment to blunder through the curtains. "Master, I have returned with wine," he announced.

FIFTY SEVEN

XXXXXXXXXX

"Ino, will you bring light?" Shelby asked. Turning to the boy, he added: "Stand still, Dolios. No need to trip on something and spill the wine."

Shelby heard Ino step through the draperies to fetch a light and shifted over to Dolios, asking him quietly, "Did you see who it was?"

"Yes, I did," Dolios replied just as quietly. "It was Iapetus. He stopped me and asked me what I was doing, and I told him I was sent to fetch wine for you. He was pleased and said he would prepare wine for you himself. Here it is."

Ino came in with a small oil light and the alcove brightened.

"I don't really want any wine right now, Dolios," Shelby said. "Just set it over there."

He rummaged in his pack and took out his SOG. This was a good time to finish sharpening the knife. He had not shaved in days and his beard was heavy. Putting a good sharp edge on it now would save time in the morning.

"Melia is coming to get me at dawn," Shelby said, as the slaves knelt at the foot of the bed watching him. Ino's eyes were still red, but her demeanor was calm. Dolios had a rascally spark in his eyes that made Shelby wonder whether he was hiding something.

"Why has Iapetus sent wine to me?" Shelby wondered. "We had a good, friendly visit at the bath, but I also stopped the kidnapping and the plot against Kratos, and now I have Ino. If Iapetus had a hand in the attacks, then I am a target for revenge. If I stay alive, I may hinder the rest of his plans, too. That's why he sent wine. It's probably poisoned. Or it was a friendly gesture and Iapetus is not involved at all."

"How did Iapetus seem to you when you saw him?" asked Shelby.

"How to do you mean?" Dolios replied.

"Was he agitated? Sleepless? Unhappy?"

"The prince is always unhappy," Dolios said.

"No he isn't," said Ino.

"Was he agitated? Unable to sleep?"

"That's hard to say. He was awake. An unhappy man wandering the palace in the middle of the night is sleepless. A sleepless man is usually agitated."

More passive-aggressive stonewalling, but also much more perceptive than he expected from Dolios. The boy had a brain, but at the moment it was a slave's brain. "I'm going to get really tired of dealing with slaves," Shelby thought.

"Ino, you have known Iapetus a long time. How did he seem to you that night in the bath? I noticed he put a hand on your leg."

Iapetus is a deep man," she replied after a moment's reflection. "He seemed happy to be there with you and Eurymedon, and he was talkative. He is not always talkative, but it is not unusual."

Shelby thought about that for a moment. "What kind of person is Iapetus behind his public persona?" he wondered.

"Dolios, what do you think of that?" he asked.

"Of what?" Dolios replied. The boy could not extinguish the rascal look in his eyes.

Shelby continued sharpening the knife. Then he stood up, towering over the boy.

"Come here," he said to Dolios, beckoning with the knife. "I want to look at something."

The rascally look vanished from Dolios' eyes. "Yep," thought Shelby, "a grown man can intimidate a smart-ass boy every time."

Dolios approached and stood before him, not looking up at his face. Shelby took him by the chin and tilted his head back, turning his face first one way and then another in the weak lamplight. He saw fuzzy down on the boy's upper lip.

"Don't move," he instructed, and with a deft swipe he ran the blade of the large knife over the boy's upper lip, threatening to lop off his nose. It happened so fast that Dolios was stunned and began trembling.

Shelby was pleased to see the dusting of fuzz on his blade. "It's probably sharp enough," he thought. "For good measure, though, perhaps I should try the boy's neck hair in a minute."

He pushed Dolios away firmly.

"Go sit back down," he said and began pacing the little alcove, putting a few last swipes on the blade. He knew he would have no more trouble with Dolios now that the boy knew who was in charge. One glance at the youth showed him the truth of it. From now on, Dolios would follow his every move, keep out of his way, answer questions directly. That contest was over.

Ino was another problem. It's not so easy with a female. Ino gave the appearance of one who wants to cooperate, but it was probably a subterfuge. That moment of intimacy in the dark had gone a long way with her, establishing a field of common feeling, however. She seemed to believe that he respected her feelings for Iapetus, and that made her more pliable, less resistant.

Different creatures needed different kinds of discipline.

What Ino did not know is that he had listened to the captured Achaean Bren's tale about the human sacrifices for the lion and about Danae's role in it. "If Iapetus is behind any part of that," he thought, "Ino's feelings for him will only stand in the way. She will not say anything that she feels is demeaning about Iapetus, nor will she allow Dolios to do so. I am sure she will lie. They will both lie, but I will be able to detect a lie from Dolios. Ino will be more difficult."

Something nagged at him, something he was overlooking.

He paced with the knife, polishing the blade with a corner of cloth.

What was it?

"Ah ha," he thought. "Laundry. The chiton and the lion. The plot against Kratos. Ino had worked in the laundry. Hadn't that been where Danae worked? Did they know one another? Was Iapetus the mysterious man Bren had seen with Danae when the slaves were delivered for the lion's meal?"

He felt the hair prickling on his neck.

"Was a ten-year-old Ino originally intended as food for the lion?"

He saw them watching him and turned his back to them, deep in thought.

"The laundry. Ino taken from him. Was that before or after the attempt on Kratos? Iapetus lingering outside his alcove just now. The wine," he thought. Ideas rushed together. "Metis' disdain. The oldest born son forced to count bushels of wheat and care for cattle. The worship of a paternalistic and vicious male god."

The slaves were still watching him intently, but when he stared at them, Ino put her hand to her mouth and yawned. Dolios was rigidly still, scarcely breathing. Shelby had scared him, but he had not scared Ino.

"If it is Iapetus, why doesn't Melia know about him?" he asked himself. "If she knows so much and can look into people's minds, why hasn't she helped Metis do something about her oldest brother? Is he simply hidden from her because he's so close, hidden in plain view?"

He took more turns around the alcove, and Ino slumped, leaning back on an elbow.

"If Iapetus is a traitor, then what will be his next step?" he wondered.

"I have a question for both of you," he finally said. "If I wanted to get in or out of the city without being seen, how would I do it?"

He looked steadily at Ino, as though he expected her to answer the question. He knew she would not. In the corner of his eye he saw Dolios shift. Without taking his eyes from Ino, he said, "Dolios? How do you do it?"

The boy jumped. "So it is true that he comes and goes," Shelby thought. The light was not bright enough to read Ino's eyes, though he thought he detected a narrowing of her pupils.

"Yes, woman, you have done it too," he thought.

Dolios explained that a passage under the temple rock leads to a series of short tunnels, one of which leads outside the city walls. The slaves used it regularly to get away from the palace for a while.

"How are these tunnels defended?" asked Shelby, his mind shifting from Iapetus to the pending invasion. "A gate? Guards?"

"Of course," Dolios said. "The tunnels have gates."

"Where does the tunnel come out?"

"On the east side of the wall. A small ravine, just wide enough for two people side by side. It runs near the tunnel and at its head is the entrance. On the wall above the ravine is a guard station, but they are not concerned about slaves coming and going, because they can see that we are not carrying weapons."

"Hmm. . . . It sounds like it would be difficult to mount an armed invasion from that entrance. Still, a few trained men can do plenty of damage if they gain access to the city without being seen. I think you should take me to see this passage. Ino, stay here and watch out for my things. I think someone has been snooping around."

The girl nodded her short blonde curls and watched them go, her eyes bright and intent under her feigned sleepiness. When she was sure they were gone, she wiped the tears from her eyes, got up, went to the wine cup, and drank deeply. Then, she took Shelby's knife from his pack and slipped out between the draperies into the courtyard.

C H A P T E R

FIFTY EIGHT

XXXXXXXXXX

Ino passed the trickling fountain, and walked down a side passage that led out to the stables, her arms crossed to hide the knife. She began to feel the effect of the wine, but attributed it to her long abstinence. If anything, the wine merely increased the sense of giddiness she felt at finally making her decision.

Across the yard from the stables were the warehouses, Iapetus' domain. There, he stored and rotated the stock of food for the city and animals and kept the city prepared for siege. It was a long custom for the warehouse manager to be chosen from the leading families of the city, and it was a role that always made its owner very wealthy. It also left him plenty of spare time during some seasons of the year, such as during the months before the harvest when everyone else was so busy. Unless war broke out, or the crops caught fire, the warehouses were never thought about by most of the population. Nevertheless, as new harvests went in, older stores rotated out.

Iapetus was born into the role. It suited him, because it was easy, people left him alone, and it allowed him to stash away enough gold to buy a kingdom of his own. He carried on an active if clandestine trade in wine, oil, and grain with neighboring settlements, a trade ignored by Metis. But Ino knew he resented the job, too, because he felt it was beneath him. He should be more important. He was the oldest son, the lead prince. In other nations, he would be the heir apparent.

Ino passed by the wagon-width main doors to the warehouse complex and slipped down another side passage. It was not the same path she had taken during the thunderstorm, but it led to the same area of the city.

At the end of the side passage was a narrow wooden door, almost closed. From within, she heard voices, and recognized Iapetus and Timon. She put her hand out to push the door open and felt a wave of dizziness, as though she were seeing double. Her stomach cramped.

"Oh," she thought, "it's not that time of the month yet." One hand went to her stomach.

She pushed open the door.

Inside the small room was a table with stools on either side. Iapetus was seated at one of the stools. Timon was just rising, startled by her presence. Other men wearing cloaks were standing around the room, perhaps a dozen of them. They all turned away and drew hoods over their heads when she entered, then they drifted out.

"Ino, my lovely," cried Iapetus, "come here." He held out his hand and turned sideways on the stool so she could sit on his lap.

"I brought you something," she said, surprised that her voice sounded raspy. She staggered as she crossed the room, and both men looked at her with concern. She made it to his lap, and he folded her into his arms. She was breathless.

"Did Icarus get the wine I sent with Dolios?" he asked her sweetly.

"He did. He didn't drink it, though. Look what I brought you." She handed him the SOG.

He pulled the newly sharpened blade from the sheath and sighed. "Oh, it is so lovely. I've been hoping to get my hands on it, but he will miss it. How did you get it?"

"He and Dolios went to look at the slave gate, and when they left I took it and brought it to you. I won't go back."

"But baby," Iapetus said, his tone pleading, "you know that it is just for a day or two longer. Then we can be together forever."

"I'm not waiting any longer," she said, and suddenly began choking.

Iapetus sprang up, easing her onto the table.

"What's happening to you? Are you all right?"

She was too weak to talk; it was hard to catch her breath. Her eyes rolled up into her head and then came back to focus on him. She clutched him hard, violently, digging her fingers into his arms, staring wildly at him and foaming at the mouth as she struggled to breathe. Her body went rigid with agony. Her skin turned blue.

Her eyes, fixed on his face, went out of focus. She heaved, then lay still.

Iapetus bent over her to see if he could detect a breath. Nothing. He smelled the wine on her lips, the faint odor of almonds.

"Is she dead?" Timon asked, his harsh, pitiless voice penetrating the stillness.

Iapetus fought back tears as he cradled her naked body in his arms.

"Yes," he said.

Timon spat.

"How did she die?"

"I think she drank the poisoned wine I sent to the big man. Maybe he forced her to drink it." Iapetus spoke with effort, looking fixedly at the dead girl, his bony hand roving over her cooling body.

"So what are you going to do now?"

"I don't know. I can't think."

"It's a slave girl, Iapetus. For Zeus' sake. Get over it. We need to get rid of the body and move on."

"She was mine, Timon," Iapetus choked out, giving way at last to tears.

Timon spat again, clearly impatient, then strolled over to look at the knife.

"This is a priceless weapon," he said. "I've never seen such a blade. The girl must have loved you, friend."

"Yes," Iapetus said, "she did. I loved her, too." He gave her blue corpse one more hug and stood, snatching the knife from Timon. "Let's pick her up and carry her into the storehouse. There's an olive oil jar big enough to put her in. If the invasion is happening as we hope, in a day or two no one will find her. People will think she stole the knife and ran away. Not an uncommon thing for a slave."

"A slave with a body like this would be welcome at any door," Timon said, grunting as he heaved on her shoulders. "She could disappear easily. Come, let's finish this. We have things to do or all will fail."

Iapetus took the girl by her long legs, adoring her slim ankles one more time, and then led the way into the dark storeroom. Enough light came from the lamps in the room to show the way. They used the hoist that moved the heavier jars to lift her body, and Timon removed the heavy lid. Lowering her into the vat spilled oil on the floor, but that was little matter to the two men.

Timon replaced the lid, and they disappeared into the shadows at the end of the room, where a carefully constructed false wall moved away to reveal a stone passage that led back into the acropolis beneath the temple. They entered silently and ghosted along the passage, back into the depths, following the hooded men who had gone before.

FIFTY NINE

XXXXXXXXXX

Thehe slave gate was not much for Shelby to see. From a spacious passage, it narrowed to a path through the rock beneath the walls, barely wide enough for two people. That path emptied into a gulch beneath the city wall at the junction of the wall with the acropolis. The gulch itself was full of debris of all kinds, some of it rotting and awful.

Shelby looked out for a few minutes, examined the entrance, and then turned to the interior of the passage where a deadfall of boulders was balanced overhead, ready to seal the entry in an emergency. He was satisfied.

On their way back, he stopped suddenly in the passage and smelled the air.

"Something is different," he said, looking around.

Dolios held up the oil lamp. In the flickering light, Shelby knelt and sniffed the air near the floor. He sniffed along the walls. He ran his hands over the stone surface. Finally, he picked up a stone from the floor and tapped on the wall. Nothing changed along the outermost wall, but tapping along the inner wall rendered a hollow sound.

"Aha," he muttered.

Scratching and knocking, he found the edges of a hidden door, but he could not find a way to open it.

"Oh well," he said to Dolios at last, "at least we know it's here. That much may come in handy. Now show me where the store-houses are."

They retraced their steps to the palace and crossed a court-yard Shelby had not seen before. Sitting on the floor in a passage on the far side they passed a pair of slave girls hugging their knees, their lower lips stuck out in pouts. Their large dark eyes stared straight ahead, their luscious black hair cascading over their naked shoulders. They were too sullen to look up.

"Eurymedon's door," said Dolios. Giggles came from inside the room.

Moments later they passed another door.

"This is Iapetus' room," said Dolios.

"He's not there," said Shelby, suddenly sure of himself. "Let's go in and have a look."

Dolios pushed open the door and stepped inside. Shelby was right — the room was empty. It smelled stale. Shabby, frayed curtains fluttered against a stone wall. The bed was a pile of skins and one cushion on a narrow platform.

"Where did he mix the wine?" asked Shelby.

"Over here," said Dolios, leading to a corner of the room where several stacked boxes made a rough table.

The search did not take long. In the box second from the floor was the vial. Shelby smelled it when he opened the lid. The bottom box was filled with gold that must have weighed a ton or more.

"Did you know this was here?" he asked Dolios, gazing at the gold.

"Everyone knows it is here. Everyone also knows that it is death to touch the box."

"How is it death?" asked Shelby.

"The Goddess has cursed it. Slaves have died from touching it. Some have disappeared and never been seen again. Everybody knows about that."

"Have you known slaves who disappeared?" Shelby asked, closing the boxes and re-stacking them.

"Yes, several. They came to the palace from the slave traders, were sent to Iapetus, and the next we knew they disappeared. Iapetus said that they had touched the box after he had warned them and that spirits from the Goddess came in the night and took them."

"Oh. Well, that explains that," thought Shelby. Now he understood how Iapetus had been feeding the lion. It was probably as effective a security system as one could have.

They were walking out the door when Shelby thought of something else.

"Doesn't Iapetus have an elderly man as a slave? I think Ino called him 'Dogbreath.'"

Dolios paused a moment. "Yes, that was his name. He has only been working here for a few weeks."

"Where is he?"

"He should have been here in the room. Maybe the Goddess came and took him away because he touched the box."

"I don't think so," said Shelby.

The scale of the treachery was taking shape in his mind, and Iapetus was at the center of it. If he was going to protect Melia, he must find and stop Iapetus.

He looked around one last time.

Why were the curtains against the stone wall fluttering?

Behind the curtains on the wall he found a section of rock face ajar, a false door that opened on a pivot. Shelby pulled it open and smelled death.

Dolios raised his lamp, and they peered into the darkness.

In the small inner passage lay an elderly slave, pink foam at his mouth, the ground about him soiled and an agonized look on his staring face. His skin was blue. Beyond the slave was a passage leading into the dark.

"Let's go," he said, and they stepped over Dogbreath into the dark passage. He pulled gently on the door to close it, leaving it slightly ajar.

The passage ascended on the right side and descended on the left. Taking the descending passage, they moved along, the flickering light of the lamp showing several passages branching off back into the deeps below the acropolis. The place was tomblike.

But not more than ten minutes later they heard voices approaching them and the noise of sandals slapping the stone. At the closest offshoot, Shelby dragged a terrified Dolios out of the passage and snuffed the lamp, clamping his hand over the boy's mouth to prevent him from making a noise.

Two men hurried by. A short, skinny one first, dragging his hand along the wall, and a large swarthy one with an oil lamp coming after. He could not be sure in the dim light, but the man in front appeared to be Iapetus. The swarthy one had a vaguely familiar appearance. "From where?" Shelby wondered. "The lion camp?"

It seemed certain that the two would head for the acropolis, following the ascending path as they were. So when the footsteps faded, he released Dolios and pulled him out into the passage, holding out his hand on the wall to guide his way. He used his little flashlight now and then to see where he was going and to traverse the occasional byway. Eventually, he spotted the men's oily footsteps on the rock, and then he was sure of himself.

They hurried down and pushed open a wooden door at the end of the passage, stepping into a large warehouse filled with huge ceramic jars.

"What are these?" he whispered to Dolios.

"These are the jars where the grain and oil are stored," said Dolios, wondering at the man's ignorance. "All our food is stored here. We are supposed to have enough to endure a siege for a year. Iapetus is in charge of maintaining the supply and guarding it."

Oily footsteps led from one of the large jars toward the door. Moments later, Shelby and Dolios looked down through the oil at the dead face of Ino.

Dolios turned ashen.

"I don't believe Iapetus would have done this intentionally," Shelby said. "Perhaps it was the man with him."

"That man was an Achaean," said Dolios, "you could smell him. Only an unbathed Achaean smells that way."

"He looked like the Achaean from the lion camp, the one who was beating the woman. If it is, then I wouldn't put it past him."

Ino should have been watching his stuff in his alcove, but she had either fled here or been carried here. That meant that his stuff was unwatched, and it might also mean that the cup of wine — he was certain now that it was poisoned — was still there. Should he go back and check, or should he pursue Iapetus and the Achaean?

He decided on pursuit. Dolios could deal with his pack, and would not be any help in the dark passages.

"I will take the lamp, Dolios," Shelby announced as he replaced the jar's lid. "You must run as fast as you can back to my alcove and get rid of the cup of wine. Do not drink it or touch it. Don't spill it. Don't smell it. It has a deadly poison in it. You must pour it out in a safe spot away from the water in the courtyard and away from people. It will kill anything it touches. If you doubt me, remember Dogbreath. Also, probably Ino. That is a horrible way to die, Dolios. Do as I say. Do you understand?"

The boy nodded.

"I am going after those men. If you can, after you have gotten rid of the wine, bring the rope and my pack and join me in the passage. You can enter through Iapetus' room. He won't be there."

His sense of urgency seemed to stir Dolios and Shelby believed that he could safely send him on this mission.

"Remember, you must dispose of the poisoned wine safely and you must not touch it or drink it. I will give you a reward if you do as I say. Do not let any of it touch your skin!"

The slave boy was off.

"I remember when I could run so effortlessly," thought Shelby as he hurried off on the trail of the two men. "Like the wind. Just like the wind."

X

SIXTY

At about the time Shelby and Dolios went to investigate the slave gate, Rhodia finally gave up trying to sleep. She lay restless in her bed in the corner of Melia's room, frustrated and angry. Tonight after posting the Meliae, she saw two palace mothers looking at her and whispering with amusement. That had done it. She had had enough ribbing about Icarus from every other female in the city.

"The big man is just exciting," she thought. "He is somebody new. And, so big! His arms are bigger than my legs! And, his smell. Oh Goddess, his smell!"

She was, of course, alone. Metis and Melia had gone off to do their Goddess thing, something that made Rhodia yawn at the very thought. "I'm glad I don't have to do that," she thought.

She enjoyed the excursion to the Achaean camp. It was thrilling to have the Meliae follow her orders, and they had devastated the camp. Sooner or later the Achaeans would discover the slaughter, and maybe it would scare them off.

Meanwhile. There was tonight.

She turned over and sighed, again. Somewhere in the darkness she heard a slave girl rouse to see if she needed anything. Water. Wine. Comfort. A back rub.

Maybe it was Ilexa or one of the other girls. Melia's friends slept in her room every night, a big slumber party. When Melia left to wait on her mother at the midnight sacrifice, they all went to sleep. Metis did not like the distraction of a big crowd of girls, so they stayed put, but Melia had duties as attendant.

"Good for her," Rhodia thought, thinking she would yawn. But she didn't.

"I will not waste any more time tonight turning over and over in this bed by myself," she thought. "I can't have Icarus, so I'll go back to Eurymedon. He's the nicest of the whole family. Really the only normal one. Ophion makes my skin crawl, Iapetus is like an empty barrel, and Kratos is so full of himself and so loud that it's embarrassing. Besides, Kratos is not here. Eurymedon is not big like Icarus, but he's slim and he doesn't smell bad. He likes me, too, which helps. At least he pays attention when I'm with him."

She slipped out Melia's door and down the stairs, and soon let herself into Eurymedon's room. The young man was in bed, spooned between two female slaves, the covers thrown down.

"Out of here, you harlots," snarled Rhodia to the slaves in a low tone, and then she snuggled in next to the sleeping man.

A little later, as they were catching their breath and enjoying the warmth of each other's company, Rhodia suddenly sat upright in the bed.

"What's that smell?" she whispered to Eurymedon.

"It's not me," he replied, dreamily, reaching a hand out to stroke her back.

"No, I know that." She said urgently. "That smell. What's that smell?"

"Eurymedon," called a deep voice quietly from behind the bed curtain.

"He's busy," said Rhodia firmly. "Go away."

Timon was taken aback by the sound of the woman's voice giving orders. "The women in this city," he thought with disgust. "Every one of them needs to be taught a lesson. Maybe we will just kill all of them except the virgins under age ten. That would be the safest."

"Eurymedon," he said again, more forcefully, "we need to go. We are setting out for our journey tonight before the war starts."

"Go away, Timon," Eurymedon replied. Turning to Rhodia, he said, "It's Timon. He's the guide Iapetus has employed to take me on my tour."

"Is he an Achaean?" Rhodia asked, bewildered, wrinkling her nose.

"I think so. He knows the route."

"You are traveling with an Achaean? With someone who smells like that?" Her temper was slipping quickly away.

"You're in the way here, woman," said Timon, assuming — mistakenly — that an assertion of male domination would get rid of her. "Go away. I have business with Eurymedon."

He threw back the curtain.

He should have thought twice about that.

Rhodia was now fully enraged at everything in the world — at Eurymedon for planning to leave, at Metis for being condescending, at Melia for being haughty, at the other women for making fun of her, and now most of all at this stinking heathen Achaean male for barging in on her, in the palace no less!, when he had been told to go away.

She flew at him in fury, leaping squarely into his face, her hands extended like claws, slashing at his face with a vigor that astonished him and knocked him backward. She maimed his face, almost blinding him with her ferocity, kicking at his genitals with her bare feet, over and over again. He went down and rolled away from her, then jumped to his feet with his knife drawn. He went for her.

Eurymedon sat stunned to this point, but when he saw the knife, he also leapt up.

"Timon!" he cried, causing a commotion in the halls outside. "Timon! What are you doing?"

"I am going to teach this puny she-cat a lesson," Timon replied, stalking Rhodia with his arms spread, the deadly knife in one hand. "I'm going to cut this bitch a new one."

He bled freely from multiple wounds on his forehead and cheeks. Blood streamed from the corner of his left eye.

Rhodia backed away in a crouch, like a cornered lioness looking for an opening. She did not care that she was unclothed. She did not care that he was male and larger. She did not care about anything but getting her hands on him again, clawing his eyes out. Unexpectedly, she realized that all the training with Icarus and the Meliae had prepared her for this.

Timon made a step in her direction, and she began the high-pitched ululating alarm call that the women of the city had used forever to warn of danger, but she shaped the tone into the word "Meliae!" It spread through the already tense city, and all who heard it took it up. In the streets outside the palace, women already restless from the rumor of war stumbled from their beds, rousing their men and grabbing weapons. The wail grew and grew and the percussion of running feet was heard in the hallway.

Timon threw himself at her with all his might, leaping to come down on her and crush her, to let his momentum carry her down while he struck with the knife.

She wasn't there. He landed where she had been, but she sidestepped and was now behind him, flipping him to the floor, the knife hand high in the empty air behind him. She plummeted onto him, pulling his arm down backward with her falling weight, the knife wrenching free, dislocating his shoulder. She straddled him, wrapping her legs around him and buried her teeth into the base of his neck, paralyzing his good arm, her fingers finding and gouging his eyes. He struggled blindly at her, hitting the top of her head, and then he felt Eurymedon's strong hands grasping his arm, breaking it, and the room filled with people.

Angry women saw Rhodia still astride the stinking Achaean and joined the fray. In moments, Timon's scrotum was ripped from his thrashing body, he was torn open, more pieces of his flesh torn away, his windpipe wrenched from his neck, his own knife thrust deeply into his heart, and a hundred or more times into other parts of his torso.

Rage comes easy, goes hard. Rhodia was still tearing at Timon when the women began pulling her off, but it was like handling an angry cat. All the pent-up fury she had felt for weeks had been unleashed, and as soon as she was pulled off the dead man she went for Eurymedon. She snarled at him with blood running out of her mouth and down her face. Her naked body, drenched in the dead man's blood and gore, assailed him.

Among other things it was apparent to the other women that Rhodia's healthy sexual energy had transformed into an apotheosis of rage. Poor Eurymedon, all he could do was cower and try to protect his face as she hit him again and again, accusing him of everything from stupidity to filthy habits to cowardice. "Oh, this will make a good story," the women thought, with admiration. "Eventually."

SIXTY
ONE

XXXXXXXXXX

In Arktos' large hut on the western frontier, Ophion awoke from a deep sleep at his father's foot. They had returned from a multiple-week trip to the citadel, stopping to check all the garrisons along the way, and they were tired. Ophion liked to sleep on the ground because the ground talked to him. Now it woke him. Indistinctly at first, he heard only the hissing of the earth, the secrets of the dead whispering underground as always. Then, he began to see awful visions of hate and fire. He sat up.

"Father!" he whispered urgently. "Father! Trouble in the city. Mother is in danger. I go now!"

He leapt up as Phorbus shook off sleep.

"Arktos!" Phorbus shouted. "Get Ophion a fast horse. Your fastest. Now! You, there," this to a sentry outside the hut, "fill a flask with water and help Ophion get on his horse. Now! Right now!"

Within minutes the horse was ready and Ophion astride it.

"Be careful, my son," Phorbus urged. "Only you can go. Kratos must stay here to lead the defense of the west, and I will ride back to the citadel at first light. You and your brothers must hold the city."

Ophion looked at him grimly. "The earth screams, but the vision is filled with smoke. It is unclear."

Then, he was gone. The clatter of his horse's hooves receded into the night.

Phorbus glanced at Arktos.

"Any news from this front?"

"Kratos took a band of men to raid the Achaeans near the bottom of the hill. He expects to be back soon."

Phorbus sighed.

"I hope someday he will learn the virtue of patience. It is better to let the enemy come to you when you have a strong defense than to go to him in the dark. Still, he has won glory before. I hope he survives to receive the praises of the women."

"So do we all," said Arktos.

Sleep was gone for them, now, so they wrapped in warm clothing against the night's chill and paced around the camp. Here and there, the men were piled up sleeping. One or two were awake, staring at their fires. They were well fed, well clothed, and none suffered in this camp yet, but as time wore on it would be more difficult. In the end, the winner was the one who outlasted his opponent, and in a only a month it would turn bitter cold on the heights.

"They wait on our harvest," said Phorbus eventually.

"True, old friend. I worry that the Achaeans are so much more numerous than ever before. Maybe we should have been killing them off all along."

"They have grown with new peoples moving down from the north. We can hold them this time, but one day we will be overrun."

"Or we will move. After a thousand harvests here, it will be difficult to move, but other peoples have done it."

Phorbus mused a bit.

"I don't like the idea of being shoved out of a home we've occupied so long," he said at last, "but I, too, have seen it. If they are too numerous to overcome by fighting, perhaps we should consider different tactics."

"What do you mean?"

"For example, we could intermarry. Perhaps our young men would not be so particular about their young women. Then once the women were brought back here, perhaps they could spread our culture to their families, and we could find a way to get along."

"I think you underestimate how barbaric these people are. They treat their women like dirt, worse than cattle. They have gods that encourage that behavior. It makes the men think they own everything they can take, so they go and take it. If they were not fighting us, they would be fighting one another. I don't think inviting their women into our valley would do us much good."

They walked a few more steps.

"Besides," Arktos continued, "can you imagine how our women would receive them? Some opinions are difficult to change, but when it comes to changing a woman's opinion about another woman? Ha!"

Phorbus chuckled. "I see why you prefer living on the mountaintop, old friend. Our hair has grown white like the winters we have fought through, but we have learned differently. You see more clearly, I think. Our women might admit a stranger or a slave to our city, but not a strange wife. You're right. It is not the place for foreign women. You can see that in how they treat the slaves."

They took another turn together, walking past a heap of quietly snoring warriors.

"It's an idle subject, anyway," Phorbus said. "We will not face those problems because we will win this war, too."

"I do prefer the mountains to the city," Arktos said, as though Phorbus had not spoken. "I like the clear air, the distance of the horizon, the way sound travels. I like it most because up here the women do not come."

As they walked, they suddenly saw a fire break out at the citadel some forty miles away. It was a single fire, growing larger by the minute.

"Attack!" cried Phorbus. "The citadel has been attacked! It may have fallen!"

He clutched his chest and shuddered, a shadow passing over him.

"It's time to ride," he said, regaining composure. "Rouse the men. I want 200 men on horseback with me. That will leave you plenty for the defense here."

"We will have 4000 men left here and there are another 400 at each of the border garrisons and on patrol. That should hold. If they have penetrated the valley already, we may have a problem. They could be massing for an attack on the city already. If the citadel has fallen, we are in for it."

They sniffed the air. In the distance the fire began in the valley.

"They are already firing the fields to prevent us from riding to aid the citadel," he said to Arktos, clasping his old companion on the forearm. "Hold this fort. In the name of the Goddess."

"Ride!" yelled Phorbus.

With an alacrity that belied his age, he was gone, his wild hair stirring in the wind with the promise of one more battle, one more chance to throttle and chop, one more surge of blood lust.

As Arktos watched, the smoke from the fields began to rise into the sky. Further on, the fire on the temple mount where Metis raised the altar fire could also be seen, blazing with the fat of the sacrificed bullock. Soon, that fire too would be billowing its fragrant smoke skyward.

"Toward the Olympian gods," thought Arktos. "North, toward the brutal gods of the sky."

SIXTY TWO

XXXXXXXXXX

Rhodia's alarm awoke a large neighborhood of wealthy families who lived adjacent to the palace, and only moments after it first sounded, the Matrons responsible for that precinct came forth in their long robes and hoods. They patrolled the streets, gathering information, updating residents. A glance at the acropolis told them that Metis was performing a midnight sacrifice.

While in her trance, she would be remote from the events in the palace, but she would want to know about them after she awoke. Meanwhile, the small council of Matrons assumed the governance of the city. Part of their duty was to investigate the disturbance in the palace.

Poor Eurymedon had suffered as sarcastic a tongue-lashing and face slapping as was ever delivered. Rhodia was just catching her second wind before going on to round two when the Matrons walked in through the crowd of amused onlookers. The bleeding corpse of the Achaean lay on the floor, his hair, limbs, and clothing strewn all over the room. Though his face was unrecognizable, his smell was unmistakable.

"Perhaps you should be in charge of the troops, Rhodia," smiled one of the Matrons at the panting girl.

The tension in the room broke into gales of laughter, some people pointing at Eurymedon's reddened face. Even Rhodia, after a moment or two, began to relax. She took one more look at Eurymedon, slapped him a last time hard across the face, and then turned away to the Matrons.

"This stinking Achaean thought he could give me orders," she said, pointing. She breathed hard, her breasts heaving.

"I believe he must have been unsuccessful," responded another Matron, wryly. "I'd say you've given the Achaean — and some others —" (she looked at Eurymedon) "a lesson in civility."

The fury began to melt out of Rhodia's face, and she realized she was standing in the room as naked as a slave. She gave Eurymedon one more baleful look, then pushed him aside to take a cover off the bed. When he tried to do the same, a Matron said: "Oh no you don't, boy. Not yet. You don't deserve clothes yet. We are going to have an explanation first."

One of the Matrons turned to the crowd and shooed them away, then all three gathered in on the young couple.

"Tell us, Eurymedon, how an Achaean, probably a warrior, got into the palace and into this room," said one very seriously. "Rhodia has done right in killing him, but you should have acted first. No, you may not cover yourself until you have answered our questions." Eurymedon's hand stopped where it was.

"I don't know how he got in, but I've met him before," he said, beginning to quiver. "This is the man that was to be my guide on my tour."

"What tour?" demanded one of the Matrons.

"My tour of the world. You know. The tour." He was confused.

"Who told you that you would go on a tour?"

"Well, I thought it was understood. Young men go on tour. They see the world. Then when they come home they can contribute more to the city."

"Contribute more?" asked another Matron. "You have to contribute something first before you can contribute more. What have you contributed?"

"I . . ." he began.

The leading Matron, Agala, held up her hand.

"Who was going to send you on a tour?" she asked.

"I thought it was understood. When a young man reaches a certain age, he goes on a tour."

"How many young men have you known who went on a tour?" she continued.

"Well, Kratos. Iapetus didn't go because there was a war and the borders were closed. Ophion didn't go, but that's Ophion. Some of the boys in the city have gone. I thought it was my turn."

"We sent Kratos on a world tour because he has fighting skill and will one day be the commander of the troops. We did not send

Iapetus, because we did not expect him to contribute anything. Ophion was not invited to go, because he protects Phorbus, and only Phorbus understands him. We have not discussed sending you. So far, you have not shown that you will be of much value to the city one way or another."

"But Iapetus told me it was time to go. To get ready. He hired a guide for me."

"This Achaean was the one he hired?" Agala's withered cheeks had two bright pink spots growing on them.

"Yes. I met him with Iapetus in the warehouses. Iapetus has a room there where his friends gather."

"How did this Achaean enter the city?" asked another of the Matrons.

When no one answered, she asked, "Has this Achaean been in the city more than once?"

Again, silence.

"How did this Achaean get into the city, if no one saw him?!" she demanded.

"Rhodia," Agala said, "get us a slave to run to the gates and ask the guards if they can identify this Achaean. Surely they would have smelled him coming in through the gates. The old men will know if anyone will. Maybe he was naked like a slave and wearing a collar when he came in. Still, his smell should have given him away. Send the slave and come back here, and meanwhile wash this heathen's blood off of you."

Rhodia left the room and Agala turned again to Eurymedon. "You, boy, have failed your city. An Achaean is in your room. Achaeans plotted against Kratos, and only the stranger Icarus saved him. Achaeans assaulted your mother and sisters, which Icarus also interrupted. Now we have information of an Achaean invasion. If an Achaean warrior has had free run of this city, then all our hidden defenses are known to the enemy. He may even have discovered the tunnels! We would have no escape, no way of surviving if the gates fall. The whole city and everyone you know could be raped and killed. This looks like treason."

"If Rhodia had not led in killing the Achaean, what would you have done?" asked another Matron. "Gone with this man?"

"You have acted stupidly," said the third Matron, who had remained out of the questioning. "Even for a male. I cannot believe this. Did it ever occur to you to ask anybody, anybody at all, about your tour?"

"No," replied Eurymedon sheepishly. His knees lost their strength, and he sank to the floor just as Rhodia came back in.

"Just as I thought, fool," Agala said to him. "Weak and stupid. What on earth can you do to make up for this?"

Eurymedon's blank eyes took on a tiny glimmer of hope. He might be allowed to make up for it.

"Rhodia," Agala said, turning to her, "will you speak for Eurymedon? If not, we will give him to the jailer to be sold into slavery."

"Or executed," one of the others said. "Depends on Metis."

She looked at the boy trembling on the floor.

"Icarus is probably out of the question," Rhodia reasoned to herself, running her tongue over her teeth. "Eurymedon is not so bad after all, if I can't have Icarus. He's just naive. He can probably be trained, and if not, why then he still has the sentence of slavery on him, if I speak for him then renounce him. What more could a girl ask?"

"Maybe," she said to the Matrons. "I need to think about it."

CHAPTER

SIXTY THREE

✕✕✕✕✕✕✕✕✕✕

Dolios did not make it to Iapetus' room with Shelby's pack. As he rushed by, three Matrons suddenly were standing in the hallway in front of Eurymedon's door.

A slave running from the Matrons meant death. No appeal. So he stopped.

"Where are you going?" asked one.

"I am to go to Iapetus' room," he said.

"Why are you carrying the stranger's bundle?" asked another one.

"Because he told me to fetch it and bring it to him there," replied Dolios in what he hoped sounded like both a convincing and true statement.

"Then we will go with you," said Agala, leaning back into the room to instruct Rhodia and Eurymedon to follow. "You can put on some fighting clothes now, Eurymedon," she added, "and bring weapons, but this is not over."

Moments later, they trooped into Iapetus' empty room. "We do not see the stranger in this room," said one of the Matrons. "How do we know you are not stealing his pack?"

"I am supposed to go behind the curtains there and through the wall," he replied, knowing his life was at stake.

"Show us," she said.

He pulled back the curtains and showed the narrow gap in the wall, where a rotating section of wall protruded.

"Open it."

He pulled on it and it started to move outward. "A dead slave is inside," he said, grunting. "Icarus and I found him when we went through here earlier."

"Icarus has been in this room also?" asked Agala. "I thought this was the palace, not the gate to the city."

"Yes," said Dolios, opting for complete disclosure. "We came in here looking for poison. He thinks Iapetus poisoned his wine and that's what killed Ino."

"Killed Ino?!"

"She's dead. She's in a vat of oil in the warehouse," he said.

"I don't understand," said Agala. "Who poisoned whom, and why is Ino dead?"

"We think she drank some wine that Iapetus prepared for Icarus. Icarus heard somebody outside the curtains at his place in the courtyard and sent me to see who it was. It was Iapetus. Icarus told me that if anyone saw me I was to say that I was going for wine. Iapetus recognized me and said he would prepare wine for his brother's savior himself. We came to his room and he poured the wine over there," Dolios pointed to the corner of the room where the chests were, "and then brought it to me. I took it. I'm glad I didn't try it on the way."

"So, how did Ino die?"

"Icarus did not drink the wine," Dolios explained. Then, he told them about going to the slave gate, going to Iapetus' room, finding the passage, and eventually Ino's body in the vat of olive oil.

The hidden door in the wall opened fully and the smell of death flowed into the room.

You better take some lamps if you go in there," he said.

"Does this amazing story have more than you have told us so far?" asked Agala.

"Oh yes. We followed this passage beyond the door. Icarus was leading. At a certain point we heard footsteps, and we hid in a place off the main passage. We saw two men go by. I think Iapetus was one. The second was an Achaean, from his smell. After that we found Ino and the two men's oily footsteps leading from the vat to the passage. Then Icarus sent me to get his pack and bring it to him here. He decided to go after the two men."

The Matrons exchanged looks. Agala looked back at Rhodia.

"Rhodia, bring weapons for all of us. We need a general alert. Let the Meliae and the guards know. Quickly!"

A step through the door brought them to the corpse of Dog-breath, the pink foam around his mouth drying dark on his face.

"Dolios, is the slave gate open?" Agala asked.

"Yes it is."

"The slave gate needs to be closed. It may already be too late," Agala stated to the other Matrons.

Rhodia had not yet returned. They looked at Eurymedon, measuring him, weighing whether he had enough sense to be trusted with a simple mission. Finally, they decided. He did not.

"Eurymedon, you go in front where we can see you. Dolios you follow him. We will follow you. One of us will alert the guards at the slave gate," Agala said.

Wordlessly, one of the Matrons moved quickly through the outer door to the room. The others turned toward the passage just as Rhodia came in with her crossbow and other weapons.

"Hurry," breathed Agala at Eurymedon's neck, and they rushed into the dark as fast as their lamps allowed.

SIXTY FOUR

XXXXXXXXXX

On the floor above, in the now deserted women's quarters, Iapetus quietly entered Kalista's room.

"Sister, sister," he whispered urgently.

"Iapetus?" she responded. "Help me get up. My stomach still hurts."

He leaned over her and scooped her up in his arms.

"Hurry," he said, "we have to get out of here. I'll carry you. Be quiet, though. I'll show you a secret passage, if we can get away before the others find us."

"What's happening?" she asked, whispering also. "Is there danger? I heard the alarm call!"

"I'm not sure," he said grimly, "but it's downstairs. I think the Achaeans have broken into the palace. I'm taking you to Mother at the temple."

Kalista's nurses roused and came to them. The younger girls who stayed in Kalista's room did not awaken. The nurses were displeased having a man in her room, but Iapetus comforted them.

"I'm taking her to mother," he said. "Everything will be all right. Bolt the door after we leave and let no one in. An Achaean was found downstairs."

He hurried out of the room carrying Kalista, pleased to hear the sound of the door being bolted behind him. At the end of the hallway, the building met the rock of the acropolis, and there, behind a statue of Hermes, a small door painted to look like stone opened into one of the tunnels. Iapetus squeezed through holding her, and then shut the door behind them, apparently locking it in place.

"I never knew a door was there," Kalista said, still whispering to him, now in the dark.

"Yes, I know," he replied, "it is only for emergencies."

She was alarmed by the tone of his voice. Something was wrong. Was there an echo in the passage, or had something changed? He seemed to be gripping her more tightly, shifting her weight.

"Iapetus, put me down," she said, suddenly wary for some reason she could not pin down. "I can walk. My stomach still hurts when I bend in the middle, but I can walk. You don't need to carry me."

"I want to carry you," he said grimly.

"No, I think you should put me down," she said. "You are not accustomed to carrying people. You might trip or drop me or something."

They turned a corner and in the distance she was relieved to see an oil lamp burning in a niche on the wall. By its faint light, she looked up at Iapetus' face, and what she saw was frightening. His eyes had a glare she had never seen.

"Iapetus, what's the matter?"

He did not answer. Instead he picked up his pace.

"Where are we going?"

He still did not answer, though he was beginning to breathe hard.

"Iapetus, you're scaring me!"

"Shut up," he snarled. "I'm trying to think."

Panting in earnest a few moments later he said, "I'm putting you down now, but you have to move. We don't have much time to get to safety."

"Why?" she asked. "What's happening?"

"I don't know, but there's been an attack in the palace. Mother sent me to get you and bring you to the temple, where we will be safe."

"Oh," Kalista said. She did not know whether to believe him, but he was her oldest brother. More like a father, really, he was so much older. She had always trusted him.

Holding her wrist, he hurried along the passage, ascending flights of stairs. Here and there were openings to the night air, which cast a faint light into the dim passage. Iapetus took one of the oil lamps, and Kalista noticed several passages opening off into the depths of the temple mount. From some of them came a breeze of much colder, clammy air, and stale smells. She had no idea where they were, except that they were ascending.

Iapetus paused to catch his breath and raised the lamp. In a narrow passage on their left, Kalista smelled a foul odor and the lamplight caught something white in the gloom, shifting, scrabbling. It was a rat and she screamed.

At the guard's post over the slave gate, all of the men heard the commotion in the palace.

"Sounds like somebody's wife found him sleeping in the wrong bed," joked one of the guards, looking toward the palace.

The guard standing next to him raised his head and sniffed.

"Do you smell fire?"

Suddenly, all the guards were alert. They could not see fire or any smoke in the city that shouldn't be there, but they could smell burning grass, that distinctive odor.

"Are the fields afire?" asked one urgently.

"We should check on it," said another.

"No, wait," said Yiannis. He had command of the guard post for the evening, and he took the job seriously. "If they need us, they will come for us. Let's stay where we are supposed to be."

"You stay," the six other guards laughed. "We know what's happening here. Nothing. Nothing ever happens here. This is the most boring station in the city. Sometimes you see slaves coming and going, and we can throw the slops down on them, but we haven't even seen slaves for a week. It's boring. All the excitement is somewhere else."

They ran down the wall to get a better view of what was going on.

Yiannis stood watching them, angry and determined to get back at them, when suddenly he was knocked to his knees by a blow on his back. He caught himself as he began to fall forward and saw an arrow sticking out of his chest. It hurt to breathe.

"The slave gate. The slave gate," he thought desperately. "I'm shot. It's an attack. Close the gate."

More arrows scattered on the rocks around his head.

Spitting blood, he crawled on all fours back into the guard station, pulling himself up on a pillar inside. He reached a lever, and with his dying effort, pulled on it.

A rope pulled out a linchpin and a deep rumble was heard below. Then screaming men. The deadfall dropped, sealing the passage below, as Yiannis collapsed, dead.

CHAPTER

SIXTY FIVE

XXXXXXXXXX

S helby heard a girl's scream echo through the stone passages. It could have come from anywhere. Here and there passages opened off to one side or the other, but the scream sounded like it came from the rightmost passage, so that's the way he went. Because he did not worry about an oil lamp blowing out, he moved fast, but he did worry about the aging batteries in his LED flashlight.

Then he heard a rumble like a rock fall, and the screams of men in terror and agony. Turning a corner, he witnessed a dust cloud blowing down the passage with more moans and screams of men. He played his flashlight through the dust and saw a pile of rocks, several men mangled or trapped in the bottom. They were soldiers, but not from the city. These were Achaeans, some with the flint-tipped spears he had seen at the pool but others with bronze weapons. Those not killed in the rock fall were dazed, but when they saw his light they panicked. Some fell on their knees, others scrambled for cover.

Looking around, Shelby realized he was at the slave gate and that these men were trapped in the deadfall that sealed it.

He switched off the light and stepped back into the dark, narrow passage, controlling his breath so as not to give himself away.

Another encounter with Achaeans, and yet again he was unarmed. Not a good plan. "Damn it. This kind of thing needs to stop happening or it will be the death of me," he thought.

Now that the flashlight was off, the passage was completely dark. If possible, the men were even more frantic than they had been.

Considering his options, Shelby decided to pick them off one by one, using the total darkness to his advantage. It seemed the easiest thing to do.

He moved forward stealthily in the dark until he detected a blubbering Achaean. He could not see anything at all, but he sensed the man's presence and reached out. His hand connected and the man screamed and leapt back.

"Who's that? Who touched me?" he cried.

Another man stumbled into him, and Shelby got his bearings. The man went down with a broken neck.

"We need to get our wits," said one voice. "That light has gone. If it was an evil spirit, it hasn't come back."

"Yeah," said another. "You go first."

Shelby backed away toward the passage. Suddenly, he blinked the flashlight toward the men, showing their terrified faces, their wide eyes. The bright light momentarily dazed them, and it revealed their positions.

He attacked again, this time without stealth. Loud, unearthly screams of attack. He was pretty sure when it was over that three more of the men had gone down. He heard groaning, and he had heard bones breaking.

Now he had a sword, too.

"The rest will be easy," he thought, withdrawing again into the passage.

It was so easy to spot them by sound and smell that he no longer needed the flashlight. Instead, he got low and crept forward in a crouch. He heard a shuffle to his right and slashed out with the sword, connecting with bone. The man screamed: "My leg! Something's got my leg! Holy Zeus, my leg is gone!"

To his left, another man swung wildly with his sword in the dark, hoping to protect himself. He took down one of his fellows, who died screaming, "It's got me! It's got me!"

"They will do this work for me," thought Shelby. "Time for a little more terror, and then I will leave them to kill themselves."

He laughed as loudly and as demonically as he could, a laugh that echoed in the passage and repeated back.

All the men screamed again and slashed madly with their weapons right and left. They were chopping one another to pieces.

"I wonder," thought Shelby as he retraced his steps down the passage leaving the howling and maddened men behind, "if that is all of them. Perhaps an advance guard penetrated this passage before I got here."

Passing the small turning through which he had originally come, he followed the wider main tunnel, feeling his way along rather than risking the flashlight again. At least now he had a weapon.

Then, he heard muttering from another group of men in the passage ahead. They were around a corner, and if he was not careful he would walk right into them. He paused and retreated into a crevice.

Something flickered on the wall ahead, probably a lamp.

"Where the hell is Timon?" growled one man. "He should have been here by now."

"Yeah, where is he?" asked another.

"Which way do we go?" asked a third. "No point in going back. The roof collapsed."

"There you are," cried a voice approaching from the far side. Shelby was startled, but not surprised. It was a familiar voice.

Iapetus. From the increased flickering on the wall, Shelby deduced that Iapetus carried another lamp. The flickering brightened after Iapetus spoke, suggesting that others with lamps followed him.

"Timon has been detained. You look to number about 100. We should have been twice that many, but never mind. You will split up into four groups. One group will go with me. These three men will lead the other three groups. They will show you where to go and what to do. This is Iros, this is Noemon, and this is Athanasios. They are experienced soldiers and from good families. They have many men who will join us if you are successful opening the gates and subduing the city defenses. Already the fires are burning in the fields, and we believe that Phorbus has fallen into the trap we set for him."

"He wasn't so lucky with his brother, though, was he," muttered the soldier closest to Shelby.

"Kratos, who should have been killed by the lion, has been distracted to the western garrison and is fighting there, trapped with a small group of men. He will not be able to come to the city's rescue. Zeus will replace this cursed Goddess at last and the men of the city will rise up to join us when they see that they will be set free from their wives. It is only up to us to do the few things we need to do to make it happen."

"Who is that girl you've got with you? The one with the gag?"

"She's one of them," Iapetus replied. "I gagged her after she screamed."

"Can we have her?" said another.

"You will have plenty of women and girls later. This one goes with me to the top of the acropolis, where her mother is the priestess. Do as you are bid, and you can take your pick from thousands."

Kalista struggled and her eyes widened with horror. The Achaeans grabbed at her, even though she was out of reach in Iapetus' grasp.

"Now line up and each man will get a partial payment. These gold coins are specially stamped. After the fight, show me your gold coin, and I will give you nine more just like it. Those are your wages for being here tonight."

He turned to Iros. "How many did you count?"

"About ninety men here. I think we lost some."

"We can do it with ninety." He looked at the man on his far-thest right. "Here," he called, "come and take your coin, then go and stand with Iros. The next man will stand with Noemon, the man after that with Athanasios, and then back to Iros. That way we will be evenly split up. First, you ten," he pointed at ten stand-ing closest to the front, including the one who asked for Kalista, "you will come with me. Here are your coins."

"Iros, take over. I need to take this little bitch up the hill to visit with precious Mother."

The men pocketed their coins and jostled one another, grinning, then followed Iapetus, who was dragging a thoroughly terrified Kalista behind him.

Shelby was blocked from following them by the large group of men slavering at the sight of all the gold in Iros' hand. He saw no way through. When the Achaeans finally moved off, he could follow along and hunt them down, killing the hindmost, but there would be too many. Instead, he must rescue Kalista again. He needed to be at the top of the mountain. Metis was there, and that meant Melia was there too.

So now there was no question about it. The city gates were to be attacked, and already enemy soldiers were in the fields. Should he believe Iapetus that Phorbus was dead? How could he know? Maybe that was just bravado.

"If Iapetus succeeds in reaching the acropolis with his mercenaries, he can do a lot of damage," Shelby thought. "Melia will not be able to hold them all off, no matter how good her arm. Without her and Metis, the city's leadership will be in disarray, decapitated. The city's only hope once Iapetus gets to the acropolis is the Meliae."

The telling out of coins took forever. With every coin, Iapetus was another four or five steps away.

"I hope the Meliae are ready," he said to himself.

SIXTY SIX

✕✕✕✕✕✕✕✕✕✕

O phion's horse told him not to take the direct route to the city. The detour would add time, but he would avoid the enemy troops. Ophion listened to his horse.

No sound passed between them, but what is communication after all if it is not a meeting of minds? Ophion was listening to his horse with his uncanny ability to hear the unheard.

As they skirted the edge of the field where a rider would have gone, he saw the glint of metal in the moonlight and knew the horse was right. Enemy troops already had penetrated deep into the heartland.

He let the horse choose the pace, which dropped to a soft canter as they passed within earshot of the enemy. No horse could move silently, and stealth was not their primary survival skill, but different gaits made different noises. Hooves striking the ground hard made more noise. An easy canter did not make much noise, but the animal moved faster than a man could keep up. That would do.

A few moments later they were clear, and Ophion urged the horse on.

They covered the distance from the western camp swiftly and approached the gates just as the ululation of Rhodia's alarm call echoed from the palace precincts.

"Open the gates, I'm coming through," shouted Ophion.

"Who is that?" came the reply.

"Ophion. For the Goddess' sake, open the gates. Do it now!"

The guards hesitated.

"You can come through the small gate, but we can't let you bring in the horse," said the voice from the wall. "We can't open the main gate. The Matrons say the enemy are out there."

"I know," yelled Ophion. "I just avoided them. I must see Metis instantly. Open the gate so I can ride the horse up to the palace."

"She's on the acropolis," said the voice, "but you must dismount and leave the horse."

"Elpenor!" cried Ophion. "This is urgent! Open the gate wide enough for the horse and stand aside. I'm coming through."

The gate began to move. A troop of soldiers armed with bows and arrows bristled on the battlement over the gate and a group of torch-bearing slaves came running through the small gate to light the area.

The guards stood aside. He walked the lathered horse through the gates, just squeezing in, and then re-mounted and urged the steed into a gallop. The guards fell back to let him pass, and before he cleared the second gate he heard the main one slam shut behind him.

He rode through the streets, yelling at alarmed people to get out of the way, past the palace, and up the stepped road leading to the acropolis, a path only taken heretofore by sacrificial animals.

"It's okay," he muttered to the laboring horse, "you won't be sacrificed tonight. Just get me there in time."

At the portal to the temple precinct, Ophion dismounted and sprang up the much steeper steps onto the flat top of the acropolis. In the distance, he saw the altar blazing with the sacrificed bullock. Beyond it, on her knees on the steps of the temple, he saw his mother, her arms lifted. She was in a trance, and twenty paces behind her, nearer the altar, knelt Melia, head bowed.

Between him and the altar were two Matrons, attending to the service and caring for Metis as she came out of her trance.

Metis was keening, the eerie sound of her voice penetrating the dark fabric of the night like a knife.

Ophion was relieved. Everything was normal. He stopped to breathe and then sank to the ground on his knees, bowing his head to earth.

Something was still not right.

Lying full length upon the ground, his ear pressed to the stone surface, he began to hear voices crying and screaming. He heard his horse shifting uneasily at the bottom of the staircase, still lathered and chilling in the night air. He heard more voices. Then it seemed that the voices were rushing toward him, crying out to him.

"Ophion, Ophion, protect your mother!" they cried.

From his prone position, he looked up again at the altar. It was blazing higher now as the bullock's fat turned to flame, the smoke erupting into the sky.

Metis' keening suddenly stopped, and he thought the earth shifted. He was certain it shifted.

Then he heard his mother's voice screaming, "What are you doing? What are you doing?"

The Matrons hurried forward. He heard Melia's voice above the din.

"Iapetus, NO!"

Sparks rose in a sudden fountain from the altar.

He ran as fast as he could toward the altar, and saw Iapetus grappling with Metis as Melia tried to beat him off. Soldiers crowded toward Melia and the altar, but they were not city soldiers. Achaeans!

Achaeans had infiltrated the acropolis!

They pushed toward Melia with their spears, and she broke off from Iapetus and darted away. A moment later, one of the soldiers went down, hit squarely in the forehead by the bolt of a crossbow fired from the temple roof. Another soldier dropped, and another. Still they charged toward Melia, and then they were under the overhang of the temple, out of the range of fire from the roof.

Ophion saw Iapetus stab Metis, again and again, and haul her body to the altar. She was still alive when he hoisted her over his shoulder, her blood dripping down him, and then staggered forward, throwing her onto the altar, raising another cloud of sparks.

Ophion saw another human form there. Small. "No! Kalista!" Kalista with her sightless eyes, her gagged mouth, her blonde hair flaring where she lay in the flaming grease of the burning bullock.

His corded garrote was already in his hand as he sprang toward Iapetus. Iapetus did not see Ophion, but instead rushed into the level esplanade nearby where he had a glimpse of Melia. Suddenly Shelby was there, too, emerging onto the acropolis close by the temple, and four large Achaeans gave up searching for Melia and leapt on him, pinning him. Two more Achaeans tried to stab him with their spears.

Iapetus scanned the hilltop with his blazing eyes, insane, completely insane. A few steps before Ophion reached him,

Iapetus spotted Melia through the columns of the temple and took after her. Ophion chased him.

Melia rounded the seated idol's legs, Iapetus close behind, and suddenly dropped out of sight.

Ophion saw him disappear too, only a few steps ahead. "Mother's murderer will pay," was the only thought in Ophion's mind as he reached an opening beneath the idol he had never seen before. A pushed-back panel revealed steps leading down. He heard Melia and Iapetus below and plunged down the steps after them.

What Ophion did not see was the corpse of Metis rising to a sitting position in the fire, raising a smoking arm in the direction of the Goddess, her hair blazing like a torch. The body stayed in that position until it melted away into ash and was lifted off the altar by the wind.

The Matrons saw it.

They were not surprised.

SIXTY
SEVEN

XXXXXXXXXX

Rhodia and Eurymedon emerged onto the acropolis followed by Dolios and two Matrons as Iapetus was stabbing Metis, the other Matrons rushing toward the altar. They saw him hoist her still-living body onto the altar. Just ahead of them, Shelby struggled to get free from Achaeans who surrounded him.

Men on each arm were holding him, but he was still fighting, lashing out with his feet. Every time one of the Achaeans lunged at him with a spear, he somehow dodged it, protecting himself with the bodies of the Achaeans grappling with him. In his fury, he moved too quickly for the Meliae on the temple roof to risk a shot, though they were ready.

Eurymedon took out one Achaean with his spear and went after another while Rhodia, coming up behind, finished off one of the Achaeans with her sword, slicing the hamstring on his right leg as he tried to evade Eurymedon. Shelby was freed, and immediately dashed toward Melia, leaving Eurymedon and Rhodia to deal with the remaining Achaeans.

The Matrons instructed Rhodia and Eurymedon to throw the Achaeans off the precipice behind the temple to the jackals below. All of the Meliae with their crossbows and their black costumes had swarmed onto the acropolis to help by this time and were hurrying toward Rhodia for orders.

Shelby was slashed on his torso and arms, but the gashes were superficial: he could function. Mentally, he fixed on finding Melia, catching his breath.

How odd, after a lifetime of mostly male companionship and immersion in the most codified of male hierarchies, that he would know in his heart of hearts that the love of this one woman had the power to rid him of the demons, could cure him of his rage and loss. How odd. Yet, he knew.

Sounds of battle welled up from the direction of the city gates. Alarms, clashes of swords, shouts and screams. The city, already alerted by the cries from the palace, awakened in fury. He assumed women were mobilizing the defense of their streets. "Surely," he thought, "the Achaeans are not already storming the city! How had they maneuvered into the fields unseen? Had the citadel fallen, or the army crossed over the western hills? When? Can Amphinomus rally for a counterattack at the gates, secure them before further harm is done?"

Not his problem he decided. "Save Melia." It was the only thing he could think of. "Save Melia." He grabbed his pack from Dolios and took off, certain that Ophion would get to Iapetus, but could he get there before Iapetus caught up with Melia?

He found the passage and plunged down it, little caring where it headed.

Steps led down to the underground lake that lay beneath the acropolis, and in his haste, he lost his footing, plunged through empty air, and landed with a resounding splash in cold water. He expected to die in the fall. Instead, he was surprised when he found that he was underwater.

Surprise quickly turned to fear, however. Light did not shine in the underground lake, and he could not feel the bottom. He did not know which way was up. All he was certain of was that he was deep underwater.

Fumbling in his pocket, he found his flashlight and turned it on to spot bubbles rising. He stroked after them and broke the surface a moment later, inhaling deeply. In the distance he heard Melia's voice echoing off stone walls as she screamed at Iapetus. They were somewhere close, but he could not be sure where.

He was a powerful swimmer, and he swam toward the sound of the voices. He heard echoing footsteps, their sandals slapping the stone, and he followed the sound.

Shelby touched a stone surface and hauled himself out of the water. Off to his left, he heard their voices again. Iapetus' voice taunting. Melia's voice defiant. Hadn't he seen Ophion? "Where is Ophion?" he asked himself.

Shuffling with his feet to keep from stepping off into the water, Shelby followed the sound to the left. He stumbled into a vertical stone wall, then put his back against it and slid along. At one point he discovered he was on a ledge so narrow that his toes hung off. Below was water, but maybe also jagged rocks, and the light from his flashlight chose that moment to begin fading. The batteries were draining. He flicked it off, believing that it was better to have weak light than no light, and he might need it later.

Eventually the ledge widened out, and he shuffled faster. Suddenly the rock at his back was gone and he stumbled into a passage. Reaching out a hand behind him, he felt the wall curling away from the lake, and he picked up speed, guiding himself by dragging his hand along the wall.

Another few turns and ahead a lamp hung on the wall.

Oh, relief. Light.

Fifty paces after that, around a bend, another lamp sputtered and smoked.

He heard Melia scream ahead and started running.

One lamp. Two lamps. Three lamps. Then no more lamps. Despite an opening off to the left again, he heard them shuffling ahead of him, down a different passage, a passage without light.

Finally, after a long way, he lost the sounds of their feet slapping the stone. He had not heard Melia's voice for some time and assumed they had drawn so far ahead that he could no longer hear them, but the fear also arose that he missed them in the dark, that they had taken a passage he missed, and that he was now lost underground in the eternal dark.

His eyes, moreover, began to play tricks on him. Ghostly green shapes blossomed and disappeared in the dark on all sides of him. Now and again, there was a gleam of red or blue, but that disappeared, too.

He felt for his flashlight and dropped it. He went down on all fours to pat around on the ground searching for it and found it at last, but now was not sure which direction he had been going. He tried the light and got a weak gleam.

The surface of the tunnel was rock and it was hard, jagged, cold, and sweaty with an odor like damp concrete.

His clothes had not dried from his plunge into the lake, and in this dank atmosphere there was no chance of them drying. If he did not keep moving, he risked hypothermia.

"Are you following me?"

He heard Melia's voice in his mind. Nothing disturbed the air, but he heard her voice.

"Yes," he replied aloud. "I lost you."

Her voice was as clear as if she were sitting next to him, conversing in a normal tone.

"Follow your heart," the voice said.

"To my right," he said.

"Then go that way. Follow your heart."

"I love you," he said. "I love you so much. I live because of you."

"Then follow your heart," she said. "I need you."

Time had no meaning to him running in the dark, only his breathing to measure time, and only when he listened. He did not know how long he ran, or how far. Behind him, he heard a growing bedlam, a clamoring and sound like steel upon stone. He ran on.

"Those are the dead," her voice said. "They are angered by Metis' murder."

He pressed on.

Something struck the wall next to his head. He did not know what it was, and he could not see it. He heard a buzzing in the dark, and then something struck again. It missed again. He pressed onward.

The noise behind him grew louder. "Don't look back," Melia's voice said.

"Run! Don't look back!" she said. "Follow your heart!"

He pressed forward, ever forward, feeling the icy breath behind him chilling his neck, his legs.

Suddenly, the passage widened. He was no longer in a passage at all, but a large room. He stepped into a stream of water, and from the far end of the room, or cavern, he saw a glimmer of light. Real light, not the imaginary green blossoms.

Then he heard a struggle.

"No!" screamed Melia. "No! No!"

Her real voice! Not in his head!

Against a distant glow he saw shapes moving, fighting. Iapetus and Ophion! He was sure of it.

He rushed forward. It had to be them! It had to be!

"NO!" she screamed again.

Where was she?

Grunting men, and a moan, and the earth began to heave.

"Melia!" Shelby cried, running forward.

Suddenly she was trembling in his arms. He lifted her and

346

rushed forward, away from the clash behind. He heard stones falling, had a glimpse of gold, and then was struck on the head. He was dazed but not out. He almost dropped her.

"Are you okay?" he breathed.

"Oh yes," she said, "oh yes!" her arms around his neck.

The ground heaved again, and somewhere in the cavern was a huge crack and a rending crash. The ground shook violently, and dust exploded around them. Something had fallen, something huge. Over the noise came the screams, and then the sound of bedlam, of thousands of screaming voices. Despair. Terror.

They were at a narrow passage and he could see moonlight glimmering off the little stream at the end of the next cavern, the painted cave. Beyond that was the pool. They had come through the mountain!

He clasped her tightly to him, feeling her bury her head in his neck, wrap her legs around him, as the ground began to heave and vibrate. The earthquake shook her loose and she dropped from his neck. She shoved him as the ground heaved violently, and he staggered forward, struck by something, falling rocks, unbelievable noise. An explosion. Choking dust billowed outward, and he was knocked down, struggled to get up. But she was not there. She was not there.

Hours must have passed, he thought, as he pulled himself upright where he had lain next to the little foot-wide stream of water. He splashed water on his face to wipe away the thick coat of dust, and cupped the clear stream to his mouth. His head ached and he coughed violently.

Ahead of him, the gray light of dawn filtered in through the narrow opening that led to the pool. Around him on the walls were incredible paintings of women, women doing everything. He limped forward, taking a last look at them. The magnificent, punctured body of a dead warrior looked familiar. Kratos? Himself? Phorbus? Over the early morning air smelling so sweet and pure, he heard the seven-note call of a golden jackal, and away in the distance beyond, the thump of a helicopter.

He had returned to the pool. The recovery helicopter had spotted him. In moments a rope would drop. He looked around, to fix the place in his mind, and then looked up.

He waved at the tech looking down at him from the twenty-first century.

✕

SIXTY EIGHT

✕✕✕✕✕✕✕✕✕✕

"Mr. Shelby, are you all right?"

The flight tech looked concerned.

"You look like you've been in a fight with a bear."

For the first time, Shelby realized the fight on the acropolis and the struggle through the labyrinth had shredded his clothes, leaving him with multiple slash wounds, now clotted from the earthquake dust.

"Nah, just a rough landing. Where am I?"

"Greece. We've got the coordinates for you. What happened?"

"I don't know. I launched from the C130 and blacked out. When I came to, the helmet wasn't working."

They had recovered his flight gear and the helmet, winched his parachute from the pool. The tech looked at the helmet, turned it over in his hands, but saw no evident damage. He took off his own helmet and put it on, then removed it.

"Seems to be working to me," he said.

Shelby slipped it on and sure enough, the helmet powered up. The heads-up display on the visor gleamed its green ciphers, tracking the flight of the helicopter and reading out elevations, heading, airspeed, GPS positions, connecting to local NATO frequencies.

He took it off and looked out at the tumbled rocks passing below.

"Wasn't working up there," he said.

THE END

www.ingramcontent.com/pod-product-compliance
Lightning Source LLC
Chambersburg PA
CBHW020327180626
46812CB00001B/89